THAT BOY

THAT BOY

JILLIAN DODD

Jillian Dodd Inc.
Madeira Beach, FL
Jillian Dodd is a registered trademark of Jillian Dodd, Inc.

Editor: Jovana Shirley, Unforeseen Editing.

ISBN: 978-1-946793-63-8

Books by Jillian Dodd

The Keatyn Chronicles®

USA TODAY bestselling young adult contemporary romance set in an East Coast boarding school.

Stalk Me
Kiss Me
Date Me
Love Me
Adore Me
Hate Me
Get Me
Fame
Power
Money
Sex
Love
Keatyn Unscripted
Aiden

That Boy Series

Small-town contemporary romance series about falling in love with the boy next door.

That Boy
That Wedding
That Baby
That Divorce
That Ring

The Love Series

Contemporary, standalone romances following the very sexy Crawford family.

Vegas Love
Broken Love

Spy Girl™ Series

Young adult romance series about a young spy who just might save the world.

The Prince
The Eagle
The Society
The Valiant
The Dauntless
The Phoenix
The Echelon

To my bandit, my angel, and my very own Prince Charming.
Your support means the world to me.

PRESENT DAY

"YOU ARROGANT SON of a bitch," I say. Well, maybe I growl it. It's hard to say for certain.

But I can tell you this. I am fuming, smoke-flying-out-of-my-ears mad as I take the engagement ring off my finger, shove it into his hand, and march toward the stage. The march to the stage feels like it takes forever because there are a million thoughts running through my mind.

Did all these people come here because they really thought I'd say yes?

Or did they come for the fireworks of me saying no?

Do they wish us well?

Or hope to see us fail?

I reach the stage and tentatively walk out on it. One of the band members hands me a microphone, and I know I *really* need to say something to all these people.

I might die of embarrassment.

Actually, I wish it *were* possible to die of embarrassment. Then, I could drop dead right now, and I wouldn't have to do what I am about to do.

Part of me wonders how in the world I got here to begin with. We have been friends for a really long time and only decided to have a real relationship all of *a week ago*.

And, well, it has been really incredible.

I mean, he is *incredible* in ways I didn't even imagine!

Okay, so I might have imagined a little.

Anyway, as of about six minutes ago, we were out on a romantic first date.

Then, he had to go and blow the whole thing all to hell by asking me to marry him.

Can you believe that?

Me neither.

And, as if it wasn't unbelievable enough that he *asked* me to marry him on our first date, he was so *damn* sure I'd say yes that he planned this huge *surprise* engagement party.

Tonight. On our first date. Like, right now!

I shudder and mentally prepare myself.

I have to tell everyone who came here tonight that there is *no way* I'm going to marry that boy!

Before I say the words, I glance at him, and my mind is transported back to the memory of my first kiss.

It's where this all began really.

boys are dumb.

4TH GRADE

PHILLIP WAS THE first boy to ever kiss me. We were swinging sideways on the swings out behind school, when out of the blue, he reached over, grabbed my swing, and kissed me *right* on the lips. Then, he jumped off his swing and ran home. It was one of those perfect sunny afternoons when school was almost out for the summer. I thought it was the best day of my life.

I was in love.

Phillip must have told someone what he did because, today, at school, everyone was singing.

"Phillip and JJ sitting in a tree, K-I-S-S-I-N-G ... "

I couldn't take it.

I was being tortured.

It was the worstest day of my life!

It was such a letdown because the day before had been a GREAT day. I had gotten my first kiss from *a boy*!

I know it was *just* Phillip, but still, I was very surprised.

And I had been so excited to come to school—until I had gotten there, and everyone started torturing me with those stupid, *stupid* songs. Even my friend Lisa was singing them.

That traitor.

And, very quickly, I went from loving that boy to hating him.

3

At least, that was what I had to tell all my friends, so they would stop singing those ridiculous songs.

Phillip must have started a trend because, later that day, Joey kissed Katie, and everyone forgot about Phillip and me.

They had someone new to torture endlessly.

I noticed that Phillip didn't tease Joey and Katie.

Neither did I.

PHILLIP MACKENZIE LIVES across the street from me. We have been friends forever.

I mean it. Since birth.

Our dads are fraternity brothers and best friends. Phillip is five months older than me, and our parents think it is just hilarious to show embarrassing photos of us together as babies.

And we are *naked!*

It's just so gross. I can't even describe it! Phillip and I want to hide—*and we usually do*—whenever they get out those stupid baby books.

Our parents hope that Phillip and I will get married when we grow up. I totally laugh at that. I have told them *so* many times that I can't marry Phillip because I'm going to marry a prince. I blame my obsession with wanting to marry a prince on Disney and Phillip's sister, Ashley.

Ever since I can remember, our parents have been getting together to play cards on Friday nights. We have pizza, which I love, and I get to play with Phillip. Unfortunately, that also means I have to play with Ashley. Ashley is four years older than Phillip and me and a pain in the rear. (I would say butt, except I'm not supposed to say that B-word.)

Speaking of B-words, Ashley is very bossy. And she *always* plays the queen. That means, she gives me the choice of being either her servant or her daughter. And who in their right mind would sign up to be her servant?

I told you how bossy she is. It would be unbearable!
So, I always play the princess.

Important Things I Have Learned in My Life So Far:

1. **Always be the princess.** Princesses have much more fun and not so much responsibility. Plus, you get to marry the prince.

2. **Never be the queen.** Queens are old and bossy and sometimes even evil. (Remember *Snow White*?) Queens think they are in charge of everything. Queens are responsible.

3. **Responsibility makes you crabby and no fun.**

4. **When you have the choice, play with a boy.** Boys are easy to get along with. They don't care if your clothes match or if your hair is a mess. Boys don't talk behind your back or make up stories about you to try to hurt your feelings. They are too busy playing sports or video games.

5. **Always trust your daddy.** Daddies are incredibly smart and handsome, and they always smell very good.

6. **Never kiss and tell.** You will get tortured by people who you thought were your friends.

7. **Never, ever, *ever* trust Mary Beth Parker.** Even if she says she is your best friend.

Last week, Mary Beth Parker told me I could be her best friend. She got me to play with her on the playground, and Lisa, who is my best friend, got mad at me. The very next day, Mary Beth Parker told everyone *not* to play with me.

I didn't do anything to her. That's just how she is.

She is very mean.

Phillip was the only person who played with me. He didn't

care what that bossy girl said. He acted like a prince that day.

I told him so, and ever since, when it's just us, he calls me Princess.

And he's the only person I'd let get away with it!

The worst day of my life.
5TH GRADE

TODAY IS THE worst day of my life.

Really, it is!

A new family has moved into our neighborhood—across the empty lot from my house and across the street from Phillip's house.

This is most unfortunate.

The parents seem like nice, decent people, but unfortunately, they had to bring their stupid, stinky son with them. Why couldn't they have forgotten to bring him or left him on the side of the road somewhere in Missouri? Maybe someone would've taken him home, like a lost kitty.

That way, he could've ruined someone *else's* life.

Phillip and I have *so* much fun playing together. We play lots of sports, games, and fun stuff that I make up. Usually, we play some version of the handsome prince coming to rescue the beautiful royal princess. But it's not like it's all girlie. Phillip gets to do some really cool boy stuff, like fight a dragon with a sword, duel with an evil warlock, and climb the tower. We even play Olympics and have all sorts of sports competitions.

But, since that nasty, smelly boy next door came here, Phillip has been acting like the only fun thing to do is play with him.

Phillip and I are both real good at sports. It's not like I can't keep up with him! Honestly, I'm bigger than he is, and I can actually beat him at almost everything, except for a flat-out running race; he is a bit faster than me.

I'm always the first girl picked when we split into teams at school, but somehow, this evil boy has convinced Phillip that he shouldn't play with girls.

Today, Phillip and I are minding our own business, playing in the empty lot between Danny's house and mine.

Did I mention his name?

Danny. Danny Diamond.

Devil Danny is more like it.

I wonder if his parents know how truly awful he is.

Poor people. They really should consider giving that boy up for adoption.

Oh, I *hate* that boy!

He makes me so mad!

Anyway, Phillip and I are playing a nice game of Four Squares, which *all* the boys at school like to play, when *he* comes walking over.

He thinks he is *so* cool!

The first day he moved here, he told me how he's a *great* quarterback.

I told him to stop bragging. It's not nice.

But he went, "I'm not bragging. I'm just confident in my skills."

Whatever.

I figured the kids at school would hate him because no one likes a bragger, right? Right?

Wrong!

Because of his bragging, his so-called *skills*, and the way he looks, *all* the girls at school are in love with him. I mean, he does have nice blond hair that always looks like he just combed it, even when he's out in the wind. And all the girls have been going on and on about his dreamy blue eyes and his *cool* attitude.

Personally, I think they're just bored with the boys we've grown up with, and they would like *anyone new*.

Although, I have to admit, the first time I saw him, I thought he was really cute, too.

But that was way before I *knew* him.

He interrupts our game by saying, "Four Squares is a dumb girl game. Wanna play football, Phil?"

It's not Phil, you idiot! No one calls him that. It's Phillip.

I'm sure that my Prince Phillip will not let him talk about our game—or me—like that. So, I wait for his reply.

"Sounds fun," Phillip says. "I'll go grab a football."

And off he runs.

No, Bye, Princess.

Nothing.

Has Devil Danny used some kind of evil brainwashing on Phillip?

Can he control people's minds?

Will he suck out Phillip's soul?

I am so mad that I could scream!

But, instead, I try to get along, so I say, "That's okay. Football sounds fun, too."

Danny glares at me, like I'm a piece of poop that he just stepped in. "*Girls* can't play football. Why don't you go home and play with your *dolls* or something?"

Well, that's about all I can take from that boy.

"Danny, you are a stupid, ugly, smelly boy."

I am so mad at him! But then something terrible happens. As I'm yelling at him, tears start coming out of my eyes. Why is that? I'm not sad. I'm boiling hot, furiously mad!

MAD. MAD. MAD. MAD!

I continue to yell at him anyway, "And I wish you would just go back to Missouri and *die!*"

What I say doesn't seem to upset him in any way.

He just looks at me with disgust and says, "Girls are such crybabies."

I turn and run home.

Fast.

I slam the back door, run up the stairs, and slam the door to my room. I throw myself across my bed and cry. I move to my window seat, so I can look out the window at those stupid boys playing football while I cry.

Why do I cry when I get mad?

Maybe he's right. Maybe I am just a crybaby.

Maybe I will just give up and let him steal my best friend from me.

No way.

Never, I think and dry my eyes on my shirt.

Just then, Daddy walks in. I'm sure he heard the doors slamming and is coming to yell at me. He hates it when I slam doors.

I try to hide my crybaby eyes from him.

He looks at me and out the window at the boys. Then he sits down next to me and wraps me in a great big hug.

How come a boy can be so stupid, but a daddy, who *actually* used to be a boy himself, can be so wonderful?

"Three's a crowd, huh?" he asks, nodding out toward the boys.

And smart, too!

"Yeah"—I sniffle—"Danny says girls can't play football. He said I should go play with my dolls. I don't even play with dolls anymore."

At least, not very often.

"I was so mad at him, Daddy. I tried to tell him how mean and stupid I think he is, but then I started crying, so he called me a crybaby. I swear, Dad, I wasn't sad; I was *mad*. I don't know how he made me cry. It's a big mystery to me! Plus, he's trying to steal my bestest friend in the whole world."

"Well," Daddy says, rubbing the stubbly stuff on his chin and thinking.

I love it when he does that. He has the most brilliant ideas!

"I know," I say, interrupting him. "How 'bout you go over there and give him a good, old-fashioned ass-whooping?"

Daddy laughs. He knows I have heard Grandpa say the same thing about me.

"Please don't use bad words like that, okay?"

"Okay," I reply sheepishly. "But I think it would be a very good idea."

"I don't think I could do that, Angel." He smiles, pauses, and strokes the stubble some more. "But that doesn't mean *you* can't."

"You want *me* to go and beat up Danny?" I'm very surprised at that man.

"No, you silly goose," he says, ruffling my hair. "But you are very good at sports, and you especially love football. Teach him a lesson. Show him that girls can play anything they want. Beat him at his own game. I think it would be good for Danny to *lose* to a girl."

He gives me another big hug and walks toward my door.

He turns around, grabs my doorway, and says, "You know, it's okay to have more than one best friend."

Well, his advice on boys might be good, but evidently, he's forgotten the laws of fifth grade.

You can have only *one* best friend.

That's okay though; his memory is probably going bad because he's getting so old. He is thirty-eight after all.

I hug my knees and watch the boys for a few more minutes while I get my courage up. I'm gonna show that boy that anything boys can do, girls can do better.

My friend Lisa likes to sing, "Girls go to college to get more knowledge. Boys go to Jupiter to get more stupider."

I don't know where she comes up with these funny things, but I love that she does. Usually, they are so good!

In this case though, Danny's gonna get more knowledge. And I am about to school him.

I get up and look in my mirror. Daddy always tells me I am beautiful, but I'm not sure I believe him. Isn't it required that dads tell their daughters that? Anyway, all I see in the mirror staring back at me is a girl who is *way* too tall and *way* too skinny and who has gross, knobby knees and some really stupid freckles on her nose.

I look some more.

Well, I suppose my blue eyes are okay, and I do actually like the color of my long blonde hair, but I just can't see beautiful.

Oh well. I'm going to teach that boy a lesson, and I should definitely look as much like a girl as I can when I do it. So, I take my hair out of its ponytail and brush it until it shines, and then I put on some Lip Smacker lip gloss. Lisa gave me this gloss.

She says, "Glossing is as important as flossing."

I think my dentist might disagree with that, but gloss does make your lips look kind of pretty.

I RUN OUTSIDE and walk right up to those stupid boys. I ignore Danny and say to Phillip, "I want to play football with you guys, okay?"

Phillip shrugs his shoulders. "Sure. I'll go out for a pass, and you can guard me."

Danny steps between us and says to Phillip, "No way. She'll just end up getting hurt and go bawling home." He glares at me. "Girls aren't tough enough to play football."

I look that devil boy in the eye.

Dad told me to teach him a lesson by playing football, but I can see now what I have to do. I cock my arm back and punch that boy right in the stomach. Then, I move in closer and give him a jab to the face. He falls onto his butt in the grass.

What can I say? Dad and I watch a lot of boxing.

The corner of his lip is bleeding a bit, and he is lying on the grass, looking up at me with a shocked expression. I expect him to go home and cry to his mommy.

But he surprises me. He wipes his mouth on his shirt and looks at me with new respect.

He slowly nods his head up and down at me.

It's like his brain is transparent, and I can see the lightbulb going off inside it.

Boys are so clueless.

Finally, he says, "You know what? *You* just might be tough enough to play football."

I have to say that I think we both learned a lesson today.

He learned that all girls aren't prissy wimps, and I learned that he *just might not* be the devil after all.

THE THREE OF us have been best friends ever since.

Happy Birthday, Lisa!
7TH GRADE

TONIGHT IS LISA'S fourteenth birthday party.

We have been planning it for months—actually, for years.

I think we started planning for her first boy-girl birthday party in fourth grade, but this is the first time her parents have finally agreed to let her have one.

This is the third one that I've been to.

Boy-girl party, that is.

The first one was a little boring; everyone was too scared to do anything fun.

But, at the last one, things got a little more interesting. We played Spin the Bottle and Seven Minutes in Heaven. I got stuck in the closet with Andrew Martin.

Gross.

I wouldn't let him get near enough to breathe on me, let alone do anything else!

I'm hoping that, at this party, I will end up in the closet with Billy Prescott. He is way cute.

Lisa assures me that she has the drawing of one boy's and one girl's name rigged in my favor.

She lied.

I end up in the closet with Neil.

Right before we have to go in the closet, Neil runs over and breaks up with Mary Beth Parker.

Tacky. Very tacky.

Phillip told me that Neil has a crush on me. I let him kiss me, mostly because I haven't liked Mary Beth Parker since fourth grade when she told everyone not to play with me.

When we come out, Neil has a huge grin on his face.

That's when things get all dramatic.

Mary Beth is very mad at me.

She is all huffy and says bad things about me.

Of course, she changes her tune as soon as she gets sent into the closet with Phillip.

Then, she thinks she's my new best friend.

God, I hope he didn't kiss her!

LATER ON, I have to play Spin the Bottle.

Yes, I have to.

Lisa is making me.

She says I'll ruin her party if I don't.

I don't need *that* hanging over my head, so I agree to play.

See? Have to.

Plus, since there are only seven kids left at the party, one of them being Billy Prescott, I figure the odds are in my favor that I still might get to kiss him.

Lisa turns off the light and puts down a bottle. Everyone gets positioned on the floor in a circle.

Neil is strategically trying to place himself across from me.

We go through four spins of the bottle without it landing on me.

Boohoo!

Then, it's Phillip's turn. He spins, and the neck of the bottle points directly *between* Mary Beth Parker and me!

I kid you not.

Mary Beth looks all excited.

I feel sorry for the poor guy. It's like he has to choose between heaven and hell. And hell—Mary Beth—will get really mad and make his life miserable if he doesn't pick her.

Phillip looks at her and then at me. He takes the neck of the bottle and moves it, so it points straight at me.

Really!

Both Neil and Mary Beth are looking pissed at Phillip, but he doesn't seem to care.

He grins and then crooks his index finger at me, motioning for me to come and get him.

I am going to shake my head, but his grin gets me every time. I can't resist him; plus, I kinda want to kiss him. So, I crawl through the center of the circle. It's like his eyes are the light at the end of a tunnel, and all I can see is him.

I'm still not sure what happened, what Phillip did, or how he did it so fast. But, next thing I know, I am lying on my back across the center of the circle with Phillip lying on *top* of me, kissing me.

The boys are hooting and hollering, but it barely registers because Phillip keeps kissing me. I'm having a hard time processing anything other than the fact that Phillip is a really good kisser and that he is *lying on top* of me.

Around us, everyone gasps and jumps up.

I think this is exactly what Phillip hoped would happen.

I am slightly dazed though, so I can't be sure.

Once everyone scatters, he stops kissing me, pulls me up onto my feet, and flashes me that adorable grin.

And I can't help but fall a little in love with him.

"So, are you secretly in love with me, or were you just trying to break up the game, so you wouldn't have to kiss Mary Beth?" I whisper.

"Oh, I am definitely in love with you," he replies with a big smile on his face as he sees Mary Beth storming out of the party.

"Liar," I say.

It's stupid, really.

8TH GRADE

EVERY SUMMER, PHILLIP'S dad sets up a tent in their backyard. But it's so hot already in May that the boys talked him into setting it up this weekend, so they can camp out. I've spent many a night in that tent with the boys, but my parents have decided that, *this* year, I'm too old to camp with them.

It's stupid really.

It's not like I *like* them.

I mean, we're together a lot, and let's face it; if I really wanted to *do* anything with them, I could just do it any old time.

But, since we are *only* friends, nothing happens.

I have tried explaining this to Mom and Dad, but they got all freaked out when I told them that, if I wanted to do something with one of the boys, I could *do it any old time*, and I nearly got grounded.

Fortunately, I haven't been banned from the tent entirely. I still get to go over there, but I have to come home to sleep, which really makes no sense either because a lot can happen before I come home. But whatever. I mean, all we usually do is eat, play cards, and talk.

I know that I'm growing up, but I don't really feel all that different. I'm a lot taller than I used to be. I'm five-ten, which seems a bit excessive to me, and it really sucks because there are only two boys in my grade taller than me. So, if I want to go out with a boy who is taller than me, my choices are *very* limited.

My mom is five-nine, and she says she loves being tall and not to worry; the boys will catch up in a few years. She is also constantly telling me to stand up straight.

It drives me nuts.

The talks the boys and I have in the tent are *much* different from the ones I have with my friends Lisa and Katie. I swear, growing up is all they have talked about for the last three years.

Who got their boobs first?

Not me.

Who got their period first?

Again, not me.

Who got kissed on the lips first?

Well, that would have been me, but now that we are older, a *silly playground kiss* doesn't count.

So, that one is also not me.

They are totally obsessed with boys and are so excited about going to high school next year because they think the place is just full of boys dying to date them.

Lisa has been counting down the days until we are fifteen and old enough to go out on real dates—131 days for Lisa, 215 for Katie, and 321 for me, at last count. The countdown is kind of silly to me. I mean, do they think they will turn fifteen, and all of a sudden, boys will be standing in line to ask them out?

What if no one does?

I haven't pointed that out to them and probably won't.

They would get all huffy at me.

AS IF I don't have enough to worry about, eighth-grade graduation is coming up. It's a big deal around here. We have a graduation ceremony and parties and everything. Normally, this is something

I would be very excited about—I love parties—but my mom has been trying to ruin my life.

I swear!

She said I have to wear a dress. I know I'm kind of a tomboy, and I love sports, but I don't mind wearing dresses. It's just that I find they're not usually very comfortable. Then, there's the whole *worrying about your underwear showing* issue. So, anyway, the problem isn't really that I have to wear a dress; it's the *type* of dress she wants me to wear. Everything she picks is *so* pink! And she keeps dragging me to the store and making me try these things on.

I think Lisa and I were switched at birth. She might very well be my mother's real daughter. They both love to shop and to go, *"Ooh! Isn't that just dar-ling?"* to anything with rhinestones, fringe, sequins, or leopard print.

Last time we went shopping, they made me try on a dress that was a combination of hot pink and leopard.

I'm pretty positive I saw that once in the Fashion Don'ts that Katie is always reading.

I swear, they want me to look like a hooker.

I told Mom that.

And, evidently, *that's* when she decided that she is very frustrated with me.

Dad told me this, and when I was like, "I know the feeling," even he got testy with me.

After our last shopping trip, she told him she has given up. And that's saying a lot because this woman loves to shop.

DAD TRIED TO intervene and asked me at dinner a couple of nights ago, "JJ, have you seen any dresses you've liked *anywhere?*"

"Not really." I shrugged and took a bite of my chicken.

"Why don't I take you shopping tomorrow night? And, if we find a dress, I'll take you to Johnny's for pizza."

I was really amazed by this development because Dad has told me for years that he is allergic to shopping. Advil must help his *shopping allergies* because he took three before we left the house.

Surprisingly, Dad and I did find something for me to wear to graduation. First, we went to the juniors section at a department store Katie recommended. I tried on a bunch of dresses, but Dad vetoed them all as too sexy, so we continued our search. I kinda liked the black one he thought was way *too sexy*, but I was hungry, so I didn't argue. Katie also told me to try the Gap, so we did, and I really need to thank that girl because that was very helpful advice. I found a pretty eyelet skirt and a really cute top.

During our whole shopping trip, Dad only held his head in his hands and muttered things to himself twice, so it was a good experience for him, too, I think.

And, now, I am actually excited for graduation.

RIGHT NOW, I'M getting some snacks together to take out to the tent.

"Phillip, come help me!" I yell across the street as I struggle to carry everything.

Phillip runs over and grabs two grocery sacks full of candy and snacks from my arms. I'm left with just the big bowl of warm, buttered popcorn. As I'm following Phillip across the street, Danny comes out of his garage, carrying a cooler.

"Why do you look so sneaky?" I ask him as we meet in the street.

Danny looks just like he did the night we decorated the Mackenzies' trees with Ashley's underwear. At first, Ashley, who was sixteen at the time, laughed like she didn't care, but that was before she realized Phillip had sent a heads-up email to everyone in her address book. She was completely horrified when all her friends, boys included, started driving by her house and honking at her lacy bras and panties.

Danny's got something up his sleeve, I can tell.

"I'll tell you later. Just act normal in case my parents are watching."

Later, after we've eaten most of the snacks and we are playing cards, Danny opens the cooler and says, "How 'bout we have some fun tonight?" He pulls three cans of beer out from underneath the pop.

Phillip, who I figure will tell us exactly what a bad idea this is because he tends to be the most conservative of the three of us, says, to my surprise, "Heck yeah."

So, of course, I say, "Sounds awesome."

We open our beers, and Danny cheers, "Here's to the good life."

I'm pretty sure he heard that on a commercial.

We drink up. A few hours and few beers later, we're basically drunk. Good thing our parents are already in bed.

See? I told you *things* could happen out here before bedtime.

The boys and I talk about who likes who and who doesn't like who—all the gossip. We don't know the answers to these questions, but we talk and laugh anyway. We share the last beer.

Actually, I am smart and only pretend to drink from it.

We are laughing and laughing when the boys start telling me about how they wake up in the morning with hard *you-know-whats*.

So, I say, "Well, that's nothing," and proceed to tell them in gory detail all about a period.

I ask them why they are so obsessed with girls who have big boobs, and they want to know why girls only like guys taller than them.

LATER THAT NIGHT, Danny and Phillip puke their guts out.

I earn honors because I don't.

Of course, I feel terrible the next day, but I will never admit it.

Mrs. Ryan Marshall?

9TH GRADE

THREE DAYS UNTIL my first real date.

I am so excited!

I am also a paranoid, nervous wreck.

I like this boy so much! His name is Ryan. Ryan Marshall.

Ryan is so good-looking, and he's a senior! He reminds Katie and me of Jake from the movie *Sixteen Candles*. I know it's an old movie, and the clothes are weird, but it's still funny and romantic, and it is worth watching *just* to lust after Jake. Lisa, Katie, and I all rank Jake in the Top 25 on our lists of All-Time Movie Hotties.

So, how does this sound?

JJ Marshall.

Jadyn Marshall.

Jadyn James Reynolds-Marshall.

Mrs. Ryan Marshall.

Doesn't that just roll off your tongue?

Speaking of tongues, they are the main reason I'm a nervous wreck. Ryan is a senior, and, well, sadly, I'm not all that experienced with boys. I mean, I'm a freshman, and I have been to dances with boys my age and have even *gone out* with boys, but I've never *really* kissed them. Not like I hope to kiss Ryan anyway.

Bobby Robinson did shove his tongue into my mouth one

time when we were kissing under the bleachers at a football game, but it didn't feel so good. I'm pretty sure he didn't have it exactly right.

So, I talked to my friends Katie and Lisa about how to properly make out.

But ... well, here is just a bit of their unhelpful advice.

"Just let him take the lead and do whatever he does."

Um, couldn't that get me into a lot of trouble?

"Just sort of kiss his tongue but try not to drool."

"Don't open your mouth too wide."

And then, "Just open your mouth wide."

See?

Stupid, conflicting information.

And this from girls who *supposedly* know how to do this!

I feel like I'm an undercover CIA agent trying to wrestle vital information out of a ruthless double agent when the fate of the free world depends upon it. All the while, the president is yelling at me in a panic, saying, *Somebody! Anybody! Just get me the truth!*

You know, this is really the kind of stuff that would be helpful to learn in health class. Much more useful information than knowing how a fallopian tube works or what kinds of cancer I can fight by adding fiber to my diet.

I mean, this is a date of epic proportions.

He's a senior, for God's sake!

My high school reputation could be ruined or made in one single night.

I don't want to be known as a terrible kisser!

Or, worse, as totally inexperienced!

I've got to do something.

Get me somebody, anybody!

I need someone who has experience and, most importantly, who will help me.

I glance out my window and see Danny's bedroom light is on.

Cha-ching.

Danny has experience, and I'm too desperate to be embarrassed.

So, I call him. "Danny, are your parents home?"

"No, they went to that parents' meeting at school with yours."

Yay!

"Good. I'm coming over. And you're, like, totally alone? Phillip isn't there, is he?"

"No, I'm totally alone. What's up, Jay?"

"Um, I just really, *really* need your help with something. Be right there."

I slam down the phone and run out of my house and over to his. I barge in the front door and take the stairs two at a time up to his bedroom. He's sitting on his bed with a varsity football playbook spread out in front of him. I can tell by the intense look on his face, he has been studying hard. Danny's goal is to be the best high school quarterback in the state and then play for Nebraska. Let's just say, he is well on his way to achieving his goals.

"Hey, Jay," he says, straightening up. "What's the top-secret meeting all about?"

Maybe this is a bad idea.

No. You've got to find this stuff out.

It's vital to our country's well-being!

Okay, that's a bit dramatic, but it is vital to my well-being.

I pace the length of his room a couple of times, wringing my hands together, trying to get up the nerve.

"Okay, here it is. I need your help, and, well, I'm kind of embarrassed to say it, but here goes. I have that date with Ryan on Saturday, and I'm afraid I won't know what to do. I mean, I've never done it before, and I'm not exactly sure how. I don't even know if he'll *want to do it with me,* but I'm hoping that he will, and, well, I want to, you know, *be prepared.* So, I need you to help me, Danny. Will you show me what to do?"

Danny stares at me in disbelief.

"This is a joke, right?" He laughs, gets off the bed, and looks down the hall. "Where's Phillip hiding?"

"No, Danny, I'm serious. I mean, if you can't *show me*, could you at least tell me if I know how to do it right?"

"Let me get this right, Jay. You want me to *show you* how to have sex?" He has a huge goofball grin on his face. "Wow. Well, I suppose that could be arrange—"

"Wait! What? Sex? Danny, what are you talking about?"

"What are *you* talking about, Jay? You're the one who said you've never done it and that you want me to show you."

"I never said that!" Well, wait a minute. Maybe I sorta did. "I mean, if I did say it, it's not what I meant."

Now, he's staring at me like I'm psycho.

I probably am.

"The truth is, Danny, I've never really made out." There, I said it. "And I *really, really* need to know how to do it right. I can't seem to get reliable information from my friends, I can't ask my parents, and Ashley's at college, so you're my only hope."

He continues the stone-faced look at me. "I thought you made out with Bobby?"

"Yeah, I did, and it was awful. And I don't wanna be awful," I whine desperately.

Then, I change directions in my thinking, trying to figure out a way to get him to teach me. So, I say with a challenge, "Hmm, well, maybe you can't do it. That's okay. I'll just go ask Phillip for help."

"Heck no," he growls. "He has about as much experience in that department as you do. Fine. I'll help you." He puts his hand up to his chin, thinking. "Hmm. Come sit down."

I sit cross-legged on his bed, facing him.

"Here. Take this." He throws his pillow at me.

Ooh. Yum. It smells just like him.

But, uh, excuse me. I've already tried practicing on my pillow, and it was no help!

"No, that won't work." He quickly snatches the musky thing away from me. "Too big. I know. Hold your hand up to your face," he orders. "Kiss it."

I look at him like he's nuts, but he nods his head, so I hold my palm up in front of my face and push my lips into it.

"Turn sideways a bit, so I can see better," he bosses, so I turn. "Okay, but your puckering is way too tight. You're not kissing your grandma, Jay."

"No, worse," I gripe, "I'm kissing my hand."

He glares at me. I think I had better just do as he said.

"Just loosen your lips. Try again."

This time, I pucker my lips but then try to make them loose. I glance over at him, my eyebrows raised in hope.

"All right, now, slightly open your mouth."

I try to slightly open my mouth. "This feels ridiculous."

"Hmm, is this really that important to you?"

"Uh, ye-ah. He's a *senior!* My entire reputation is at stake here."

"Well, okay then." He jumps off his bed, shuts and locks his door, and turns off the light. There's plenty of light coming through his window from the streetlight, so I can still see him. But I must appear alarmed because he says, "Look, I just don't want anyone walking in on this."

He looks at me like he's a soldier being sent off to war, and I should be proud of his bravery and selflessness.

Actually, I am.

"Plus, you need to relax. Maybe, in the dark, you won't feel so stupid." He plops back down on his bed next to me and continues, "Tilt your head a little to the left."

I tilt my head.

"Lick your lips, so they're not all dry."

I lick.

"Stop smiling and close your eyes."

I close them.

"Come on, Jay, I shouldn't have to tell you everything! Pucker those lips."

I pucker.

"No! Not so tight."

When he touches my bottom lip with his finger, I nearly jump off the bed, my eyes flying wide open as he yells at me, "Lesson number one? Don't do that! You scared the crap out of me. You have *got* to relax!"

He reaches out and puts his hands on both of my shoulders, feeling that they are in fact extremely tense. "God, you're way tense!"

Puh-leeze, how could I not be?

I mean, doesn't this whole effed up situation require some tension on my part?

"Sorry." I breathe deep and shake my shoulders, but it doesn't help. I am still tense.

Danny's hands are still on my shoulders, and he starts rubbing them.

I can't help but melt—I mean, uh ... relax.

"I know. Let's try some positive visualization. Close your eyes again." He speaks slowly in a hypnotic tone, "All right, picture yourself at the movies with Ryan. So, it's dark, and the movie is playing—"

"Wait! What are we seeing?"

"Does it really matter?"

"Uh, yeah. If you want me to visualize, I need the whole picture."

"Fine then. Something scary, so you'll want to hang on to him."

"Okay." I nod and smile. "That sounds good."

"So, at the scary movie, he puts his arm around your shoulders." Danny moves to my side and puts his arm around my shoulders. "You turn your face toward him and look into his eyes."

I turn my face toward Danny.

"He smiles and leans in to kiss you." Danny pushes my hand up to my face, pressing my lips into my hand.

I like this visualization stuff. I pretend my hand is Ryan and start to give it a good kiss, but then I think about how ridiculous I must look and start laughing again.

Danny does a big, huffy breath at me and shoves my hand away from my mouth. "Stop laughing."

I keep my eyes shut tight and bite my lip while Danny continues in the hypnotic voice, "Okay, I'm going to touch your lip, and I want you to open your mouth a bit."

I giggle again.

I can't help it! I really can't!

"Oh, screw it," he says.

I open my eyes and watch him shake his head at me.

"This is just too hard to explain."

I am ready to scream, *I'll stop laughing. Please, please, please don't give up on me*, when he pulls me toward him and covers my mouth with his.

Oh. My. Gosh.

He's kissing me!

Danny is kissing me!

And, wow, practical knowledge. This is even better!

He kisses me with soft lips and a slightly opened mouth.

Oh.

He is a good kisser.

I kiss him back.

He impatiently taps my hand.

I take it I'm supposed to do something.

Why am I here again?

Oh, yeah, the tongue thing.

I cautiously stick my tongue out, and somehow, he grabs the bottom of it with his tongue and sort of sucks on it.

Oh my, that's nice.

He taps me again.

I stop for a second because I'm not real sure what to do. But then Danny puts his tongue into my mouth, so I try to mimic what he did to me ... and, hey, it works!

I think I'm kind of getting the hang of this.

And wow! It feels *really* good.

Obviously, *this* is the right way to do it. I knew Bobby Robinson didn't have a clue.

Danny and I practice for a little while longer.

I never knew learning could be so much fun!

ALL OF A sudden, I hear something.

But it's hard to be concerned about a stupid, random noise when Danny is lying on top of me, kissing me, one hand tangled in my hair, the other hand up my shirt.

But then I hear something else, and my brain awakens.

I tear my lips away from Danny and turn my head. Danny kisses down the side of my neck while I peek over at the clock next to his bed.

The clock says nine thirty.

Nine thirty?

Wait. What?

Nine thirty?

Nine thirty!

That can't be right!

When I left home, it was seven thirty!

Have I been making out with Danny for two whole hours?

Crap!

Are Danny's parents home?

Danny and I both hear the next noise.

Danny's mom calls out, "Danny."

And I swear to God, she must apparate from the garage because, in less than an instant, she is at his door, trying to open it.

But it's locked.

She tries the handle again and says, "Danny, may I come in?"

Danny says, "Sure, Mom, just a sec."

He seems way too cool about this. He gives me his Devil Danny grin along with a last deep kiss and jumps off the bed.

Only problem is, my leg is still wrapped around his, and he sorta tumbles out of the bed instead.

And I don't know why—maybe I am slightly high from kissing him—but I find this quite funny and can't help but giggle.

Danny grins back at me as he picks himself up off the floor.

Well, he's grinning until his mom hears my giggling and says madly, "Danny Diamond, unlock the door this instant. Who is in there with you?"

Danny is not supposed to have girls over when his parents aren't home.

Shit. Shit.

Well, double shit.

We stare at each other for a second.

This is gonna look bad.

I've got to think of something quick.

Work, brain, work!

I see Danny's binoculars on the floor, half-hidden beneath a sock, and I grab them. Then, I spy his little telescope on a shelf next to an old Punt, Pass, and Kick trophy. I jump up quick and sweep it onto his bed.

All this while he walks over to the door and unlocks it.

I am amazing and brilliant, I think.

Especially considering the fact that, for the last two hours, my brain has been nothing but mush.

Danny's mom bursts into the room.

She sees me sitting on his bed and grimaces, like she walked in on us naked.

She seems kinda angry as she turns to Danny and says, "What's going on? Why are you and JJ in here with the door locked and the lights off?"

Although her voice is stern, there's a slight panic in it. I can only imagine what she thinks we were doing.

I mean, she could be *partially* right. But what was going on was, you know, *only* for academical—I'm not sure if that's a real word or not—purposes.

Really!

However, I don't think we could explain it that way.

Danny stands there. I know he is thinking, *Busted!*

I can tell he hasn't come up with a plausible excuse, and I certainly can't let him get into trouble.

He was only helping out his friend.

And he was really, really, really helpful.

So, I lie easily, "We were just spying on Phillip, Mrs. D." I innocently hold up the binoculars and point across the street toward Phillip's window.

Thank God Phillip is sitting at his desk, doing something on his computer.

She walks to the window and looks over at Phillip.

I give Danny a hopeful glance.

He winks back at me.

"Okay, so why was the door locked?"

"Um, well," I lie some more, "so no one came in and blew our cover. You can see how the hall light just lit this room up." I sweep my arms out into a circle. I'm kind of getting into this.

Danny and I even duck when Phillip glances, seemingly on cue, our way. I knew Phillip could read my mind because I have been sending him telepathic messages to do *just* that!

Only I hope he wasn't reading my mind earlier. I'm not sure I want him to know the things I might have been thinking about Danny.

Uh, yeah …

"He keeps looking over here. He might know it's us," Danny whispers, like he's afraid Phillip can hear us. "We've been sending him secret admirer instant messages."

I go further with Danny's lie. I laugh and say, "It's been pretty hilarious because he's been trying to juggle between our messages and his girlfriend's."

But then I glance at Danny's computer and suddenly realize it is not even turned on.

Crap!

I need to come up with something good to get her out of here fast!

Oh. I've got it.

"We also caught him perusing some *fairly entertaining websites.*"

I don't say, *As in porn,* but the way I have my eyebrows raised and a big grin on my face, I'm pretty sure she gets my drift because, all of a sudden, her face goes white, and she looks embarrassed.

Apparently, this was *way* too much information.

"Fine," she says. "I'll leave the lights off, but the door stays open."

Thankfully, she goes back downstairs. Probably straight to the phone to call Mrs. Mac and get Phillip in trouble.

"Thanks," Danny says, blowing out a big breath of air. "I couldn't come up with a good excuse. My mind was just blank."

"Well, you caught up quick. The ducking was brilliant."

"What can I say?" Danny high-fives me. "We're a good team."

A good kissing team, is what I'm thinking, but I doubt that's what he's referring to.

"Um, I suppose I'd better get home. I, uh, didn't leave a note or anything. I mean, I, uh, didn't expect this to take so long."

Funny, I didn't feel at all embarrassed when we were making out, but I feel a little awkward now. Part of me wants to run and hide; the other part of me wants to lock the world away, so I can kiss him some more.

You know, for practice's sake only!

"Come on, I'll walk you home," Danny says, not the least bit awkward.

I follow him down the stairs and out the door.

"Uh, thanks for that and everything. I, um," I stutter and wring my hands. "Danny, do you think I did okay? I mean, will I do all right on my date?"

"You know, *I don't think so*, Jay." He shakes his head and hangs it in apparent sorrow.

I look at that boy, shocked.

He continues with a sly grin, "It might take many more *long*, grueling hours of practice for you to get it right. But"—he raises his hand to his heart—"I can tell you're committed to learning, so I'll just have to take one for the team and give you some more private lessons."

I stare at that goofy boy.

"You know what they say, practice makes perfect. Let's see … how about every day after school?"

"Um, you have football practice," I reply with a *duh* in my voice.

"Damn," he says, moving his arm in an aw-shucks fashion and snapping his fingers. "But, hey, you know, anything for a friend."

"Danny, you are so noble, but I think you'd better go to practice. You can't play for Nebraska someday if you don't."

I look him in those beautiful blue eyes. It's almost too bad I kept my eyes closed while I was kissing him. "Seriously though, thank you. I was so freaked out when I got to your house, and now, I'm, like, totally relaxed."

"Ah, yeah"—Danny laughs—"two straight hours of kissing will do that."

"It didn't seem like that long," I say, shaking my head in disbelief.

"Never does. Um, let's not, you know, mention this to anyone."

"Duh."

"I doubt Brittany would approve of my tutoring you in this particular subject." He laughs, referring to his sorta girlfriend.

"I think you're probably right. And you should know that I appreciate your selflessness in my time of need."

"You'll do fine on your date." He kisses me on the cheek, throws his arm around my shoulders, and says in a practiced Southern drawl, "JJ, darlin', when you're ready ta move on past kissin' and want ta do some more *practicin'*, you just come and see ol' Uncle Danny. Anytime. Keep it in the family, love."

Oh, jeez, now, he's British.

I just shake my head at him. He really cracks me up.

"You're sick. You know that?"

"Yeah, well, that's why you love me," is his smart-aleck reply.

We are at my front porch now. I just smile at that boy, and walk in my front door.

UP IN MY room, I lie on my bed and close my eyes. My lips feel all tingly. In fact, I feel like we're *still* kissing. I think it's kind of like when you've been on a boat all day, and even though you're off it, you still can feel it rocking.

I'm really looking forward to my date now.

When Phillip calls me at ten o'clock for our nightly phone call, I tell him I have a headache and am going to sleep. I don't want to ruin the way I feel with mindless conversation.

127 days without getting grounded!

SUMMER BEFORE 11TH GRADE

DANNY, PHILLIP, AND I are sitting on the hood of Phillip's car in the parking lot of the baseball field, drinking and eating sunflower seeds. The salt's burning my lips, but it doesn't stop me from sucking it off the seeds. I had an early softball game and then stayed to watch the boys' baseball game against Park City, a neighboring small town. Everyone else has left, so the lot is dark and deserted.

We haven't left because we are *still* trying to figure out what we're going to do tonight.

We live in Westown, Nebraska. It's a small town, not far from Omaha. My parents say we are really lucky because we get the best of both worlds—small-town life with big-city amenities. Westown has an old downtown and a newer part up by the highway that goes through town. This little strip consists of your basic small-town stuff—bank, bowling alley, ice cream store, and gas station. This is the area we cruise when there is nothing better to do.

Which is a lot.

Down the highway a little farther are Johnny's Pizza, the high school, and the viaduct that takes you out of town.

Tonight, there is a party at Billy Prescott's house, and a bunch of the guys on the baseball team are going up to Johnny's for pizza first.

It's a small town, and if we feel like going out, those are our only real options.

Actually, that is not true.

I mean, there's an infinite number of places we could go and things we could do. We just say that because we like to complain that there is nothing cool to do around here. I am assuming that other teenagers say the same thing even if they live somewhere amazing, like Paris or New York.

The problem tonight is that the boys aren't motivated to go home and change.

And, personally, I have no desire to go anywhere. I love hanging out with them.

Our backs are against the windshield, and we are staring at the brilliant stars. It's a clear, warm summer night, and you can see millions of them.

Oh, in case there are any men out there freaking out about Phillip's paint job, please note that we are sitting on a blanket to protect it.

Phillip loves his car.

It's a very nice car, although I forget what kind it is. But, since it's blue, I really don't care. I mean, if you are going to go to the trouble of having a car, shouldn't it be red?

Red cars are so sexy. I am so hoping for a red one soon. I *really* want a red Mustang convertible, but I'm sure I will get something boring and reliable, like a four-door something or other.

I keep hinting to my parents about getting me a car. I turned sixteen three whole months ago.

They say they have taken it under advisement.

I'm pretty sure that means no.

We are just sitting here, spitting seeds and chatting occasionally.

That's one of the things I love about hanging out with boys.

They don't feel the need to fill every second with words and talk.

Like my girlfriends.

Sometimes, they talk so much, it makes my head hurt.

Speaking of girlfriends, it's Friday night.

Girls' night.

I'm truly breaking a cardinal rule by not being out with them. I'm pretty sure it's written in our town's laws that Friday night is girlfriend night, and Saturday night is date night. Kind of like in *Footloose*, where there is a stupid town law against dancing.

You know what my favorite part of that movie is?

Well, duh, it's definitely not the dancing. I love her red cowboy boots. I mean, I know I sort of live in the country, but I don't own even one pair of cowboy boots. Someday, I'm going to buy myself a pair of red ones, just like the ones in the movie.

Hey, they could match my red car!

Sorry. Where was I?

Oh, yeah.

I sort of had to lie to Katie and Lisa about what I was doing tonight. I couldn't really tell them I was just hanging out with the boys. They would've given me a hard time. Besides, they were going to a party some Park boys had invited them to, and I thought *that* could only lead to trouble. And, since I'm lobbying so hard for a car, I have to be responsible. I have been very responsible lately and have not gotten grounded in four months.

Which is like a record for me.

And I'm really quite proud of this accomplishment.

Besides, even though it's supposed to be *girlfriend* night, all they want to do is go out and look for boys. Or talk about them. Why can't it be friend night, and why do girls think they can only be friends with other girls?

The only time one of my friends has any interest in being a boy's friend is when she has her sights set on him as a boyfriend.

First, she pretends to want to be his friend, so he will notice her. And, sometimes, they even do become friends, but once she accomplishes that, she will try to make him her boyfriend.

I don't get it.

Danny finally breaks the silence. "So, you're missing girls' night out, huh, Jay?"

"What exactly do you guys do anyway?" Phillip asks.

"Usually drive around town and look for cute boys," I reply.

Danny wonders aloud, "Then, how come, when we drive around, looking for you, a lot of times, we can't find you? It's like you're nowhere to be found."

"Well, sometimes, we go to other towns and shop for imports." I grin.

"Imports?" Phillip questions as he spits a seed.

"Yeah, that's what Lisa and Katie are doing tonight. Going to the party in Park. They're not happy with the current supply of boys here, so they're shopping for imports. Get it?"

"You know, I've heard them say that before, but I always thought you guys were looking at, like, BMWs," Phillip says, shaking his head.

"You would," I say, rolling my eyes.

"Girls are goofy," Danny states. "And I thought Katie was dating Neil."

I shrug. I have no answer for that. 'Cause she is. But she was seriously crushing on the cute third baseman from Park City, so she was hoping sparks might fly at the party tonight. And then Neil will probably be history, which is too bad. Neil is a sweetheart.

"So, let me get this straight," Phillip says wisely. "On Saturday night, you go out with your *boyfriend*, and on Friday night, you go out and look for your *new boyfriend*."

"That pretty much sums it up," I say. "Or try to see what your current boyfriend is up to. You never know. He could be out with another girl. Speaking of that, Danny, did you tell Tiffany you would be hanging with me tonight?"

He shakes his head.

"I didn't think so. But I understand because that's the thing with girls; you could tell her you're gonna hang out with me, and it would turn into one big jealous mess.

"Phillip, your girlfriends always get mad at you about that. It's just easier not to tell them. They tend to be so dramatic. I mean, either they are crazy in love or terribly jealous or got dumped or can't get the guy they like to notice them. And, God forbid, if he finally *does* notice them, they get together and have a one-night stand, and then he doesn't call, then they feel even worse."

I don't say it because this is top-secret girl knowledge, but this happened to Lisa recently. This older guy she had been crushing on forever talked and flirted and kissed her at a party, and then he offered to take her home. I tried to tell her not to go with him, but she didn't listen. And, of course, they went parking. She was a little drunk, and, uh, well, things happened. *One-night stand* kind of things. *Losing her virginity* kind of things. Then, he never called. She has been beating herself up about it for weeks. So, I'm hoping she will meet a nice, cute boy in Park City to restore her faith in men.

"Whoa," Phillip says, suddenly very interested in what I'm saying. "Go back to the *one-night stand* part."

"Yeah," says Danny. "Who's having one-night stands, and why aren't they having them with Mac and me?"

I can't help but laugh at Danny on that one because, well, I guess he's not a *one-night stand* kind of guy. He's more the guy that you date for a week, fall in love with, and have sex with, and three weeks later, it's probably over. And, somehow, it's okay with you because you had three glorious weeks with him. And you would do it all over again.

Typically, girls hate guys like this. They feel used or taken advantage of. But not Danny's girls. They all love him, even after he leaves them. That leaves most of us wondering, *How does he do it?* I'm sure, if we did an in-depth investigation into this phenomenon, we would find out it's some kind of magic combination.

Killer abs + devil grin + easygoing, aw-shucks attitude + sparkle + great arms + amazing kisser + star quarterback + dreamy blue eyes = irresistible.

He is so cute.

"Jay," Danny says, interrupting my thoughts. "Hello? Pay attention. We are talking about one-night stands."

I can't tell them about Lisa. So, I make up something.

"Oh, uh, well, maybe not one-night stands actually. I mean, sometimes, there is sex involved, but usually, it's just that maybe there is an older guy that a girl crushes on, and he pays attention to her at a party and offers to take her home, but of course, they end up parking, and she just does more with him than she planned, and then he never calls. Or even worse, he's a total gentleman, and they just talk and kiss, and she thinks he's the one, and then he never calls. All I am trying to say is that, when I go out with the girls, we can't just sit peacefully on the hood of a car, stare at the sky, and enjoy life. They are always stressing and obsessing about something. They dissect every conversation, every stare, every word."

"You're a girl, and you're not like that," Phillip tells me. "Maybe you need some new friends."

"No," I say, shaking my head. "I think that they're probably normal and that *I'm* just weird."

"Yeah, well, we know that," Danny teases and then pelts me in the face with a wet sunflower seed from his mouth. "But we love ya anyway, Jay."

Go Westown Warriors!

11TH GRADE

WHAT A GAME!
What a close, exciting, exhilarating game!
Danny was amazing!

We were behind by a touchdown at halftime but ended up winning by six. And Danny won the game practically single-handedly!

There had been only two minutes left in the game when Coach called a quarterback sneak. Danny ran through the line, broke the huge linebacker's tackle, and went running forty yards down the field. He was dodging tackles, dragging guys behind him, and twisting out of their arms. It was an amazing run, and we all thought he was going to score—until we saw the safety barreling sideways across the field, ready to hit him at the five-yard line. Danny was not to be stopped though. He'd put his left arm out and his shoulder down and run right over the guy and into the end zone.

Touchdown!

It was brilliant really and pure Danny. Sometimes, I wonder if he's not challenged enough because, when he really wants something, it's like this light clicks on; Wonder Boy comes out, and he goes into *can't be stopped* mode. In this mode, I have seen him make amazing plays. He's a very talented quarterback.

That would be a great play to put on his scout tape. Every college in the country would want him.

Okay, so I might be a bit biased, but a lot of big-name colleges already do.

He's verbally committed to play at Nebraska, but he still has a couple more recruiting visits to make. I don't think he'll change his mind though. He's wanted to be on their team since he was a little boy.

AFTER THE GAME, Danny, Phillip, and I come home early—as in *way* before curfew—to sit in the hot tub at my house. The boys stop off at their houses to throw on their swimsuits. As I'm walking over to my house from Phillip's, I realize there is noise coming from my backyard.

It's music—'80s hair-band ballads, I think.

Tragic.

Then, I hear a man's and a woman's laughter.

I stop.

Oh.

I see that it's dark in the backyard, and I know my parents probably aren't expecting me home this early. I mean, it is a full hour and thirty-eight minutes before my curfew, and I am never early. I probably shouldn't just barge in on them. I wouldn't want them to barge in on me, but of course, they would. And I am adult enough to understand that parents ... *you know*, but it is just something I refuse to think about.

I mean, yuck.

Gross.

I reconsider going back there. I certainly don't want to see something that could very well scar me for life. As I get a little closer, I realize that there are numerous voices laughing.

Whew, they're not alone. I'll just kick them all out of the

backyard, so we can use the hot tub.

It's late, they're old, and it's, like, so way past their bedtime.

Okay, so it's not that late, and they're not *that* old.

I decide it's safe to go through the gate and am just opening it when I catch a whiff of something. At first, I wonder if they have a fire going, but then I notice it has a sweet smell to it, like burning hay.

No way!

What I see when I bound through the gate is almost too freakish to describe. Our parents are all in the hot tub.

Naked.

There are empty Corona bottles scattered all over the edge of the hot tub.

Glass bottles, I might add.

Glass!

How many *millions* of times have I been told to never have glass by the hot tub? Because, if a glass broke in the tub, you could never get it all out, and the whole thing would be ruined!

Obviously, these rules don't apply to our parents.

Then, I notice that Phillip's dad, Mr. Mac, is taking a hit off a joint.

Ah, there it is.

They are all laughing at something and are apparently already half-baked. I'm practically standing in the water with them, and they *still* have not acknowledged my presence.

Hello?

Naked parents.

Pot.

Alcohol.

I might very well be traumatized by all of this.

Somebody wanna call a shrink?

Just as I am about to say something, Mr. Diamond stands up to grab another beer.

Yikes.

I close my eyes real quick. There's no way I need to see this man naked.

I don't want to see him naked.

But I peek anyway 'cause, come on, he looks like Danny—all grown up. I open my eyes and see him standing there in all his glory.

In a swimsuit.

Dang!

I look a little closer and realize they are not naked after all. I can see some stringy things tied around Mom's neck.

But still ... pot. They are so busted.

I jump onto the hot tub stairs and say, "So, kids, this is what goes on when I'm not here. You all are so grounded."

Mom chokes on her Corona. Phillip's dad nearly swallows the joint. Everyone else, my father included, is giggling. My father laughs often, yes, but *never* giggles. They seem to think this is hysterical.

Okay, so I have to tell you, this is not exactly the picture I had in my mind of what my parents do to while away the time until I get home. I mean, sometimes, I picture them sitting in matching rocking chairs, rocking and pacing, checking their watches with worry, counting down the seconds until I'm home safely.

Lately though, I picture them as wild referees with stopwatches and big whistles.

Last Saturday, I was coming in the door very quietly—not sneaking in, mind you, but just trying to be polite and not disturb them—when it was like this huge prison spotlight came glaring on me, and Dad jumped out of nowhere.

He blew a referee's whistle at me, and a scoreboard buzzer went off as he said, "Jadyn, you are twelve and a half minutes late."

"According to whom?" I asked politely. "My watch"—which I

might have set back ten minutes or so—"says I'm right on time."

"According to NASA, that's who," Dad said, pointing to the GPS, satellite-tracking watch thingy he had.

Anyway, it's just that I don't really picture them having a life without me. I mean, I know they get together with friends to watch movies or play cards. I can picture them chatting or killing time watching *Storm Stories.*

But certainly not smoking and boozing it up in my hot tub.

Okay, so it's not really mine. I just like to think that it is.

Dad laughs and asks why I am home so early. "Fight with Brian?"

"No, Dad. It's Friday night. Friend night, remember?"

"Oh, I do!" says Phillip's mom, Julie. "I used to *love* girlfriend night. We would always go out and look for cute boys."

I shake my head and figure I'd better say something quick, or we'll all be launched on a full-scale trip down memory lane.

So, I change the subject by saying, "I hope someone is going to tell me that you're all suffering from glaucoma."

The parents chuckle at this and apparently are not the least bit embarrassed about being caught by me with a joint. I can tell you that, if the tables were turned, I'd be in big trouble.

And, excuse me, but isn't this illegal?

"The boys and I came home early, so we could sit in the hot tub." I turn to look at Danny's parents and say, "You know, your son took quite a beating out there tonight and is really sore." I'm trying to make them feel guilty. "But I guess, since it's obviously *occupied,* we'll just hang over at Danny's."

"What are you guys going to do?" Dad asks me, more politely than normal.

I pause and think, *What the hell?*

And then I grab three Coronas and a lime from the cooler. Bold, I know, but what are they gonna do, stop me?

"Well, Dad, we'll probably start with these beers, have a few shots, do a little X, have some wild sex. You know, the usual." I give him a smirk.

"Fine," Dad says, rolling his eyes at me.

Everyone laughs. Um, well, actually, everyone giggles.

What? You think I'm joking?

Sadly, I am. I am also a little irritated by this whole scene. I mean, don't you ever grow up? Shouldn't I be the one out, getting stoned and drunk with *my* friends?

Sadly, my parents' social life far surpasses mine.

That thought is very pathetic and totally tragic.

I start to head to Danny's but turn back around and say, "And, tomorrow, when you're all sober"—I wave one of my fingers back and forth at them while trying not to drop the beers—"I think we need to revisit the whole *Just Say No* concept."

I RUN OVER to Danny's house and bang on the back door with my elbow.

Phillip lets me in. Phillip and Danny are both standing there in just their swim trunks.

Damn.

It's like walking into an Abercrombie ad. Have I mentioned I love my life right now?

"We're just grabbing some towels," Phillip tells me.

I set the Coronas and lime on the kitchen island.

"Sweet," says Phillip. "My parents left me a note that said they were over at your house. What's going on over there?"

"Oh, nothing much. They're all in the hot tub. Naked, drunk, and baked," I reply flatly.

"No way!" says Phillip, his eyes big.

"Okay, so they're not naked, but at first, I thought they were." I smile, but the boys don't seem as appalled by our parents' behavior as I am, so I open the beers and grab a knife out of the drawer. I slice lime wedges, put one in each beer, and hand them to the boys.

"So, no hot tub?" Danny asks crabbily as he takes a swig of beer. "Figures."

"Let's watch a movie," Phillip suggests as he pulls a sweatshirt over his head. He turns to me with a sweet grin. "And you can make us some popcorn and nachos."

As if I can turn him down when he grins at me.

Well, actually, I can't.

"Let me guess, *American Pie* for the hundred millionth time?" I ask, knowing full well what the answer will be.

I make snacks, and we head toward the family room. I notice that Danny is moving very slowly. He's obviously sore, and he seems to be irritable. Unusual for him after a big game, especially a game he won practically single-handedly. I'd expect him to be flying high.

"What's wrong with you?" I ask him. "You had such an incredible game. Why are you being such a crab?"

"It was a rough game," he snarls at me and then says softer, "I'm just kind of sore, I guess."

I plop down on the couch between the boys.

"Do you want me to rub your back?" I ask Danny nicely.

Lots of times after a game, we'll watch movies, and I'll rub Danny's or Phillip's shoulders. I doubt Phillip is at all sore. He's Danny's number one receiver, but he got double-teamed all night and only got open in the flats—close in to the line of scrimmage, not way down field like usual. That's why it was such a tough game.

Most teams can't shut down the Danny and Phillip combination, but tonight, they did. Because they have played together so much, it's like Danny always knows where Phillip is going to be, even before he gets there. They make some amazing plays together and have a lot of confidence in each other. It's really pretty cool to watch.

ABOUT MIDWAY THROUGH the movie, I say something to Danny, and he snaps at me, "What?"

"Jeez, Danny, I just asked if you took some Advil."

"No," he says a little nicer.

"I'll grab you some," I say and reassuringly pat his forearm.

He practically jumps off the couch when I touch his arm.

"What is wrong with you?" I yell.

"I'm just a little sore there!"

I squint my eyes at that boy. *What's going on?*

"Danny, let me see your arm."

He sighs madly but gingerly holds it up for me.

I examine his forearm. No wonder he's such a crab. His arm is quite swollen. So, I touch it very gently, and crap, it feels hot to the touch.

This is not good.

And the skin is all shiny-looking.

Just a little sore, my ass.

This arm is broken.

"Danny! No wonder you're being such a butt. Your arm is broken."

My screeching gets Phillip's attention away from the TV where a hot girl is taking off her shirt.

"Did it happen on that last play? When you stiff-armed that guy? His helmet hit your arm, didn't it?" Phillip asks in rapid-fire succession.

"Um, yeah, I think so," Danny mutters. He turns to me and says, "It can't be broken, Jay. Coach thought it was just bruised."

"Yeah, well, I hate to tell you this, Danny, but he's wrong."

NEXT THING I know, I'm sprinting back over to my house. I bang through the gate and stand in front of the hot tub again.

Everyone stares at me like I'm spoiling their fun, and they wish I would leave.

I ignore that possibility and announce, "Hey, guys, um, I think Danny broke his arm."

I know *that* will at least get their attention.

"What?" they all say in alarmed unison.

Oh, sure, *now*, we're all concerned.

"Not his throwing arm?" Danny's dad asks.

God forbid!

And then Mr. Mac asks, "How?" before I can get a word in edgewise.

I answer them both, "No. It's his left forearm, and it happened when he stiff-armed that guy in the fourth quarter right before he scored."

Dad asks me, "Did they look at it in the locker room? Did Coach think it was broken?"

Coach is a great guy. He's coached winning teams at Westown for years, and everyone respects him, but excuse me, is the man a *doctor?*

I think not.

"No. He thought it was just a deep bruise, but I don't agree," I say, shaking my head like I'm an expert.

I practically am really.

"It's hot to the touch, and the skin is all swollen and shiny. So, either you're gonna have to share some of your *stash* with him to get him through the night or he needs to go and get an X-ray. And definitely some pain pills. The boy is *very* crabby."

"JJ, can you hand me the phone?" He announces, "I'm going to call Dr. Rohm and tell him to meet us at the hospital."

"I don't think that's a good idea, Chuck," Mrs. Diamond says to her husband. She turns to me and says, "JJ, do you think you could take him? We weren't planning on going anywhere tonight, and none of us"—she looks pointedly at Mr. D—"should be driving."

Obviously.

So, I say, "Yeah, we'll take him."

"Thanks, honey," she replies. "His insurance card is in the cubby by the desk. He's eighteen, so there shouldn't be any problems. We'll have Dr. Rohm meet you there."

"Drive carefully," Mom tells me.

I think it's ridiculous that they can't take their son to the hospital, and no one is giving me any credit for caring enough about him to discover that his arm is broken. So, I decide to point this out, just to let them know they all owe me big.

I raise my arms in the air and say, "FYI, everyone, just wanted to let you know that I've earned myself a Get Out of Jail Free card."

"What do you mean?" Dad asks, suspiciously eyeing me.

I point at him and look him in the eye, so he knows I am serious. "I mean, *next time* someone wants to ground me, I'm turning that card in."

PHILLIP DRIVES WHILE Danny and I sit in the backseat. Danny's head is resting on my shoulder, and his sore arm's lying across my lap while I gently stroke his swollen fingers.

Yeah, I know ...

Many, many girls would practically kill to be in my position.

And let's face it; even I am not immune to Danny's charm.

But, right now, that's like the last thing on my mind because I know all too well what broken bones feel like. I've broken my right arm, my left wrist, and three different fingers while playing football with these boys. And I couldn't even begin to count the numerous sprains, bruises, cuts, and stitches. So, instead of feeling slightly turned on, I just feel like I'm going to cry.

And that's weird because I didn't even cry when I broke my own bones.

OH, AND FYI, to all you doubters out there, Danny's arm was

indeed broken.
  I was right!
  I love it when that happens!

Let it snow!

DECEMBER – 11TH GRADE

I'M SITTING IN my room, curled up on my window seat, reading a great book. I'm having a hard time putting it down because I'm dying to find out if Madison will end up with Chase and if they'll be able to solve the mystery and return the stolen diamond before the Mafia hit man gets them. I only have a few chapters left, and although I want to peek at the ending, I could never do that.

It would ruin a perfectly good story!

Just as I am getting to a really steamy part, where Chase *accidentally* walks in on Madison while she is in the shower—*accidental, my ass*—my phone rings.

It's Lisa. *Dang it!* She is so chatty. I might never get her off this phone!

She is regaling me with the story of Christmas at her father's crazy relatives', and I am half-listening, half-reading when a huge snowball splats on my window, scaring me to death and causing me to drop both my book and the phone. I bend down, pick up the phone, and put it back up to my ear just as another snowball hits my window.

"What was that?" Lisa cries in my ear.

"Sorry. I dropped you. Someone is throwing snowballs at my window. It scared the crap out of me."

"Well, who is it?" she snaps impatiently.

I glance out and see Danny holding a football up in the air, grinning at me. Phillip has so many clothes on that he looks like the Michelin Man.

"It's Phillip and Danny. I think they want me to come play football with—"

"Strip football?" Lisa screeches, interrupting me. "I'm coming over. Now."

I hear a click in my ear and know that she has hung up on me. Kind of rude, don't ya think?

But I will probably forgive her because she has a huge crush on Danny, and the idea of seeing him with no shirt on is almost too much for her to handle.

I think it's hilarious.

I mean, he's just a guy. Okay, he's a hot guy.

I open my window and yell to the boys, "Be right down."

STRIP FOOTBALL.

Sounds indecent, I know.

But we don't strip, like, naked or anything.

Well, at least not completely.

Strip football is a game we created a few years ago. It is usually played on a sunny day when there is snow on the ground. The rules are a bit sketchy at best, mostly because Danny and I tend to make them up as we go. The basic gist of it is, if you mess up—like miss a well-thrown pass, get intercepted, fumble the ball, or miss an important tackle—you lose an article of clothing. Danny and I tend to argue—okay, so we fight—during this game because what constitutes a bad play or pass is a bit of a *gray* area.

And, well, Danny and I both always think we're right.

That's where Phillip comes in.

I am convinced that the United Nations should send Phillip to the Middle East. In under an hour, he would have a peace treaty signed with all parties thinking they got the best deal. It is simply due to his fine negotiation skills that Danny and I don't kill each other.

He is truly amazing. Smart, too. Somehow, I think, since he never gets involved in the arguments, he always stays warm and dry while Danny and I are running around in the snow with nothing on but a T-shirt, jeans, one sock, and, if we're lucky, maybe a mitten.

The fun part about playing the game in the winter—we have played in the summer, but the game is over pretty fast—is that you have lots of layers to strip off before you're out of the game.

Our moms used to yell at us because they were afraid we'd freeze to death. It's a major embarrassment to be called inside by your mom. Much worse than losing outright. But, thankfully, they gave up on us, assuming we were old enough to come in the house before frostbite set in.

I quickly put on multiple layers. First, a swimsuit and then a T-shirt, bike shorts, sweatshirt, sweatpants, snow pants, jacket, socks, boots, and mittens. I pull my hair back in a ponytail and throw on a baseball cap, and then I add sunglasses and a scarf for good measure.

You have to be very careful about how many layers you put on because there is a fine line between perfect and too many.

Too many layers, and you can't bend your elbows or knees.

And, if you can't bend them, it makes it very difficult to throw, catch, and run. Then, you can end up stripped so fast that the extra layers didn't really do you any good in the first place.

WHEN I GET outside, I see that it's not just Danny and Phillip who are going to play, but some other guys have shown up, too.

As you can imagine, strip football is a bit of a novelty game and is developing quite a following. You'd think, since there is stripping involved, that it would be a coed game, like strip poker, but this game is for guys only.

Well, except for me. And it's more of an I'm a manly, macho, tough guy, and I can stand to be out in the cold weather, playing football with practically no clothes on kind of game.

The boys have already split into two teams by the time I plod over through the snow. We had a beautiful white Christmas, and there's about four inches of new snow blanketing the grass.

The teams seem to be split—juniors versus seniors—with Phillip, Neil, Joey, and me on one team and Danny, Dillon, Kevin, and Brandon on the other.

We huddle up and start on offense. Joey plays quarterback and makes a perfect throw to Phillip. Phillip catches it but fumbles it, and off comes a coat. The game continues like this. Every few plays, someone loses an article of clothing. I'm doing pretty well. I have only lost my jacket, cap, and scarf. Phillip, who I knew was way too bulked up, has lost all three of his jackets and is now performing much better.

Our team is also winning—twenty-one to fourteen!

LISA SHOWS UP with Katie. The two of them are dressed like they are going to some posh ski resort in Aspen or somewhere. Katie has on trendy, furry boots, and Lisa has some sort of sparkly stuff on her cheeks. I swear, they are such girlie girls! It cracks me up!

They keep working on making me that way, and apparently, they've had some success because, just the other day, I bought a pair of jeans with rhinestones on the pockets.

Mom loves them!

They also tell me that I must wear at *least* mascara and lip gloss every day.

So, I do. And I am getting pretty proficient at eye shadow as well.

Did I mention that both of them decided to try out for cheerleading last year and made it?

Of course, I don't hold that against them. They both tried basketball with me as freshman, and it was kinda sad. I would much rather be a cheerleader than a benchwarmer, too.

And they feel it has definitely raised their popularity factor.

They have Lisa's trunk open and are getting out what, upon first glance, appears to be full tailgating paraphernalia, but it is really just two lounge chairs, a table, and a couple of thermoses full of hot chocolate with, knowing them, a little Peppermint Schnapps.

That will earn them bonus points with the boys.

I politely ask them if they would like to play with us, knowing full well, there's a snowball's chance in hell that they will.

This is when Danny, for no apparent reason, starts purposely picking on me.

Well, actually, there is a reason.

Lisa drives him nuts.

She really hoped that, once she became a cheerleader, she would have a shot at dating Danny, but it hasn't happened so far. And, between you and me, I don't think it ever will. Even though she's now a cheerleader, she's still not Danny's type.

But Lisa is an eternal optimist, and Danny is currently girl-friend-less.

Stranger things have happened.

SO, DANNY STARTS throwing the ball to Dillon, who I'm guarding—and, shh, sorta crushing on right now. He is so cute!

Oh, sorry.

So, I'm a tall girl, but Dillon is about six-four.

Yes, Mom was right. The boys have finally caught up. Anyway, he's a full six inches taller than me, so, aside from my being distracted by his cuteness, Danny's passing the ball to him so far above my head that I have no chance to defend it.

And it's really pissing me off.

SOON, WE ARE losing by a score of twenty-one to twenty-eight, and I'm left with just my socks and boots, snow pants, and swimsuit top.

Danny throws a great pass to Dillon in the end zone.

And, well, you know what they say; desperate times call for desperate measures—or maybe a little creativity.

Dillon jumps up and catches the ball, but he lands *just outside* the out-of-bounds line.

Really! I swear.

Okay.

So, my fingers might be crossed behind my back, but whatever.

I say, "No good. Out of bounds."

"No way!" Danny raises both of his arms straight up in the air. "Touchdown."

I shake my head at him. Dillon isn't exactly sure where he landed. I was really the only one who saw.

Danny comes bounding down toward me, looking for Dillon's boot prints, which I have already *conveniently* obscured.

"TD." Danny smirks. "What's it gonna be this time, Jay? How about the swimsuit top?" he teases, daring me to take off my top.

Like that would ever happen—other than maybe in his dreams.

I walk up to him and hand him the football. "In your dreams, *sweetie.* He was out of bounds. No touchdown."

"Prove it because the field judge—*me*"—he smiles a fake smile—"saw him land in bounds."

He is so competitive and a liar, I am sure. He couldn't have seen.

"Oh, yeah? Well, the line judge didn't have a clear view," I say, nodding toward Phillip. "The side judge over there was watching the cheerleaders." I point at Neil, who's flirting with Lisa and Katie. "And since there is *no* instant replay"—I give him a curt smile—"I'm just gonna have to call a do-over. It's only fair."

"You're a cheater," Danny says, squinting his eyes at me.

I raise my eyebrows at that boy and say, "Yeah? Well, that's better than being a liar."

I mean, really, it is.

Phillip finally comes over to intervene, and I get my way.

Yes!

We do the down over, and Danny does the exact same play.

I told you! He's after me!

But, this time, I'm expecting it, and I jump up as high as I can in front of Dillon and manage to just tip the ball away from him.

"That wasn't your fault, Dillon," I tell him. "Danny loses something on that one. It was a terrible throw."

Dillon is on my side instead of his teammate's on this one because all he has left on are his jeans and his boots, and he really doesn't want to give up a boot.

I jog back up to midfield and tease Danny, "That didn't work out quite the way you planned, did it, Danny boy?"

He hates to be called that. His mom called him that when he was little.

"So, what's it gonna be, Danny? Your shirt or a shoe?"

That boy gets a nasty look on his face, but then the look changes, and he smiles a wide, slightly evil smile at me.

Devil Danny is back, I think, and he's standing right in front of me.

I glance at Lisa. She can barely contain her excitement. I mean, this is what she has been out here braving the cold for.

Danny stands in front of me and very, *very* slowly pulls his T-shirt up over his chest. He is doing a striptease just for my benefit. Although I'm willing to bet that Lisa will warp things in her mind and be convinced that he is showing off for her.

Most of me wants to collapse in a fit of giggles when he gets the shirt off and swings it above his head like a lasso. But I have to admit, when he takes his shirt off, even though I have seen it a million times, it kinda takes my breath away.

Just for a minute.

Somehow, he is still tan, and the sweat on his naked chest glitters in the sun, just like it glitters in the snow all around him.

That shouldn't be that much of a surprise really. I mean, Danny pretty much glitters all the time. His last name is really quite appropriate.

God, he has a great chest!

I know Lisa, Katie, and I will discuss it in excruciating detail later. It's not even that Danny's all that big, but the muscles in his arms and shoulders are *just perfect*, and his body is lean in *just the right places*. That brings us to that faint little line of blond hair running from his chest, down through that beautiful six-pack of abs, and to God knows where else.

Don't even want to think about that.

I realize that Danny has tossed his sweaty shirt on my head. I take it off and fling it over to Lisa, who catches it and cuddles it with affection.

I stand there and grin at that boy. "Chilly, *honey?*"

"Absolutely not, *darling*. You?"

WE ALWAYS PRETEND to love each other after a fight because it makes Phillip happy. In these games, it seems that Danny and I always argue until we are cold enough to call a truce and gang up on Phillip.

LATER IN THE game, Danny hands off the ball to Brandon, who promptly fumbles it. With this fumble, he is down to only his jeans and one wet sock. I'm sure his feet are quite cold.

Brandon wants to call the game, but Danny fervently tries to talk him out of it because their team is winning. If a player bails out, that team automatically forfeits the game regardless of the score.

I just smile, watching him try to convince a freezing and shaking Brandon that he's not really cold.

He tells him, "It's all mental," and, "Tough it out."

"No way, man. I can't take it any longer," Brandon finally says.

Yay! We win!

Our team huddles up, and we hoot, holler, and high-five each other.

"DO YOU SEE my sweatshirt?" I ask Phillip.

My teeth are chattering now that I'm not running, and I realize how cold I am. Phillip bends down and lifts my sweatshirt up out of the snow where Dillon carelessly flung it. It's all wet and cold.

We both sadly look at it.

Then, he does the sweetest thing.

He says, "Here, Princess," and takes his own warm sweatshirt off and pulls it over my head.

Now, I know everyone gets all hyped up over Danny, but Phillip, who is his workout partner, is a few inches taller than Danny and carries more weight. Quite honestly, Phillip's muscles are bigger, and I kinda like them even better. I get a little peek at his abs because, when he pulls up his sweatshirt to take it off, his T-shirt rides up with it.

Yummy. Very yummy.

You know, being friends with cute boys does have its benefits.

Phillip wraps those muscular arms around me and rubs his hands up and down the sides of my arms, trying to warm me up. He's saying something to me about a great team, but he's standing so close to me that, for a minute, I kind of get lost in his eyes.

I swear, he's so sweet that, if he wasn't my friend, I think I might kiss him.

"Thanks, Phillip," I say, blinking away that thought. "I think we need to hit the hot tub!"

"Come on." He grabs my hand and drags me behind him. "Let's get a head start."

When we're halfway to my house, he yells, "Last one in the hot tub is a loser." He looks back at Danny and his team and says, "Oh, sorry. *I forgot.* You already are!"

Hey, princess!

FEBRUARY – 11TH GRADE

I GRAB MY phone and am just getting ready to dial Phillip's number for our nightly phone call when the phone rings in my hand and startles me. I look at the caller ID, expecting to see Phillip's number, but instead I see *Renner, David.*

Who the heck is David Renner?

Was that the name of the hot guy Lisa and I met at the sporting goods store the other day?

She used to detest going to the sporting goods store with me, but she's recently discovered that it's one of the few place guys actually *like* to shop. I mean, how many guys has she ever met in her girlie stores?

Exactly none!

So, while I was trying on jogging shorts, she was trying on boys. Well, not literally, but she did get herself a date and, well, supposedly one for me, too, with this guy's friend. Who, I might add, is clearly not capable of getting his own dates. I mean, he is not very fortunate in the looks department. So, aside from the fact that I already have a boyfriend, I'm sure I will be coming down with something highly contagious this Friday.

Then, it hits me.

Renner.

Allison Renner. Phillip's girlfriend, right?

Is he calling me from her house? No, it's past ten, his school night curfew.

As if he needs one. I swear, he's the only person I know—and quite possibly the only teen in the entire universe—who *prides* himself on being home *before* curfew.

I look across the street and see that his bedroom light is on.

I answer with a polite, "Hello?"

"JJ, this is Allie," Allison says, using the name her friends call her.

No duh.

"Hey, Allison. What's up?" I answer, trying to sound pleasant but purposely not using the name her friends call her.

'Cause this is weird. I mean, she and I aren't good friends.

Honestly, we're not friends at all. In fact, I really don't care for her much. She's very annoying, and she talks a mile a minute. It's like she hardly needs to breathe. The boys at school make crass remarks about what else that would make her good at. Boys are sick. Anyway, she acts like she owns Phillip, and they've only been dating for, like, three weeks. I don't think she'll last much longer though.

I've never spoken to her on the phone before, so naturally, I get the feeling I'm being set up. You know, like when your friends call you on a three-way call but pretend that only one of them is there, and she tries to get you to say bad stuff about the other friend, who is secretly listening, and then they both get mad at you.

"Um, JJ, I have a quick question for you; it's about Phillip— well, I'm sure you guessed that, and I mean, I know you guys are neighbors and good friends, and, well, I really need you to tell me something because I really like Phillip, and I don't want to be stupid and not believe him, but I also don't want to be stupid and be, like, cheated on."

God, she talks fast!

"Allison, Phillip is not cheating on you!"

He wouldn't! He's not that kind of guy. I mean, *granted*, he'll be dumping her soon, but it will be because her clinginess is driving him mad. As in she is always complaining he spends too much time with me. But that's beside the point.

"What would ever make you think that?"

"Well, I just called him, and he answered the phone in this sweet, sexy voice, and he never talks to me like that."

"What did he say?"

This should be good. Did he call her another girl's name?

"He said, 'Hey, Princess,'" she says, imitating his velvety-smooth voice.

Oh, boy.

Surely, he didn't. He would never tell.

I'd kill him!

I glance over to his house and see his bedroom light flickering off and on, off and on.

I'm assuming that is some form of SOS.

I hear my computer ding, and I'm sure it's a message from him. I've got to stall this girl.

"Um, Allison, did you ask him who this *Princess* is?" I ask as I run over to my computer.

"Yeah, I did."

"Well, what'd he tell you?"

There is an instant message from Receiver—Phillip. It's just one-half of a word.

Ash.

I send him back a message from Cess. Everyone thinks it stands for Excess, to which I tend to do everything, but Phillip set up my account, so it's really short for Princess.

I write, You owe me!

"Um, JJ, you know who it is, don't you? So, could you please tell me first, so I know if he's lying to me?"

"Sure, Allison," I say, bored. "Phillip's sister, Ashley's, nickname is Princess," I lie.

Totally lie.

Her Royal Queeness possibly.

Her Royal Highness, Ruler of the World, perhaps but *never* a lowly princess.

"Oh, thank goodness," she gushes. She's all happy now and rambles on, "I mean, I wanted to believe him, but I just didn't know what to think, and I mean, his voice sounded all sweet and gentle, and I guess it would make sense that he talks to his sister that way."

Not.

They fight like crazy.

He really loves her, but he says that it's his job to annoy her. And he does.

But I'm not really listening to Allison ramble. I'm lost in thought. I never realized it before, but Phillip does have a special voice he uses when he speaks just to me. It's one of the reasons I love talking to him before I go to sleep. It's sort of soothing.

I don't think I would've ever qualified it as *sexy*.

Puh-leeze. That's just silly.

But, when I talk to him, it's kind of like I do a brain dump—tell him about my day, the good, the bad, and the ugly—and then he tells me what I should do. Of course, I usually don't do it, but talking to him is kind of like getting a mental massage.

Allison says, "Thanks, JJ. See you at school."

I HANG UP and call Phillip while I type, *It's me! Pick up!*

He answers, "Hey, Princess."

Okay, so it is kind of dreamy.

"You owe me," I tell him.

"No, you owe me. I could've just told her the truth."

"Yeah, well, then I would've had to kick your ass, and I'm afraid that might be damaging to our friendship and your reputation."

He laughs at me.

Quite possibly because my chances of kicking his buff ass are very slim indeed. But, since I could do it when we were young, I cling to the idea that I still could.

He finds this humorous and told me recently that he would love nothing more than for me to try. Of course, then Danny piped in with the kind of nasty comment only a boy could make, so I let it slide.

"Enough of your girl problems," I say. "Mark called me tonight and wants to hang out on Saturday."

Mark was a hot coworker of mine at my short-lived attempt at waitressing. He's nineteen, in college, and totally hot. Did I mention that? Thick, wavy blond hair, big muscles, great body, hot car.

He's what Lisa would call a trifecta.

Hot face. Hot bod. Hot car. Trifecta, baby.

Unfortunately, he seems to only see me as his cute little work friend.

Yeah, it blows.

But I'm totally infatuated with the guy. I can't help it.

Whenever he calls, I drop everything and change all my plans in order to go hang out with him.

Last time, I even ditched my new boyfriend, Dillon. And Danny gave me all sorts of crap about that.

He was like, "Dillon is my friend. You can't just be doing that."

But, honestly, I didn't think it was that big of a deal because Mark and I always just sort of hung out together. And Dillon told me, as long as it was just a friend thing, he was cool with it.

Unfortunately, it has been just a friend thing.

Until last time, that is.

And, this time, he's asked me to go out to dinner somewhere kinda nice, which makes it sound like an actual date. So, I am really excited!

"What should I do, Phillip? I'm kinda supposed to go to a movie with Dillon."

"Kind of?"

"Okay, we have a date," I reply curtly.

"So, what'd ya tell Mark?"

"Um, that I'd let him know," I lie.

"You know, I don't know why you always jump every time that guy calls, and then when he doesn't call, you get all depressed. What's that line he always says?"

I sigh. "'When you least expect it, expect it.'"

"Yeah, what the heck does that mean anyway?"

We've been over this many times before, but I reply, "It means, just when I'm at the end of my rope, waiting to hear from him and close to believing I'll never hear from him again, that's when he calls."

And he does. He's got it down to an exact science.

"I'm just saying, that isn't exactly the best way to treat a girl you like."

"That's the problem, Phillip; we're *just* friends, so it's not like I can complain about it."

"I thought you kissed him last time you went out," Phillip says.

Uh, yeah. And I've been reliving it every night and during all my classes for the past few weeks. He was such a good kisser. And it was perfect, exactly how I had imagined it. I thought, *This is it. He wants me. We'll be together, and it will be amazing.*

Then ...

One week ...

No call.

I told myself that, if he didn't call in two more days, I would never speak to him again.

Then …

Two weeks …

Still no call.

By then, I gave up hope of ever hearing from him again and convinced myself that it was just a dream. I also decided, if he did ever call, I might speak to him but only to make sure he was still alive because I was a concerned citizen. But, after that, I was going to give that boy a piece of my mind!

Finally, after two weeks and three days, he called and asked me to dinner.

I wanted to scream at him, *You freaking jerk*, but I caved and said, "That sounds great."

I'm so dumb.

Hey, wait a minute. I know Phillip never forgets *anything*, but I don't recall telling him this piece of information. I haven't even told Lisa. I was keeping it to myself.

Hoarding it.

Plus, I seriously didn't want Danny to find out. Or Dillon, for that matter.

"Uh," I stammer, unsure of how to answer.

"No, you didn't tell me he kissed you," he says, reading my mind.

I swear, he can sometimes.

"I saw him all over you when he dropped you off."

"Phillip, were you spying on me?"

"Actually, no," he says in a believable tone. "I was seeing if your light was on."

Sure.

"Phillip, what should I do?"

"What you *should* do is tell him you're busy—*for once*. But what you're gonna do is break up with Dillon and go out with him. Right?"

Okay, so the boy has me figured out. And he's right. That is what I'll do. How can I help it?

Hot face. Hot bod. Hot car. Trifecta. *Triple threat.*

"So, what are you gonna tell him?"

"Well, I already kinda said yes," I say, telling the truth this time.

"Told you. You're hopeless! Night, Princess."

"Night, Phillip."

I GO TO bed, thinking of Mark and willing myself to have a juicy dream about him. But, instead, I have some warped one where Phillip rescues me from Mark's car because Mark has turned into some evil werewolf/vampire creature.

Bizarre.

SO, MY DATE on Saturday with Mark didn't go so well. I suppose my dream should have been an indication of what was to come. It seemed Mark decided, unbeknownst to me, that he wanted to be *more* than just friends.

A lot more!

He took me parking *before* dinner. I said no way, and he took me straight home. Aren't guys supposed to at least buy you dinner before they expect that? I was so upset. And, of course, Danny is mad at me for breaking up with Dillon, and Dillon is still mad at me for breaking up with him.

Maybe I'll just give up on boys.

Okay, maybe not.

I mean, they're just so cute!

If you've got it, flaunt it.

SUMMER BEFORE 12TH GRADE

TODAY IS THE perfect day for lying out in the sun. It's almost eighty degrees, and there is a soft, cool breeze. I don't plan on wasting a day like today!

So, I'm in my room, putting on my new swimsuit. I'm really excited about this suit. It's my first *real* bikini. I've always worn a two-piece, but they are more of an athletic cut. This is one of those wonderful, skimpy, stringy things. I've never bought a string bikini because I've always looked stupid in them. Let's face it; you've got to have a figure to wear a suit like this. I've never had much of a figure unless you consider the shape of a board an attractive figure. Yes, I've heard all the sayings.

"Flat as a pancake."

"String bean."

"Toothpick."

"Tall drink of water."

"Beanpole."

That's one I don't really get. I mean, I understand the bean part and the pole part, but what is a beanpole anyway? You'd think, since I'm from a place where beans grow in fields and that I have actually *walked* beans, that I would know, but I don't. Speaking of walking beans, I truly believe Congress needs to step in and enact some child endangerment legislation against that job.

Have you ever walked beans?

It's the most disgusting thing on earth. I lasted one day—well, half a day really. I just couldn't see mucking around in the mud in the blazing sun with all the bugs, chopping down weeds with a scythe.

Yes, a scythe.

Do you *know* what a scythe is? It's, like, a huge, sharp, curved pirate sword.

And they hand them out to kids!

I am very fortunate that I didn't chop off one of my legs while cutting down those stubborn weeds. That or the guy's leg in the row next to me. And I have to tell you, when you think weeds, you think maybe a few here and a few there, like at home in your landscaping. But, no, there are about a gazillion weeds in each row. And these weeds aren't just little things either, but often corn stalks. And it takes a lot of work to chop just one of them down. And I swear, each bean row must be, *at a minimum,* several hundred miles long.

At least, that's what it felt like.

After about four hours of walking beans, I have to admit, I was ready to use the scythe on myself, just to make the misery stop. But then I figured I'd forever be remembered as the girl who killed herself in a bean field.

Not exactly the legacy I was hoping for!

So, I quit.

I'll take babysitting some cute kids as a summer job any day. You take the kids to the pool, flirt with the lifeguards, and get a wicked tan. You go have ice cream, take the kids home, and put them down for a nap. Then, you sit in the air-conditioning and watch *Oprah* and your soaps. A much nicer working environment, I think.

But back to the beanpole thing.

I looked it up on the internet and guess what. There is such a thing as a beanpole. It's all one word. *It is a thin pole used to support bean vines.* Just what you would think, I guess, but I can tell you that I never saw one of them during my bean-walking experience!

Where was I?

Oh, yeah, my bikini body.

It seems a strange thing happened this year. I went from a nonexistent A-cup to a nice, full B. Granted, Katie and Lisa have had boobs like this since about sixth grade—okay, so my body is a little slow—but I have to say, they were worth the wait! For once in my life, I actually fill out a bikini top on my own—as in no padding—and it looks pretty good, I think. I *almost* feel sexy in it. Mom was with me when I found it. At first, I thought it might be a little too skimpy, but she liked it on me.

She said, "If you've got it, flaunt it because, once you have kids, your body will never be the same."

This from a woman who is five-nine and a perfect size six. She goes and works out three times a week with a group of friends.

Although, from the sound of it, I suspect there is more gossiping and coffee-drinking going on than actual exercising. However, she must be doing something right because she still wears a bikini herself and looks good in it. When we go on vacation to the beach, it's really kind of embarrassing because the young guys pay more attention to her than they do me.

Maybe there is hope for me.

Of course, I'd prefer not to have to wait twenty years before I get a boy to notice me in a swimsuit.

In all seriousness, I know there are large, really important issues in the world. World peace, terrorism, nuclear arms, and global warming. But, honestly, finding the perfect swimsuit has got to be at the very tip-top of most women's list regardless of race, religion, political, or sexual orientation. So, in finding this perfect bikini, I really feel I've done my part to help conquer this great world issue.

I'm thinking about the bikini's big inaugural event. It will first be viewed by the public—and, specifically, Jake, who I've been dating off and on for about three months now—at a big river outing some of us are having next weekend. Today, my plan is to hide in the backyard and fill in my tan lines, so it really looks great.

I am prepared to lie in the sun all afternoon if that's what it takes.

I am so proud of my strong convictions!

I have the whole place to myself. Mom is at a volunteer meeting, and Dad is at work. Jake would be pissed to learn that I'm home alone and not begging him to come over—you know, so we can *be alone*—but I'm not in the mood to deal with *that* today. It's too perfect of a day. So, I put the stringy thing on and appraise myself in the mirror.

Not bad.

The bikini is of the string variety, like I said. It's supposed to look like the American flag. One side of the triangular top is blue with white stars. The other side is red with white stripes. The bottoms are also red and white stripes, and all the strings are made from the star fabric. It is really very cute.

I HEAD OUT to the backyard, move my chaise into the sun, and cover myself with a mixture of baby oil and iodine. I know, *I know*; no sunblock is a bad thing. But my mom used it when she was young, and she doesn't have cancer or anything. Plus, it works great!

I lie down on my stomach first. Next to me is a table with an ice-cold Diet Coke and a trashy novel to read if I so desire. Playing is my current favorite mix CD.

Ah, perfection.

I close my eyes and start to daydream. I'm envisioning Jake's possible reactions to the tiny bikini. They have ranged, so far, from him wrapping me in a towel because he is so desperately jealous and doesn't want anyone else to see it to attacking me with kisses out on a raft to his fainting in amazement of my body to—

"Hey, Jay," a male voice says.

I open one eye and see Danny's head peeking through the gate.

"Come play catch with me and Mac."

Oh, come on. Can't you see I am very busy?

"Ah, Danny, I can't. I've got oil all over me."

"Please, Jay. I've got football camp coming up, and I haven't thrown a pass in two weeks."

"What about Kelly Majesky?" I reply smartly, referring to his latest in a long string of female conquests.

Really, if Danny were a girl, he would totally be considered a slut.

"*Football* passes, Jay," he says smoothly, rolling those baby-blue eyes at me. "Come on."

"I can't, Danny. I really need to work on my tan today. I'm all set up here."

"When we're done, I'll take you and Phillip to The Shack for ice cream," he bribes in a singsong voice. "My treat. *Come on.* You can get a tan while playing football. You play in a swimsuit all the time." He pauses. "Of course, with all that oil on, you'll be harder to tackle. Maybe you'll give Phillip a run for his money. For once."

For once?

A challenge, huh?

Hmm.

"I want a double cheeseburger, fries, a chocolate shake, and maybe even a hot fudge sundae. Deal?"

"Pig," he replies but nods his head in agreement.

"Fine, I'll be there in a minute."

I lay my head back down and try to revive my daydream. Unfortunately, it's long gone.

I look at my back. No change yet, but I guess Danny's right. I can play with my suit on.

Play and fill in the tan lines at the same time.

I am so efficient!

So, I get up from my comfy spot, walk over to the picnic table, hook my finger through a belt loop on my favorite cutoffs, pull them off the table, and drag them behind me. I walk over to my fence and fling open the gate.

Danny and Phillip are casually tossing the ball to each other in the empty lot next door. The lot has a luscious carpet of grass that Phillip and Danny work hard to keep immaculate, just for this purpose.

I start to walk toward them, and then I think, stop, and yell, "Shoes or no shoes?"

You have to decide this in the beginning because, if you don't have shoes and the other guy does, it can be a very painful day for your toes. If the boys are feeling very serious about their practice, it's shoes.

Most often though, it's no shoes.

I keep standing there, holding my shorts, waiting for an answer.

"Hello?" I say, waving my shorts in their direction.

But the boys are both just standing there, staring at me, their mouths agape.

Is one of my boobs hanging out or something? I take a quick look down at myself. No, everything appears to be in order.

What? It's like they can see me, but they can't hear me.

"Shoes?" I yell again because maybe they *didn't* hear me.

"Uh," says Phillip, looking down at his own feet like he can't remember if he has them on. "Um, no shoes."

Phillip gives Danny a sideways glance, and Danny smiles back at him.

What's up with those two? I probably missed some stupid boy joke. Whatever.

I jog over to them in my bare feet, pull on my shorts, and zip them up. "Okay, I'm ready."

"Uh, new swimsuit, Jay?" Danny asks with his eyebrows raised at me, half a smirk on his face.

"Yeah. Do you like it? I got it for the Summer Bash next week."

Danny doesn't answer my question but asks one of his own, "Your dad seen it yet?"

"Well, no, but he's not going to the party. So, do you guys like it? Does it look okay?" I stare at Phillip. "Phillip?"

Phillip is still looking at me, sort of shocked.

What's the deal? Does it look bad?

Phillip starts to open his mouth to say something. At first, nothing comes out, but then he says, "I think I like that pink one you have better."

Jerk!

The pink one he is referring to is practically a granny-style one-piece. I give that boy a mad face.

Danny looks at Phillip and shakes his head at him. Then, he winks at me and says, "Go long, right, Jay."

I do, and we play catch for about thirty minutes, running various plays and routes. It's usually fun and a good workout for me. But, the whole time we're playing, Phillip's bikini comment is festering in my brain.

I brilliantly intercept a pass, and I nearly scream out loud, *Ha-haha-haha, Phillip! You jerk!* But I withhold my comments and give him a smirky grin instead.

That apparently doesn't bother him in the least because he shrugs his shoulders at me, his body saying, *No big deal.*

And that really pisses me off.

So, on the next play, as we're running side by side down the field, I carefully stick my foot out with the intention of *accidentally* tripping him.

Only it doesn't quite work as I imagined because my leg gets tangled up with his, and we both go down.

BOOM.

I land on my side with a thud and literally bounce off the grass.

And it must knock the wind out of me because I can't seem to breathe.

I try to take a breath, but before I can, Phillip rolls me over on my back, pins my arms above my head, and sits on me.

At first, I think he's going to tickle me or something, but then my oxygen-deficient brain registers his brown eyes flashing black.

Uh-oh. I don't think he's very happy with me.

I painfully suck in a breath of air just as he leans down close to my face.

Warm, minty breath blows on me when he yells, "You did that on purpose!"

"What are you talking about?" I ask ever so innocently.

Who? Me?

"You're being mean! I don't know what your problem is, but I won't let you hurt us both. I'll be damned if I miss senior year football with a broken leg because you can't play nice."

"Poor little Phillip. Can't play with the *big* girls?"

"I play *fine* with girls," Phillip answers with a smirk of his own.

A little too fine lately, if you ask me.

He might be getting too cute and confident for his own good.

He pushes my hands into the ground. "I'm serious. No more cheap shots."

"You can't tell me what to do, Phillip."

"Maybe not, but I'll tell your dad you've been a poor sport."

Oh crap. He's got me on that.

"Fine. Get off me."

Phillip stays where he is and says in his calmer, sweeter voice, "What are you so pissed about anyway? Are you mad at Danny?"

Is he serious? I mean, is he really that clueless? How could he possibly not know what has me so upset? And, really, why do I care what he thinks anyway? He's just a big, fat dork who dates clueless girls. Girls who wouldn't know a tight spiral pass if it hit them in the, uh, well, you know.

"Hey! You guys gonna get a room, or do you wanna play some football?" Danny yells from across the yard.

Danny. Wow. I almost forgot he was here.

But I'm glad because his comment jerks me out of my feeling-sorry-for-myself mood, and my cockiness comes rushing back. I raise an eyebrow at Phillip and then let my eyes wander down the length of his body.

I mean, he is on top of me.

He gives me the evil eye, gets up, and throws the ball back to Danny. "I've had enough," he says.

I hop up and follow Phillip to where Danny's standing.

All of a sudden, my legs feel itchy.

Crap.

A bunch of loose grass clippings are stuck to the oil on my legs. *Not particularly attractive,* I think as I try to brush them off.

Danny, trying to ease the unusual tension between Phillip and me, laughs and points at me. He calls me the Grass Monster or something equally juvenile and stupid.

Phillip finally laughs, too, and then says, "I'm starving!"

"Yeah, me, too. Let's go," Danny agrees. He bends down, grabs his T-shirt off the grass, and slides his feet into a pair of flip-flops.

"I've gotta run home and grab a shirt and some shoes," Phillip tells us.

I start to head to my house to grab a shirt, too.

Danny responds to Phillip by saying, "Jay's driving that hot new Mustang of hers." Then, he runs up behind me, snaps me on the butt with his T-shirt, and follows me home.

"What was that all about?"

"Oh, he was just pissed because he thought I tripped him on purpose."

Danny looks at me like a human lie detector. "Did you?"

I chuckle. "Maybe ..."

I shove my shoulder into his and say, "So, I know what *Phillip* thinks of the bikini, but you never gave me a straight answer. So, do you like it? Come on, Danny, I value your opinion, and I really don't want to wear it to the party if it looks stupid on me."

Danny thinks for a moment, like he's not sure what to say.

I mean, come on!

Any other girl in a bikini, and Danny would be giving me much more information about the bikini than I would ever want to know. You'd think he'd at least be able to answer one simple question about *my* bikini.

Finally, Danny turns to me and says blandly, rolling his eyes, "Jake will love it."

Yay!

"But you'd better just have water at the Shack, or you might outgrow it before the party."

I flash angry eyes at him, but I can tell by his smirk that he's just teasing me.

"Cheapskate. You're just trying to get out of buying me lunch."

You're not wearing that.

SUMMER BEFORE 12TH GRADE

"MOM," I YELL as I bound down the stairs to the kitchen. "Can you tie these strings in tight double knots for me?" I'm holding my bikini top up to my chest. The straps are trailing behind me.

It's the day of the Summer Bash, and I'm running late—as usual. Jake will be here any minute, and I am so not ready.

Mom is standing at the kitchen sink. Dad is sitting at the table, drinking a cup of coffee and reading the Sports section.

He glances up and quickly reverts to the paper. Then, his head comes flying back up. He looks at Mom and then at me and says, "You're not wearing that, are you, Jadyn?"

No, I just put it on for fun and am having Mom tie it for no reason.

But I don't have time for any hassle right now. I'm late enough as it is.

So, I say in my sweet, polite voice, "Yes, a swimsuit is required attire for a beach party."

I give him my *I'm your little angel, and I can do no wrong* look as I slide over with my back toward Mom, holding my top against my chest with one hand and my hair up with the other.

"Double knots, please," I say quietly to her.

I don't want it coming undone at an inopportune time.

Dad says to Mom in an edgy tone, "Don't you think that swimsuit is a little skimpy, Ronny?"

My mom's real name is Veronica.

Veronica James Reynolds.

James was my great-great-grandma's maiden name. All firstborn girls since my great-grandma have had James as their middle name, thus *my* weird middle name. And, evidently, giving your daughter a boy's name for a nickname also runs in the family. I seriously didn't even know my name was Jadyn until I went to kindergarten. Daddy always calls me Angel, and everyone else always calls me JJ.

I'm only Jadyn when I'm in *big* trouble.

I know what's coming next.

I don't let Mom answer Dad's question. I jump into the conversation by saying, "Mom helped me pick it out, Dad. She thinks it's cute."

"Well, it might be *cute*, but I don't think it is particularly appropriate for someone your age," he declares like he is the ruler of the free world.

Unfortunately, of my free—*I think not*—world.

"Dad, come on. I'm seventeen. Besides Mom said I should wear ..." I glance at Mom.

She is clearly giving me the *shut up* signal, crossing her hand in front of her neck and her eyes bugging out. That, or she is threatening to kill me.

Uh, okay, I get it, I think.

So, I finish, "Uh, I should wear this suit for *sunning* purposes only." I nod.

Which I will be doing at the lake.

All day and maybe even into the night.

"Besides, I have a tank top and board shorts that I will wear over it to swim in."

"Well, you can wear them to sun in at the lake, too, or you're not wearing it at all. I think it should only be worn for sunning in the backyard." He thinks about it, squints his eyes at me, and adds, "And definitely no playing football in that thing."

Uh, yeah ... well, it's a little late for that.

I've got to get out of here!

Mom saves the day by saying, "Maybe you should come swimsuit shopping with me and JJ this week, Paul. You can help us pick out something you feel would be *appropriate*." She gives Dad a look of defiance, one eyebrow raised in challenge and her arms crossed in front of her chest.

She's got him so beat.

He'd never go shopping with us in a million years. He still says he is allergic because he equates shopping with torture.

"Uh," he backtracks, "why don't you let me see it with the shorts? It'll probably be okay that way."

Yeah, I'm sure it will.

After promising to keep the shorts on and finally getting his approval, I fly back up the stairs.

When Jake arrives, I rush out of the house, so he won't have a chance to talk to my dad.

Needless to say, I don't wear the shorts at the river, and Jake likes the suit just fine.

LATER IN THE week, I have what starts out as a great dream. I'm in the empty lot, playing catch with Phillip and Danny. We're having so much fun because Danny and I don't fight about anything.

It's like the perfect day.

Strangely, Danny disappears, and I relive tripping Phillip—sort of on purpose—like the other day. He sits on top of me and holds me down.

Then, the dream gets really weird.

He leans in to yell at me but starts *kissing* me instead. And, well, he does some other stuff, too.

What a nightmare!

Phillip is like a brother to me.

I don't ... I mean, I can't ... well, I *shouldn't* think about him like that.

It's practically incestuous!

But, evidently, I'm pretty warped because not only did I *really* enjoy the dream, but I also keep finding myself wanting to have it again.

And it's freaking me out.

It really, really is.

Seniors rule!

SEPTEMBER — 12TH GRADE

THE MUSIC IS cranked up, and the top is cranked down. Phillip and I are in my car, driving to Lincoln, Nebraska, on Thursday afternoon.

Why are we going to Lincoln?
We are going on a campus visit.

Now, for the rest of your questions, the answers that I give will depend on who you are. For example, if you are a teacher, parent, or guidance counselor, you will hear the following:

Why are you going on a campus visit?
Well, Phillip and I are really looking forward to having the opportunity to get a firsthand view of the place. I mean, every campus has online tours and information, but there really is no substitute for visiting when it comes to getting a real feel for what the school is like.

And what will you be doing there?
We will be taking a guided tour of the campus as well as taking part in a group orientation session. We will also try to sit in on a class and check out the food and the dorms. We will look at the

activities available to us and try to meet with an advisor or professor in our chosen major. Oh, and I especially want to check out the library and the bookstore.

And how will you make the difficult decision of which college to attend?

Well, I'm sure I will make a lengthy pros and cons list for each school we visit, but basically, I will choose the school that has the best combination of academics in my chosen field and overall best feeling. You know, how comfortable I feel there.

Okay, so that's a college campus visit in *theory*. The reality of this trip is probably going to be a bit different from that.

Why are you going on a campus visit?

To visit Danny, spend three nights with him, go to a football game, meet boys, and PARTY!

And what will you be doing there?

Going to parties, checking out cute boys, seeing the dorms, partying, meeting cute college boys, and PARTYING. Oh, and going to a football game and checking out the cute boys when not enthralled by the game.

And how will you make the difficult decision of which college to attend?

I will base my decision on whichever college has the best parties and the cutest boys. Oh, and where I feel comfortable with the parties and the boys.

And the guidance counselor at school tries to make us seniors think the process is so complicated. I mean, it's really quite simple.

But the good news is that college visits are an excuse to go party at college *with your parents' approval!*

With even your teachers' approval.

All of our teachers are so happy that Phillip and I are setting such a *good example* for the other students and taking the initiative that they waived all of our homework for the weekend.

"You don't need to worry about that pesky stuff," Mrs. Reece told me. "You need to *fully immerse yourselves* in the collegiate experience."

Yes, she actually said those words. I told Phillip I planned to *fully immerse myself* all right! Of course, that's when he looked a little nervous.

And my parents are also proud that I am taking my college choice so seriously. I mean, I did sort of tell them that I had to start early, so I could try for early scholarships.

Do they even have early scholarships? And, if they do, I'm thinking I had to apply for them junior year, but oh well. I'm not even sure.

I suppose I'll have to get online and look that up while I'm there because I know that will be the first question they'll ask when I see them. Phillip and I have to be on our best behavior Saturday when we meet our parents and the Diamonds for tailgating before the game. It will be imperative that we act like this is serious.

I'd really like to know who came up with the whole guise of the college recruitment visit.

They were brilliant!

Under no other circumstances would your parents allow you to go away for the weekend, completely unchaperoned!

Now, don't get me wrong. When looking at colleges, you should decide what is important to you and organize and prioritize.

I have made a list of the things that are a DON'T MISS!

This includes an entire campus tour, fraternity row, Memorial Stadium, Student Center, local bars, coed dorms, and any party we can find!

Now, I appreciate the fact that academics are important, but I really believe that the college's social—*can you say party?*—atmosphere is stratospherically more important.

And let's face it; I can get an education anywhere, right? But I'm going to have to *live* with these people for four—*hopefully only four*—years. So, it's imperative that I *really do* find a place where I will feel comfortable.

Of course, Dad made Phillip have a sit-down with him to discuss the rules for the weekend. Although, really, I think Dad would let me go just about anywhere if it meant I wasn't with Jake. Let's just say, he hasn't exactly made Jake feel like part of the family. But that's a whole other story.

"So, what did he tell you again?" I ask Phillip for the hundredth time because this really cracks me up.

"*I am holding you personally responsible, Phillip.*" Phillip does a perfect imitation of my dad's deep voice. "*She'd better not get drunk, stoned, pregnant, or die.*"

I laugh some more.

Little does he know, Phillip—who is still by far the most responsible of the three of us—has turned into a full-fledged partier this year.

It's going to be killer.

Danny called me last night. He was laughing, telling me that Dad had talked to him, too. He basically threatened them both with bodily harm if they let anything happen to me.

Here's the other great thing: Phillip and I are staying with Danny.

Yes, my parents are letting me spend the night with a boy. Okay, it's a boy they trust—sorta—but I just find this all so hard to believe.

Our goal is to get to Lincoln in time to see part of Danny's football practice. We lied and told him that we would be there later because we want to surprise him.

Danny told me we're going to sit on the roof of his dorm after practice to get some sun. "So, wear or bring a swimsuit," he said.

When I questioned him further on what college girls wear, I got no answers other than, "Uh, shorts, jeans, you know."

No ... I don't. That's why I'm asking!

But I gave up, and in the end, I let Lisa pack for me, which is a really scary thought in and of itself.

ONCE ON CAMPUS, Phillip makes me drive around forever, trying to find a suitable place to park. I'm sure, if we had planned this better, we could have gotten a visitor parking pass, like the website talks about online. But, well, we didn't.

"Phillip, they don't know who we are. I'm parking up close. I mean, I'm going to get a ticket regardless of where I park." I'm completely confused by the array of threatening parking signs with cryptic letters on them. "So, why not park close?"

As usual, I frustrate that boy. Regardless of his newfound partying skills, Phillip is still a *follow the rules and go by the book* kind of guy.

Dad's probably right. I'll be perfectly safe with him, and I won't get into any trouble.

Darn it!

"Look!" Phillip cries out.

What? Really cute boy?

"There. Over there. A visitor parking lot, and it's fairly close. Go park there."

I'm tempted to argue 'cause it's not that close, but I don't need him mad at me already.

So, I say, "Great job, Phillip!" and park.

WE GET OUT of the car and walk down the wide, main pathway that leads through the campus and ends at Memorial Stadium.

The campus is really beautiful. I've been here for lots of football games, but I've never really paid attention. There are huge, colorful trees and wide stretches of green grass. I love the cool, old buildings with their neat architectural features. I wonder how they keep such old places looking so clean and shiny.

There are all sorts of students. Some appear to be rushing to class; others are just milling about. We see a group of girls pretending to study in their bikini tops. Phillip is looking at them and not where he is going and about trips over the curb.

"Real smooth," I tease.

I also notice a group of cute boys kicking around a soccer ball.

I packed clothes to dress appropriately for all possible collegiate activities. I'm wearing jean shorts and a very fitted vintage T-shirt. I hoped this outfit would blend in. I don't want to be walking around here, looking like a dumb high school girl! I notice that most of the girls are dressed similarly.

Oh, and look! There is an adorable couple walking toward us, holding hands. They stop to kiss, and they are looking at each other like they are in *love*!

Oh, I so want that to be me.

I am so going here.

Where's the sign-up sheet? I'm in!

We work our way down to the stadium and the practice fields. I've never seen a college practice before, so I'm really excited.

WELL ...

Now, I have to tell you that, if you ever plan on stopping by the university to see the team practice ...

Don't bother!

The place is like FORT KNOX!

I'm serious. There is so much security; I don't think even the President of the United States himself could get in without a pass.

Actually, I know he couldn't. He's from a rival state!

The Department of Homeland Security ought to come here and take some lessons because I'm telling you, if our country's borders were guarded like this, we'd never have to worry about anything.

The security guys have walkie-talkies and earpieces and everything.

I try to explain to one of the big men that I am a friend of one of the players, but that doesn't seem to matter. He just looks at me with a face that says, *Sure you are. Like I've never heard that one before.* When that doesn't work, I ask him what is such a big secret. I mean, a football play is pretty much a football play, isn't it? And, please, I know that Nebraska has always been a powerhouse in collegiate football, but are there really *that many* people trying to spy on them? Is it really an issue?

Evidently.

So, Phillip and I sit around and wait between some cool old columns with our backs facing the practice field until the guy tells us it is officially over.

Danny is redshirting this year, so he plays quarterback for the scout team. Besides leading the scout team, his job this year is to practice, eat well, bulk up, get stronger, get faster, and memorize the playbook upside down.

We find Danny walking up to the stadium from the practice field. He is pleasantly surprised to see us early.

"Well, we tried to watch practice," I tell him.

"You shoulda told me you were coming early. I could've gotten you a pass," Danny says like we should have known this.

Coulda, woulda, shoulda.

"See, JJ?" Phillip says. "Sometimes, it pays to plan ahead."

"Shut up, Phillip. I didn't see you doing any planning. You could have taken care of it," I tell that bratty boy.

"Hey," Danny says, grinning, "want to play catch in the stadium?"

Now, that gets my attention.

"Memorial Stadium?" I ask Danny. "Can we do that?"

"Yeah." He shrugs like it's no big deal.

"Uh, yeah!" I scream.

So, we walk over there.

Well, I kinda run.

This is *so* exciting. I have been watching this field on TV since I was old enough to remember. And I've been to lots of games, but nobody told me you could walk on the field!

I stand in the middle of the field and spin in a circle.

This is awesome!

I grab Phillip and say, "Come on."

I drag him into the middle with me. We stand on the big red N.

"Look around, Phillip!" I say with excitement. "Did you ever realize just how huge this place is?"

I am overwhelmed.

"Ye-ah," Phillip says. "I've been to football camp here, re-member?"

Fine, Mr. Know It All.

Mr. Been There, Done That.

But I don't care. I don't let his lack of enthusiasm bother me. I just can't believe how huge it is! I mean, the perspective is totally different from here than it is in the stands. What a rush it must be for the football players to hit the horseshoe in the tunnel, run out to the roar of the crowd, and look up to see all those zillions of people dressed in red.

Okay, so maybe not zillions, something like eighty thousand. Whatever.

Don't rain on my parade because this is truly thrilling for me.

"Hey, Jay," Danny says, walking toward me with a football in hand. "Go out for a pass."

So, I do with Phillip guarding me. I run as fast as I can down the field of *Memorial Stadium*!

And I look for the throw. I'm thinking this is not the best pass that Danny has ever thrown. And, well, it is a bit long, but I'm getting way into the moment, and I do not worry about the turf stains I might get on my T-shirt. So, I dive for the pass and just miss it. At first, it makes me mad because I don't like to miss, but then I think, *I just slid across the turf at Memorial Stadium!*

Wow!

Brushing myself off, I walk back to Danny, who seems to think something is funny.

As I hand him the football, he says very seriously, "You missed, Jay. You owe me your shirt."

What?

"No way, Danny! You never called SF"—strip football—"before the play," I tell him.

"Yeah, I did," Danny says. Then, he turns to Phillip and says, "You heard me, didn't ya, Mac?"

Phillip grins and nods his head. "Yeah, I think I did."

Ugh. He is such a liar!

"Well, even if you did, that was a horrible pass, and I shouldn't have even tried to catch it."

"Yeah, but you did." Danny smirks.

I look around the field again. There are a bunch of players still hanging around, but no one is paying any attention to us. The only person even watching is some equipment dude, who has a bag of footballs for Danny to throw.

"You just want to see my bikini top, don't you, Danny?"

"No, not really. I mean, I'll see it later anyway," he says very convincingly. He raises his eyebrows and shrugs his shoulders. "Just trying to play fair."

I look to Phillip, but can see he is going to be of no help in the matter.

Whatever.

"Fine," I say.

I'll show him.

I throw my shoulders back, hold my head up high, pull the elastic from my hair, and shake out my ponytail. I saunter toward Danny with what I hope is a sexy smile. Crossing my arms in front of me, I grab the bottom edge of my T-shirt and *very slowly* pull it up, revealing the skimpy, stringy American flag bikini top underneath.

Practically like a stripper.

God, if Dad saw me now, I could forget grounding. He'd have me chained to my bed for the rest of high school.

Danny grins at me in amusement. He loves that he won this round.

I pull the shirt over my head and punch it into Danny's stomach. "Here. But, if you throw another one like that"—I give him a pointed look—"I'm coming back for your pants."

I hear equipment dude mutter something that sounds strangely like, *God bless America*, and I can tell the mulling about has stopped, and people are watching.

But I don't really care about that. I just need to win.

I line up opposite Phillip, and just a second before Danny is ready to call the snap, I whisper sneakily across to Phillip while touching my chest, "Hey, Phillip, my boobs aren't hanging out of this or anything, are they?"

As I anticipated, Phillip looks straight at them. I mean, he's a guy. He can't help himself. So, he is caught a bit off guard when I tear past him. I run full-bore down the field, but I feel him gaining on me. I turn, jump up, and catch a *perfectly* thrown pass from Danny.

Shoot.

I really wanted that bossy boy's pants.

Only one week until prom!

APRIL 20TH

BIG PARTIES IN Westown are usually held in a cornfield somewhere out in the boonies. This party is kind of hard to find, but I can see there are already a ton of cars here. As Lisa parks, my mind is on Jake. Jake and I have been dating off and on for over a year.

I really like Jake, but do I *love* him?

That's the big question.

I *tell* him that I love him, but I'm not sure that he's, like, the *real* love of my life. I just can't really picture myself married to him. I mean, he's *no* prince. But he's a decent high school boyfriend, and we usually have fun.

Well, we have fun when he's not being a jerk.

That is why our relationship has been as much off as it's been on.

Jake was quarterback of this year's football team. Granted, they sucked, but can you imagine how hard it was to follow in Danny's shoes? To follow a record-setter and state champion? Danny was a great high school quarterback, he'll be a great college quarterback, and it wouldn't surprise anyone if he went on to be a great pro quarterback.

Jake probably won't even go to college. It's not that Jake's not a smart and athletic guy. It's just like he's missing something, like the drive to succeed. His bangs are always falling onto his face, and you never know for sure what's going on behind those smoldering, dark eyes. He's a sexy combination of athlete and bad boy. He has a hot, casual look about him.

Like he'd skip school and say, *Who cares? Let's go on a picnic.*

Not that he's ever done that.

Or, *Hop on my motorcycle, and we'll just ride with nowhere in mind to go.*

Okay, never done that either.

I think that's the big difference between Jake, Phillip, and Danny. Jake has nowhere in mind to go. Phillip and Danny both seem to know *exactly* where they are going.

When I think about the kind of guy I want to marry, I think I might prefer someone who knows where he is going. I mean, a prince pretty much has his whole life planned out already, doesn't he? And this is important because I have no idea where I'm going or what I want to do with my life.

I do know some things. I know I want to go to college, but I'm not sure where. I'm not that bad though; I do have it narrowed down to two. I want to have a successful career, but doing what? Maybe be an architect, but how do I know if it's right? I want to marry a great guy, but I don't know who. I want to have kids someday and be a great mom, but I'm not sure I'll know how.

You know, life is weird. There are times I feel so grown-up and like I know *everything* I need to know, but then I think about the future and realize how little I do.

Sometimes, being a teenager sucks.

But back to Jake.

IT'S TAKING ME forever to figure out what to wear tonight. Normally, I would just be in jeans, a cute, fitted T-shirt, and tennies.

But not tonight.

Tonight, I want to make an impression. Tonight, I am *finally* going to do it with Jake.

Why am I finally going to do it with Jake?

Well, I'm still not one hundred percent sure on that. I mean, Jake definitely wants to, and I *have* made him wait for over a year. Sort of. It's like, every time I start to think I am ready, we usually get in a fight about it and break up. But, this time, we have gone a whole month without a breakup, and he is really wanting to. It's pretty much all he talks about. And I don't know why I have waited so long anyway. Lisa has been doing it for a long time now. Katie's doing it with Billy Prescott, and they've been dating for only, like, two months, but she is very certain he's the love of her life. I turned eighteen a few weeks ago, so, I mean, I'm officially an adult and all. I just don't really feel like one yet. And then there's the whole *am I really that in love with him, and is he really the one* thing. So, even though I'm not sure about every detail, I do feel like it's time. Part of me just wants to get it over with!

Months ago, I told Katie and Lisa that Jake wanted to *take our relationship to the next level,* so they dragged me to Victoria's Secret. At their urging, I bought a fuchsia-and-black stretch lace bra and matching low-rise, thong panties. Lisa says wearing the high ones and showing them is so tacky.

I've had the bra and panties for months now. They've just been sitting there, in my drawer, waiting patiently. They've been there so long that, every time I open the drawer, even *they* ask me when I'm finally going to do it. So, after much deliberation, I have decided tonight is the night.

AFTER MANY CLOTHING changes and panicked calls to Lisa, she takes pity on me and comes over early. She does my makeup, and I try on more clothes, finally settling on a pair of low-fitting, dark denim jeans, some obnoxiously high-heeled black sandals that she scrounged around and found in Mom's closet, and a shrunken raspberry cashmere sweater. I love the sweater. It feels so soft on my skin that I keep wanting to hug myself, but I suppose me feeling myself up would look a little weird, so I just keep petting the sleeve a little.

LISA AND I re-gloss our lips, make sure nothing unfortunate is hanging out of each other's noses, get out of the car, and head toward the party.

As usual, the Warner twins are in charge of the door.

The Warner twins, Gary and Larry, are seniors, too. They come from a big farm family, and, believe it or not, they have siblings named Cary, Barry, Harry, Mary, and Jerry.

Kinda *SCARY* ... get it?

Scary rhymes, too.

Oh, never mind.

They are both huge farm boys, about three hundred pounds apiece, and the *pipeline* for our football team's offense. Basically, they are so big that they'll either knock you down or run you over like a pair of freight trains. To look at them, you'd think big, tough, and dumb as doorknobs, yet they are both at the top of our class academically, crazy practical jokers, and really just great big teddy bears. I love those guys.

Lisa and I say hi to the boys and hand them our money.

I ask, "Is Jake here yet? I didn't see his truck."

Gary looks confused. "You're *supposed* to meet Jake here?"

The boys exchange pointed looks.

Larry looks me up and down and changes the subject. "Hey, you look hot tonight." He then gives his brother another weird glance.

"Thanks. What's going on? Come on, boys, spill the beans."

"Um, JJ. Gosh, I don't want to tell you this, but Jake is here, and, um, well, maybe I should start by telling you that I've never liked Jake much," Gary stammers.

I give him a frustrated look. "Keep going."

He grimaces. "All right. Well, Jake is here, but he's with another girl."

"Yeah, some slut from Park," Larry pipes in. Larry adds with his hands cupped in front of his chest, "And she has got the biggest cans I have ever seen. And you can see the top part of those thong underwear thingies right here"—he turns and points down to his own side—"above her jeans. You know, like ..."

"Lar-ry," Gary interrupts with a *don't say stuff like that* scowl to his brother.

Okay, my practical jokers. I'm not that gullible.

"Really?" I say, testing them. "So, what does she look like?"

Gary and Larry blankly look at me.

"We just told you, JJ," Larry says.

"I mean, her face, boys."

They look at each other like they don't have a clue what her face looks like. I know it's a joke for sure.

"Look, I know you two. Very funny. Ha-ha. Come on, Lisa, let's go get a beer."

We head to the keg and find Phillip there. He hands Lisa a beer.

What a sweetie.

Phillip looks so cute tonight in a deep purple polo shirt with a pair of those plaid patchwork shorts. Yes, I picked out his outfit. I must say, the dark purple color looks so good on him. Phillip is really quite cute. And I know he wanted to look especially nice for this girl he has been talking to and is hoping to hook up with tonight.

It makes me kinda wish I wanted to hook up with an adorable boy like Phillip rather than Jake.

But I'm not backing down. Tonight is the night.

For better or worse because I seriously cannot go to college as a virgin.

I grab a red plastic cup, tilt it under the tap, and let him fill it with beer.

He whispers in my ear, "We need to talk."

"About what?"

"Jake. He's here with another girl, and she's *all* over him. It's pretty obvious it's a date."

Phillip gently touches my arm and tells me this news in a hushed tone, like a doctor who just lost a patient would tell the family.

"Shut up, Phillip. You're just in on the twins' big joke, right?"

"Princess, I'm not joking. When did you and Jake break up anyway, and why didn't you tell me?" He looks at me closer and says sweetly, "You look gorgeous, by the way."

I melt slightly because that is *exactly* the look I was going for, and then I say very seriously, "Phillip, we so did not break up. I am—or was—supposed to meet him here tonight. We spoke about it just a few hours ago. I mean, I didn't tell Jake, but I decided tonight is *the* night."

But, in my mind, I wonder. I really don't think Phillip would joke about something like this. Honestly, he would probably tell me about the joke, so I could play along. I look at the ground. The reality of what this could be is sinking in.

"You're serious?"

"Come over here." He takes my hand and guides me away from the keg and everyone's ears.

"Let me get this straight. He didn't break up with you? He told you to meet him here and then brought another girl to the party? That's it. I'm going to kill him."

"Phillip, calm down. Are you sure he brought her?"

I'm thinking this can't possibly be true, yet at the same time, there's this sinking feeling in my stomach.

"Maybe she's just over there, trying to pick him up. That

happens sometimes. Girls like Jake. I'll just walk over and see what's going on. Surely, there's a logical explanation for this."

I turn to walk toward Jake.

Phillip grabs my arm. "There's not a logical explanation for this. They came here together. I *saw* them. The boys up front were really pissed about it, but they thought you must have come to your senses and broken up with the loser. They figured he'd brought her to try to make you jealous. Plus, he's been kissing her like crazy." He sighs. "Well, at least one good thing will come out of this."

"What's that?"

"You're *not* doing it with Jake."

I roll my eyes at that boy. He has always been very much against my doing it with Jake. He told me, if I wanted to lose it that bad, I should do it with a friend, a guy who would at least treat me right, but I can't go asking Joey or Dillon to just do me.

How awkward would that be?

So, then Phillip made me a pros and cons list—well, I should say a cons list; I had to add the pros because he couldn't come up with any pros for Jake.

Maybe he was sort of right after all.

"Where are they anyway?"

He leans next to me and points. "Over there, on the other side of the bonfire. Can you see him?"

I follow his finger with my eyes and say sadly, "Yeah. God, she really does have big boobs."

Phillip sympathetically looks at me. "You know what? He's not worth it. Let's go get you out of here. We'll go get some ice cream or pizza or something."

Like ice cream could fix this mess. Well, it can fix *just about* anything, hmm. You know, it might be worth a try.

No. I need to get to the bottom of this first. Plus, that wouldn't be fair to Phillip. Even though he's going to prom with

Carrie Sadler, I know he was hoping to hook up with Megan Masters tonight.

"Phillip, let me be clear about this. I'm not going *anywhere* until I talk to Jake."

I think.

"Why would you do that?" Phillip asks me, like it's the stupidest thing he's ever heard in his entire life.

"Because I think I deserve to know what the hell's going on. Don't I? Wouldn't you want to know?"

"What do you want? Some big confrontation? You screaming or crying or making a fool of yourself while he sits there with that cocky grin of his, ogling his big-boobed date? Who, I might add, has the reputation of being the biggest slut in the whole frickin' county."

I throw my full cup of beer down on the ground in frustration, stomp my foot, and say, "No! That is *not* what I want."

Shoot.

I need to think.

"I'm gonna go for a walk, Phillip," I tell him as he walks over to pick up my cup. He could never litter.

"Good. Let's go," he says, following me.

"I thought you wanted to hang out with Megan tonight. And it's not fair for me to mess up your plans just because my boyfriend is a jerk. Well, ex-boyfriend, I guess."

Phillip grabs my hands again and says in that smooth, adorable voice of his, "Princess, there's no one I'd rather hang out with more than you. You know that."

I look at him and feel warm inside. He really is the sweetest friend.

And I really don't know how to deal with all of this, so I'm not even sure what I should tell him.

I need to think.

"Um, I'm just gonna walk out to Lisa's car, grab my lip gloss, and think about this."

Phillip looks at me like he's not sure he believes me.

"Just give me fifteen minutes. If I'm not back, you can charge out on your horse and rescue me." I stop and give Phillip a hug. "I love you, Phillip. You'll always be my best friend. And you must be a very good friend if you are willing to choose hanging out with me over getting laid. Especially when we know I'm going to do nothing but sob and complain about my stupid, cheating boyfriend. So, I just ... I, um, I appreciate it, okay?" I back up and lightly punch his shoulder. "I'm just shocked, and I need to figure out what to do. I promise, I'll be back, and hopefully, when I come back, I will have some sort of a plan. Just don't go killing anybody yet, okay?"

He nods.

I kind of lower my head and look at the ground, scuffing the dirt with Mom's strappy sandals because I'm not so good at this part. You know, the admitting-I-might-have-been-wrong part.

"Thanks for telling me. I'm glad I didn't go charging over there."

SO, I START walking to the car.

In my mind are a bazillion questions.

How could I have been so stupid? Has he been cheating on me the whole time? Some of the time?

What am I going to do? To say?

How could Jake do this to me?

What an asshole.

Okay, Jadyn James Reynolds, pull yourself together.

What's your plan?

My plan so far is ...

Get to Lisa's car.

Have a big, quiet temper tantrum.

Maybe scream silently and cry my eyes out, somehow without messing up my mascara.

Darn! I knew I should have worn the waterproof kind.

Then, I will put on some stupid lip gloss and go back into the party. I might even confront Jake. I will hold my head up high and stand up straight and tall.

Grandpa used to tell me to do that. "Walk into the place like you own it, JJ, and people will think that you do." Of course, he also said, "If you can't dazzle them with brilliance, baffle them with bullshit."

I have to admit, I am kind of good at that. People tend to underestimate blondes. They just think we are naturally dumb, and, well, on occasion, I might have used that to my advantage.

But back to Jake.

Can I convince him that the slut doesn't bother me?

Can I walk in there like I own the place?

I can't let him know he's upset me; that's for sure!

I'M ALMOST BACK to the entrance and about to walk past Gary and Larry when I see three guys heading our way.

I'd know that strut anywhere.

What to my wondrous eyes should appear?

Danny!

I can't believe it! He's here! As a quarterback, he's known for his perfect timing, and I'm so glad it has spilled over into my life. His timing couldn't be more perfect. Because he's just the guy I need to see tonight. Hanging out with Danny is practically therapeutic. I get so wrapped up in having fun, competing, or conspiring with him that I forget about everything else. I think I might need that tonight! And the fact that he brought a couple of hot friends? I mean, it's pretty much a given that they don't go unnoticed by me.

So, I try to forget about Jake and Boobs and remind myself that I look damn good tonight.

If Jake can enjoy himself, I think, well, maybe I can, too.

Two can play that game, right?

Maybe one of Danny's friends will think I'm cute. Maybe I can make Jake jealous.

Do I want to make Jake jealous?

Yes.

Do I want to make him apologize and beg me for forgiveness?

Yes.

Will I take him back if he asks?

Absolutely not.

Hmm.

I'm almost sure of that.

I WALK UP next to Gary and Larry, who stare at me with concern. I don't say anything to them.

I just raise my arms high in the air and yell loudly, "So, what? You've had enough of hot coeds and wild fraternity parties, and you just wanted to drink from a keg in a cornfield?"

Danny hears me and starts running toward me at full speed. I'm afraid for a moment that he's going to tackle me, but he stops on a dime in front of me and pulls me into a big bear hug.

Then, he pushes me out to arm's length, looks me up and down, and says, "Jay. Damn! You look … *hot*?" He says it in a way that is half-statement and half-question. Like looking hot is unusual for me.

Okay, so it is.

"What, are you drunk already? Danny, I know spring practice is over, but—"

"Sexy as hell *actually*," Danny interrupts, nodding his head and grinning lasciviously at me, finally deciding that I indeed look good.

Wow. Maybe Lisa is right. Maybe I should dress this way more often.

"This is John and Michael," Danny says, introducing me to his hot, muscular friends. "John, Michael, this is Jay. I don't think you've ever met."

Did I mention that John is quite cute?

"*This* is Jay?" John says. "Wow. The way you talked, I thought Jay was a dude."

"Definitely not, boys." Danny grins, his eyes running lazily up and down my body. "*Definitely not.*"

Hey, stop that! You're making me nervous.

"Where's Jake anyway? I'm surprised that, with you looking like that"—he looks me up and down again—"he's not attached to your hip."

Before I can answer, Danny turns to Gary and Larry and gives them high fives and slaps on the back. "How the hell are my two favorite linemen?"

The twins grin proudly.

Crap. Skip the part about picking up one of the friends and trying to make Jake jealous.

I can't do this.

Can there be quicksand in a cornfield?

I didn't think it was ecologically possible, but I'm pretty sure I'm sinking into some right now.

No, JJ, you're just losing your mind. No biggie.

Well, that's reassuring.

I've got to get out of here.

So, I announce to no one in particular, "Jake and I broke up."

"Sweet. When? Why didn't you call me, Jay?" Danny smiles and turns back toward me.

"Tonight, *apparently*, when he brought some other girl to the party."

Danny's face has questions written all over it.

Questions I'm not prepared to answer quite yet.

And do I really want to tell Danny my humiliating story in

front of two hot guys?

Uh, no.

"Um, the Ringling Brothers here," I say with a nod toward Gary and Larry, "can give you all the gory details. I gotta go."

And I just walk away. I must be more upset than I realized because I just walked away from two college hotties.

But, yeah, I actually did it. Just walked away.

You'd think Lisa's car was my salvation. I just need to keep it together until I get there.

God, this sucks.

First, I was confused about whether to do it with Jake. Then, I *finally* made the decision, and he does this.

I officially need to give up on him.

Granted, I probably should have a long time ago, but, God, what am I gonna do now?

What am I gonna do every Saturday night? Who will I talk to before I go to bed?

Oh, well, yeah, still Phillip, but I mean, before that?

All right, decision time.

What am I going to do?

I need options.

Okay.

Option one: go in there, make a scene, punch him in the face, and tell him off.

Phillip would like that option—well, except for the fact that he wants to be the one to punch Jake. Either would probably make me feel good, but unfortunately, sometimes, when I get mad, I start crying. And, if I cry, Jake will think he hurt me, and I can't have that.

Option two: ignore him, like he is of no interest to me. Then, wait and see what he does.

Hmm.

Maybe?

Option three: listen to Phillip, call it a night, and go home.
All options suck!
Okay.
Here's what I'll do: I'll hang out with my friends and completely ignore Jake. I'll act like I'm having a good time and see if he comes and talks to me.
I'll listen to my friends bash Jake, maybe get good and drunk, then go home and cry on Phillip's shoulder, as usual.

The walk to the car is difficult because it's pretty dark now and hard to see the ground.

I'm trying to walk sexy but nonchalant—you know, in case there are any college boys looking my way—while thinking about Jake at the same time. But, when you walk in a cornfield, you really do have to focus on where you are going, especially in four-inch heels, or you will trip on a clod of dirt or an old, dried-up cornstalk and fall flat on your face.

Finally, I make it to the car.

Now what?

I am cold. I am mad and sad and hurt and embarrassed. I feel stupid. I am mad and ...

Is that normal?

Can anyone normal feel this many emotions all at once?

And here's the big question.

Reality checkpoint.

Am I upset because I loved Jake or because he dumped me?

Just think, JJ!

Danny's voice calls out to me. I turn around and see him jogging over, noticing he hasn't once looked at the ground.

Figures.

I lean my back up against the car and take a deep, cleansing breath. *You're gonna have to keep it together a little while longer,* I tell myself.

Danny strides up to me. "Hey, don't leave. Jake's a dick. He's *always been* a dick, and he will *always be* a dick. You should be glad you're rid of him."

"Gee, thanks. I think I know that now."

"Just be done with him for good this time, okay? He doesn't deserve you." He studies my face. "You okay?"

"Yeah, I think so." Then, I whine, "Could he not have had the decency to a least break up with me first? And did he have to pick a total slut to rub my face in it? Why would he do this to me?"

But, in my mind, I think I already know the answer.

Simple really.

Because I wouldn't do it with him.

Because, seriously, what girl in this day and age would make a guy wait that long?

What is wrong with me?

Danny looks grimly at me. "The twins told me who he brought to the party. I'm assuming you guys still haven't done it."

Excuse me! I know we are friends and all, but do we really need to discuss this?

This is my virginity here. I should have a little privacy, I think.

But I sigh and say, "No, not yet."

I sigh again and realize that at least I can talk to Danny about this stuff better than I can with Phillip. Danny listens.

Hell, Danny is willing to teach when necessary.

Phillip, on the other hand, got upset with me for even *considering* doing it with Jake.

"Oh, Danny," I say, taking a big breath.

And, darn it, if everything I've been thinking doesn't just come rushing out of my mouth.

All in one big jumble.

"We haven't *yet*, but he has been bugging me about it so much. Every time we go out, it ends in a fight because I say no, and he gets pissed. So, of course, I'm constantly thinking about it, and I finally decide, why not do it? Why keep waiting? So, guess what, Danny. I decided tonight was the night, and I tried to dress hot, and I've got on the *greatest underwear*, and I'm all mentally prepared, and WHAT?" I say, my hands flying out in front of me. "He shows up with some imported girl, and no one can even tell me what she looks like because they can't seem to get any further than her boobs and her thong—which I'm also wearing, by the way, but I wouldn't let it hang out like that. And the whole reason I didn't do it with him in the first place is because he never made me *feel* like I wanted to. I mean, come on, Danny, aren't guys supposed to do something to a girl that makes her *want* to? I mean, I kind of thought maybe it was just Jake or something, but since he's obviously *doing* Miss Teen Boobage, he must be fine, and it's probably just me."

I take a big gulp of air, slump up against the car, and look up at the star-filled sky.

Shit. I can't believe I just said all that.

Danny moves in a little closer to me. He smiles and shakes his head. He's got a bright, contagious smile. Usually, when I see it, I can't help but smile back at the boy. But not tonight.

He moves in a little closer.

A lot closer actually.

I'm about to say something else, but as I open my mouth to speak, he puts a finger up to my lips to shush me and says, "Jay," in the sexiest way.

Then, he kisses me.

And oh. My. God.

The boy can kiss.

He can so kiss.

I almost forgot how good he could kiss. I swear, I can feel it all the way down to my toes and in some other very interesting places in between. And I think I get it. God, I could let him kiss me forever, and I'm pretty sure I would let him do just about *anything* else.

I never, ever felt like this with Jake. Maybe *that's* why I've been holding back.

Then, damn it, he stops, and thinking out loud, I say, "Well, doesn't that just suck?"

"Huh?"

"Oh. *Sorry.* Not you. You're great, Danny. I've just realized I've probably wasted a year of my life on an idiot who is a really bad kisser!" And then, with a gasp of realization, I throw my hand up over my mouth and say, "Oh God, did it rub off on me? Have I become a terrible kisser, too?"

Like I need something else to worry about.

Danny wraps strong arms around me.

Did I mention that, all of a sudden, he now looks, well, like a *man*?

Wow! When did that happen, and why did I not notice it before?

He's grown up.

A lot.

He pulls me back in close. "Well, I can't be sure." He laughs. "The line judge didn't have a clear view, the side judge over there was watching the cheerleaders, and since there's no instant replay available"—he shrugs his shoulders and tilts his head—"I'm just gonna have to call a do-over."

Real original, Mr. Smooth. But I like it.

"You're a cheater," I say.

"Better than being a liar," he fires back.

And then he kisses me again, except it's even better this time because there are no thoughts in my mind about Jake.

I mean, Jake who?

Eventually, to my dismay, he stops kissing me.

I bite the edge of my lip and say nervously, "So, what's the call?"

I get the kind of intense look that is usually reserved for football.

"You kiss fine. Better than fine actually. Uh, how 'bout we go get a drink?"

Uh, no. How about we just stay here and drown my sorrows in your kisses?

"Um, yeah. I need to get back in there anyway—before Phillip sends out the cavalry."

"You know, Phillip and I really care about you. We hated you dating a guy like Jake. We've never had any proof, but I'm pretty sure this isn't the first time he's cheated on you."

Figures.

I grab my lip gloss out of the car, put it in my pocket, and shut the door. I stop, grab the car handle, and start to open the door as I say aloud to myself, "I suppose I'd better grab my jacket."

"You don't need a jacket, Jay," Danny says, taking my hand. "I'm pretty sure I can keep you warm."

God, am I swooning?

I'm not exactly sure what swooning is, but I might very well be doing it.

He leads me back toward Frick and Frack, who I am sure have been watching everything.

Gary says to Danny, "You know, Big D, the shit's gonna hit the fan if you do that"—they both roll their eyes in the direction of the car, indicating that they saw us kissing—"in there." They lean their heads in the direction of the party.

"I'm pretty sure I don't care what Jake thinks," Danny states emphatically.

As we walk by them toward the party, Gary smiles, slaps Danny on the back, and says, "Well, Big D, if you need it, the pipeline's got your back. And, hey, JJ, did we ever mention that there might have been a few times during the season when we *accidentally tripped* and Jake got sacked?"

I grin at that thought. Looking back, I give those boys a salute. I always knew I liked them for a reason.

Danny and I laugh and head toward the keg where our friends have gathered. Michael and John are standing around it, chatting with Phillip, and seem to have already hit it off with Lisa and Katie. I wonder where Billy, the love of Katie's life, is.

Phillip leans in toward the keg and pumps it again for Lisa as he suspiciously eyes me.

I'm okay, I mouth silently to him.

He nods his head toward Danny, whose arms are wrapped around my waist, and mouths back, *I see that*. But his eyes are big with questions.

Accusing-type questions.

I know he's wondering why Danny is holding me, but he probably thinks Danny did the same thing he would have done eventually. And that is to drag me back in here and help me have some fun.

Or not.

Phillip wanted to take me out of here.

I watch as Phillip and Danny do the whole male back-slap, high-five, fist-bumping stuff.

"Hey, Mac."

"What's up, Big D?"

Gary and Larry, done with their door duty, come join our little group.

Larry holds up a big bottle of Jack Daniel's as he says, "Let's get down to business," takes a big swig, and passes me the booze.

Now, I'm not much of a drinker, maybe just a beer or two, but my, this does go down smoothly tonight. I'm standing in front of Danny, who has us both wrapped inside his brown leather jacket.

Did I mention that Danny smells really good? He has an amazingly sexy, crisp, citrusy smell. And I flash back to standing in

Hollister with him, helping him pick out a scent girls would die for.

And, now, I am the girl dying for it.

Fate?

EVERYONE IS SEEMINGLY having a great time. The guys are telling old jokes and old stories. But I'm having a hard time listening to them because, as they are talking, Danny slides the hair off my neck and peppers it with little ticklish kisses. I think, right now, they are telling about the time Gary and Larry convinced a carload of city boys that they could drive straight through a huge hay roll, and the hay would fly out all around them, just like on cartoons. P.S. For you city folk, it's a lie. They might as well have run into a tree. Fortunately, no one was severely injured. Everyone laughs, and I almost forget about Jake.

Almost.

The bottle goes around again, and I take a little swig. When Danny kisses me, his mouth feels hot from the whiskey, and the hot feeling of our mouths combined with the cool weather is incredible. I can't help but wonder if Jake has seen us, but I'm assuming he is too busy with the sleaze. Phillip, on the other hand, is watching us like a hawk. A hawk with a scowl on his face. Or I guess, technically, it would be a beak.

Oh, whatever.

I'm not sure why he's scowling, and I'm too enthralled with Danny to care. I mean, I know Phillip watches out for me like a big brother, but I really don't think he needs to worry about Danny. He loves the guy.

Lisa announces that she has to pee, grabs my arm, and drags me off to a remote corner of the cornfield.

I'm sure she has to pee, but I also know that she is *dying* to know how I've ended up with Danny.

Sure enough, as soon as we are out of earshot, she screeches,

"Ohmigawd, JJ! Danny! How did that happen?"

"I'm not exactly sure." Because I'm not. "But you might be right about the clothes and makeup."

"Told you. So, did you just jump him in the parking lot or what? God, I've had a crush on him since, like, eighth grade."

Her and every other girl in school.

"Do you know how lucky you are? I mean, Danny is one hundred percent pure, unadulterated hotness."

I laugh and wonder if she even knows what unadulterated means. Probably one of her SAT study words. I'm tempted to ask her, but she's still gushing.

"I mean, I always thought you were lucky just to *live* by him because you got to see him mow with no shirt on."

"Don't get all revved up about this, Lisa. I practically had a meltdown out there in front of him. He's just trying to make me feel better. Help my ego," I say, trying to convince myself that's *all* there is to this. It just doesn't really feel that way.

"Like you've ever had *ego* problems."

Well, I am usually quite confident. But Lisa doesn't understand how I have perfected the *game face* from years of playing sports. And trust me; I'm wearing it big time right now so that she can't see the hurt and confusion I'm feeling over the whole Jake-dumping-me thing.

"I really think he's just being a good friend."

Lisa, not deterred from her fantasy, says, "Yeah, well, you don't usually see *good friends* kissing like that. And, come on, you've been good friends for a long time *and* had a lot of boy issues, and you've never made out with him before."

"Uh ..." I kind of squint my eyes and look guilty before I realize it.

"Shut up!" Lisa's eyes get huge. "You made out with Danny and didn't tell me? When?"

"It's not a big deal. It was a long time ago."

"How long ago?"

"Freshman year, but I begged him to. I needed to know how to French kiss."

"And that worked? I should've tried that one because I know you'd kissed boys before that."

"Not really. I had that date with Ryan Marshall, and I was just a wreck about it."

"So, he *told* you how, or he *taught* you how?" She has a goofy grin on her face, and I know she is dying for details.

"Taught me."

Her eyes get big again.

"Okay, I give up." I hold my hands in the air. "Enough questions. We made out for a couple of hours, and it worked. When I went on my date, I knew how to make out properly."

"Why didn't you tell me?"

"It was really no big deal; plus, he was dating someone at the time."

"Who?" she asks, like this very old news is some juicy piece of gossip.

"I don't remember. Some cheerleader, I think."

"Which one?" She is still enthralled.

"They're *all* the same one, Lisa." I shake my head because Danny's girls are pretty much all the same. "They just have different names ending with the letter Y."

She laughs and nods, knowing exactly what I mean. "Okay, so Jake? You were all set to ... *you know* with him. So, are ya bummed?"

"No, not really."

"Ohmigawd! I have a brilliant idea. You can do it with Danny!"

"I am not going to be doing it with Danny."

I don't think.

But I'll admit this: *I feel like I could.*

"I probably shouldn't even be kissing him, but I am glad that I didn't do it with Jake. I knew it wasn't right with him. Not enough sparks."

How did I date him for over a year? Well, off and on anyway.

Lisa nudges my elbow and raises her eyebrows, grinning at me like a Cheshire cat. "Any sparks with Danny?"

"Lisa, with Danny, I might very well burst into flames."

"Well, the way he was drooling over you, I'm thinking it's way more than a friend thing. And it's about freaking time!"

"So, what's up with you and John? You two are looking friendly." I nudge her back. "He's very cute."

"He is adorable. Did you see the muscles on him? I just want to squeeze them all. And he wants us to come down to Lincoln before school gets out and party with them."

"Just be careful. He is a college boy," I warn. Not that it will make a bit of difference.

"Okay." She wiggles. "Now, I really do have to pee. See you back there."

I'm walking by myself back toward the party when Phillip seems to step out of thin air.

"JJ," he says.

Ooh, I'm in trouble when I'm JJ, not Princess.

"How 'bout I take you home? You've had a rough night with Jake and all, and, well, you're starting to drink a lot." I start to speak, but he holds his hand up in the halt position and finishes, "And you know Danny is one of my best friends, but I'm not sure I trust you with him tonight."

"What? You think I might damage his reputation? That big stud Danny has to stoop to dating useless virgins?"

"That's not what I meant."

"Phillip," I say, exasperated, "can you *please* let me scrape a little fun out of what is left of my night? Danny is a good guy, and you know it."

"Yeah, well, tonight, he looks like he could eat you alive. I'm not sure I like it, and I'm *really* not sure *you* can handle it."

"Phillip, I'm fine, and I haven't been drinking a lot. I've had two tiny sips of Jack, but I didn't drive, and I'll get drunk if I want to." Of course, I don't want to, but he doesn't need to know that. "And, anyway, what's so wrong with having someone look at me like that? Maybe I *want* to be wanted."

Phillip is getting really bossy, and I hate that, so I say, just to spite him, "You know how I told you tonight was *the* night?" Okay, I know what I'm about to say is not even close to being true, but I say it anyway, just to give him something to think about and because, honestly, I have been thinking about it, too, "Maybe it still is." I shrug my shoulders, like my virginity is something that requires very little thought. "Who knows, Phillip? Maybe I'll just switch the guy."

Phillip's eyes get huge at that comment. I know I'm not being very nice to him, but he's pissing me off. I turn on my heels. They've sunk into the dirt, and I nearly trip, but I maintain control and start to walk away.

I stop, turn around, and continue, "And stop scowling at me every time I take a drink. I'm a big girl, Phillip. I can take care of myself."

I march off in the direction of the keg.

When I get there, Danny runs his hand across the bare skin at my waist, giving me instant goose bumps across my entire body. He hands me the bottle.

I take another sip and pass it on to John as Danny whispers in my ear, "So, tell me about this great underwear."

That gives me goose bumps all over again.

I don't get to respond because our conversation is interrupted by Lisa complaining, "I'm cold. Let's go warm up by the fire."

Danny looks at me seriously. "Jake's over there. Can you deal with that?"

Uh, no.

Yes.

Maybe.

"Uh, yeah," I say as we walk to the bonfire, "although I'm really not cold."

"Yeah, me neither." He throws his arm around my shoulders, winks at me, and smiles a devious grin.

Uh-oh. He's got a wild idea; I can tell. He's giving me the look. The look he's given me on so many other trouble-making occasions.

"What?" I say knowingly.

"Ya know, maybe it'd be good for Jake to think there's a reason you never did it with him."

I squint my eyes, trying to understand what he's getting at.

"Like, maybe you were doing it with, oh, say, someone older. Someone you might go to visit *often* at college."

"Someone like you?" I say, getting it.

Danny grins conspiratorially.

Hmm. Nice idea, but I'm not sure Jake will believe it. Well, actually, he might believe it 'cause he's jealous as hell of Danny. And I did kinda lie to Jake about my trips to Lincoln all year. In fact, I might have led him to believe I rarely saw Danny, that I spent most of my time partying with Lindsay, a girl from my volleyball team, who, honestly, I never saw even once.

Jeez, our relationship has obviously been of the *don't ask; don't tell* variety.

Nice.

I carefully study Danny. "You know, I'm not so sure we should mess with Jake's temper."

"Don't worry, Jay, I'd love for him to make a move. Most of the guys on the team would've beaten the crap out of him years ago, but Coach would've killed us. But for him to believe it"—he stops, pulls me close, and kisses me—"I might have to do a *little* more than kiss you."

Sorry, I'm a bit foggy. What were you saying before your kisses wiped all rational thoughts from my mind? Oh, yeah, doing more.

"Whatever."

"So, don't freak out and slug me or anything. Deal?"

"When was the last time I slugged you?"

"Uh, eighth grade. Phillip convinced me I should try to look up your skirt."

"Oh, yeah. Well, you deserved it, and it worked. You haven't done it since."

"Not that you know about anyway." He smirks.

"So, what kind of things are we talking about?" I coo.

"You'll see, or maybe I should say, *feel,*" he answers cryptically. Then, he slides his warm hands up the back of my sweater.

He grins, which melts my heart and numbs my brain, and then drags me over to join everyone by the fire.

I swear, if he keeps kissing me, there will be nothing left of me but one big puddle. I'm not exactly sure what we're getting ourselves into, but Danny always has great ideas, and, well, I'm having fun.

I once read a quote from that said, "Ever notice how *what the hell* is always the right answer?"

I think that should be my theme song for tonight.

I wonder if anyone's ever set it to music.

But, hey, as long as I'm warm and Danny keeps kissing me, let's throw caution to the wind.

What the hell?

Right?

And, speaking of kissing Danny, did I mention how wonderful it is? How I can feel it all the way down to my toes?

Oh, yeah, I think I did.

Did I mention that I feel a little dizzy?

Maybe that's more the whiskey.

No, it's not. I mean, I've only had a couple of little sips.

I think I'm just intoxicated by Danny.

I mean, what girl wouldn't be?

And what exactly did Phillip mean by, 'He looks like he could eat you alive'? Does he think Danny might actually want me? Like, more than just kissing me and trying to make Jake jealous, so I will feel better?

Me?

I'm not even a cheerleader.

And definitely not a C-cup!

He'd be breaking *way* out of his comfort zone.

What about the fact that I'm having conflicting thoughts about him? I mean, he's a great guy, and he is older and has more experience than a high school boy, and if the kissing is any indication, then I think we could have a winner!

Unfortunately, he is also my friend.

My good friend.

Would I want him to be more than that?

Uh, yeah! Right?

But I don't really have time to contemplate that thought because, as Danny and I slide to the front of the group, the bottle of Jack is passed around again. I put it up to my mouth for another sip when I notice Phillip out of the corner of my eye. He's giving me the eye and ever so slightly shaking his head.

Okay. Fine. So, I pass it along without taking a drink.

I thought everyone would give me a hard time about it, but no one even seems to notice. Evidently, Phillip is the only one concerned about my drinking habits for the evening.

WE ARE NOW in plain view of Jake and his loser friends. Of course, pre-Boobs, I thought they were my friends, too. I find myself staring at Jake through the fire in a daze. I catch him looking back at me, but before I can read his expression, Danny twirls me around to face him.

The boy wastes no time.

I know he knows that Jake is watching, but I have to wonder ...

Is he doing this just to piss off Jake?

Or is it because he's actually enjoying it?

Danny kisses me thoroughly and *very much* seems to be enjoying it.

I know I am.

In fact, I feel like my knees could give way at any minute. He puts his hand on my back, between where my sweater stops and my jeans begin, and rubs slowly. Then, while still kissing me, he runs that hand up under my sweater. I find myself thinking about how wonderful it feels, wondering what Jake must be thinking, and deciding that I really don't care.

I might very well be developing multiple personalities from all this trauma.

My thoughts are interrupted by the feel of Danny's hand sliding down my back, past the waistband of my jeans, and into thong territory. I don't move, but I stop kissing him and suck in a deep breath. Danny quickly moves his hand onto the outside of my pants. But then he chuckles in my ear, glances at Jake, and slides his hand down to the bottom of my butt, where it meets my leg, and gives it a little pinch.

I toss my head back and kinda laugh and scream at the same time.

It definitely gets Jake's attention.

The laugh is not for show though because it really tickles.

I know. It's a weird place to be ticklish. It's kind of like when I stand behind Lisa and stick my index fingers into the sides of her waist. That girl can't help but scream out loud. It is also funny because Phillip and Danny are the only friends of mine who know this about me, having been ratted out by my dad years ago during a particularly competitive Thanksgiving Day game of flag football. Instead of grabbing my flag, Dad pinched me there, which caused me to fumble the football.

Danny and my team lost because of it.

He *still* gives me crap about that.

Jake does not know this fact about me, and I'm sure what Danny is doing must look bad.

I'm still sort of laughing and thoughts are swirling around in my brain. I bring my head back toward Danny and realize he is, like, right there.

He puts his lips on that little spot right at my jawline, almost up by my ear, where I am even more ticklish.

Believe it or not, this is a spot that Jake, in over a year, has never found.

And I have *never* told Danny about it.

I giggle out loud and think fleetingly that, if he can find that spot so fast, then maybe we belong together.

You just can't fight fate. At least, that's what Lisa says.

I just want to scream aloud, Danny, you big stud. Take me to bed or lose me forever.

Uh. Like, now.

Seriously.

Who cares about making Jake jealous?

But, evidently, our PDA was all Jake could take.

He grabs my shoulder, jerks me toward him, and says, "JJ, what the hell?"

I can feel Danny right behind me. He's so mellow about this. He just wraps his arms around my waist, pulls my back in tight to his chest, and leans his chin on my shoulder.

Like this is an everyday occurrence.

God, I wish it were.

Of course, that is exactly what he wants Jake to think.

I can only imagine the look he's giving Jake.

If it were me, I would have my thumbs stuck in my ears with the rest of my fingers waving at him, going, *Na-na, na-na, boo-boo.*

But I doubt Danny is doing that.

Because my ego has been substantially boosted by Danny's attention, I look very blankly at Jake and let out a breathy sigh. "Well, Jake, Danny was just kissing a very ticklish spot on my neck. One that you've never managed to find, and, well, you're interrupting."

I raise my eyebrows at him and shrug my shoulders in a *what's a girl to do* gesture.

So many boys; so little time.

Scratch that.

One boy and not nearly enough time.

Jake studies Danny and me, and then he says very calmly, "I didn't realize the two of you had stayed so close."

Of course, this is *exactly* the opening Danny has been waiting for.

"Well, I *guess* you could call it that." Danny chuckles. He looks down at me, kisses the side of my neck, and runs the back of his hand down my side, from boob to waist, very slowly and suggestively.

Jake is clearly pissed. His face looks twisted, but I don't think he'd dare throw a punch at Danny, especially now that the two linemen have come to stand directly behind us.

So, Jake, being the loser that he is, goes for the weaker link.

Me.

JAKE SPEAKS VERY loudly, so *everyone* within earshot of the North 40 can hear, "Well, hotshot"—Jake snorts—"don't think you're gonna get anything from that." He scowls at me.

Like I am an inanimate object.

"As you can see," he continues as Boobs magically appears at his side, "I had to go elsewhere."

Jake tosses his arm around Boobs, and they both laugh at me like I'm some big inside joke.

Sadly, I probably am.

Of course, I'm humiliated by the fact that my alleged virginity is being discussed in front of half the student population.

Do I have a witty comeback?

What should I say?

Maybe I'll just punch him.

No, bad idea.

But I don't have to say a thing because Danny steps up to the plate.

He pulls me a little closer. I didn't think I could get any closer, but, hurray, I could!

He runs his hand across my thigh, sending chills up my spine. He laughs out loud at Jake and says, "Hey, Jake, ya think maybe there's a reason she's never done it with you?"

I can see by the look on Jake's face that the thought never crossed his mind.

Hey, wait a minute. I could be a player, too.

Or not.

Danny cocks his head and shrugs at Jake. "Might explain all them trips to Lincoln …"

He then looks at me in a way that can only be described as hungry, and I give him a kind of slow, sexy smile that I didn't even know I was capable of.

It takes a few seconds for the implication of what Danny said to sink into Jake's little brain. When Mr. Rocket Scientist finally puts two and two—well, one and one—together, his head looks like it's going to explode—or, quite possibly, implode.

He flies toward Danny. I instinctively duck down just as someone grabs my arm and pulls me out of the way of the flying fists.

Of course, who else?

It's Phillip.

He tightly holds my arm and practically drags me out of the party.

We get to his car, and he orders, "Get in. We're leaving."

I can tell he is mad at me, and I probably shouldn't argue, but I cross my arms in front of my chest and say, "What about Danny?"

I am so not done with that boy yet.

"And me? And maybe I want to see Jake get the crap beat out of him. And, hey, Prince Charming, why aren't you in there, helping to defend my honor anyway?"

Okay, I might have gone a little too far with that one. Sometimes, my mouth gets away from me.

Phillip is very obviously not happy with me.

"Get. In. The. Car. Now!"

"Okay, okay. Fine," I say to Mr. Bossy as I slide into the seat. After he slams my door, walks around, and gets into the car, I finish, "But I'm not going home yet."

Jake is a big. fat. lying. cheating JERK!

PHILLIP DRIVES DOWN the gravel road that will take us back into town. It's deathly quiet in the car. He hasn't said a word to me, and I'm not about to break the silence. I'm mad about the way he treated me at the party. I know he thinks he's helping, but was it really necessary to drag me out of there? I've seen fights at parties before and survived them.

Okay, so I've never been the direct cause of one before, but that's beside the point.

I'm sure it broke up quickly and is already over. The guys are probably back to drinking, telling stories, and having fun.

Without me.

It's not fair. I could be kissing Danny right now.

I really, really liked kissing Danny. I was also very much looking forward to what might have happened next, as in I just might have taken Lisa's advice and attacked him. I *need* to get back to the party, back to Danny.

Phillip pulls his car off to the side of the road, puts it into park, then turns to me, and says, "Stop glaring at me."

"I'm not glaring at you."

But I might very well be giving you mad glances.

"Yes, you are."

"Well, you're glaring back."

"Look, I know you didn't want to leave, but, unlike you, I did the right thing tonight," Phillip brags.

What is he talking about? This has nothing to do with right and wrong. Except that he was wrong to make me leave.

"The right thing?"

"Yes, whereas you never thought once about whether any of the things you were doing were right or wrong."

He is chastising me.

I have had about enough of jerk boys tonight, thank you very much.

"I didn't do anything wrong tonight, Phillip, if that's what you're insinuating."

"Really? Did you once stop to think that getting Danny into a fight could possibly get him injured and ruin his football career?"

I stare at him. And, uh, no, that thought did not cross my mind, but I will not share that piece of information with him.

"You ought to think about someone besides yourself for a change," he says, adding insult to injury.

"I didn't make Danny do anything. He wanted to. In fact, the whole make-Jake-jealous thing was his idea!"

This boy is infuriating!

He says to me, "Whatever. I'm not going to fight with you about this."

He puts the car in gear and starts driving again.

Not only are we done fighting, but evidently, we are done talking, too.

"So, where do you want to *go?*"

"Back to the party."

He glares at me, so I say, "I really should let Lisa know where I am. I was supposed to ride home with her, and I don't want her to worry." What I don't say is, *I wanna see Danny, I wanna kiss Danny, I might even want to, uh, do it with Danny.*

I am not ready for this night to end. Why did I let him drag me to the car? What was I thinking?

"I already told Lisa that I would take you home."

Wait. How did he do that? We never stopped to tell her, and the fight broke out quickly, so that means he planned this.

He's not just a jerk.

He's a premeditating jerk.

"*Before* the fight started?" I call him on it.

"Yes."

"So, you *planned* this?"

"Well, let's just say that I was smart enough to figure out exactly what was going to happen tonight. So, where?"

I really don't know what to do. I just know I won't give him the satisfaction of taking me straight home. Maybe the fight will break up the party, and everyone will head back into town.

"Let's go to The Gas Stop. I'm hungry."

"Great." He gives me a cocky grin. "I need to get gas anyway."

"You would have to turn it into something practical," I mutter under my breath.

Of course, he hears me. "What's that supposed to mean?"

"Oh, I don't know, Mr. Spontaneous."

I get the glare again.

"Well, I was *almost* spontaneous tonight. I *almost* dragged you out of the party before the fight started, but I decided to give you the benefit of the doubt. Obviously, *that* was a mistake."

We pull up to the gas pump. Phillip jumps out and starts the pump. Then gets back into the car. I'm checking out the parking lot between the Gas Stop and the bowling alley and see, sadly, that no one is around.

Darn. Now what?

I'm supposed to be hungry. That's why I wanted to come here, but food does not sound the least bit appetizing. Not even Hostess CupCakes.

I must be more distraught than I realized.

Phillip snarls, "I thought you were *hungry*."

I can tell he knows I was lying.

"What can I say? You made me lose my appetite."

See? Something is your fault. You're not perfect.

Jerk.

"I see." He smirks.

The smirk on his face is pretty much the last straw, so I let him have it.

"Phillip, can't you ever do something just because it feels good? Why do you have to think through and analyze every situation to death?"

"What? Would you rather I was like you and never thought anything through? You were in trouble at the party, and you know it."

"Maybe I wanted trouble, Phillip,"

"Well, you know what? That would have been fine, but then you had to drag Danny into the whole fiasco."

"I dragged Danny?"

The boy is playing rough.

Fine.

"Yeah, I dragged Danny, kicking and screaming, straight to my lips and forced him to kiss me. Many, many times."

I don't know why I think this will upset Phillip. I mean, I know he doesn't *like* me, but I do know something about Danny and me together bugs him.

So there.

"Besides, this mess isn't my fault. It's Jake's. He started the whole stupid thing." I shake my head at him. "And Danny's a big boy. I can't *make* him do anything."

"Oh, you'd be surprised at what you can *make* Danny do," Phillip says like I'm some harlot.

"Phillip, *he* kissed *me*. Not the other way around. Granted, he might have done it because he felt sorry for me, but no one, especially not me, made him." I stop and look closely at Phillip to gauge his reaction. "And what would be so wrong about Danny and me together anyway?"

Phillip looks exasperated. He shakes his head in disbelief and chuckles. "You'd kill each other, for one, because you'd fight constantly. It'd never work. And you'd completely screw your friendship."

"Well, at least Danny and I feel strongly enough about things to fight about them. It shows we have passion, that something is important to us. You know, Phillip, it's okay to have feelings."

Phillip doesn't respond.

So, I say, "You know what? I give up. All you ever do is make me feel bad because I'm not perfect like you. I don't need it anymore, and I'm not sure I want to be your friend either. Take me home." I madly cross my arms in front of my chest with a *humph*.

"I thought you didn't want to go home," Phillip says in a snotty little boy voice.

I don't get a chance to respond to Jerk Boy because his cell rings.

Maybe it's Danny!

He sighs at me, looks at his phone, reads the caller ID, and whispers, "It's Dad," before he presses Talk. "Hey, Dad."

I listen to his side of the conversation.

"Yeah, I do. She's in the car with me now." He glares over at me. "I was just about to take her *home*."

He gives me the snotty little boy look again. Then his expression drops as the color drains from his face. I watch his eyes bug out like he's hearing that aliens just landed on Earth or something else unbelievable.

"Uh. O-kay." He looks at me sideways and lets out a sigh. "We'll be there as fast as we can, Dad. I will."

I ask, "What? What's wrong?" I'm worried because whatever his dad said didn't sound like good news. I wonder if there was a terrorist attack or something equally horrific.

Phillip takes a deep breath, like what he has to tell me is so very bad.

"Your parents were in a serious car accident." He blows out a big breath. "They are being life-flighted to University Hospital. My parents were following them home when it happened. They'll meet us there."

"What?"

Phillip flies out of the car and quickly shuts off the gas pump. We leave the Gas Stop fast, and he's already speeding by the time we hit the viaduct going out of town.

I look at his speedometer and then at him with a *what are you doing* look.

Phillip never speeds.

Reading my mind, he says, "I know I'm going a bit fast, but Dad said to hurry."

That can't be good, can it? My world feels like it's slipping out from underneath me, and to top it off, Phillip is mad at me. That's fine. I'm mad at him, too. But, at the same time, I'm glad he's here. This is scaring me.

Because life-flighted …

That's bad, isn't it?

Just as we climb the hill and go speeding by the high school, a police car's lights come flashing on behind us.

"We don't have time for this."

"What do you mean, Phillip? How bad is it? Phillip?"

He pulls over and rolls down his window. Then, he turns to me. "Bad. Really bad."

"Bad as in broken bones? A bit smashed up? Paralysis, coma?" I pause and think, *Oh my God …* "Or like dying bad?"

"I don't know."

The officer walks up to the window and shines his flashlight in our eyes. "JJ?" the policeman asks.

I hold my hand in front of my squinting eyes, trying to see whose face the familiar voice is coming from.

Phillip says to the officer, "You know JJ?"

"Sure. Went to high school with her dad. Still play Wiffle ball together."

Phillip looks up to the roof of his car and mutters, "Thank you."

In a very businesslike tone, he tells the officer, "Mr. and Mrs. Reynolds were in a bad car accident and are being airlifted to the hospital. I was told to get JJ there. Fast."

"Not the accident that has the interstate shut down?"

"Um"—Phillip gulps—"yeah."

"Damn. Leave your car here and come with me," Officer Myers tells Phillip. "*I'll* get you there."

"Come on," Phillip says, pulling me out of his car and putting me into the squad car next to him.

"Is there anything you're not telling me?"

He tells me that everything will be okay, but his body language is sending out an entirely different message. He is way tense. I can tell that he is biting down hard on his back teeth. It's making his jaw look very stiff. I can't tell if it is because the accident was a bad one or because he is so mad that he hates me now and can't even stand to speak to me.

"Let's just get there," he says, not really answering my question.

OFFICER MYERS, WHO I do recognize now that he's not blinding me with his flashlight, does play Wiffle ball with my dad. I think his first name starts with a J, like John or James, but everyone calls him Cookie. Don't know they come up with these nicknames. Everyone who lives in a small town—the guys who play Wiffle ball on Sundays, in particular—seem to have them. I think I remember hearing that they call him Cookie because in, like, fifth grade, he stole the neighbor girl's boxes of Girl Scout cookies and ate them all.

I don't know why I'm thinking about all this. I feel bizarre. I have tons of adrenaline rushing through my body. Part of me feels like I could jump the tallest building or run faster to the Med Center, but the other part of me feels numb. Like I can't move. Like I'm paralyzed.

The police car goes fast, the lights flash, and the siren blares. I usually hate hearing sirens. They have always kind of scared me, but for some reason—maybe because it never stops—it's almost comforting this time.

I pray the whole way there.

Please let them be okay.

Whooh, whooh, whooh.

Please let them be okay.

Whooh, whooh, whooh.

Please let them be okay.

It's like the siren and my prayer have a sort of rhythm.

I close my eyes. Maybe I'm having a bad dream. Maybe this whole messed up night is just some bad, horrible, crazy dream.

I will myself to wake up. I slowly open my eyes, only to see Phillip staring out of a police car window with a scared and numb look on his face.

So, it's not a dream.

Okay, I need to mentally prepare myself. Be rational. Whatever this is, I can handle it. Obviously, they are hurt badly if they are being airlifted. But lots of people get better after bad car wrecks. You see it on television all the time. Broken bones heal; scars can be fixed.

They are going to be fine. Everything is going to be fine.

I see the hospital up ahead. We're almost there. I feel a hand on my shoulder, so I lean my head toward it and touch my cheek to it. I take a long, slow breath and feel myself relax. I feel comforted. As we pull up to the emergency entrance, I put my hand up to my shoulder for more reassurance, but my hand only touches my fuzzy sweater.

That's weird. For a minute, I thought it was Mom's hand I touched. She always holds my shoulder like that. But I shake my head at that thought because, duh, she's obviously not here.

I hear Phillip tell Cookie, "Thanks for the ride."

Oh, boy. Here we go.

We get out of the car and walk through the emergency room doors. I see Phillip's dad right away. He's pacing, waiting for us, and he doesn't look so good. Truthfully, he looks terrible, like he's been crying. His shirt's untucked and dirty, his hair's a mess, and—oh God, it's not dirt. It's *blood* all over his shirt.

He was there, I remember.

"How are they?" I ask immediately as he takes my hands in his.

He closes his eyes, takes a deep breath, opens them, and says somberly, "JJ, honey, your mom didn't make it."

Didn't make what?

Oh.

God, no!

That can't possibly be.

There's got to be some kind of mistake!

But I don't have time to think because he drags me down the hall.

"Come on. Hurry. You need to see your dad. He's been asking for you."

We're riding up the elevators to Intensive Care when he adds, "He's not doing well, JJ."

I cannot even handle this.

He rushes me into ICU and lets the nurse know I'm here. She leads us to Dad's room.

Oh my.

All my self-talk in the police car did nothing to prepare me for this.

Saying Dad doesn't look good is a major understatement. He looks ... well, like he's going to die, and I am instantly petrified. His head is wrapped in bloody bandages. The majority of his face looks swollen and bruised. There are tubes and wires hooked up to him everywhere, and the room is filled with all sorts of beeping monitors.

Part of me thinks this can't possibly be my dad.

I mean, Dad is big and strong.

He's invincible. My very own superhero.

I can't handle seeing him like this. He looks ... helpless.

I stand frozen in shock in the doorway. I am totally unable to move. Mr. Mac puts his palm across my lower back and gently guides me closer to Dad's bed. Then, he turns and walks out of the room.

I stand there and stare at Dad for a minute, not quite sure what to do.

"Daddy?" I finally say.

Dad slowly blinks open his eyes and looks at me.

He's okay! He's awake!

I grab his hand and pull it up to my cheek. I feel relief. It's going to be okay.

I close my eyes and feel warmth go through me as his hand touches my face even though his fingers feel cold.

That's weird. Dad's hands are always so warm.

"Angel," he says and smiles a little smile at me. I mean, really, only the corners of his mouth go up a bit, but I know it's supposed to be a smile.

"Daddy, everything's gonna be all right."

He looks straight at me with eyes that seem to say, *No, it's not.*

Not unlike the look he gave me when he told me that Pookie, our beloved dog, had died when I was nine.

Wait. He doesn't think he will be all right? Or is it just because he knows about Mom? Does he know about Mom?

Is Mr. Mac even sure about Mom?

He looks very tired and closes his eyes, so I sit there, holding his cold hand to my cheek, staring at his swollen face, trying to think positive thoughts, and praying like I have never prayed before.

His eyelids flutter open for a second, and he whispers softly, "Love." He takes a shallow breath. "My Angel." His eyes close again.

I keep his hand on my cheek and let him rest.

I'm sure he needs lots of rest.

But I can take care of him for a while. I mean, he has taken care of me for my whole life. I don't know what we are going to do without Mom. It's going to be horrible, awful, but I'll figure it out. He and I will somehow get through it together.

I look at his chest.

Is he breathing?

My eyes get big, and I feel panicked as I watch his chest, waiting for it to rise again, for him to take another breath. I wait for what seems like forever.

Come on!

The monitors start screeching, and an alarm sounds.

Nurses and doctors come tearing into the room. I hold my breath as I sink down into a chair in the corner, pull my legs up on the seat, and wrap my arms around them. A nurse grabs me and hustles me out of the room.

I say a new prayer.

Don't leave me, Daddy. Don't leave me, Daddy.

Please don't leave me. You can so not leave me!

I say it over and over in my mind while I sit in the ICU waiting room.

I think that's a horrible name. Waiting room. Sitting around and *waiting* for someone to live or die. It's terrible. And I will never in my life forget the smell of it. It smells like hospital disinfectant and microwave popcorn. Someone has just made some, like they're having a party. I see two people over in the corner, eating it and watching TV. They're even laughing!

That, quite frankly, is something I might never do again. I might very well be devoid of emotion.

What is wrong with me?

My mom's dead, and my dad could be, and I have not shed a single tear.

My mom is dead. I can't believe I just thought those words.

There really has to be some kind of mistake. Can they mix up people in the hospital? Don't they do that with babies sometimes? Maybe, in all the commotion, they mixed up Mom. Maybe she's going to walk down the hall and tell me she's okay, that everything is okay, that it was all just a big mistake.

But I don't think that is going to happen.

I feel so ... I don't know ... twisted.

Speaking of twisted, you know the movie *Twister?*

I know, not my typical romantic comedy genre, but when you live in the Midwest, tornadoes are scary fascinating, and in the spring, that movie plays on basic cable every other weekend.

So, in the movie, they had no warning.

And that's why they are out chasing dangerous tornados.

Anyway, I think that's what happened. An invisible F5 tornado just plowed straight through my life, sucking up everything important to me.

And I had no warning.

No menacing clouds, no rain, no hail, no debris.

And I'm the freaking twisted-up cow that goes flailing in front of Jo's truck. Like I got picked up way over there and was tossed out of the tornado, landing clear over here, shaking my head and wondering, *What the *#!$ just happened?*

How fitting. I'm the debris.

I look around for Mr. Mac. Did the F5 suck him up, too?

No. He probably went to get Mrs. Mac and Phillip.

Phillip.

Oh crap.

I am such a freaking idiot.

Phillip was really mad at me.

And, even though some of the stuff he said pissed me off, as usual, Phillip always has the situation figured out, and I hate to admit it, but he's usually right. That is why I do get mad at him sometimes. I hate not being right.

Phillip and I never fight. And that was, like, a fight. And I said some mean stuff to him. Like I told him I didn't want to be his friend anymore.

Why in the world did I say that? I didn't mean it.

I've got to tell him I'm sorry.

But what if he won't forgive me? What if he hates me now?

He barely spoke to me in the police car.

He probably does hate me.

Regardless of the fight, I mean, he is my best friend, and I don't know what I would do without him.

Especially now.

I mutter another prayer.

Please don't let him hate me. Please don't let him hate me. Please don't let him hate me.

THE ELEVATOR DINGS, and I stand up in front of my chair and watch the doors open. Standing inside the elevator are Mr. and Mrs. Mac and Phillip.

I try to read Phillip's face as he steps off the elevator, but I'm unable to judge what he's thinking. I do notice that his eyes don't look angry anymore, so maybe there's hope.

Phillip doesn't say anything.

He rushes to me, wraps me in a one-armed hug, and pulls me close.

I close my eyes and whimper in his ear, "I'm so sorry, Phillip. Please forgive me. I didn't mean what I said. Please forgive me. Please forgive me."

"Princess," he whispers back, "you know I could never stay mad at you."

And that's when the tears come.

Standing there, in Phillip's arms, this whole nightmare becomes, well, real.

Nothing is ever real until I tell it to Phillip, I think. *Why should this be any different?*

"She's dead, Phillip." I sob into his shoulder. "I think he might be dead, too."

Mr. Mac says loudly, "What?"

"He might be dead, too. He talked to me—well, he said my name, and he sorta smiled at me. I thought that meant he was going to be okay. But his hands were so cold, and his hands are just like Phillip's. They're never cold. Then, he stopped breathing, I think. A bunch of alarms went off, and they made me leave. But no one has come out to tell me *anything.*"

Because Phillip is smoothing down the back of my hair with the palm of his hand, I actually manage to get the words out.

Mr. Mac drops into a chair, runs his hand through his hair, hangs his head down, and keeps it there. He's changed out of his, you know, dirty shirt and is wearing a green scrub top. It looks really out of place on him because he's always a very polished suit-and-tie kind of guy.

Mr. Mac has known my dad longer than I have, I suddenly realize.

We sit in uncomfortable waiting room chairs and wait and wait for what seems like an eternity.

Everyone handles the stress of waiting differently. Mr. Mac

paces up and down the hall, jingling some change and keys in his pocket. Mrs. Mac plays hostess. She makes us all coffees and then cleans up a mess that isn't really there. Phillip sits next to me and holds my hands. I just stare into space, my mind in overdrive, trying to figure out how I am going to deal with this.

FINALLY, A NURSE comes out. She tells us they revived Dad. I feel hopeful, but then she quietly adds that his outlook isn't good, and a doctor will be out to talk to us soon.

"Is there a chapel here?" I blurt out, feeling a sudden need to have a chat with God.

"Down the hall and to your right," she tells me.

"I'm gonna go down there, okay?" I tell the Macs.

"Can I come with you?" Phillip asks me. "Or do you want to be alone?"

"Come with me. I might need backup," I tell Phillip hastily as I march off.

"What do you mean?" he asks as he follows me down the hall and to the right.

"I'm pissed, Phillip. I'm mad at God, and I want him to know it!"

Phillip follows me into the empty chapel.

I walk to the front and hold my arms in the air.

"Okay, God?" I say to the sky. Not that I expect an answer, but I need to get this out. "I mean, what in the hell did they do to deserve this? Why them? Why me?"

"JJ! You can't say stuff like that in here. It's totally disrespectful."

"You know what, Phillip? He pretty much took my parents away from me tonight in one fell swoop. I think I've earned the right to say a few bad words. I mean, jeez, could it get any worse?"

Phillip sighs. "You know God doesn't cause accidents. They're just that. *Accidents*."

"So, what happened, Phillip? Who or what caused this *accident*? And like God couldn't have saved them if he wanted to? Haven't you ever heard of miracles? Don't you think he could've even spared just one?" I yell at both Phillip and God.

Phillip studies my face and begins, "Well, a woman lost control of her car. Crossed the median." He gulps. "They collided head-on."

"Oh, figures. And I suppose she wasn't even hurt. Probably walked away without a scratch while my mom is dead, and Dad is ... oh, I don't know what he is exactly."

"Actually, they were on the interstate, going seventy-five miles per hour when they collided. They say she was killed instantly." He intensely looks at me and continues in a measured tone, "Her four-year-old daughter was in the backseat and *miraculously* only has a few cuts and bruises."

Oh, sure, throw my miracle request back in my face.

"So, it could be worse. You could be a four-year-old with no mom."

Leave it to Phillip to find the one damn ray of sunshine in my whole dark life.

"Fine," I sigh. "So, it could be worse. Regardless of my age, Phillip, I can't handle this. How am I supposed to handle this?"

I am starting to freaking freak!

"I'll help you." He grabs my wrists and leads me to a pew. "My family will help you. You know our parents agreed to take care of each other's kids if anything happened to them. Your being eighteen doesn't change how they feel about you." He runs the back of his hand across my cheek and then holds my chin, forcing me to look up at him. "We love you. I love you. We'll get through it together." He breaks a little smile. "You know, Grandma Mac used to say, 'God never gives you more than you can handle.'"

"My grandma used to say something like that, except hers was, 'What doesn't kill you makes you stronger.'" I shake my head. "It looks like I'm about to get a whole helluva lot stronger."

"Jadyn," Phillip says, stroking my cheek again.

Jadyn? Phillip has never called me that.

"You're the strongest"—he smiles—"and most stubborn person I know. I think maybe you'll realize just how much strength you already have."

I don't know if it's thinking about Grandma or what Phillip said or the way his touch relaxes me or just having it out with God, so to speak, but I feel a little better.

I say another silent prayer. *Sorry for yelling. This is just such a shock. Please help my dad, and please help me.*

Maybe I can get through this. I mean, let's face it; do I really have a choice?

No, I have to.

For my parents, I suppose.

"Thanks, Phillip. We'd better get back. I don't wanna miss the doctor."

HE HOLDS MY hand as we walk back to the waiting room, and that gives me strength somehow.

Mr. and Mrs. Diamond must've just arrived. They are crying and hugging the Macs.

They see me and hug me, too.

"Oh, JJ. We're so sorry, honey. I just can't believe this," Mary says tearfully.

We update Chuck and Mary, and I complain that we still haven't heard from a doctor.

"That's ridiculous!" Chuck tells us and marches straight into ICU.

Danny's dad is an attorney and a lot like Danny, a very take-charge kind of guy. I'm glad he's here because I don't think Mr. Mac is going to be able to take charge of anything. He's not dealing so well.

While Mr. Diamond is in the ICU, Mrs. Diamond is on her cell, trying to reach Danny. "Straight to voicemail," she complains. "I can't—" She starts crying again. "I can't just tell him this on voicemail. And I talked to him right before Julie called. He said he saw you guys at a party in town."

Phillip nods at her.

Jake. Danny. The party. It seems like a lifetime ago.

"Why he hasn't bothered to stop and see his mother while he is in town, I have no idea," she mutters. "Anyway, I know his phone's not dead. Why have one if you're not going to keep it on and answer it?"

"He's probably back at his dorm by now. Why don't you try there?" Phillip suggests.

"Why don't *you* try?" she says to Phillip. "Maybe he's just avoiding his mother."

Phillip takes out his cell and punches in Danny's number. I hear him leave a message.

"Hey, it's Phillip. Your mom's been trying to reach you for a reason. Call me as soon as you get this. It's Jay's parents. Um, there's been an accident, and it's ... uh, not good. Call me, no matter how late."

MR. DIAMOND WALKS out of the ICU. He's lost his swagger.

"The doctor will be out in a few minutes," he announces. Then, he walks over and sits down beside me. He puts his big hand on my knee, but I'm not sure if it is meant to comfort me or bolster him. "You need to prepare yourself, JJ. The news isn't going to be good." He swallows hard, and tears well up in his eyes. He starts to cry as he says, "They don't think he's going to make it and want to talk to you about organ donation."

"Jesus, Chuck! Don't you think they should try to save him before they start auctioning off his body parts?" Mr. Mac yells. He madly throws his coffee cup in the trash and storms down the hall.

We all ignore his outburst. We know he's very upset.

I watch him walk down the hall, sigh, and say to Mr. Diamond, "I think he wanted that."

"He did. I took care of your parents' estate planning. You're going to be okay, JJ." He looks at me with worried eyes and adds softly, "Well, at least financially."

I sort of roll my eyes because, I'm sorry, finances are the least of my worries right now.

The ICU doors part, and a doctor walks out.

I stand up and rush toward him. "Is he okay?" I ask.

"Jadyn Reynolds?" the doctor asks me.

I nod my head.

"Let's sit down."

I cringe at that. On TV, bad news always follows that saying.

I sit down next to Phillip, who grabs my hand and tightly squeezes it.

"Your father suffered severe brain trauma, and his body is shutting down. We've revived him once, but we need to discuss what you want done if it happens again. Did he have a living will?"

I look at him, kind of puzzled because I'm not exactly sure what that is.

Danny's dad stands up and says, "Yes, he did. Here. I brought a copy." He hands the living will to the doctor.

"What's that for exactly?" I ask.

Chuck turns to me and says very slowly, "Well, your parents didn't want you, or each other, to ever have to make difficult decisions about medical care should something like this happen. So, they put their wishes in something called a living will. Your dad did not wish to be held in a vegetative state."

Oh my gosh, I think. *Vegetative state?*

"So, bottom line is that he's going to die?" I ask incredulously.

Please let this be a bad, bad dream.

"Yes, it's inevitable," the doctor tells us.

"When?" I ask and then hammer him with a whole slew of questions. "Can I go talk to him? Can he hear me? Is he in pain? What are we supposed to do? What am I supposed to do?"

"Yes, you can talk to him." The doctor is young, good-looking, and has compassionate eyes. If I wasn't in such distress, I'd probably be flirting with him. "He's highly medicated, and he won't be in any pain. He's slipped into a coma, so he won't talk back, but we believe coma patients can hear you. So, go talk to him, tell him you love him, and say good-bye." He stops and sighs. "I know this is tough, but he signed the back of his driver's license, indicating his wish to be an organ donor. We need your approval for that. He was a strong, healthy man, and his organs could help many families whose loved ones will die without them."

I zone out most of what he said because all I can focus on is the word *was*. He *was* a strong man.

Was?

I turn and glance at Phillip. "Was?" I put my elbow on my knee, hold my chin in my hand, and close my eyes.

How am I supposed to do this?

I cannot do this.

A voice inside my head—probably the same stupid one that can never say *no* to a dare or take *no* for an answer—says, *You have to.*

"You didn't answer the when part," I say.

He shakes his head and purses his lips. "Not long. Maybe a few hours; maybe a few minutes."

"When do you need to know about the organ donation stuff?"

"When you make a decision, let his nurse know, and she'll get you the appropriate paperwork. You can all go in to see him, but please, no more than two at a time." He gets down on his knees in front of me, touches my hand, and says seriously, "Jadyn, I'm very sorry about *both* your mother and father. I was here when they both came in, and we really did everything we could."

And I realize that this has been hard on him, too. "Thank you. I appreciate everything you did," I manage to say.

Mr. Mac comes walking back down the hall. Mr. Diamond heads him off and updates him on the situation.

"I'm going in there," I state.

I want to see Dad, but I feel sick to my stomach. Part of me feels like, if I just pretend this isn't happening, then maybe it won't be. The other part of me needs to say good-bye. I feel like a big, fat chicken.

Get ahold of yourself. You are so not a chicken.

I walk up to Mr. Mac, look at him with well-practiced puppy-dog eyes, and give him a hug. He really looked like he could use one, and truthfully, I'm hoping to soften him up a little.

"Would you come in with me?"

Okay, so maybe I'm a bit chicken.

"I don't know if I can, JJ," he answers truthfully. "It tears me up to see him like that."

"Me, too. But we have to. We'll do it together, okay?"

He nods his head, and we walk into the ICU.

I hate to say it, but Dad looks worse. His skin is very gray. I don't know why this is such a shock to me, but it is. I nod my head to Mr. Mac, indicating he can go first.

He puts his hand on my dad's shoulder and says, "Hey, buddy. Not our best night ever, huh? And we have had *some* nights, haven't we?" He pauses, remembering and smiling. Then, he continues, "Things aren't looking so great for you, so I want you to know I'll take care of your Angel, as promised."

Huge tears stream down his face, and he doesn't bother to wipe them away.

It's really hard to watch a grown man cry.

He slowly backs away from the bed, so I walk over and perch

gently on the edge of it. The hospital smells like cleaner and medicine and disinfectant, yet through it all, I can still smell my dad.

It's not even his cologne.

It's just him.

I lay my head across his chest. "I love you, Daddy. So much. I don't know what I am going to do without you and Mommy."

This sucks.

No one should ever have to go through this. It's just so horribly, incredibly awful.

The organ donation thing comes to mind, and I think, if I can save *even one* family from having to go through this, I should do it.

I walk straight out to the nurse and say, "Let's do it. Let me sign the papers."

While I'm signing, she says, "You know you're doing a wonderful thing. In a few minutes, people across the country will get the call they have been hoping and praying for. Because of you."

"No. Because of my dad," I say and walk back in to be with Dad.

HE DIES A few hours later.

PHILLIP'S PARENTS DRIVE us home. We get to their house, and like a robot, I wash my face, brush my teeth, and pull on a pair of Phillip's sweats and a T-shirt. Danny's mom whips up some sandwiches. They look good, but I have no desire to eat. I sit there on the sofa and don't say a word.

Really, no one says a word. I think we're all in shock.

Finally, Mrs. Mac breaks the silence. "I think we should all try to get some sleep." She turns to me and says, "JJ, the doctor gave us some sleeping pills for you. I think you should take one."

I shake my head. "There will be a lot to do tomorrow. Oh, I guess it already is tomorrow. I mean, like, later today. Anyway, I helped my parents plan Grandpa Reynolds's funeral last year, so I know there'll be lots to do, and I don't want to feel all groggy."

I took a sleeping pill once after I broke my arm and had a hard time staying awake the next day.

Danny's dad says, "JJ, we can do *everything* for you, honey. You don't have to."

"Yeah, I do," I tell them. "I think I need to."

Phillip's cell rings. "Danny," he says to me.

He gets up and walks into the dining room to talk. Obviously so I can't hear. As usual, Phillip is trying to protect me.

Like I'm not already painfully aware of what happened tonight.

He walks back into the room and hands me his phone.

"Are you okay?" I ask Danny.

"Ohmigawd, Jay. Yes, are you okay? No, that's a stupid question. Of course you're not okay. I am so sorry. God, I should've been there with you."

"You couldn't have known."

"I'm headed out the door now. I'll be there as fast as I can."

"Don't do that, Danny. It's been a long night, and I don't want to worry about you driving. And we're all just getting ready to go to bed, so get some sleep first and come in the morning, okay?"

"O-*kay*," he answers.

There's silence on the other end, and I wonder if the call dropped, but then Danny sighs, "Jay?"

"Yeah?"

"It wasn't just about making Jake jealous. See you in a few hours."

Phillip takes the phone away from me and gives it to Mrs. Diamond.

"All right. It's been a long night." Mrs. Mac stands up and claps her hands together. "Everybody to bed."

THE DIAMONDS GO home, and I ask pathetically, "Is it okay if I sleep in Phillip's room? I don't wanna be alone."

"Sure, honey," Mrs. Mac says, hugs me, and heads to her room.

Phillip grabs my hand and leads me upstairs. He lies on his bed, props a pillow behind his back, and holds out his arm. I snuggle into the crook of it, put my head on his chest, and close my eyes.

Phillip doesn't say anything to me. He just runs his fingers through my hair over and over again.

It is incredibly soothing, and at some point, I must fall asleep.

I WAKE UP a few hours later, still lying on his shoulder.

"You're awake," he whispers.

"Why ..." I start to say, looking at him and wondering where I am.

Then, it all comes rushing back.

"Oh God. It really happened?"

"Yeah, it did." He strokes my hair again.

God, he's sweet.

"It seems like so long ago, but I'm sorry I yelled at you after the party."

"I doubt it was for the last time." He chuckles.

"Phillip."

"Well, at least I hope it wasn't the last time because it would mean you weren't with me."

I roll my eyes at him. I don't get mad at him that often. Just when he disagrees with me.

"I'll always love my Princess." He smiles. "Even when she's mad at me." He winces and says seriously, "I'm really sorry about everything. This is going to be so rough, but I want you to know that I'm here for you. My family's here for you."

AND THEY WERE there for me.

Especially Phillip.

He stood by my side and held my hand through it all. As I picked out caskets and gravestones, planned the funeral, chose the pallbearers, picked the music, the scriptures, the speakers, and even when I had to decide what clothes they should wear.

And, every night, the only way I could go to sleep was lying on his shoulder.

I never could've gotten through these last few days without him.

Celebrating their lives.

APRIL 23RD

"MAY THEY REST in peace," the pastor says, finishing the eulogy.

Now, it's my turn.

I walk slowly up to the podium at the front of the church, turn, and gaze out at all the people who came to the funeral. My parents really did touch many people's lives. Mrs. Mac and Mrs. Diamond tried to discourage me from speaking at the funeral, which, quite frankly, just made me want to do it more.

Because, really, how could I not?

Hopefully, I can say everything I want to say.

Deep breath.

Game face in place.

Okay.

"I want to share a quote with all of you from a book I've been reading. It goes, 'Do any human beings ever realize life while they live it—every, every minute?' We're all busy people, and it's easy to get so wrapped up in *life* that we forget to live. My parents knew how to live. They enjoyed the little things in life, like sunsets, great parties, telling jokes, hanging out with friends"—I can't help but smile—"and even silly things like giving piggyback rides. I'm pretty sure they wouldn't want us sitting around here, crying over the fact that they are gone. I think they'd rather we celebrate the fact that they lived—every, every minute—and would challenge us all to do the same."

The lights dim, and the presentation starts. My cue to step away from the podium and take my seat.

When we were at the church, planning the funeral, it was very sad and somber. And I don't know what hit me, but I looked at Mr. Mac sitting there, not smiling, and I just thought, *This is not what Mom and Dad's lives were about.*

If Dad were here, he and Mr. Mac would be laughing and joking about something. They had more inside jokes than a group of seventh-grade girls.

I know you have to do the religious part, and I wanted to do the religious part. But they sorta felt disconnected. The religious part felt more about what was next for them, and I'm happy that they are in heaven and all that, but what about us, the ones they left behind?

We don't really want them in heaven. We want them back with us.

I want them back with me.

So, I told our pastor that I wanted to do something that would make people feel good. To help them remember the fun times, to see that my parents enjoyed their lives.

They loved to celebrate.

So, I wanted to do something that would celebrate my parents' lives.

Phillip, Danny, and I would be outside, shooting hoops or playing a game of H-O-R-S-E, and Dad would come out and be like, "It's gorgeous out; a day like today is worth celebrating."

I always thought *celebrate* was sorta code for, *If I say I'm celebrating something, then my wife won't complain to me about sitting here, smoking a stinky cigar.*

But that wasn't it. Because, before you knew it, Mom would be out there, sitting on his lap, drinking a wine cooler, and celebrating with him. Then, pretty soon, half of the neighbors would show up, and they would all be drinking and eating and *really* celebrating the fact that they were together, that it *was* a beautiful day. I think they definitely appreciated daily life and not just special occasions. They made everyday occasions special.

So, even though it was painful, Katie, Lisa, and I went through all our photos and selected a few that showed my parents doing just that.

Celebrating their lives.

Phillip scanned them all into the computer and created a slide show of them set to music.

Notes play and pictures flash by:

Mom as a baby.

Mom with no front teeth, with pigtails, on her bike.

Mom with her high school friends in their graduation caps and gowns.

Dad as a chubby, bald baby.

Dad dressed as a cowboy with Uncle John dressed as an Indian.

Dad playing basketball in high school.

Then, the two of them together in college, looking goofily in love.

Dad and Mr. Mac in college, togas on and cigars in their mouths.

A big group of Dad's frat brothers, all holding red cups and making silly faces and gestures.

Mom and Dad at a fraternity formal, Mom with bright blue eyeliner and big hair.

Mom with her best friends on spring break at the beach.

Mom catching the bouquet at the Macs' wedding and Dad pretending to be scared.

Their college graduations.

MOM WITH AN amazingly happy look on her face, holding out her engagement ring, while her friends are gathered around, looking at it.

Mom and Dad dancing and kissing at their wedding.

Dad carrying Mom over the threshold of their new house.

A group of their friends in a hot tub on a skiing trip.

Daddy holding me at the hospital the day I was born.

Mom and Julie holding Phillip and me as babies.

Mom teaching me how to walk.

Daddy holding my hands in the air, teaching me the signal for a touchdown, when I was two with a Nebraska game on the TV in the background and everyone around him dressed in red.

Daddy teaching me how to ride a bike.

Christmas morning, wrapping paper everywhere.

My parents at Disney World, watching the parade, with me asleep over Daddy's shoulder.

Dad, Phillip, Danny, and me playing soccer in the backyard.

Daddy blowing out the candles on a very pathetic-looking cake I had frosted.

Mom and me at my eighth-grade graduation.

Our families all standing in front of a fountain in Kansas City with the Plaza lights aglow around us.

A Thanksgiving Day flag football game with all our families.

All our neighbors together for the annual block party.

My family with the Diamonds and the Macs this past Fourth of July.

I glance at Phillip, who's sitting next to me.

When I was going through all the pictures, I realized how much Phillip and I had been together. He was in practically every picture with me even if he was lurking in the background somewhere.

The screen flashes.

Dad, by the grill, holding a plate of very badly burned hamburgers with Danny's dad and Danny laughing.

The slide show is incredible. Phillip didn't want me to watch it before the funeral, and now, I see why. It's like he got me the perfect gift and didn't want me to open it early.

What would I ever do without that boy?

I reach over and put my hand on top of his.

He glances at me, and I mouth, *Thank you*, to him.

He smiles at me as he wipes tears from his eyes.

AT THE VISITATIONS, all the ladies were telling me what a lucky girl I was to have such a devoted and supportive boyfriend. At first, I told them that Phillip was not my boyfriend, just one of my best friends, but most of the ladies I said that to sorta rolled their eyes at me.

Like Phillip was really my boyfriend, and I was trying to keep it a secret.

When Mrs. Mac told someone that Phillip and I were just very close friends, the lady sneered and practically insinuated that *close* meant, uh, *close*, as in, based on the way he was always touching me, we must be sleeping together.

And, well, we are—kinda. Since I can't go to sleep without his shoulder next to me. But, you know, not in the way that lady assumed.

So, finally, both of us gave up.

It was easier to just agree than to try to explain.

So, when people asked him how his girlfriend was doing, he would say, "She's hanging in there."

And, when people said I had an amazing boyfriend, I'd smile and agree.

And, of course, Phillip had to give me a hard time about that.

So, last night, when it was just us, he was referring to himself as my amazing boyfriend, my support system, my devoted lover, my, uh, *close* friend.

He really does make me laugh. And being able to laugh occasionally, in a situation like this, has helped release some of my pent-up stress.

At least I haven't blown yet.

THE VIDEO ENDS, and the pastor requests that everyone join us at the *place of rest.*

And, seriously, this is the part I have been dreading.

This is the part that freaks me out.

The place of rest.

As in the cemetery.

Where they will be buried.

And I will never see them again.

Okay, yes, I know they are dead. I know they aren't coming back.

I know they are never going to talk to me again.

But, for some strange reason—and I know this sounds kind of sick—having their bodies still here, like at the funeral home and here at the church, it's like they are still a little bit here.

It kills me to look at Mom and Dad lying there, in their caskets, not smiling at me, not teasing me, or not telling me they love me.

But, at the same time, they are still here.

Well, sorta.

I mean, I definitely believe in God and heaven and all that. And I believe that their souls have gone to heaven and that, someday, when I die, we will be reunited.

But that doesn't mean I am ready to let their bodies go into the ground.

It feels so harsh.

It feels like the wrong thing to do.

Because it feels like that is all I have left of them.

And I'm hanging on by whatever threads are left.

As Phillip walks me to the limo, I tell him, "Phillip, I don't know if I can do this part."

And, of course, Phillip and I can't carry on a conversation because people are wonderful. They keep coming up to me, hugging me, holding my hands, and telling me what wonderful people my parents were, how sorry they are for me, how my parents are watching in heaven—all that stuff people say at funerals to try to make you feel better.

And it does. I know they are being sincere, but still, I have a horrible feeling of dread inside me.

Because this is it.

After we bury them, I am going to be all alone.

Phillip pulls me aside, next to the limo. "Princess, you can do this. You've got this. You stood up there and gave that little speech without crying. This will be easy compared to that."

I whisper, "But, Phillip, this is not the easy part because, when they bury them, I am going to be alone. All alone."

And, really, that is the part of all this that scares me the most.

Phillip tenderly cups my shoulder with his hand and pulls me into a hug. Then, he smiles at me, touches the tip of my nose with his finger, and says, "Don't think you can get rid of me that easily. As long as I'm around, you'll never be alone. I do have my reputation to uphold as your, uh, very *close* friend, you know. Heck, I'm going to be around so much; you'll probably be begging me to leave." He gives me a sly little grin.

I give Phillip a little smile, but I don't get to reply because Aunt Sara and Uncle John barrel between us and hop in the limo.

Phillip rolls his eyes at them and then says, "I guess it's time to go."

I follow them into the limo, and it takes all my strength not to pull Phillip in with me.

To protect me.

I have to sit with *just* them, as in just Aunt Sara and Uncle

John, for the next part of the service.

I really don't know why I agreed to it, but it was important to John that it be just family, so I did. I figured, since I planned everything for the funeral of his brother without his input, it was the least I could do.

But, now, I wish I hadn't been so nice.

Especially when I get in the limo and Uncle John doesn't say a word to me. On the ride to the cemetery, I thought maybe he would say something about how I was brave to stand up there and speak, which so many other people have said.

Or how amazing he thought the slide show was because it showed them as we all remembered them—so full of happiness and life.

But no. Nothing.

I don't think I like Uncle John very much.

AT THE CEMETERY, I take my seat next to John under the tent covering the two freshly dug graves.

We wait for the twelve most important men in my life, the pallbearers, to get the caskets out of the hearses. There's Mr. Diamond and Danny; my dad's fraternity brothers, Mr. Mac, Scott, Lance, and Barry; my friends, Joey, Neil, and Brandon; my dad's work friend, Jeff; and his best high school friends and weekly basketball teammates, Todd and Mike. I really thought my mom's friends should be able to carry her casket, but it was explained to me that pallbearers were traditionally men, and I would be smart not to stray from that because caskets are apparently heavy. So, I made my mom's best friends honorary pallbearers, which I hope made them all feel special, too.

Of course, Phillip was going to be a pallbearer. But, when we were planning the funeral, they told me the pallbearers all sat together, which meant that I was going to be sitting in the front row all by myself.

Well, I mean, John and Sara were going to be there, too, but I wasn't expecting any love or support from them.

That's when I begged Phillip to take on an even more important role.

WHEN WE WERE lying in the hammock, looking at the stars the other night because I couldn't sleep, I told him that he'd been my rock through all this and asked if he would continue that most important job and please sit with me at the funeral and hold my hand, so I wouldn't fall apart.

Actually, I kinda begged.

Something about having Phillip squeeze my hand helps me keep it all together.

The pallbearers each grab a handle as the caskets are slid out of each hearse.

They start the long walk up the grassy hill. Before today, many of the pallbearers didn't even know one another, but right now, they look like brothers, all in dark suits and all with the same solemn look on their faces.

I forget what they told me the caskets weigh, but I remember them saying they were easily supported by six men. What they didn't say was that the emotions they seem to be carrying are much, much heavier than the caskets ever could be.

They all look like they are carrying the weight of the world.

I'm sure that, if I could see my own face, it would probably look the same.

THE PASTOR HAS started speaking, and I'm trying to pay attention.

I listen to the words and prayers he says, trying to find some comfort in them. But, well, honestly, I'm not really feeling it.

Because, internally, I am freaking out.

The pastor asks us to stand for the final prayer, and I know it's getting close.

As planned, the caskets will get lowered into the ground. John, Sara, and I are then supposed to sprinkle dirt over the top of each. Then, we are supposed to slide one of the long-stemmed roses out of the floral arrangement and drop it into the hole as well.

I wanted to fight that part, too.

I was fine with the dirt because I got the whole ashes-to-ashes and dust-to-dust thing, but the rose bothered me for some reason.

Throwing the rose in, I thought, would feel like it did when you threw a coin in a fountain and made a wish.

I mean, how sweet would it be if I could wish them both alive, throw the rose in, and have them pop out of their caskets, alive and laughing?

I don't know. The rose felt wrong to me, but I agreed to do it.

I don't know where my willpower has gone.

I did ask why people throw the rose, and I didn't really get a clear response. No one seemed to know why. They just knew people did it.

FINALLY, JOHN GOT frustrated with me and told me it was out of respect. *"And you want to be respectful, don't you?"*

But then I looked it up on the internet and found out the reason you stay to watch them get lowered into the ground is not out of respect. This process is supposed to be harsh and difficult for the mourners. It is supposed to force them to face the reality and finality of the death. That, in turn, is supposed to help the grieving process.

We'll see about that.

All I know is, when you start doing Google searches on caskets, pallbearer etiquette, and funeral traditions, something in your life has gone very wrong.

As you can imagine, lots of people have been giving me advice about how to handle this. About how to handle death.

And how to feel.

How to deal.

And I can't remember all of it, but one piece of advice has evidently stuck in my mind.

I was sitting on the couch at the Diamonds' house. We had all eaten dinner there and were getting ready to go to the visitation. Danny wrapped his arm around me, pulled me in tight, kissed the top of my head, and told me everything was going to be all right. Mrs. Diamond, who had lost her own mother when she was only twenty-two, was sitting next to us, giving me advice, but I was having a hard time concentrating because Danny looked so sexy that I wanted to just jump on top of him and start kissing him.

Sadly, I haven't kissed Danny since the night of the party. With him going back and forth to Lincoln for classes and off-season football workouts and me constantly being surrounded by people who are worried about me, I haven't even had a second alone with him.

But, when I look over and see two butterflies flitting around a nearby gravestone, well, I remember what she said. She told me to let myself see a little of God every day. And, for some reason, watching those butterflies offers me more comfort than any of the prayers.

But then, while I am standing there, getting my courage up, I watch in horror as John and Sara walk up to the caskets, do what we are supposed to do, and then walk away.

Uh, hello?

Wait a minute!

They were supposed to wait for me.

We were supposed to do that together!

And then *boom!*

All my comfort and courage are gone.

I seriously feel like I could faint or puke or die myself.

I am frozen in my spot, and I want to scream out loud.

I can't do this!

I can't handle this!

This is so not the way my life's supposed to be!

I am not supposed to be burying my parents.

The pastor clears his throat to get my attention. He is waiting impatiently for me to come up and do what I am supposed to do.

He might as well have yelled at me, *Move it, missy.* It would have felt the same.

I know you're probably not supposed to cuss at a religious ceremony, but I can't help but scream aloud in my head.

My hands start to shake, and I think my head might explode.

I am also seriously contemplating jumping into the dirt myself, so they can just bury me with them.

I feel a hand on my back, so I turn my head, and there's Phillip.

"I can't do this," I whisper.

"We'll do it together, okay?" The same words I used on his dad at the hospital.

Phillip holds my hand and guides me up to the caskets.

Well, maybe pulls me up to the caskets is a more accurate description.

I am seriously shaking.

He gives me a handful of dirt, and together, we sprinkle some dirt on the caskets.

And I don't know where it comes from, maybe the butterflies, but I decide to stick to my guns.

I pick out two roses, put them up to my nose, and breathe in their wonderful smell, but I don't drop them into the dirt.

I can't.

I'm keeping them.

Taking them home with me.

I'm sorry, but I don't need any more harsh reality.

I've had enough of that.

So, I repeat the mantra I've been telling myself all week—through the planning, the visitation, and the funeral.

Don't lose it. Stay in control. Put on your game face and get through this.

You can do it.

And, now, with Phillip holding my hand, I think maybe I can.

We turn away from the caskets, toward everyone. I take a deep breath, clamp my back teeth down tight, hold my head up high, and walk away from my parents for the very last time.

And I didn't know it, but apparently, after I was supposed to dropped the rose, the people who attended the graveside service were to come up and do the same thing.

Say good-bye and drop a flower.

But they don't.

They follow my lead.

When people start coming up to me to give me their condolences, most all of them are also carrying two flowers.

And I realize I've started a trend.

I look around the cemetery grounds and see that nearly everyone mingling about is taking two flowers home with them. For their own, in remembrance.

And that comforts me more than the butterflies.

God, I am going to miss them.

Even Mr. Mac, who comes marching up to me because he is furious with John, is clutching two roses in his hand. He tells me, "JJ, you're riding home with us and not in the limo with that jerk John. I can't believe he just left you up there by yourself. *Some* family."

He shakes his head at John and herds me to their car.

THE FUNERAL LUNCHEON is at the Mackenzies' house. It has a much lighter tone because, for everyone here, the worst is over.

But I know that, when everyone leaves, my worst will just be beginning.

Because, regardless of how sweet Phillip is, now, I'm alone.

Truly alone.

Last night, Uncle John offered to take me back to Seattle with him. I don't know John that well. I see him once a year, if I'm lucky. I'm not sure why, but he and Dad weren't that close. All I've ever heard him say is something about John being selfish and only worrying about himself.

I never used to understand, but I get it now.

Phillip's mom was not happy about his offer.

Here's how the conversation went:

"JJ is staying here with us. That's what her parents wanted," Mrs. Mac said firmly.

"JJ, you're eighteen. You can do anything you want. I think it would be good for you to get away from all of this for a while. Get a fresh start," Uncle John said, scowling at Mrs. Mac.

Mrs. Mac grunted. "Well, I disagree. JJ, you need to stay with us. We love you." Then, she cried.

How come everybody around here can cry so freely? People must think I'm a horrible daughter because I haven't cried since the hospital.

I just haven't been able to.

I'm either very callous or still in shock.

Or something might be seriously wrong with me.

Or maybe not. I think it's just that I have become an empty shell.

My body is still here, true, but I'm pretty sure most of me died when they did.

AND AN EMPTY shell should not be fought over, so I pretended to be grown up and replied diplomatically with something like, "I need to stay here and finish high school, Uncle John. Maybe I could visit you this summer."

IT'S GETTING LATE, and by now, most of the funeral-goers have left. I'm sitting out on Phillip's front porch, alone for a few minutes. It feels good to just sit here, in the rocking chair, not having to be polite, not having to say, *I'm fine,* when I'm about to fall to pieces.

Danny strides through the front door.

I know that I'm in mourning, but mourning or not, the boy is overwhelmingly hot.

"Hey," he says.

"Hey," I say back. "Please don't ask me how I'm doing, or I might have to hurt you. I'm tired of lying and saying fine."

"Do you know that, in the last two days, Phillip and I counted you being asked *how are you* over one hundred sixty-seven times? Then, we lost track."

"It feels like it."

He grins at me. "So, *how are you?*"

I roll my eyes at him. "Fine."

Phillip told me that Danny and Jake hadn't done all that much fighting. Evidently, Jake ended up with just a black eye, and that was courtesy of the pipeline. I'm so glad Danny wasn't hurt. Phillip was right about that. I never should've let him risk getting hurt for something so stupid. I mean, if I have learned nothing else throughout this whole ordeal, it's that life can change in the blink of an eye.

Danny takes my hand, pulls me up, and wraps me into a hug. I practically melt against him. Then, he pushes my chin up with his hand and kisses me deeply.

My mind is immediately rendered incapable of thought. It's the first time in days that my brain has finally shut up and stopped thinking.

Now, this is my kind of therapy.

Kissing Danny feels so good. I was really hoping we'd kiss again. I mean, on the phone, it sounded like he wanted to, but this is the first time we have.

"You've been amazing through this, Jay. I'm proud of you. Quite honestly, I'm not sure how you're doing it." He smiles and winks at me. "But then, I always knew you weren't a prissy wimp."

"Not always," I say, reminding him of what he thought of me when he first moved here.

"Well, nearly. Anyway, it didn't take you long to convince me."

I smile in spite of myself, and feel a chink in the armor I've been wearing.

"Thanks, Danny."

"Seriously, how are you holding up?"

"Honestly, I don't know how I'm doing, Danny. But, when you just kissed me, I felt alive for the first time in days."

He grins big at me and pulls me into another long kiss. Then, he says, "We haven't really had the chance to talk about the party. I wasn't sure what you were thinking. What are you thinking?"

"Um, well, I mean, you told me on the phone that it wasn't just about making Jake jealous, but I guess I have felt a little awkward around you. I didn't know what you were thinking."

He wraps his arms around my waist and pulls me into a tight hug. A much different hug than the hugs I have been getting all day. Those have been the kind of hugs where just your shoulders and arms touch. This is the kind of hug where your hips touch and your stomachs touch, and you feel like your bodies are molded together.

"This doesn't feel awkward to me," he says and kisses me some more.

"Danny, why did you kiss me at the party?"

He is still holding me close, and I am praying no one comes outside and interrupts us.

"I don't know. I felt like it."

"That's it? You felt like it?"

"No. I mean, that didn't come out right." He sighs. "Jay, truth be told, I've maybe been wanting to kiss you for a while. And I got there, and you looked hot, and then you had that cute meltdown, so I kissed you. And it was amazing, and I was having fun and thinking this could be something, and I should have just taken you home with me, but instead, I thought we'd mess with Jake first, and then the fight happened, and then Phillip whisked you out of there, and then your parents—and I haven't gotten to talk to you about it. And, every time I see you, Phillip is holding your hand, and everyone thinks you two are together, and I just keep thinking it should have been me there. Holding your hand, making you feel better. Why did you ask Phillip to sit with you and not me?"

"I didn't do it to upset you. I wanted everyone to sit with me, but they told me pallbearers had to sit together." I eye him. "Were you jealous?"

He nods a little and rolls his eyes up to the ceiling, looking uncomfortable.

"Danny, I asked Phillip because I know exactly where I stand with him. He's been part of my life forever. He's like a brother to me. And he has this way of calming me down, of relaxing me." I look at him with a naughty grin. "You don't exactly relax me."

As in he excites me—a lot.

"Mmhmm, I know what you mean," he mutters before he starts kissing me again.

We kiss for a while.

And, while we are kissing, I keep hearing Danny's voice in my head saying, *"This could be something."*

That is good, right?

That means that it was more than him feeling sorry for me.

Didn't he also say he had been wanting to kiss me for a while?

Could we really turn our friendship into something more?

Something amazing?

As in something that might last longer than his typical three weeks?

The long, amazing kiss eventually comes to an end. Danny still has me wedged up against his body, and I'm loving that.

He says, "Now that we have that straight, I have a favor to ask you."

Sure, anything, I think to myself.

"So, I have this problem. I'm dying—"

"Bad choice of words, Danny," I interrupt him and surprisingly let out a little chuckle.

"Oh, sorry. But I *am* dying to go to prom, and no one will ask me."

Yeah, right.

"And, well, I figured, since you probably don't have a date either …"

"I'm not going, Danny."

"Come on, ask me."

"I'm not gonna ask you. Going to prom is, like, the last thing I want to do."

Phillip walks out on the porch. I expect him to freak out over me being in Danny's arms, but he looks relaxed.

"So, did you ask her?" Phillip asks Danny.

"Nah, she asked me." Danny gives me a smirk.

"I did not!"

"Mac, my man, I'm still trying to convince Jay she needs to take me to prom."

"Danny, it's sweet of you to want to go."

"Jay, I'm not just being sweet. I really want to go with you, and I think you should go. It's your senior prom. It's a big deal."

"In light of recent events"—I sigh—"it just doesn't seem like that big of a deal anymore."

"I think your parents would have wanted you to go," Phillip says, ganging up on me.

I start to say no again, but I wonder if maybe they would have wanted me to go. Mom shopped with me forever to find the perfect dress. She probably would have been disappointed if I didn't wear it.

"Don't you think it's a little callous to go to something as frivolous as prom so soon after my parents' deaths? It seems, you know, disrespectful."

I can't. I shouldn't.

"Everyone thinks you need to start getting your life back," Danny states.

"I don't have a life anymore."

"Bullshit. You have lots of friends who care about you, and I'm pretty sure, if you could ask your parents, they would tell you the same," Danny says, getting slightly worked up over this.

I look at Phillip. "You agree with this?"

I thought it would *never work.*

He nods.

"Actually, *both* Phillip's mom and my mom agree. Your parents wouldn't have wanted you to miss it," Danny informs me.

Phillip butts in, "And we're not gonna let you go with Jake."

Okay, now, I get it. Evidently, Danny is the lesser of two evils.

"I mean, come on," Danny says, "you've got everything for it, right? Everything's already planned?"

"Yeah." I waver.

"Great!" Danny says. He gives me a chaste but still delicious kiss. "I've got to head back to Lincoln. Call me. Let me know how you're doing or just to talk. Anything, okay? Is there anything I can do, anything you need?"

"No, I think your mom and Mrs. Mac have thought of everything."

And they have.

I owe those ladies big. But I know they did everything not just for me, but also for my parents. They loved them, too, and it was their way of showing it.

"Saturday. Six o'clock. Don't keep me waiting," Danny says with a grin as he leaves.

PHILLIP GOES BACK in the house to get a drink. I look across the street at my house. The lights are on, and I'm drawn to it like a moth. I halfway feel like I can just run over there, bang open the door, and hear my dad yell at me. So, I run home, bang the door ... and hear nothing but silence.

I look at the kitchen and can practically see my memories.

Me sitting up on the counter, helping Mom mix a special chocolate cake for Daddy's birthday. I can't wait to lick the leftover batter off the beaters.

Mom and I making sugar cookies at Christmas while Dad sets up the tree.

I turn my back on the memories and run up the stairs to Mom and Dad's room. There, more memories come rushing into my mind.

Bringing Mom breakfast in bed on Mother's Day. I tried to surprise her, but I had to tell her to stay in bed. I made her peanut butter toast and milk—although I think I ate most of it.

Me running and diving under their covers at bedtime because I wanted to sleep with them and not in my own bed. Daddy would pretend he couldn't find me. He'd bounce on the bed, grab under the covers, and tickle me silly. Then, I would jump on his back and get a piggyback ride to my room.

Me lying in bed, sick with the chicken pox, getting to watch TV all day while eating crackers and drinking 7UP.

Mom and me playing cards and watching movies.

Mom and Dad telling me to come snuggle up between them when I had a bad dream.

I feel like I'm in a bad dream right now. I close my eyes.

I think I've become a memory junkie.

Even though the memories make me want to cry, they also make me feel warm inside, and I like the feeling. I go sit on the floor of Dad's closet, watching him in my mind.

He was getting dressed in his tuxedo. He looked so handsome that night.

Mom running over to get the back of her dress zipped up. I loved the way he kissed her on her neck and told her she looked beautiful and how she blushed. They seemed so in love.

I grab one of Dad's big flannel shirts and put it on over my blouse. I've worked so hard throughout this whole ordeal to maintain control, to keep it together, to represent my family proudly, to be tough and hold it all in.

I can't do it any longer.

I run back into their room, throw myself across their big bed, and lose it.

I mean, I totally, completely lose it.

I break down and cry and sob and wail like I've never done before. I have never, ever hurt so much. I didn't even think it was possible to feel this much pain.

You'd think, eventually, my tears would run out, but they don't. I just cry and cry and cry.

And cry.

I'M STARTLED BY a noise. I flip around and see Phillip staring down at me.

He sits on the bed and shakes his head at me as he gathers me into his arms. "I wondered when you'd finally lose it."

I can't seem to choke out a response, so I just bury my head into his shirt and sob.

What am I going to do?

APRIL 26TH

ON FRIDAY MORNING, I wake up, feeling groggy. Finally took that sleeping pill.

I glance over at the clock and see it's nearly ten, so I go downstairs to the kitchen.

On the breakfast bar, I find a note from Phillip's mom.

It says, *Had some errands to run. Back by two.*

Four hours by myself.

What am I going to do?

Normally, I would relish having four hours of peace and quiet, or I would call and have Jake come over. But now? Well, Jake—although he did come to the visitation and was very polite—isn't an option, and I don't think I can relish the quiet.

I'll just feel lonely and start thinking about my parents.

Plus, I'm feeling edgy. Like I need to *do* something.

Like I can't sit here alone.

Maybe I'll go to school today. At least there's always a lot going on there. I've been feeling edgy since the funeral. It's weird; when I'm at home—*home* being Phillip's house for the time being—I feel like I need to go and do something. Then, when I get there, all I want to do is come home. I feel like I should be out, looking for something.

Unfortunately, I'm afraid what I'm looking for can't be found. I can't have my parents back.

If I hurry and get ready, I can be at school in time for AP English. It's my favorite class. We've been reading the play *Our Town*. The main character, Elizabeth, dies, but she doesn't want to leave the living. One of the most important lines in the book, the one I quoted at the funeral is, *Do any human beings ever realize life while they live it—every, every minute?* The quote is Elizabeth's way of saying we should put more emphasis on the value of daily life. After dying, she finds out that life's not just about special events or occasions. It's about seeing the wonder in daily life and not wasting opportunities.

You know, like stopping to smell the roses.

I wonder if I have been too busy living life.

Did I take my parents for granted? Probably a bit. But, as we tried to show at the funeral, my parents' philosophy on life had been to work hard and play hard. And we always did. Even when we were working on a project, like staining the fence—which is a really horrible job—we had fun. My parents always did a lot with me. Dad helped coach my soccer and basketball teams and always had time to play with me in the backyard. Mom stayed at home, and there was often warm cookies and milk waiting for me when I got home from school. I loved coming in the door after school and trying to guess what she had baked based on the smell. She always talked to me about my day and gave me great big hugs for no reason. And they both told me they loved me—a lot. I think they lived life fully.

I make a promise to myself to try to always do the same.

And I guess that means getting back to living.

So, I go to school. I manage to sign in at the office without attracting any attention and am early to class, the first one here. I slide into my desk and open my notebook. None of my good friends are in this class. They think it's stupid to work so hard your senior year, but I'm getting college credits for the class, so I think it's worth it. Besides, the teacher is great, and even though the class work is difficult, she has a way of making it fun. I also love it because we read novels, and I love to read.

Because most of our class time is spent discussing the novels and because there are only eleven kids in the class, Mrs. Reece will often let us have class outside or in the commons area. A few weeks ago, we talked her into going to the bowling alley for lunch and checking out a *slice of life* in Westown. It was really fun.

The first bell rings, and the students slowly file in.

A man walks in and stands up front.

Great. Substitute teacher. That means today's class will be completely worthless. I so should have stayed home. What was I thinking?

After the tardy bell rings, the substitute, whose dress and actions are very stiff and formal, introduces himself as Mr. Gustafson.

He starts in a droning voice, "Today, we are going to talk about the essays you will be writing regarding the play *Our Town* by Thornton Wilder. Mrs. Reece says that you have discussed how this play shows a slice of life. For your essays, you will write about a slice of your own life. Mrs. Reece wants us to use this class time for brainstorming, which will help you decide what to write about in your essays. I'm going to ask each of you to share a slice of your life with the class. We'll cover sports, home life, friends, family, weekends, dates, et cetera. Let's start with something easy. Who would like to volunteer to tell the class about their weekend? Share a slice of your life? Anyone? Anyone?" he asks hopefully, looking around.

Of course, no one raises their hand because they know, however they tell it, their weekend will sound boring and lame. And no one wants to be that. But my insides are squirming for entirely different reasons. Obviously, my weekend was anything but boring, but I'm darn sure I don't want to share it.

So, as he walks around the desk and grabs the seating chart, I'm pleading in my mind, *Please don't pick me. Please don't pick me.*

"Well, if there are no volunteers," he says, "I will pick someone. Let's see ... how about Miss Reynolds? Stand up, please, and tell us about your weekend."

You've got to be kidding me.

I don't stand up, but I say, "Um, I really didn't have a *typical* slice-of-life weekend. Could you choose someone else?"

"Nonsense. Please stand up," the sub says.

The class becomes dead silent.

I still don't stand up, but I say, "Um, how about I tell you about a different slice-of-life weekend?"

"No, I would like to hear about *this* weekend."

He's being difficult, so I say with a pissy voice, "I thought the whole point of this exercise was to show the typical and mundane goings on in life. I'm telling you, my weekend wasn't typical. It was anything but."

I mean, it's not that most of the class hasn't heard about my weekend. I'm sure there's some great gossip going around, and if it wasn't all about me, I would probably want to hear it, but there is just so much involved, and I'm not sure I can get through it without a breakdown.

"Miss Reynolds, you are being insubordinate and just plain stubborn. Even if your weekend wasn't typical for you, I'm sure others have had similar experiences. We are all friends here."

Like he'd know.

I seriously doubt there are any others who have had a weekend like mine. In fact, I'm sure of it. I'm also getting mad at this man.

Very mad.

"Stand up now and tell us about—"

Suddenly, Ricky Leeman stands up behind me and says, "I'll do it. Let's see ... on Friday, we had a track meet—"

"Mr., um ..." the substitute says, consulting the chart again,

"Leeman, sit down."

But Ricky doesn't sit down. He leans up from behind me and says quietly, "JJ, you don't have to do this. Just leave. Come on, I'll go with you."

Ricky surprises me. He's being so kind but risking getting into serious trouble. The sub is furious with him.

The class is murmuring a bit; they know he's about to blow.

I mean, this man is supposed to have an education of some kind; you would think he'd have a clue that something is up.

But no, he's too puffed up on power to take a look around him.

"That will be enough. You've all had plenty of chances to volunteer, and I'm in charge of this class. I will not tolerate such a blatant lack of respect. Mr. Leeman, if you do not sit down and stop the interruptions, you will go to the principal's office."

"Can I go to the principal's office?" Part of me wants to run away, but now, because my insides are boiling mad, part of me kind of wants to tell this idiot all about my *slice*.

Just for shock value.

"Absolutely not. You will stay here. Please begin. Now, Miss Reynolds."

"Fine."

The grief inside me is suddenly gone, and all that's left is anger.

"Where should I begin? Well, like I said, this weekend was so not typical." I roll my eyes. "Thank God. I don't think I could live through another one."

"Teen angst," the sub interrupts. "I like it so far."

Smart-ass. Well, we'll see if you say that when I'm done.

"Well, let's see ... I went to a party where I got dumped by my boyfriend. Needless to say, *that* upset me, and I was going to leave, but then a guy friend of mine showed up, told me not to leave, and, well, kissed me." I can't help but smile a little smile about that. It was the one bright spot of the whole damn weekend. "Okay, so ex-boyfriend saw me kissing said friend and tried to humiliate me in front of everyone. When that didn't work, he started a fight. Another friend dragged me out of the party and back to town. We stopped to get gas, and his cell phone rang. It was his dad who, believe it or not, had been looking for *me*. It seemed that my parents had been in a car accident." I swallow hard. "We sped through town and got pulled over by the police. Luckily, it was a nice Westown officer, who drove us to the Med Center."

I glare straight into the evil substitute's eyes and smile an obviously fake smile as I continue, "When we got there, I found out that my mom had died. Oh, and my dad died a few hours later."

I can feel the tears wanting to come, but I push them back.

Just stay mad, I tell myself.

"That is not very funny, Miss Rey—" he starts to say.

I look at him and smirk. *Told you!*

I interrupt the idiot and say, "You're very right. It is so not funny. But it's the truth." And, with a curtsy to the class, I say, "And that is a slice of my life."

I GRAB MY books and storm out the door.

I can hear the teacher ask the class if it was true.

I hear him mutter a curse word before the door closes.

I STOMP IN an angry daze out to the empty commons area, sit down, and let out a big sigh.

Ricky Leeman is on my tail. He sits down, puts his arm around my shoulders, and says, "God, what an asshole. You okay?"

"Yeah, I'll be fine. So, do ya think the sub liked my slice of life?"

"Well, he dropped the F-bomb in front of the class, so I'm

guessing not. I don't think we have to worry about him coming back."

"I appreciate what you tried to do in there, and, well, no offense, but how come you're being so nice to me?"

"Um, well, I feel really bad about what happened to your parents, and, well, I'm kinda in charge of you this period."

"In charge of me?"

I don't like the sound of that.

"Well, yeah, I mean, I am the only guy from the team in AP English, but I would've volunteered anyway."

"What in the world are you talking about?"

"Uh, um … I take it, you didn't hear about the meeting?" He grimaces.

"Evidently not. Enlighten me, please."

"Um, well, maybe I wasn't exactly supposed to tell you that," he says, suddenly nervous. "You know what? I think I'm gonna go get Phillip. That's what I'll do. You stay here."

He gets up but sees Phillip heading down the hall toward us.

Phillip rushes over. "Shelby came and got me out of study hall. What are you doing here? Are you okay? Do you want me to take you home?"

Being mad is much easier than feeling sad, so I say in a perturbed voice, "No, Phillip, what I want is to know what's going on around here."

Ricky touches my arm. "Hey, I'm gonna go. Sorry about your parents, JJ."

Chicken.

"Uh, thanks, Ricky. I really appreciate what you did." I turn to Phillip. "Phillip? I asked you a question."

"Oh, it's not a big deal or a big secret or anything. We were just kind of keeping it quiet because Danny knew you'd react like this because you're stubborn and hardheaded."

"Danny?" I shake my head, trying to understand. "What does

Danny have to do with this?"

"Well, he sort of met with the football team."

"The *football team*? Why?"

"Well, not everyone—mostly just the seniors and a few juniors, and, well, Coach and Principal Mazer, too."

This is mind-boggling.

"Why?"

"Well, Danny knew he'd have to go back to Lincoln right after the funeral. He felt like he was abandoning you and worried about how you'd do when you came back to school. He just wanted to make sure you'd be okay and that someone was around if you needed anything."

Most of me wants to throw a fit and scream, *I can take care of myself,* but the other part of me feels grateful and loved. Because, awww, that was really, really sweet of Danny. That's how my life has been this week. An emotional roller coaster. Two stupid sides to every feeling I have. I think I liked myself better when I just thought my side was always right.

"You know what, Phillip? I do think I wanna get out of here. I'll see you at home later. I shouldn't have come here today. And I've been lucky; I haven't run into Jake."

"Uh, yeah. Danny might have had something to do with that, too."

I arch an eyebrow at him.

"Fine." He rolls his eyes at me. "He invited Jake to the meeting and told him, in no uncertain terms, to leave you alone. That's the other thing the guys are supposed to make sure of."

I sigh. *I need to get out of here.*

"I'm gonna sign out."

I almost get out of school without being seen by the faculty, but when I round the corner, I run smack dab into Principal Mazer.

Crap. I suppose I'm going to get in trouble for my insubordination to a substitute teacher.

But Mazer surprises me by giving me a hug. "JJ, I'm surprised to see you here. We didn't expect you until Monday. Everything going all right so far?"

"Um, uh, there was a little *incident* in AP English. I want to apologize in advance, and when you hear about it, um, just know he pushed me."

Principal Mazer looks confused by my statement, but I don't elaborate.

I just say, "If it's all right, I think I am going to leave now."

"Sure, honey, feel free to come and go as you please for a while, and if there is *anything* you need, let us know. All of us around here care about you."

"Thanks. That means a lot to me." My standard funeral response, but I can't seem to come up with anything better.

Phillip tells Mazer that he's leaving with me.

"Follow me," Phillip bosses me as I get in my car.

I FOLLOW PHILLIP'S car in a daze. Pretty soon, we are at Westown Park. We park and get out of our cars. Phillip grabs my hand and leads me to the swings.

I sit down on a swing and am pleasantly surprised when Phillip starts pushing me.

I close my eyes and enjoy swinging. I love how swinging makes my stomach feel all fluttery. I remember once, when I was little, I told my mom that I'd been swinging so high that I thought my feet had touched heaven.

I swing higher and point my toes upward.

I hope they still can.

Phillip is swinging beside me now, and I realize this is exactly what I needed. I don't know how he does it, but Phillip always seems to know *exactly* what I need.

Come to think of it, enjoying a ride on a swing is *very much* like stopping to smell the roses.

I hope my parents are proud.

you look really hot.

APRIL 27TH

BECAUSE I GREW up around Danny and Phillip, I discovered the truth about the male language very early in life. What I learned is there are three basic responses that most guys will use when shouldered with the major task of having to answer the question, *How do I look?* by the fairer sex.

Although I have never confirmed it, I am convinced that boys are taken aside in school—probably in fifth grade when the girls watch the film about getting their periods—and are taught the following three responses:

You look like crap.
Translation: You look bad. Just go back to bed and start over tomorrow. I really shouldn't be seen with you like this.

You look fine.
Translation: You look good enough to be seen with.

You look hot.
Translation: I want you.

They also must teach them there is only one acceptable variation to these responses and to use it sparingly. The variation is simple. They just throw a "really" into the sentence.

The following are examples I have witnessed:

JJ, you REALLY look like crap.
Translation: You must be very hungover or sick or having an extremely bad hair day. I really don't want to be seen with you.

REALLY, JJ, your hair looks fine.
Translation: Your hair looks the same to me as it always does even though you spent an hour fixing it, so stop messing with it, and let's go because you look good enough to be seen with.

And …

(Insert cheerleader's name here) *looks REALLY hot.*
Translation: I REALLY want her.

So, when Danny shows up at my door and says five simple words—you might think, with my insider knowledge, I would have expected them—I'm truly surprised!

"Jay, you look really *hot!*" he exclaims, looking me over from perfectly done hair to perfectly painted toes.

Now, normally, I would be excited by this compliment because it's not something I typically hear.

But what I'm thinking is, *My God, I have spent, like …*

Four hundred dollars and months of shopping, which is still not a pastime I find enjoyable, on a fabulous halter dress in a beautiful, stretchy coral fabric with coral and silver beading. This dress actually makes me look like I have hips.

Sixty dollars on a special bra, so I'd show no straps.

One hundred twenty dollars on a pair of strappy, high-heeled silver sandals with rhinestones.

And, yay, even in five-inch heels, Danny's still taller than me, unlike my previous date, Mr. Unfaithful.

Seventy-eight dollars on a silver clutch, which is only big enough to hold some lip gloss and a cell phone.
Sixty dollars on a silver gossamer wrap in case it gets chilly.

Okay, so I have absolutely no idea what gossamer is either. But Lisa said that's what it's called, and she should know. All I know is that it's a very sheer fabric that has no chance in hell of ever keeping me warm.

Two hundred forty dollars, plus tips, to get my nails, toes, hair, and makeup done.

And all Danny can say is, "*Jay, you look really hot*"?
You'd think that maybe he could have come up with something a little more original, like, *Wow, that color looks amazing on you.* Or, *Your face looks flawless*—which, incredibly, it does—or, *I love how your toenails are the exact shade of coral as your dress, and my, aren't they painted perfectly?*
But, no, I am hot.
Still, coming from Danny, it does make me feel good. For two reasons really.
One, it is the second time—in a week, no less—that he has used my name and "hot" in the same sentence. Except for something like, *Jay, it's really smokin' hot out here; why don't you go grab us some drinks?*
And, two, I think it's the only time I've ever heard him say those words in reference to someone other than a supermodel, cheerleader, or playmate.
The boy really does need to broaden his horizons a bit.
Did I mention how handsome Danny looks? He's wearing a black tuxedo with a cool silver-and-black-patterned vest and tie. I love the way his shoulders look so broad when he wears a suit.

Danny grabs my hand and kisses me. "So, are ya ready?"

Um, I have been, like, *getting ready* for the last six hours.

Hello?

Can't you tell?

But I don't say that because I know he's wondering if I'm ready to face everyone at the dance.

"Okay with all of this?" he asks again.

"Yeah, and by the way, I'm glad you're forcing me to go." I grin.

"Ah," he says, holding his hand to his chest like I have just stabbed him. He flashes an infectious smile and winks at me. "We've gotta run over to my house. Mom wants to take some pics."

Just as we finish pictures, Phillip is at the door.

Phillip—my articulate, sensitive, linguistic, emotional man— what do you have to say about how I look tonight?

"Wow," he says, "you look ..."

Okay, here we go. He's searching his brain for the perfect word. Come on, I know you can do it! How about the perfect shoes?

"Hot. Really hot."

Oh, for God's sake, what is it with boys?

PHILLIP LEAVES TO go pick up his date, and Danny and I head to dinner.

A lot of our friends are going out to dinner in big groups, but because Jake wanted to be alone with me, Danny and I are going out alone. Of course, Jake, Mr. I Can't Plan Ahead, wouldn't make any plans for prom, so I arranged everything.

And guess what. Rumor has it that he was cheating on me, like, the *whole time*! And, apparently—get this—he's *honest* with the other girls. He *tells them* he has a girlfriend. And they're okay with that!

So, he's been doing it with pretty much everyone *but* me. So, here's my question. Why was he bugging me about it so much? I mean, supposedly he had a whole legion of skanks to choose from. Why not let me—his sweet little girlfriend, whom he professed to *love more than life itself*—stay safely ensconced in my imaginary virginal bubble world? Why keep pressuring me?

Why?

God.

I really should've skipped trying to make him jealous and gone for option one: walked straight up to him and punched him in the face. Hard! And I'm not talking a little slap across the face like what girls in movies who get mad and slap their lying, conniving, cheating boyfriend and yell, *You bastard!* give.

I'm talking, *BOOM.*

As in he's leaving with a bleeding nose.

That's what I'm talking about.

Sorry, I digress. I might still be slightly bitter.

However, it does make me feel better, knowing that I'm going to prom with one of the nicest and hottest guys around. Danny will be, hands down, the best-looking guy at the dance. Although, I have to admit, Phillip will be a close second. I swear, he just keeps getting cuter.

It's probably for the best that Danny and I are going to dinner alone.

I'm not sure I could handle all the questions.

Like, *How are you doing? Are you and Danny serious? Is it true that Jake has been dating that girl for, like, four months?*

I'd have to answer, *Um, I don't know,* and, *Uh, I don't know,* and, *Well, I don't know.*

I'm a fountain of non-information.

DANNY AND I have a great time at dinner.

He teases me.

I feign irritation and tease him back.

He kisses me, and I melt.

He feeds me dessert.

I've decided I'm very glad we're alone. I've been able to forget about my life for a while, and it's been perfect. I mean, when you're around Danny, it's really hard to think about anything but him. He's got this easy, seductive way about him. Like he's a warm, inviting swimming pool, and you can't wait to jump him.

In. I meant, jump *in*. You know, jump *in* the pool. The, uh, warm pool.

Crap. I've become one of those girls. Those girls who hang on his every word and think he can do no wrong and wouldn't care if he did.

Those are the girls I make fun of.

I do a great impersonation of a swooning, mute, hair-flipping, eyelash-batting, stomach-holding-in, and boob-sticking-out girl. Phillip thinks I'm hilarious when I do this.

And, somehow, I've become one. Well, not completely. Co-herent words are still coming from my mouth, and I'm not flipping my hair.

Okay, so I can't flip it since it's up in pins.

My point is, I haven't been totally hypnotized by his charm.

I'm holding my own.

My dad used to call Danny a *chick magnet*. Eighties slang for what would probably now be referred to as a player. Anyway, I've thought it's a good way to describe him. But I've always been like his opposing magnet. We tend to butt heads.

Tonight, I think I've become like, you know, a wimpy paper clip or something. I can't help but be drawn to him, and I'm totally incapable of resisting his pull.

WE FINISH DINNER too early to go to the dance, so we retreat to the limo, and Danny tells the driver to just cruise around. We really aren't paying attention to where he is going because we are sitting in the back, drinking champagne, and seriously making out.

You know, I never wanted to be cliché and do it on prom night, but let's just say that the issue is currently under advisement.

What it really means is that I haven't made up my mind yet. I have determined though that, *if* I wanted to, Danny could be the perfect guy for it. I mean, I love the guy. And why not do it with a friend? Someone you trust and are comfortable with.

Not some stupid, slut-loving boyfriend.

And didn't Phillip tell me I should think about doing it with a friend?

So, why wouldn't I?

Well, 'cause maybe you're afraid of ruining your relationship?

See? I really can't decide.

WE GO TO prom, and I have fun dancing with Danny. I especially enjoy how he holds me when we slow dance and how he keeps playing with the loose strands of hair that have fallen out of the back of my updo.

Memo to self: updos and passionate limo kissing are not a good mix. Especially when your date is enthralled with your hair and can't seem to leave it alone!

And I am totally not complaining about that even though it is rather hypnotic.

I manage to get in a slow dance with Phillip while his date is throwing up in the restroom.

Too much champagne for her. Silly girl.

Speaking of champagne, Danny and I drank a whole bottle, but I feel fine. Although, come to think of it, Danny had most of it, and occasionally, he's been taking nips from a flask of vodka hidden in his tux pocket.

Hey, where's mine?

Why aren't we sharing?
Come on! Get me drunk and take advantage of me.
Please!
He seems sober enough but sorta nervous. That's so not like him. *Why in the world would he be nervous with me?*
I might be a bit confused but certainly not nervous. It's just Danny, for goodness' sake.

BILLY PRESCOTT AND Katie are named prom king and queen, and at a little after eleven, Danny and I leave, get dropped off at the hotel, and go to our room. A bunch of us went together and booked the whole floor of the hotel. We got the whole hotel thing past our parents by swearing we were all just going to crash in the rooms, and that way, they wouldn't have to worry about anyone drinking and driving. At least, that was my explanation.

God, I miss them so much.

Anyway, there's kind of an awkward moment when we first get to the room. I know we're just supposed to crash here, but you can't exactly ignore the big bed in the center of the room and what it implies. I mean, there might as well be a neon arrow pointing down to it with the words, *HAVE SEX HERE*, flashing at us.

Okay, now, I *am* nervous. I seriously need a drink. Thank goodness Danny brought more champagne to the room.

As he opens the bottle, I sit on the bed. He seems much calmer now, back to his confident self, as he pours champagne into little plastic cups.

"Cheers," he says. In one long drink, he drains his cup and then sets it on the nightstand.

I barely get to take a sip before Danny grabs my cup. I'm about to protest, but he looks at me, runs a finger across my cheek, and sweetly kisses me.

The kisses don't stay sweet though.

We're really kissing.

And, when he starts kissing down my neck, my sensible mind goes completely fuzzy. Especially now that he's running his hands through my hair and tossing the bobby pins he finds onto the floor.

Ahh!

It's like he's *undressing* my hair!

Pretty soon, his kisses get, well, urgent, and his hands, well, they have been everywhere *but* in my hair.

Oh, I like this.

But ... decision time.

I start to panic, so I stop the kissing, grab my cup, and take another drink.

A *big* one.

Relax, JJ.

Danny pours himself another cupful of champagne, which is good. It gives me a second to think without his kisses clouding my judgment. But I only get a second because he slams his champagne, sets his cup down, and starts unbuttoning his shirt. And I just sit there and watch.

Yes, I have seen Danny shirtless many times, but I am still dazzled.

Because he is not just whipping off his shirt 'cause he's hot; he is taking his shirt off *for me.*

He's getting naked *for me.*

And, well, when his shirt hits the floor, I'm pretty sure my judgment walks right out the door.

We kiss and do stuff some more.

It all feels so good, and evidently, my body decides to take control.

I hear a husky voice, which I'm shocked to realize is my *own*, suggest, "Why don't I change into something more comfortable?"

Where did that come from?

You always hear that in movies, and just once, I'd like to see somebody come out in baggy old sweats and a T-shirt. But, no, it is always beautiful lingerie.

Which I happen to have in my bag.

What? I was just trying to be, you know, prepared for every possibility.

Plus, if I am going to do this, then I'm going to do it right. Not be half-undressed in a twisted-up prom gown.

So, I go in the bathroom, brush out my hair, run my toothbrush across my teeth, and slide into the silky lingerie.

I hurry.

I swear, I am in there for only, like, three minutes.

And I've been imagining what the scene will look like when I go back out to Danny. I picture him lying on his side, diagonally across the bed, his arm propping up his head. His muscles ripple, and his eyes have that come-hither look.

You know, the sexy way all those soap guys pose while waiting for their lovers to slip into something more comfortable.

I take a deep breath and open the bathroom door.

I can't believe I'm finally going to do this.

And with Danny!

Gorgeous, wonderful, incredible, hot, sexy, addictive Danny.

I saunter out, making my grand entrance, expecting to see Danny looking at me in awe, his eyes full of lust, passion, and love.

I gaze out and see Danny lying across the bed, his back toward me, wearing nothing but a pair of sexy, silky boxers. His tuxedo is piled on the floor at the end of the bed, and there's a condom lying on the nightstand.

I want to scream and clap out loud because I'm pretty sure that means Danny wants me.

Me!

In the bathroom, I worried a little because he hadn't said, you know, *Let's do this.* I just sorta assumed he wanted to based on the things he was doing to me, and I was thinking how embarrassing it would be if I came out here, all lingeried up, and he, like, turned me down.

So, I feel happy!

God, even that boy's back is sexy!

I coo, "Danny."

I'm practically vibrating with excitement as I wait for him to roll over to see how amazing I look, to pull me into bed with him, and to finish what we started.

But he doesn't move.

Okay, so maybe he has a different version of this in his mind. I'm willing to play along!

So, I hop over his tuxedo and saunter sexily around the bed.

Here I come!

No way.

You have got to be kidding me.

I don't see eyes full of lust, passion, and love. Instead, I see that Danny has thrown up in the trash can and is passed out on the bed.

Seriously?

But I'm not about to give up yet.

"Danny!" I say as I plop down on the bed and give his shoulder a push.

But he doesn't wake up. His mouth falls open, and he starts to snore loudly.

Great.

Just freaking great!

I stomp back into the bathroom, take off the damn lingerie, and angrily shove it back into my bag.

That's it!

Victoria's Secret and I are through!

I'm definitely going to start wearing ratty, old-lady underwear because, every time I wear the good stuff, I can't even pay to get it seen!

While contemplating my lack of sexual prowess and my slim hopes of ever having any, I put on my swimsuit, a pair of khaki cargos, and a little black tank top.

The post-prom party is in Billy Prescott's suite. His room's got a hot tub. We're supposed to show up any time after midnight.

And I figure, if I can't manage to lose my virginity, then I am damn well going to get drunk.

While I did bring clothes to wear to the party, honestly, I was hoping that I would be too wrapped up in Danny—and I mean that both literally and figuratively—to attend.

Now, I have nothing better to do, and it's only eleven forty-five.

I don't want to be the first one there!

And dateless, no less.

I hope Jake's not there. That's all I need.

No. He's probably off somewhere, doing it.

AS I WALK out of my room, I see Phillip walking down the hall, alone.

I whistle and say, "Hey, you looking for a good time?"

"Actually, I am," he replies very seriously.

I don't think his night has gone exactly as planned either.

"Where's your date?" I ask as he walks toward me.

"Well, after she spent most of the night puking in the restroom, I decided to call the game. I took her home. And where's your hot date?"

"Threw up in the trash can and passed out. Wanna go to the party with me?" I bump his side with my hip.

"I have a better idea. Did you bring a swimsuit?"

"Got it on. What do you have in mind?"

"Well, I didn't tell anyone, but my room has a hot tub, too."

I look at him in surprise.

He shrugs. "I didn't want anyone to know because they'd all want to party in it, and it was just supposed to be, you know, for Carrie and me."

"Well, aren't you the sneaky little bad boy?"

I mean, he didn't even tell me!

I feel bad for him.

He really did have big plans for tonight.

"I guess I'm just gonna have to be your date for the rest of the evening, Phillip, seeing as you are my, uh, close friend."

I smile at the sweetie and grab his hand, and we start walking back to his room.

PHILLIP AND I sit in the hot tub and talk. It's wonderfully warm and relaxing in here. I lean back and put my head on his broad shoulder.

I must have gotten a little too relaxed because I think I might have dozed off.

Whoops.

"Hey, Princess," Phillip says, gently waking me, "let's get out of here and get some sleep."

"Fine, but I'm sleeping in your room. Mine smells like puke."

"All right, but it'll cost you."

"How much?" I squint my eyes, ready to deal.

"Didn't I hear you telling Katie about some sexy lingerie?" He gives me a sexy grin.

"Phillip, I have so given up on lingerie. It's like a bad boyfriend; all it ever does is let me down. You get me in sweats and one of your old T-shirts. You got a problem with that?" I point my finger into his chest.

"No, ma'am." He smiles and gives me a salute.

We lie in bed, and I put my head on Phillip's shoulder.

What is it about Phillip's shoulder that makes me instantly relax

and fall asleep?
I'm so lucky I have Phillip.

AT ABOUT FOUR a.m., Phillip and I are awakened by a *knock, knock* on our door.

It's Danny, looking for me.

Phillip points to me as I sit up in bed. I smile and wave at Danny with sleepy eyes.

My sleepy eyes are awake enough to see Danny looks great. He's thrown on shorts over the boxers, but he still has no shirt on. *Damn.*

Why, oh why, did he have to pass out?

"You know, Phillip," Danny says with a nasty grin, "a lot of girls say that it's their lifelong fantasy to be with two guys at the same time."

He turns to me and winks. "What do you say, Jay? This could be your lucky night."

I've known the boy long enough to know when he's messing with me.

"I'm game," I say and quickly sit up in bed. "As a matter of fact, it sounds really hot. Why don't *you two*"—I wave my finger back and forth between them—"start by making out while I watch?"

Danny and Phillip look at each other in disgust, and I smile to myself.

"Ah ... never mind, Jay," Danny says, stifling a yawn. "How 'bout we just crash? I'm sleeping here, too. Um, our room kinda smells. Good thing you had big plans for tonight, Phillip," Danny says, suggestively elbowing Phillip and eyeing the bed, "and got the king-size bed. Where is your date anyway?"

"Shut up, Danny," Phillip replies as he turns off the light.

AFTER THAT, THOSE boys tell anyone who will listen about how I "slept" with both of them on prom night.

When I wake up the next morning, instead of being snuggled up to my date, I'm lying on Phillip's shoulder and wrapped up in his arms.

Really, the same place I've slept for the last week.

I move over next to Danny before he wakes up.

Even *he* doesn't know about that.

We need to talk.

APRIL 28TH

I'M LYING ON the hammock in my backyard, drinking a Diet Coke and flipping through a *People* magazine. I'm trying not to think about my parents. Trying to pretend it's just a lazy spring day. Unfortunately, I keep expecting my dad to come out on the patio, bottle of beer in hand, with Mom following him, wanting to hear all about prom.

Life can really suck sometimes.

But I don't know what I can do about it.

I've been feeling really helpless. And a bit lost.

Like I was a little boat that was tied up on shore with all the other boats, but somehow, my rope came undone, and now, I'm out in the middle of the ocean, no land in sight, just floating. Completely untethered to the life I'd always known.

I told Mr. Diamond that, and he pretty much called bullshit.

Told me my parents did so many things for me so that if, God forbid, something like this happened, then I would be able to keep my house, go to college, and stay with my friends, my support system. He told me they were extremely well insured, and I would be okay financially. He told me that he was here for me and that all my friends were here for me but that I had to officially grow up now. I have to handle the things my parents always did, like making sure the house gets cleaned and the lawn gets mowed and the bills get paid. He said, as much as the Macs were trying to protect me, I was eighteen, and I needed to behave like it. He said my parents raised me to be strong, confident, and independent and that I should do my best to make them proud of me.

And, at the time, I was thinking, *Okay, maybe I'm not the little boat; maybe I am more like that game we used to play when we were little.* Jenga, I think it was called. You stack up all these blocks, and you try to pull them out of the stack, one by one. When the stack gets too weak or you pull out the wrong one and it gets out of balance, the whole stack comes tumbling down, and you lose.

I sorta feel like that is what has been happening to me. Some cosmic force has been pulling out random blocks, trying to get me to cave, to fall down.

But here's the thing I have decided.

My parents wouldn't have wanted me to fall down. So, I'll be damned if I do.

But that doesn't mean I'm still not incredibly, earth-shatteringly sad.

THE GATE RATTLES as Danny walks into the backyard.

"Hey," he says, his hair blowing back in the breeze. He naughtily dives on the hammock, nearly flipping me over and making me scream in the process.

I lean over to kiss him, but he backs off.

What the hell?

"Jay, we need to talk."

Great. One date, and he's breaking up with me. Not that we were going out, but you know what I mean. Someone, somewhere, is laughing hilariously, shoving around the blocks of my life.

"Look, I'm sorry about last night. I shouldn't have drunk so much. I really wanted you to enjoy prom, and I hope you still had fun."

"I did have fun, and I really appreciate your begging me to take you," I joke, but then I say seriously, "I don't think I would have gone otherwise, and I'm glad I didn't miss it. I have been sitting here, thinking a lot about my parents, and I think you were right. They would have wanted me to go." I laugh, "Although Dad always said you were trouble. I wonder what he thinks about me going with you."

"Your dad loved me."

"Yeah, I know."

I want to say, *I love you, too*, but I'm afraid he'll take it wrong and think I'm like *in* love with him. And, yes, he is super hot and sweet, and I wished for a long time that I could be with him, but I'm not sure if I have much to give right now. And, if I'm going to have a relationship with Danny, trust me, *giving* is what I want to be doing.

I can tell by the look on his face that there's still something wrong.

What now?

"Something else is bothering you," I say. "Spill."

"Jeez, Jay. You just have me so, uh, overwhelmed," he says as he runs his hand through that gorgeous hair.

"What do you mean?"

"I just didn't expect to feel this way about you."

I'm trying not to ask too many questions. I mean, something is clearly bothering the boy, but I'm sorry, I've got to ask this one.

"What way is that?"

"Too much. Way too much. And way too fast. Which brings me to my problem."

Uh, scratch that. I have plenty to give. I don't see a problem with this.

No problem at all!

But I think I know what the problem is. He feels bad because he passed out last night. I still haven't decided which one of us should be more embarrassed about that. Him for passing out or me for getting passed out on. But I'll tell him that we can soon. Heck, we could go in my house right now and do it if we wanted to.

"Danny, it's okay. You ..."

"Jay, this is hard for me. Just let me finish, okay?"

I nod with my mouth shut.

"Okay, so here it is. You know how I worked hard during spring practice and performed really well in the spring game and the guy who was the starter last year did really badly?"

"Yeah."

What's this got to do with us?

"Well, I haven't said anything, but I'm pretty sure I'll be first on the depth chart this fall."

It takes a second for that to sink into my brain.

"You mean, like, *the starting quarterback at Nebraska*? Danny, that's awesome! It's huge! It's what you've always wanted, what you're meant to do."

"You think so?"

"Uh, yeah. Greatness is in you. Don't you know that?"

Danny oozes confidence.

"Maybe, but, well, here," he says shyly.

And he is *never* shy.

He fishes a folded-up piece of paper out of his wallet and hands it to me. "Look at this."

I unfold the paper and see it's a picture of me—in my flag bikini top, no less—jumping up to catch a pass with Phillip just behind me.

It's a really great picture of us.

Weird. I don't usually photograph so well.

"Where'd you get this?" I study the picture closely. "Hey! This is from that day in Lincoln when you pissed me off enough to run down the field in my bikini top in front of half the football team.

Right?"

"Yeah." Danny laughs, remembering. "You told me if I missed you that time, you were coming back for my pants."

"I was serious. Where'd you get this picture?"

"Oh, it seems one of the school paper's photographers found you to be a *very* interesting subject," he says with one eyebrow raised at me, like he finds this very humorous. "He took a ton of pictures of you and gave me a few of the best. This is my favorite. Oh, and I was supposed to tell you that he wants to go out with you." He shakes his head at me and teases, "You've grown up to be quite the little heartbreaker."

I roll my eyes at him.

"Look at the picture, Jay."

I do.

"It's a fun picture. I love the look on Phillip's face."

"I mean, look at you. You look gorgeous. Perfect." He lies back on the hammock, pulling me down with him, and says, "You are also looking at my goal. *Perfection.* Wanna know what I see in the picture?"

I nod.

"I see a perfect pass, a perfect catch, and two perfect friends. When I first went to college, I wasn't throwing well. Probably trying too hard instead of just doing it. But I couldn't figure out what was wrong, why things weren't easy anymore. I talked to the team shrink, and he asked me if I'd ever used positive visualization. Of course I had. In B-ball, Coach K was always telling us to picture ourselves making every shot before we went to sleep at night. In fact, our team motto was, *If you can dream it, you can do it.* And, in high school, whenever I was flustered or out of sync, I would just picture myself throwing to you or Phillip in the yard. It relaxed me. I realized I hadn't been doing that or having much fun playing lately. He told me to focus on a time when I had thrown a perfect pass and to picture that in my mind when I started to get out of sync."

He pauses and points to the picture in my hand.

"*This* is the picture I visualize. When I think of us playing catch, I relax and have fun with the game. I'm on target."

I raise one eyebrow at that boy. "All the millions of times we've played catch, and I have to be in a bikini in this visual? Isn't there something kind of sick and twisted in that?"

"Maybe." He laughs. "I'll never forget the first time Phillip and I saw you in that bikini. You had been lying out, and you were covered in oil. I think I had to bribe you to come play catch with us. But, man, when you walked through that gate in that bikini, glistening in the sun, Phillip and I both just stood there in shock. I think it was the first time I *really* realized you were a girl—a *hot* girl." He smirks at me. "Well, and maybe a bit during your kissing lessons."

"Lesson," I remind him. Only one.

"I know I was jealous when you asked if we thought Jake would like the bikini. If I remember right, Phillip practically told you it looked awful. He didn't want you wearing it for Jake either." He pauses and grins. "I kinda have a thing for that bikini and, well, the American flag in general now, as a matter of fact."

He catches me by surprise and pulls me into a wonderful, sweet, and way-too-short kiss. He shakes his head at me, like he just can't decide what to do, and says, "Last night, I, um … God, this is way harder than I thought it would be."

I am about to make a naughty joke about what might be harder than it should be and suggest we maybe check it out in my bedroom. But, as I am about to open my mouth, he pulls me into his arms and kisses me again, and for once in my life, I don't say a thing.

I am so proud of my restraint.

Maybe I will reward myself with some chocolate later.

We lie there, wrapped in each other's arms, for a while before he speaks again, "I think you're awesome, Jay."

I hear a big *but* coming …

"But I don't think we should date."

I knew it.

"Why?"

He sighs. "Part of me thinks we'd be great together, but I know we'd fight. You *know* how we fight."

"Yeah, I know how we fight." I laugh. "Danny, I don't understand. You love a challenge. Why do you always date girls who worship you? Where's the challenge in that?"

"There isn't one; that's the point. I have enough challenge in other areas of my life. With the girls I date, I just want simple, smooth, and easy." His hand goes out in front of him, making a calm water gesture.

"Easy to get along with or just plain easy?"

"Both is good." He laughs. "But, either way, not words I would use to describe you. Oh, I don't know." He shakes his head. "A lot could happen. But I do know this. If we dated, it would ruin the picture. Probably ruin my game."

Football. There's the real reason!

Doesn't that just suck?

Then, he adds sweetly, "But, most importantly, I'm afraid it would ruin us. I love you, Jay. I love our friendship"—he shakes his head and closes his eyes—"and I really, really, don't want to do anything to screw it up."

Figures.

The one nice guy I try to date is too nice.

Thank God he passed out last night, and we didn't have sex.

"Danny," I say diplomatically, "in the last eight days, I've gotten dumped by my boyfriend for a slut, buried both my parents, *and*"—I smile at him—"just recently learned one of my best friends has a sick perversion for me. I really don't think I could handle a relationship right now."

I'm totally lying. I could so handle a relationship with Danny. Well, I think I could. Really, I don't know. But I let him off the hook because I don't want to ruin our friendship either. I seriously don't know what I would do without him and Phillip.

Especially now.

He kisses me on the cheek and gets off the hammock, being careful not to tip me. "You know you love me."

"Yeah, I know. And you're damn lucky I do."

'Cause he is.

"Here's a thought," he adds seriously.

"Yeah?"

"You'd be good with Phillip."

And, with that, he leaves.

What the hell is that supposed to mean?

It's all Greek to me!

COLLEGE FRESHMAN

THE REST OF my senior year flew by. I slowly adjusted to not having my parents around, but it was hard. Sadly, what they say is true. Life *does* go on all around you, whether you want it to or not.

I'm trying to take it day by day. Some are better than others because I have this constant empty ache inside me, but I keep going. Phillip's and Danny's families have been awesome though, and I haven't ever felt completely alone, like I was so afraid I would.

Before I knew it, I was a high school graduate, and then I was down in Lincoln and *officially* a college girl!

Choosing my college was pretty much a no-brainer. It has a beautiful campus, outstanding academics, and, well, the football team. I mean, I couldn't imagine myself at another school, going to a game and cheering for their team. Especially now that Danny is the starting quarterback. Phillip is here, too, so that made the choice even easier.

I'm living in a dorm with a pretty cool roommate. At least, she seems that way so far. We went through rush together, and even though we pledged different sororities, we are getting along well. We have similar backgrounds, having both grown up in small towns. We like boys and clothes, and—*thank God*—she hates mornings almost as much as I do.

Oh, and news flash: I've started going by my real name, Jadyn, instead of JJ. I think it sounds much more mature.

Phillip blew out his knee while playing basketball this past summer and isn't going to walk on as originally planned. He's okay with not playing football anymore. He went through rush and ended up pledging the same fraternity that our dads were in. Our dads always had great, wild stories about their time here, and I'm sure we only heard the watered-down, tame versions of most of them.

Tonight, I'm going to experience a wild fraternity party firsthand.

At least, I hope it's wild!

Phillip's frat is hosting a party tonight, and apparently, most fraternity parties have some kind of theme. Some of the themed parties they're hosting this year are Secs and Execs (everyone dresses up as business people), Get Lei-d (obviously a Hawaiian party), Heaven and Hell (where's Mary Beth Parker when you need her?), Around the World (which has something to do with drinking a different shot in every room of the frat house), and, of course, the timeless favorite, Toga.

This one is called Frosh Frenzy.

ALL WEEK, PHILLIP has been *forced* to interview freshman girls. I say *forced* because the pledges have to, but it's not like Phillip minds. Interviewing is a great excuse to start talking to a cute girl. He has this little notebook, and he has to fill out a sheet on each girl he interviews. They're kind of like the slam books that we had in ninth grade. The pledge asks each girl a variety of questions. Innocent things like name, hometown, high school activities. And what they call *vital statistics*, like cup size, height, weight, hair color, phone number. And then personal information, like what you like in a guy, your idea of a great first date, how far you will let a guy go on the first date—things like that. This part varies and tends to border on the risqué.

The interview process is supposedly a time-honored tradition. I remember Dad telling me that he met Mom when he interviewed her, but I always thought maybe he'd worked on the school newspaper or something.

Now, I understand, and, quite frankly, I *really* wish I knew what she'd said because my dad was a total catch.

Phillip told me the interviewing process helps the pledges get to know their fellow classmates. I very sarcastically pointed out to him that, if they really were trying to get to know their fellow classmates, they would interview a few *fellows*. But he just laughed at me.

Of course, all freshman girls, me included, are intrigued by the fraternity system and eager to answer the questions.

Especially from adorable Phillip.

And he is adorable. I mean, Phillip has always been a very cute boy, but he seems to be getting even better-looking, the older he gets. He's leapfrogged the line separating cute from hot and has landed deeply into hot territory. I swear, if he keeps this up, I might just have to keep him for myself.

Anyway, I've had to endure sitting by him in the Student Center while he does his interviews. I hope I never gush like that over a boy. And some of the answers these girls give? I'm sort of embarrassed by them, and I don't embarrass easily! Sometimes, an active will see a girl he thinks is hot and specifically tell the pledge to interview her. The active writes his initials at the bottom of the page, which lets everyone know that he saw her first.

And they say girls play games!

The party is a meet-and-greet party. Only interviewed freshman girls are invited. It's held under the guise that they are trying to make their pledges more social, but I really think it's so the older guys can hit on the young, naive freshman girls.

AS WE WALK down to the frat house, Phillip is telling me a whole bunch of rules he thinks I need to follow for the evening.

I swear, you'd think he was my father!

I'm half-listening and half-thinking about the cute guy I met in Chemistry class today. Somehow, I need to get him to be my lab partner. That would make Chemistry 101 *a lot* more interesting!

I hear Phillip saying, "Don't go upstairs with anyone. Don't go on any so-called *tours* of the frat house. Don't drink anything that you didn't pour yourself. Never leave your drink out of sight. Check in with me every half hour."

I'm bored by Phillip's rules, and my mind wanders back to Chemistry Boy. I wonder if we get to pick our lab partners or if they're assigned. Maybe by alphabetical order. *Shoot*, I think when I realize I still don't even know the cutie's name.

"Are you listening to me?" I hear Phillip ask.

"Uh, of course." *Now, what did he just say?* "You told me about checking in with you. I'm listening," I lie. "Please, go on."

So, he does.

On and on and on.

"No getting drunk. No table dancing."

Like I'd ever do that!

"Don't get into a game of Quarters."

Well, maybe that ...

"Be wary of the upperclassmen."

No way!

"Stick by me ..."

Boring!

I thought, at college, you were supposed to abandon all rules. At least the ones you had to follow in high school. My mind wanders back to Chemistry Boy again.

I can't help it!

Maybe we can choose our chemistry partners based on *chemis-*

try. Get it? Of course, I'm not sure if we have chemistry because all I did was smile at the boy, but he did smile back. It's a good start. Now, I just need to find out his name and then—

"Ah!" I scream.

Phillip has stopped walking and stepped directly in front of me. I awaken from my daydream to collide and then nearly fall over the top of him.

"What are you doing?" I yell at him as he grabs my shoulders to stop me from falling and taking us both down.

God, he is strong. When I finally marry my prince, I hope he has strong arms like Phillip's. Oh, and great abs, too. I wonder if many princes come to school here. Now, that would be something useful to put in the student directory and be a good recruiting tool, I would think.

Phillip is talking loudly to me.

"What are you thinking about, and why are you spacing out? This is important stuff." He sighs big at me.

"I appreciate that, Phillip."

He's still holding my shoulders and totally in my face. I'm half-tempted to kiss him just to throw him off guard, but he'd probably get mad at me, and I don't need that right now, so I don't.

"But, you know, I'm not exactly the best rule-follower. Why don't you just pick the most important one, and I'll do my best?" I say with a wave of my hand.

He lets go of me, gives me that eye, and says, "Fine. You're leaving with me." He pauses for effect. "Have you got that?"

I nod my head.

"Repeat it," he bosses.

Being the smart-ass that I am, I raise my right hand up, like I'm taking an oath in a courtroom, and say, "I swear to tell the truth, the whole truth, and nothing but the truth. I will leave the party with you."

"Continue."

I sigh. The boy knows me too well. "Even if there is a cute boy I would rather leave with." Thinking of a possible loophole, I say, "Hey, Phillip, what happens if I don't want to leave the frat house? Depending on how it goes, maybe I'll want to *stay*."

Phillip is getting irritated with me; I can tell. I kind of like seeing him a little irritated, and, fortunately, I seem to be able to irritate him easily. He is usually so reserved.

Shoot!

I just realized that I am also very dumb because I *really* should have kept that loophole to myself. I might need it later.

That's the problem with my mouth. Sometimes, it talks before my brain can think.

"God, do I need to get a lawyer just to get you to agree to something? Here it is. JJ, you are leaving with me when I am ready to leave. Got it?"

"Yeah, I got it."

Jeez, he's my knight in shining armor whether I want him to be or not.

PHILLIP AND I walk into the frat house and are greeted by two pledges. They are sitting at a table in front of the door and matching girls with their pledge interviews. One of the boys takes a Polaroid picture—I didn't even know those cameras still existed!—of each girl and writes her name on it with a permanent marker. I get my picture taken, and we head into the party. We grab a beer and stand off to the edge of the party room, chatting and taking it all in.

I keep catching a guy staring at me from across the room. Of course, being the terrible flirt that I am, I forget all of Phillip's rules and bat my eyes at the guy. I watch as another guy hands him one of those permanent markers.

What? Is he signing autographs later?

Across the way, I recognize two girls from my History class. A group of us have been whiling away the boring lectures by writing notes to each other about what kind of nasty things we'd like to do to the hot grad assistant. Due to my lack of experience in this area, I can easily say that I'm learning *way* more than expected in History class.

I glance back at the cute guy. Maybe it's time I get some of that experience.

"Don't look now, Phillip," I order, "but who's the guy over there in the green polo shirt?"

"Why do you care?" Phillip suspiciously asks me in his snotty little boy voice. I swear, sometimes, I think he's twelve.

"I don't know." I shrug. "He keeps looking over here. I'm just wondering who he is."

Phillip does as he was told and waits a minute.

At least the boy can follow directions.

"Do you think he's cute?" he asks before he looks.

"No, not really," I lie.

Phillip rolls his eyes at me, glances over toward the green polo, and, says, "Ah." He nods his head up and down and frowns. "That is Matt Fuller. He's a senior and our Pledge Advisor." He looks at me with squinty eyes and tries to read my mind. "He specifically asked me to interview you."

"Really?" I smile way too big because, now, he totally knows I was lying about the cute part. "When? I'm pretty sure I'd remember him." I quizzically look at Phillip.

"I don't remember exactly, but I think he saw me giving you a piggyback ride across campus." Phillip shakes his head at me. "I really don't know *why* I let you get away with the stuff that you do."

"Because I'm irresistible, Phillip." I smile and shrug my shoulders. "You can't help yourself. Besides, you didn't go across campus. You only went about fifty feet before you pretended to have a heart attack from supporting my weight and collapsed on top of me in the grass."

"Oh, yeah. I remember. I think you've gained some weight."

I slug him in the shoulder.

He ignores it and continues, "Come to think of it, I think that's when Matt saw you." He gives me a big grin. Like he just now remembered it. "You probably didn't notice him because you were too busy rolling around on the grass with me."

"I'm pretty sure I was trying to get you off me."

"Well, it must've not looked that way to Matt because he asked if you were my girlfriend."

"Oh God. What story did you make up this time, Phillip?"

He smirks. "Oh, I just told him that, even though you're madly in love with me, *I* don't want to be tied down, so we're just friends. Of course, what I should've said was, *Please, just take her. She's more trouble than she's worth.*"

I give Phillip the finger.

Then, I turn my back on him and stare over at Matt. I'm intrigued and excited by the fact that he wanted me interviewed. That means, he's at least somewhat interested. Matt is really hot. I'm guessing him to be about six-two, and he's built like an athlete. In good shape but not too big. He has thick, wavy brown hair, and I'm not sure if it's his authoritative stance or the crispness of his polo, but he looks like he grew up with a rich daddy. I can picture him driving a little BMW to the club for golf and tennis. He could probably be in an ad for the company that made his shirt. He would look right at home, standing in the backyard of a big summer house on the ocean, playing croquet and holding a martini.

Not my typical rough-around-the-edges guy. But, hey, I'm at college to experience new things, right?

Phillip, who has apparently been successful at reading my mind again, says, "I really don't think you want any part of that,

Princess. He has a playboy reputation, and the rumors of his sexual prowess are practically of legendary proportions. All the pledges are in awe of him—or at least of the stories about him."

"Everyone? Even you, Phillip?"

Phillip just shakes his head at me.

I frustrate that boy, I think.

I smile though because I like what I'm hearing about this Matt. Hopefully, it's not all hype. Maybe there is a bad boy under all that polish!

Phillip frowns. "Unfortunately, I think he has you in his sights. So, be careful, or better yet, just try to avoid him."

"Phillip, I am not going to avoid him." I glance up to see Matt looking my way again. This time, I catch his eye. I hold his stare for a second, smiling, until he looks away, seemingly embarrassed.

Some playboy.

He is cute though.

What the hell?

He probably made up his own reputation just to impress the pledges.

I think *what the hell* has become my personal mantra. I might have T-shirts made up soon.

"Okay. Then, at least stop giving him those eyes. You're making me sick."

I ignore Phillip's eye comment. "I'm sure the rumors are exaggerated, and besides, he's probably not that interested in me anyway. I bet he asked for lots of freshmen to be interviewed. Plus, he doesn't look like my type …"

"What? He's not an idiot?" Phillip interrupts, taking a cheap shot at my taste in guys.

I frown at him, put my hand on my hip, and flash a little attitude. "You know what? Just for fun, I'll bet you five bucks that I can make him come over here now and talk to me."

We'll test out some of my newly discovered powers of male-persuasion.

"Really? And just how are you gonna do that?"

Like I can't.

Let's see ... I have already smiled and given him the eye. Apparently, Katie and Lisa have taught me well. Next step, make him worry that my availability is questionable.

I face Phillip and lean my body close to his. Really, I pretty much just press the whole front of my body up against the front of his. I should probably mention that Phillip has an excellent body to be pressing up against.

"Well, Phillip," I whisper slowly into his ear, "I'm just going to whisper in your ear."

"And rub up the front of me, too?" he whispers back. "I think I'm liking this plan."

"No, I'm not going to do that. I'm simply getting very close to you, telling you, I don't know, something very private."

"Are you talking dirty to me?" He laughs and wraps his arms around me. That mind-reading thing comes in handy sometimes because he totally understands my ruse.

"Yes, I am! So, grin like you like what I'm saying."

"Why don't you kiss my neck while you're there, just for good measure?"

"Good idea. You don't mind my using you, do you, Phillip?" I ask as I put my lips onto his neck up by his ear.

I hear his breath catch.

I don't think he minds.

His neck smells really good. I love the way Phillip smells. All manly and musky and quite yummy. For a minute, I almost forget about that Matt guy.

"Not at all," Phillip purrs. "Although, if it doesn't work really fast, I might be forced to drag you back to the dorm and have my way with you."

I admit, I think it would be fun to let Phillip have his way with me, but we're just friends, and we don't want to ruin that, so yeah.

I laugh and start to say, "Phil—" when he interrupts me.

"You're good," Phillip says, surprised. "Here he comes."

"Liar." I don't even turn around because I'm sure he's teasing me. It couldn't have worked that fast.

But it must have because, instead of answering me, Phillip switches me into one arm, leans around me, and shakes Matt's hand. I turn around and am face-to-face with a Greek god.

He is even better-looking up close. Because, up close, I can see he has these amazing emerald-green eyes and a sexy five o'clock shadow.

"Matt Fuller," Phillip says, introducing me, "this is my friend Jadyn Reynolds."

Matt holds out his hand to shake mine.

I put my hand in his. "It's nice to meet you."

Matt shakes my hand and then lowers his hand to his side without letting mine go.

In fact, I don't think he has any intention of letting it go.

What is this boy up to?

He gazes at me with those smoldering green eyes and quickly gets rid of Phillip. "Hey, Phillip, why don't you go get some beers? The lady's empty." He clinks my empty bottle with his full one.

"Uh, sure," Phillip says. He knows he is being dismissed, so when he gets behind Matt's back, he gives me a look that says, *Remember the rules.*

I look at Matt and then down at my hand. "So, do I get my hand back?"

"I don't think so," he says, oozing sex appeal out of every pore.

Now, I would have thought this kind of bold move would turn me off a guy, but it seems to be having the opposite effect. I'm kind of impressed. It's goofy, but this is something I could see myself doing to make an impression.

"So, I'll just have to stay here all night, huh?" I say innocently but knowing the sentence has major innuendo.

"Well, at least until you get to know me properly," he replies and blinks lazily.

"Oh, great," I say, rolling my eyes in mock boredom. "Next, you'll ask me my major."

"No, I already know. Engineering."

Mr. Smarty Pants, huh?

"Well, either you read my interview or you are psychic."

"Guilty."

Not only is he still holding my hand, but also, he is totally invading my personal space. It's making me slightly crazy. I'm having a very hard time trying not to look at his mouth. I fear, if I keep looking at it, I might do something rash, like just start kissing it. I am also fighting a growing impulse to rub my cheek up against all that stubble on his face.

"I did read your interview. In fact, you might be interested to know that this fraternity house was built in 1957. It has some very interesting architectural details."

Oh, really? Let me guess ... you want to give me a tour?

"You know, I've heard about this house practically my whole life. Phillip's dad and my dad belonged to this fraternity and lived here."

"Well, in that case, I bet you would love a tour." His gaze is predatory.

Now, I do remember hearing that rule. *No tours.* I'm looking around for Phillip, hoping he'll return with my beer. I'd really like to have something to keep my mouth occupied.

"Maybe later," I say politely, not completely refusing. "So, this interview stuff, seems to me it's just a way for you guys to get the inside scoop on the new crop. Let me guess; tomorrow night, you will sit around a fire and score the girls?"

He has an expression of surprise on his face that leads me to believe that is *exactly* what they will do.

"Who told you that?" he whispers, leaning in closer to me.

I can feel his warm breath on my neck, and I can smell him. He smells different from Phillip—more like soap, but still nice.

"You really do that?" I laugh in disbelief, yet I can totally picture it. It is so very much something boys would do. I'm on a roll now, so I take another stab in the dark. "And the scores, are they based on looks or how, um, *friendly* the girls are?"

"You're not supposed to know about this," he whispers in my ear again.

I really don't think it's a big secret. I think he's just trying to get to me.

It's working.

"I'd say we rank the girls on their ability to *make friends*," he states like a not-so-truthful politician.

"So, hypothetically, let's say I kiss you tonight, what kind of ranking would I get?" I flirt.

"One star."

I give him an insulted look, and then I try to make my face look sexy.

"What if I'm really good at it?"

"Still only one star," he responds, like, *Sorry.*

"I see. So, what if I were to, say, strip naked and dance on a table?"

He grins. "Although that is something I would very much enjoy seeing, I'm afraid it would net you no stars. It's kind of like the difference between a spectator sport and a contact sport."

Ah, I get it.

"So, are you going to kiss me?"

"No," I respond, shaking my head like it is the furthest thing from my mind.

I am so lying because it's right up there at the top. All I can think about really.

"Well, how are you going to earn any stars? You strike me as a competitive girl."

Oh, I am such a tease.

"I didn't say I wasn't going to kiss anyone."

"Ah," he says, holding his chest, "break my heart."

Yeah, I'm sure.

"Actually, I'm joking. I doubt I'll kiss anyone tonight."

"What? Surely, you don't want to be the *only* girl here without a star to her name?"

He thinks this comment is like a dare to me. That I will be dying to get a kiss, so I can be like everyone else. I somehow doubt every girl here will get kissed tonight, but obviously, he has yet to figure me out 'cause that sounds like a challenge to me.

"You know, I think that is *exactly* what I'd like to be."

"So, do you always get *exactly* what you want?"

Uh, no, not really, but I think my luck is changing.

Matt is grinning at me like I'm the new Christmas toy he really wanted but can't play with yet because he hasn't read the instructions.

"If I have anything to say about it, yeah, I guess I usually do," I answer truthfully.

I'm feeling a little full of myself tonight, and I'm having fun.

And it's true. If I want it and I can do something to make it happen, I usually will.

Jerk boys who date sluts and car accidents are things I just can't control. Mr. Diamond has been telling me that over and over.

"Only deal with what you can control, JJ."

"So, let me guess," he says, finally releasing my hand and pretending to hold an interview sheet to the side of his head like a psychic. "Ah, yes, I have it. Prom queen, cheerleader, dated the quarterback, voted Prettiest Eyes. Am I close?"

"One, you already told me you read my interview. And two, those things weren't even on there."

"So, humor me."

"Eh, fifty-fifty." I hold my hand out flat and tilt it back and forth. "No to prom queen, hell no to cheerleader, yes to the quarterback," I say with a roll of my eyes and then a pointed look. "But Jake turned out to be an asshole. And, yes," I say, batting my eyelashes, "to the eyes."

Matt leans into me, pushes my long bangs out of the way, and gazes straight into my eyes. "Yeah, total bedroom eyes."

I try not to get flustered, but this guy is kind of unnerving me. Okay, really unnerving me.

So, I go back to being a smart-ass, hoping to defuse this time bomb standing next to me.

"How about you? Have you already picked your victims for tonight?" I lower my voice and whisper huskily, "I heard you're practically a legend around here."

He shrugs and looks slightly embarrassed.

Figures. If I were a guy, he'd be entertaining me with stories about past victims, but since I'm a girl, the predator has turned into Mr. Shy and Innocent.

"So, is there a record for the number of stars given out by one guy?" I say, changing the subject. But then I think and add, "Please don't say my dad."

He chuckles. "Well, there are two records actually." He looks around, like he's about to give me top-secret information and then whispers meaningless names, numbers, and dates into my ear.

"And your personal best?"

"You ask a lot of questions." He squints at me in irritation.

I decide to make him a bit more uncomfortable. I stand closer to him and gently poke my finger on his chest. "Hey, you're the one who wanted me to get to know you."

He looks me in the eyes, trying to stall, but finally says, "It's private."

"Okay, so now, you've got me curious."

He shrugs.

"Fine. I'll just have to take a guess."

"Hmm." I lick my lips and then put my finger to my mouth and rub my bottom lip, supposedly thinking. Really, I just want him to look at my mouth. "Practically legendary status but no records." I lean into him and whisper a wild guess into his ear.

I can tell immediately that I nailed it or came pretty darn close. The instant shocked look on his face is a dead giveaway.

My, my.

"Seems like we *both* tend to get what we want."

I can't help but smirk at him. He is fun to tease.

He is embarrassed and obviously doesn't want to talk about it.

I look around and see that Phillip is kissing a girl with bouncy brown hair. Jeez, when did the boy learn to work so fast? Maybe this fraternity thing will be good for him. I mean, I'm very impressed.

I'm also half-tempted to go check in with him right now, just to make a point, but I don't.

He should have some fun.

"So, how am I going to get a kiss from you," he whines, "if you won't kiss anyone?"

"Look, I promise, pinkie swear," I say, holding up my pinkie, "I owe you a kiss."

"You know, I haven't quite figured out if I should attack you or go into business with you," he says as he grabs my pinkie with his.

I grin at that.

He laughs, and for the first time, I see a wonderful, genuine smile on his face. I like it.

"Come to my room," he says in a silky voice. "I have some really good tequila. We'll do a quick shot or two."

Sure we will, and what else will we do?

I am contemplating my next move when a really great song starts playing. "Come on, dance with me first." I pull his arm toward the dance floor.

He stands firm, pulls me back, and says, "I don't dance until I've had a minimum of two shots. Sorry, it's a rule."

"Well, rules were meant to be broken."

But he shakes his head.

So, I take a different approach and purr innocently, "You mean, you can't wrap your arms around me"—I gently run my fingers down the sides of his arms—"put your body close to mine and sway slowly"—I smile, close my eyes, and sway slightly in front of him—"until you've had two shots?"

"It's not a slow song," he says, but he is weakening; I can tell.

"Close enough," I reply and drag him out there.

We dance slowly to the fast music, and he takes full advantage of the closeness by letting his hands do a lot of roaming.

I don't mind it though. There's something about him that I really like. He's, like, challenging. This isn't your typical brainless, stupid game-playing but more like a chess match.

Your move, my move, your move.

I actually have to think about this.

I find it intriguing, and let's face it; most of the guys I've dated weren't exactly brain surgeons. This mental sparring is very stimulating.

In many ways.

AFTER A FEW songs, I excuse myself to use the restroom and run some lip gloss across my lips. When I get back out, I don't see Matt anywhere. Maybe I scared him away. I'm half-hoping that's the case.

I reach down and grab a beer from a cooler on the floor next to me. Just as I stand back up, I realize Matt has snuck up on me and is standing very close to my side.

I laugh and shake my head at his persistence. "Don't you have somewhere you need to be?"

"Yeah," he whispers in my ear and holds his mouth there.

"Where?"

"In you." His voice is low and silky.

I didn't realize two simple words could sound so damn sexy.

But then my eyes get big at that comment when I realize what he meant.

Whew, is it hot in here all of a sudden?

I think I might be speechless.

That never happens.

I know.

I know what you're thinking. I am, too.

It's a total line.

But I have to admit, it's given me goose bumps and made my stomach flutter. Plus, I love having my ear whispered into. Something so hot about that.

I recover from the blatantly suggestive comment, back up, and nod my head in appraisal. "A quick *and* a dirty mind. I like that."

He swings around to face me, very much invading my personal space again, and pins me up against the wall.

"So, am I ever gonna get this kiss you promised me?" He's practically begging.

"Jeez, you are so obsessed with a stupid kiss." I roll my eyes at him. "Can't you just relax?"

He doesn't say anything, just looks at me with smoldering eyes. Eyes that leave me no doubt what the answer to the question is.

It's no.

Unequivocally, no. He can't.

Sweet!

"Fine," I say diplomatically as I reach into his pocket to retrieve the marker.

He is looking both surprised and happy at where my hand is but then looks disappointed when I pull out the marker and hold it in front of him. I make a grand gesture of taking the lid off. I grab his hand, write *IOU A* on his palm, and then bring my mouth down to his hand.

I am being so bad; I almost shock myself.

I close my eyes and slowly press my lips into his palm.

I swear, I think I hear him groan.

Ha! Who knew practicing kissing your hand would ever pay off?

I open my eyes, look at him through lidded eyes, and hold his gaze for a few seconds. I assess the pink kiss mark on his hand and then very unceremoniously drop it. "There. You have it in writing. I owe you. Now, how about that shot?"

YES, I DO go to his room. Breaking one of Phillip's rules.

But what the hell, right?

His room is decorated like a typical guy. Crap tossed most everywhere. He walks over to a mini fridge and pulls out a chilled bottle of some supposedly expensive tequila and a lime. He grabs two shot glasses, salt, and a knife, and here we go.

In preparation for the shot, he quarters a lime, pours the shots, and hands me the salt. Just as I'm about to lick my hand, Matt grabs it and slowly runs his tongue across it, all while staring straight into my eyes.

Wow.

He is so hot.

And his intentions are so clear.

He pours some salt on my hand and quickly does his own. We clink the glasses and down our first shot.

I'm wondering, *Does he always have this stuff lying around, or was it purchased just for tonight?*

The good news is, I saw him break the seal on the tequila, so I don't have to worry about *anything getting put into my drink*.

We do another shot after he toasts to IOUs, and somehow, I persuade him to go back out to dance.

See? I escaped his room without harm. I'll have to tell Phillip that his rules are stupid.

Or not. I would probably get a lecture on how lucky I was this time.

It's getting a little late, and the music has slowed down. We dance some more, very close.

I'm feeling the tequila, and dancing close to him like this is starting to drive me nuts.

Time for that kiss, I think.

"So, are you planning on collecting that IOU tonight or some other night?"

He thinks I want him to ask me out on a date.

"Uh, some other night?"

"Wrong answer. Try again."

This time, he answers with a wide, sexy smile. "Tonight." He nods. "Definitely tonight."

"Good. We're getting out of here though. If we're not in the frat house, the kiss can't go on my record. Right?" I give him my best bedroom eyes, trying to convince him, although I think he'd agree to just about anything at this point.

He nods at me, and I drag him out the front door. We're barely out the door when he pushes me up against the wall and tries to kiss me. I quickly put my hand up to his mouth to stop him.

He looks at me with frustration. I grab the IOU and hold it up to his face.

"I owe *you*, remember? Not the other way around. Why don't you relax and let *me* kiss you?"

I pull him around the side of the house. Behind some bushes.

Tacky, I know, but, hey, they are there.

I intently gaze at him. He follows my gaze down to the front of his polo, which I unbutton. I start the IOU by spreading his shirt open and kissing the upper part of his chest. Next, I move up to his neck, all very slowly and very deliberately. Eventually, I work my way up to his mouth.

I'm fairly sure I've paid my IOU in full.

And I enjoyed it. A lot.

I leave the party later—much later—but with Phillip, as planned.

AFTER A FEW dates with Matt, whether or not I would *ever* lose my virginity was no longer an issue. It happened after three dates, and then we were pretty much inseparable. I was convinced that, just like my mom, I had met the love of my life as a freshman. Matt treated me well and had almost earned Phillip's and Danny's stamp of approval. But, when we got back from Christmas break, he informed me that he had *sort of gotten engaged* to a girl from home.

Sort of meaning, *I gave her a ring, she planned the wedding, she bought a dress, and she booked the church for June.*

I have to admit, I was crushed. I really thought he was the one. That's also when Phillip decided to tell me he always knew Matt was too slick to be trusted. I asked Phillip to please give me an honest opinion of the next guy at the beginning of the relationship, otherwise to keep his big mouth shut with the *I told you so* when it ended.

However, looking back, I'm now convinced there should be a university-wide mandate—just like the one that says that freshmen should live on campus, so they can experience the social aspects of college properly—that freshman girls should not date one guy exclusively.

Because, if you liken the boys available to date at your high school to a meal, then you'd be choosing that meal from a half-filled vending machine.

But, at college, choosing a boy to date is like choosing a meal from the biggest, most incredible all-you-can-eat buffet ever imagined.

And there will be no dieting for me!

Hmm, let's see ... I think I'll start with a couple of frat pledges, the buff wrestler in Sociology class, and the more mature but totally hot History grad assistant. Then, maybe one of those football players—that hottie who always seems to be on the treadmill next to me when I work out. Maybe I'll even have some of that cute photographer.

College is so awesome!

It's really too bad they try to ruin it with classes!

Go Team!

COLLEGE SOPHOMORE

SOPHOMORE YEAR, THERE are more big changes in my life. They are good changes though because I decided to make them. First, I sold the house I grew up in. This was a difficult decision, but it was getting hard to keep up and was really just sitting there empty all the time.

The Mackenzies and Diamonds helped me go through everything. They advised me about what I should pack up and keep and what I should sell.

For example, I kept all the pictures and videos of our family, the cedar hope chest Dad had given to Mom before they were married, Mom's wedding dress, Grandma's dining room set and china—things like that. The rest got sold at a big auction. The Diamonds offered to buy the empty lot next door. They didn't want to miss our annual Thanksgiving Day football game!

Mr. Diamond has been handling the estate and helping me with financial decisions. He really is doing his best to fill in for my dad. I don't know what I would do without him. He advises me to take some of the money from the sale of the house and buy a townhome in Lincoln. It's new and within walking distance of the university.

In a ploy to keep me safe, I'm sure, the Macs and Diamonds

suggest that Danny and Phillip live with me, which is fine by me. We get along great, and our place is so cool!

It has three bedrooms and a very open floor plan.

At first, the boys say they didn't care how it is decorated.

"Whatever you think is right," Danny said.

So, just to prove a point, Mrs. Mac and I got a swatch of this really ugly pink-and-purple floral fabric and managed to tell the boys with a straight face that we were thinking of ordering a couch in it.

All of a sudden, they cared.

With the moms' guidance, we had the walls painted a neutral golden color and the trim white. The kitchen has dark wood cabinets and stainless steel appliances. It was supposed to have a wall separating it from the living room, but since we picked it out while it was still being built, we changed it, so there is a long bar area instead. The *formal* dining room has a pool table in the middle of it, and the walls are decorated with beer signs and football memorabilia.

The living room looks like a Pottery Barn catalog with two red leather club chairs and soft, slouchy khaki ultra-suede couches. There are fun pillows and funky curtains that Mrs. Mac made, using a bold geometric-patterned fabric in khaki, red, and gold.

And God forbid I should forget to mention the huge TV, gaming system, and surround sound.

I should warn you, if you are on a budget of any kind or have any kind of time constraints, don't take boys with you to the electronics store!

Just go by yourself and buy a damn TV.

With the boys involved in this decision, what should have been a simple task took three very lengthy trips to the store and nights of online comparisons, and I'm certain we could have fed a small country on what was spent.

Anyway, I really like the way it has all turned out. We even brought the big hot tub from my house and put it on the patio. We use that thing all the time!

We don't have big parties or anything. I've seen what parties can do to a house, and I want no part of that! But there always seems to be people over. Danny believes in taking good care of his offensive line since they have to take care of him, so they're over most Sundays during football season. They play pool and watch pro football games all day. I usually end up cooking and am always making yummy treats for everybody.

Phillip's frat brothers tend to hang out at their house, but a few of them come over for FAC—Friday Afternoon Club. And, of course, with so many cute boys around, many of my sorority sisters enjoy frequent visits as well.

I am definitely sick.

COLLEGE JUNIOR

I FEEL LIKE I'm freezing to death. My body is achy, my throat and neck are really sore, and I think my glands are swollen.

I hate to admit it, but I might very well be coming down with something.

It's a Tuesday night, and instead of being at the bar with Phillip and some friends, I'm in the library, doing research for a paper that is due in two weeks. I'm actually trying to get a head start on it, which is something I never do. I tend to wait until the last minute.

I have always said that I do my best work under pressure.

And, really, I do.

The teacher for this class is adamant about us using the library and not just the internet for our research. We have to have five sources that came from the library, so I'm trying to get the five stupid sources out of the way, and then I can use the internet to do the bulk of the research.

But I'm starting to feel really bad. Actually, I haven't felt great for a couple of weeks, but I've been doing my best to ignore it.

Maybe I'm allergic to the library. I wonder if that could get me out of this stupid paper.

Probably not.

I give up on the resources and go home to an empty house. I take off my clothes, put on a pair of really warm sweatpants, and then raid Danny's room for an old practice jersey. I love those shirts because they are big and soft and silky. The shirt is huge on me but feels great. I ease myself into bed and snuggle under my covers in an attempt to get warmed up.

I DOZED OFF for a little while, and when I wake up, I feel even worse.

I am definitely sick.

I wish Mom were here. She always spoiled me when I was sick.

I really miss her and Dad.

Then, I think of the next best thing and call Phillip's cell.

He answers with a cheerful, "Hey."

There's a lot of laughing and noise in the background. It sounds like they're already having a great time.

I hate missing a great time.

"Phillip," I whine, "when are you coming home?"

"Not for a while. Are you done at the library? You gonna come join us? You know we're all at Kegger's, right?"

"Oh," I say quietly.

"What's wrong?" He reads my voice and knows since I didn't say, *I'll be right there*, something must be wrong.

"Nothing, Phillip. I just don't feel very good." I sorta start to cry. "Um, well, I feel really bad, and I'm all alone." I sniffle.

"I'll be right there." I hear him tell everyone, "I gotta go," before he shuts his phone.

I'm really lucky to have Phillip, I think as I fall back to sleep.

I FEEL A hand on my forehead and wake to find Phillip at my side.

"My God, Princess, you're burning up! Have you taken your temperature?"

I shake my head and close my eyes. My eyelids burn.

Phillip runs in the bathroom and grabs a thermometer. Then, he sits on my bed and says, "Here, open your mouth."

I do, putting the thermometer under my tongue, while Phillip uncovers me.

My whole body is shaking. I really have the chills.

The thermometer beeps, and Phillip reads it.

"Oh my gosh, it's one hundred and five. I'm taking you to the hospital!"

He scoops me up out of bed, carries me to the car, and gets me to the hospital.

AT THE HOSPITAL, I'm given some medicine to help bring the fever down.

The doctor is concerned that I might have meningitis because my neck hurts so badly.

A nurse took some blood and swabbed both my nose and my throat. I am hoping the tests show something because I really do not want a needle stuck into my spine!

I'm admitted to the hospital, and I am in a room by myself. I'm feeling a *bit* better because my fever is down to one hundred two degrees. At least it doesn't hurt to blink anymore.

My doctor, Dr. Daniels, steps in and tells me to start thinking of whom I might have had close contact with recently.

He hands Phillip a little hospital notepad.

"How close of contact?" I ask him.

"Physical contact," he says simply as he reads my chart.

Maybe I'm delirious from the fever, but it seems like he's making this difficult.

So, I ask for more clarification, "Like just being around them or *actual* physical contact?"

He stops reading my chart, looks at me like I'm blonde, and says, "Physical contact. Like kissing."

"We might need more paper for that, Doc," Phillip, the comedian in the corner, says.

"Shut up, Phillip." I glare at him.

But he continues, "Just bring in the student directory. We can use a highlighter. Might go faster."

I try to ignore Phillip and ask the doctor another question, "How far back does this *contact* have to go?"

"Oh, just a couple of weeks," the doctor says.

"Why?"

"Well, meningitis can be very contagious and dangerous. It can spread quickly at colleges, but we can treat anyone you've been in contact with if we need to. We'll have a better idea of what we're dealing with when your tests come back."

"What about Phillip?" I nod toward the comedian.

"I doubt a kiss on the forehead counts," Phillip says with his bratty voice.

"Are you two related?" the doctor asks Phillip and smiles.

"No, we're roommates," I say before Phillip has a chance to make another smart-aleck remark.

"You're right," the doctor tells him. "A kiss on the forehead should be safe. How are you feeling? Any symptoms?"

"Well, my back is pretty sore from carrying this lug in here," Phillip responds, nodding at me.

"Shut. Up. Phillip."

He is so embarrassing me.

The doctor's beeper goes off. He frowns at it and says, "Excuse me. I'll be right back."

I'm thinking about who I kissed last week when a memory comes rushing into my head. I put my hand up to my mouth and say, "Oh God, Phillip. Where's Danny? Have you seen him today? Is *he* feeling okay?"

Phillip looks at me, stunned. He's wondering why I would be worried about Danny, but then he puts two and two together and asks incredulously, "Danny? You kissed Danny?"

I smile half a smile and shake my head.

"On the lips?"

Hey, I'm sick here. Stop asking me so many questions.

"Uh, yeah."

"When?" He gives me a stern look. "And, more importantly, why?"

Okay, so I appreciate the fact that he was concerned about me, left the bar, and brought me here, but I don't think this is any of his business, and I tell him so.

"None of your business, Phillip."

He looks unhappy with me. Maybe I'll just mess with Mr. Nosy a little.

So, I sigh, like I'm ready to spill my guts. "Fine. It was a few days ago, and it was nothing really. Just Danny being Danny."

"What the hell is that supposed to mean?"

"It means, he just walked in the door and kissed me. You know Danny. He doesn't have to have a reason. He just does stuff."

Phillip is sitting in the corner with his mouth open. The look on his face cracks me up, but I try not to smile.

It's good to know that I can be very sick and still have a sense of humor.

After his constant slamming of me in front of the doctor, well, he deserves this.

"It's not that big of a deal, Phillip. We just kissed some, and, well," I say with a shrug, "one thing led to another, and we spent the afternoon in bed."

Don't I wish?

Kinda.

Really, I'm not sure why Danny and I never have slept together. We have definitely hooked up on occasion, but it's never gone that far. And Danny hasn't kissed me in front of Phillip since prom night. Our relationship, from a kissing standpoint, is kinda weird, if I think about it. I guess the whole *it will ruin us* thing sits in the back of both of our minds. But we have a little tradition of making out when he's depressed or he's had a bad game or he is hurt or something. I think I'm comforting to him. He always tells me that he can't deal with other girls after a loss, so we meet in our booth at the back of the bar or at a party or somewhere, get drunk, and make out. Then, we come back home and act like it never happened.

Danny is a typical superstitious athlete. He'll wear the same socks if he gets on a winning streak, and he's never had two losses in a row if we kiss after a loss. So, I hate to admit it, but sometimes, I am not as upset as I should be when the team loses 'cause I know Danny and I will have fun that night. Maybe that's it. We both know that it's just for fun.

I always tease him and tell him he needs to marry a girl just like Phillip—someone calm, organized, and responsible.

Of course, that's when he tells me, "You need to marry Phillip."

And, if I am really being truthful, I sometimes wish Phillip would kiss me.

I mean, how many guys would ditch the girl they were dating to come home and take care of you?

But that is a whole other topic.

I glance at Phillip, whose eyes have gotten even bigger. I didn't think it was possible, but they do.

He is *so* jealous. It's hilarious, and I can't help it. I feel a wicked pleasure in that.

"Don't look so freaked out. Neither one of us is dating anyone seriously, and you know, there's always been this attraction ..."

My story is interrupted by the doctor walking back in the room. He picks my chart up and continues reading it.

I have to tell you, the look on Phillip's face is totally priceless.

I really wish I had a camera.

I bite my lip and try to suppress a smile.

Phillip sees my smirk. "You're shitting me, aren't you?"

Then, he gives me that glare. The glare that always makes me spill my guts whether I want to or not.

Normally, I try to fight it but to no avail, so I don't even try today.

I am much too weak.

"Yeah, I am." I smile at him.

"So, are you going to tell me what *really* happened?"

"Yeah, sure. It really is no big deal. He came home the other day when I was getting ready for my sorority meeting. I was vacuuming the living room because some of the girls were coming over afterward, and you guys left chip crumbs all over the floor. Danny laughed at me and said I looked like a '50s sitcom, vacuuming in a dress and high heels. He walked out the door, then swung the door back open, and said, 'Lucy! I'm home!' Then, he walked over, grabbed me around the waist, dipped me, and kissed me. Like Ricky used to do on those old *I Love Lucy* reruns. He was just being goofy."

And, um, confession time.

It wasn't *just* a kiss.

He did do the whole Lucy thing, but while I was still leaning back, he asked me if Phillip was home.

I shook my head.

Then, he picked me up, carried me to the couch, lay on top of me, and kissed me intensely. It was totally unexpected and so hot.

I really thought we might cross the line that time. But, about the time things were heading in that direction and just after Danny whispered, "I think it's about time we, you know," and then, "Your place or mine"—as in whose bedroom were we going to do this in—we heard Phillip's car door slam. We both bolted up off the couch and ran to our own bedrooms before Phillip bounded in the door.

And, *poof,* the mood vanished.

The doctor has been listening to my story, and he's standing there, very still. He eyes the number twelve football jersey I'm wearing and cries out, "Are you talking about Danny *Diamond?*"

"Yeah," Phillip and I say at the same time.

"But the Oklahoma game is this weekend. He can't be sick!"

Obviously, this man bleeds red, like most everyone in the state.

"Get him here!" he orders.

Phillip calls Danny on his cell and tells him to come to the hospital.

As he is talking to Danny, the doctor says, "Tell him to come to this room, like a visitor. We certainly don't want the media to get wind of this."

Actually, he is right about that.

DANNY FINALLY SHOWS up at the hospital about an hour later with flowers for me.

He's so sweet!

By this time, my tests have come back, and it's been determined that I do not have meningitis.

Thank God!

Instead, I have a severe case of strep throat, and evidently, strep throat can be very dangerous and have serious complications if not treated.

As in you can get rheumatic fever and go into heart failure.

Something I did not know and really wish I hadn't discovered.

I'm dehydrated and weak, so they hook me up to an IV and give me two shots of antibiotics.

One in each butt cheek.

Um, not cool.

I'm still trying to figure out why they didn't just put the antibiotics in my IV. I'm pretty sure it was the doctor's way of paying me back for possibly getting Danny Diamond sick.

"Danny, I'm Dr. Daniels. I've been taking care of your friend Jadyn here," the doctor says, shaking Danny's hand.

Phillip and I glance at each other and roll our eyes.

The man is a doctor, and he's kissing up to Danny. That tells you how important football is in our state. Phillip and I are used to it now. We just try to fade into the background. Sometimes, I don't know how Danny does it. How he manages to be so nice to people who just come up to him even if he's, like, right in the middle of dinner or a date or something.

He takes it all so well though. Luckily, he has the kind of personality where no one is a stranger. He'll shake old guys' and little kids' hands all day long. He tells us that being a quarterback is a privilege, and he needs to act like a role model and honor the legacy of all the great players in history or something like that.

Actually though, he really believes it.

I'm really very proud of the way he handles himself. He always speaks clearly and intelligently to the media, and they seem to love him. Of course, it helps that the team is winning, and Danny is playing well.

And he has a standard line he uses when the media asks him what he wants out of his football career. "I just want to bring the national championship trophy back home."

They eat that kind of crap up. Of course, that really is what he wants.

The media is tricky though. Over the years, we've seen them be totally ruthless to *very* talented quarterbacks who, frankly, just didn't have the right team combination to win.

So, Danny is smart enough to know that, as far as the media is concerned, you're only as good as your last game.

My thoughts are interrupted by the doctor asking Danny for an autograph. For his kid.

Sure it is.

Danny looks at me wearing his shirt. "Hey, Jay, give me your shirt. I'll sign that."

Excuse me, but I'm wearing it!

After much ado and embarrassment, I'm now in a stupid hospital gown, and the doctor is proudly holding a Danny Diamond autographed shirt.

I hope it has strep throat germs all over it!

Danny, as usual, is getting all the attention.

The team doctor shows up at the hospital. My doctor called him. Even though Danny says he feels fine, they decide to do a strep test on him.

"We can't risk him getting sick this week."

Hello? I'm the sick one here. Do we really need to be worried about Danny? He looks just fine.

And I do mean fine.

I don't know where he was, but damn.

He's wearing an aqua-blue T-shirt that is just the right side of tight and that makes his eyes a blazing blue.

And I must be feeling better because I didn't really notice that before.

Just my luck, he tests positive for strep and ends up in the bed next to me.

Phillip smirks at the two of us. "How adorable. Matching antibiotics, IVs, and hospital gowns."

"Shut up, Phillip," Danny tells him.

Thank you!

Danny looks over and grins at me. "Well, I guess that'll teach me to kiss you."

Phillip, the comedian again, slams us both by saying, "I would've thought you'd learned *that* lesson by now."

BUT DON'T WORRY, all you fans out there. Danny was in tip-top shape for the game on Saturday.

I still didn't feel that great, so Phillip stayed home with me and watched the game on TV.

Thank goodness we won, seventeen to six; otherwise, I would have had the whole state mad at me instead of just Phillip.

But, since I live with him, it's almost as bad.

Actually, he isn't really mad at me. He's just pretending.

He can never stay mad at me.

Diamonds are a girl's best friend.

COLLEGE SENIOR

ONE DAY IN early April, Danny surprises Phillip and me by asking us to help him pick out an engagement ring for Lori. We go to the jewelry store where he shows us the stone he's already picked out. It's a lovely two-carat marquise cut diamond. Danny is stumped on what to do for the setting. He's bound and determined to present her with a ring, not just a diamond, so we shop around and talk to the salesman.

None of the settings seem right to me, so I get frustrated and draw what I think the setting should look like on a piece of paper.

It's a platinum band, not too wide, with three baguettes coming out from each side of the solitaire, like a shooting star.

"I love that," Danny says. "Do you have something like this?" He shows my drawing to the sales guy.

"No," says the eager-to-please salesman, "but we can make it."

While we are waiting for what seems like forever for him to write it up, Danny turns to me and says, "So, what's your idea of a perfect ring, Jay?"

I nearly say I've never really given it any thought, but I'm bored, and, well, what girl hasn't given it at least the teensiest of thought? So, I draw up my perfection. A two-carat emerald cut diamond in a platinum setting. From each corner of the solitaire are baguette diamonds that form an X on each side before intertwining and becoming one at the back.

Incredible, if I do say so myself!

"Wow. That's cool, too." Danny intently studies it. "You know, it looks like you."

I smile.

This from a guy who never gave a diamond a second thought unless it had something to do with baseball. Now, he thinks he's an expert.

AFTERWARD, WE HEAD to the bar to discuss Danny's plans for popping the big question. Danny and the team did bring the national championship home, just like he always planned.

GO, TEAM!

We all went to the bowl game and had an incredible time. Danny graduated in December and will be going through the professional draft later this month. He's hoping the draft goes well, and he is excited to know which team he'll be playing for when he asks Lori to marry him.

He's planning to propose on the anniversary of their first date, May 23. His plan is to take her on what seems to be an impromptu picnic—one that will be quite elaborate, thanks to our help—and propose.

IT SOUNDED LIKE the perfect plan until Lori came crying to me because she'd just gotten another candle.

Lori and I are sorority sisters, and I'm proud to say that, with her, Danny finally broke out of his SSE—simple, smooth, and easy—rut.

You didn't think I'd ever let him forget that, did you?

He begged me to set them up after meeting her at a party last year.

Lori's a great girl.

Smart. Premed. Sky-high GPA.

She has a wicked sense of humor, which I love and which is a surprise from someone who looks so straightlaced.

Really, I was sorta joking when I told Danny he should marry Phillip, but, personality-wise, Lori is just that. A girl version of Phillip.

Probably why we get along so well. We're complete opposites. She's the responsible to my reckless, the organized to my chaos, the calm to my manic, and the serious to my flippant. Plus, the girl can seriously party, so we have had a lot of fun over the years.

She's a natural beauty, just gorgeous, both inside and out. She has long strawberry-blonde hair, a sweep of cute little freckles across her nose, and beautiful brown eyes. She's five-seven and weighs one hundred twenty pounds on a *fat* day.

And, although she does have Danny's *prerequisite* C-cups, she is nothing like the girls he used to date.

One, she has a brain.

Two, she's never been a cheerleader.

Three, she knows zero about football.

Four, there is nothing simple or easy about her.

Five, she didn't fall all over him when they met. In fact, she ignored him! She knew who he was, sure. I mean, you can't live on campus and not know who the quarterback is. But she had heard me talk about him enough to know that a guy like him, who dated so many different girls, really wasn't the kind of guy she was looking for. She pictured herself with someone serious. She figured she would meet a guy in med school, and they would become brilliant doctors together. She seriously had no desire to date him.

Really!

That is what I think really intrigued him.

She was his first real challenge.

And, really, once I begged—and quite possibly bribed—her to go on a date with him, she could see what the fuss was all about.

So, she decided, *What the hell? I know he never takes a girl seriously, so I'll have a little fling with him.*

But, for the first time in his life, Danny made a girl wait. He told her she was different, special, and after a month of him dating no girls, except for her, she finally dragged Danny in his room by his ears and said, "If I'm so special, let's get to it."

And I guess they did.

And they have been pretty much inseparable ever since.

They make an adorable pair and get along quite well in spite of their differences. He tries to teach her about football, and she tries to teach him Latin.

The thing about her that amazes me is how she always looks dressed up. Even in a T-shirt and sweats, she looks dressy. She just has this class about her, and, fittingly, she is president of our sorority.

IN OUR SORORITY, whenever someone gets promised or lavaliered, pinned or engaged, they pass their candle.

It sounds sort of weird, but it goes like this.

Basically, the whole sorority stands in a big circle with the lights dimmed. We sing songs, and when the candle has gone around the circle the right number of times, the girl who is one of those things blows out the candle as a way of making her big announcement. When you are the girl who needs to pass your candle, you try to keep it a secret until the ceremony. The tricky part is, you have to get your candle to the president. Sometimes, if it's a younger girl, she just tells the president. But most of the upperclassmen are more secretive because they want to surprise her, too.

Today, Lori got a candle in her house mailbox, and she doesn't know who it came from.

She plops down on my couch and says, "It's just not fair. Ever since I saw my first candlelight ceremony, I've dreamed that, one day, I would get to do it. And, since I met Danny, well, I just assumed it would happen. I was so sure that, once he got drafted, he would pop the question."

Danny was the second pick in the first round of the draft. To my delight, he drafted higher than the cocky running back who won the Heisman Trophy.

Sorry, but Danny totally should have won that.

He's going to be playing for Kansas City, and Phillip and I are so excited since we'll be able to go to lots of his games.

"But, instead, he's gotten so that he won't even talk about our future together. We used to talk all the time about where we hoped he'd go, how we'd want to live, how many kids we'd have." She starts gesturing big with her hands. "And, Jade, I bought it all. Now, I don't think he wants to marry me anymore." She sighs. "I think he just wants to be some rich, *single* pro player. KC's most eligible bachelor. Whatever. I'll probably end up married to a boring doctor, and I'll see Danny on an episode of *MTV Cribs*. He'll be in a huge house. A house with no furniture, except for a pool table, a big TV, and a stripper's pole. There will be nothing in his fridge but beer and Gatorade. How pathetic will that be?"

She's starting to babble.

I smile at her. It's reassuring for me to know that someone so smart can also not have a clue when it comes to boys. *Does she really not know how totally crazy Danny is about her? Is she really that blind?*

"I know I shouldn't ask, Jade, but do you know anything? Has he said *anything* to you? I can't sleep, I'm eating too much, and I can't concentrate on studying for finals. I'm going to be a moose with a bad GPA." She sighs again. "So, should I just give him an ultimatum or what?"

Wow, what do I say?

Lori is one of my best friends, and I really want to make her feel better, but I can't give the big secret away. I'm sure the reason

Danny's stopped talking about their future is because of the whole surprise factor.

"Lori, you know Danny is pretty strong-willed, and he really doesn't like to be told what to do. I think you should definitely *not* issue him an ultimatum because, even if he wants to marry you, well, that would just piss him off and make him not want to ask you. Why don't you focus on school and, well, just let Danny quarterback the relationship for a while? Let him run the game. It's what he likes to do."

Her face tells me that this is not very reassuring.

So, I pat her hand and add, "You know, someday, he's going to throw you that perfect long bomb into the end zone, and it will have been worth the wait." I look seriously at her because *this* I know for sure. "He's worth it, Lori. He is so worth the wait."

"Yeah, I know. I'm just sick of sophomores getting engaged."

WHEN DANNY GETS home from Lori's that night, he bounds into my room and plops down on my bed, jolting me awake.

I squint to look at the clock. "Danny, it's, like, two a.m. What do you want?"

"Tell me about this candle-passing stuff. Lori was talking about it. She didn't come out and say it, but I got the impression it's something she wants to do."

Duh!

"Of course she wants to, but our last meeting is next week, so unless you move up the proposal date, she won't ever get to."

"Why is this such a big deal, Jay? And what exactly do you do anyway?"

What I want to say is, *Can't we discuss this at a time when my mind is functioning?*

But my eyes adjust to the light, and I get a good look at Danny. I can't help but smile. He reminds me of a little kid sitting on the edge of my bed, waiting to get told a great bedtime story.

He's also looking at me sweetly with *those* eyes.

I swear, I'd do just about anything for that boy when he looks at me like that.

Fine. Now, it is.

"Don't you remember the candlelight ceremony at spring formal when Bobby Allen and Linsey Newman got engaged? You were there. Didn't you watch?"

Of course, I *know* he didn't watch.

He and Phillip, who I had begged to go with me for lack of a decent date and who looked so hot that I wished it were a real date, were up at the bar, doing shots with all the other guys. I know they never even looked over.

"Well, uh, I remember you all got in a circle and sang, and then I think we hit the bar. I just don't get the big deal," he says with frustration creeping into his voice.

This is going to take a while, so I sigh, sit up, and put my pillow behind my back.

"It *is* a big deal to us girls, Danny. We have watched with wonder as upperclassmen announced being lavaliered, pinned, and engaged, and each time you see it, you wish it were you. They always look so happy and in love, and let's face it; *love* is what every girl dreams of."

Well, that … and the rock and the dress and the presents and the honeymoon …

"Okay," Danny says, struggling to create a new game plan in his mind. "So, could she pass her own candle without *knowing* that it's her candle? You know, could it be a surprise?"

Maybe it's the fact that I'm sleep-deprived, but the boy is making no sense.

"Danny, she really can't be surprised because she wouldn't know it was her candle to blow out. So, it would just go around and around, like some bizarre nightmare. You know, like the one where you take the same final over and over and over again, but you never get it finished."

"Stick to the point, Jay."

"Oh, yeah." Then, my mind comes up with a brilliant idea. "Unless you want to ask her to marry you in front of the sorority *during* the candlelight ceremony."

He gives that some thought.

"I could do that," he says bravely. "Do you think she'd like that, or would she prefer I ask her in private?"

"Well, the question isn't really if she'd like it, Danny. Of course she would. The question is, are you sure she'll say yes? You know, you ask in front of all those people and she says no, it could be a bit embarrassing for you." I can't help but tease him a little.

"Uh, I think she'll say yes," he says, but I can tell he's slightly worried.

"But, honestly, even if she said no, half of the sorority would be in love with you themselves and be glad to take you up on your offer. I'm not sure if it can be done though," I ramble on. "At least, I've never heard of it being done, but I guess it could be because the candlelight ceremony doesn't have to be done in private. We have done it at formals and stuff, so my final answer is yes, I think you could and *should* do it."

"What about the serenading part that Phillip's frat does? Is that important?"

"Well, if you were in a fraternity, yeah, it would be important. But what are you gonna do? Have the football team serenade her?" I laugh at the thought.

"Well, maybe. Come on, Jay. Help me pull it off."

He gives me that look, the one I have seen so many times, usually before we do something that we probably shouldn't be doing. But, for once, this is a case where we definitely should. He and Lori are amazing together, and I am so happy that he's finally found a girl who's perfect for him. And, if I can help her wish come true, too, of course I am in.

But I have to give him a hard time first. "Do I have a choice?"

"Not really," he says as he jumps off my bed.

He leans down and kisses my forehead. He looks so happy as he bounds out of my room. "You can go back to sleep now."

Yeah, like that's possible. Now, I have a million ideas racing through my mind.

I yell after him, "Hey, Danny, is the ring ready?"

"Yeah," he replies from the hall.

"Do you have it?"

"Yeah."

"Can I see it?" I ask, trying not to sound as frustrated as I am with his one-worded responses.

"Nope."

"You're such a loser!"

"Ah, come on, you know you love me," he says with his sweet voice.

"Yeah, I do." I'm such a pushover.

"Night, Jay."

Is that for me?

APRIL 24TH

THE WEEK PASSES by quickly. Operation Engagement is in place, and the day of our last sorority meeting is upon us.

I'm just getting back home from studying at the library. Well, I was sort of studying. Actually, I was *supposed* to be studying, but instead, I was flirting with—and then making out with—this hot guy from my Tech Design class. I've been trying to get him to ask me out all semester. Turns out, he recently broke up with his girlfriend and finally appears to be interested. I was so hoping that would happen!

Lori is sitting at the breakfast bar, apparently waiting for me.

I see the candle box on the bar in front of her.

Uh-oh. I don't even get to say hello. She's across the room in a flash.

"Look at this!" she says, thrusting the box into my hands.

I'm looking at the box I wrapped in beautiful fuchsia paper. The wrapping paper has little gold pineapples on it. Inside, I know is a thick fuchsia taper.

Attached in a ring at the base of the taper are fuchsia and orange tropical silk flowers with cascades of purple, orange, and fuchsia ribbons.

I've never seen a more beautiful passing candle in all my years, if I do say so myself. I also know that these are the colors and flowers of Lori's dream wedding.

I am *so* bad!

"Pretty box. Is that for me? Late birthday present?"

"No!" she snarls, opens the lid, and shows me what's inside. "Don't be coy with me, missy. I think you already know exactly what this is."

I give her my best puzzled look.

"This is your work, Jadyn. This candle is beautifully decorated, and I know you made it." She squints her eyes at me, puts her hand on her hip, and speaks in a threatening tone, "Whose is it?"

"My work? I've never decorated a candle before"—*well, except this one*—"in my life. What are you talking about?"

"This bow"—she points—"looks exactly like the bows you made for all our Christmas presents."

Damn!

This girl is too observant and maybe too smart for her own good. I briefly wonder if she's already conducted forensic research on the box. I figure, next, she'll tell me she's dusted it for fingerprints.

Damn! I knew I should have worn gloves.

"Let me see your hand," she demands, grabbing my left hand, probably getting ready to fingerprint and incriminate me.

But, instead, I see she is glaring at my very empty ring finger.

She shocks the hell out of me when she asks, "Did you get engaged, Jade?"

She looks at me seriously. It's really hard for me not to just laugh hysterically in her face, but I refrain from doing so because I'm a good friend, and I realize that she's in distress.

But her next question very nearly blows me away.

"Did you and Phillip finally come to your senses and get together? Are *you* passing this candle tonight?"

Okay, ha-ha, maybe she's not that smart.

Her hands are on her hips, so I get the impression that she is quite serious. Gosh, I wish I were recording this, so we could all laugh about it later.

"Me engaged? And to Phillip of all people? Are you serious? I'm dating, like, two—well, maybe three—different guys right now; none of whom is Phillip. And, by the way, they make bows like this," I say in a know-it-all voice while flipping the ribbons, "at any flower or craft shop."

Looking closely at the candle, she says with a sigh so big that it blows her bangs up off of her face, "Jadyn, this blows."

That's funny. Candle. Blows. Get it? Oh, never mind.

She shrugs, lets out a huge, sad sigh, and drops onto the couch.

Uh-oh. Here we go. Meltdown time.

"It's in my wedding colors—tropical flowers even! It's like a bad joke staring at me, saying, *Ha-ha, you'll never get to pass your candle.*" Then, all of a sudden, she completely changes directions, regroups, and says conspiratorially, "Okay, so we have to find out whose this is. Go ask around. I'm going over to the house to see what I can find out."

And, with the look of a possessed woman, she gets up, takes the candle box, and leaves.

I grin to myself. I'm not too worried about what she'll find out. Nobody in the sorority knows what will happen tonight but me.

And what the hell was that anyway about Phillip and me coming to our senses? *Whatever.* She so knows we are just friends. I don't understand why people always think there is something between us.

I think, if there were, then I would know.

Duh.

I call Danny on his cell and nearly die laughing, telling him about Lori's visit.

She is going to be so surprised!

I can hardly wait!

BECAUSE LORI HAS verbally abused nearly every sorority member and still no one seems to have a clue whose candle it is, there is much interest in tonight's ceremony, and every member is present and accounted for. Our usual long-lasting and sometimes even a little boring business meeting is rushed through in record time.

I hope Danny's ready early.

Finally, it's showtime!

In usual presidential fashion, Lori announces that there will be a candlelight ceremony tonight.

But everyone already knows this and is forming the circle. Someone dims the lights while Lori lights the candle and starts the singing.

I knew that, as planned, Danny would be hiding just behind the door to the kitchen with the house mom, Doris, who, even though she is old, is still female and as such adores Danny.

I told him not to get distracted and to peek and listen carefully, so he would come out at just the right time.

Lori starts passing the candle around the circle to her right and says, "Promised or lavaliered."

I'm strategically standing next to Lori on her left. I know she will practically die when the candle makes it all the way around to me on *Engaged*.

The candle makes its first lap, and as Lori starts the second round, she says, "Pinned."

Once again, the candle makes its way around to Lori without getting blown out.

She pauses, holding the candle for an extra second, and then says with dramatic flair, "Engaged."

Then, she starts it on its third go-round.

Whenever we get to *Engaged*, there is a special magic in the air, and even though we are all singing, there is kind of a collective, *Oh!*

This time is no exception. We know it's the big one!

The candle is almost back to me, and I am *freaking out*! I'm using my mind to try to send Danny major telepathic messages.

Come out now!

Come out now!

But it doesn't seem to be working. The candle is just being passed to me. Lori is giving me a look that, by all rights, should knock me dead. She waits for me to blow out the candle.

What a joke that would be!

Me engaged? Ha! And to Phillip!

Although, I mean, that wouldn't be an awful thing. He is really hot and adorable.

But, oh, yeah, everyone is staring at me. They now know that either Lori or I got engaged. I look at Lori and smile at her. She gives me another death look.

I'm frantic!

So, I decide to stall. I take a breath in and pretend like I'm going to blow it out, and—*thank you, God*—Danny suddenly parts through the other side of the circle.

I shouldn't have freaked. I should have known his timing is always impeccable.

I watch him walking toward us. Danny moves like a panther. Graceful yet feral. I mean, girls can't help but stare, and trust me when I say that all eyes are riveted on him.

Well, all eyes but Lori's.

She's still got her eyes laser-locked on the candle she thinks I am about to blow out. I keep the candle in my hand, look at her, and bug out my eyes toward Danny.

She sees him and gets a look of horror on her face.

I can tell she is thinking, *Oh my God, why is he here? Did something terrible happen?*

He stalks up to her, and she whispers, "What's wrong? Why are you here?"

Danny doesn't answer her.

He looks her straight in the eye and slowly bends down on one knee.

The singing stops, and there is a collective gasp of breath from the girls. They've all figured out what is about to happen.

Lori still isn't completely sure what Danny is doing, and if she's figured it out, she can't believe it's really happening. She just stares at him in disbelief.

Danny takes her hand and says, "Lori, you are the most beautiful and brilliant woman I have ever known. I love you more than I ever thought was possible, and I keep falling further in love with you every day. You've made me so happy. I'm hoping you'd like to keep me that way for the rest of our lives. Make me a happy man, Lori. Marry me?"

Lori and most of the sisters have tears streaming down their cheeks.

Danny stands up.

Lori intensely looks at Danny, throws her arms around him, and screams, "Yes!"

The girls go, "Aah," and just as they are finishing, a loud-mouthed sophomore yells, "Where's the rock, Danny?"

Danny backs away from Lori, into the center of the circle. Then, he starts doing what he does best—playing in front of a crowd.

"Come on, ladies," he says, leaning back and holding both arms out in the air. "I have just pledged my undying love"—he brings both his hands to his heart—"to this woman in front of all of you. Do you really think she needs a ring?"

All of us, Lori included, scream, "YES!"

Danny nods, pulls a gray velvet ring box out of his pocket, drops back, and ...

I don't believe what I'm seeing.

For the first time in my life, I see Danny's hand shake as he throws a pass.

He does manage to pass the ring box to Lori, but the pass is wobbly and a bit too high.

I fight my natural reaction to reach up and grab it.

Sadly, this pass is not meant for me.

Lori, bless her heart, who has probably *never* caught a football—or any ball, for that matter—in her life, suddenly develops the reflexes of a cat. She leaps up and snatches that ring box right out of the air. It's amazing what a girl can do with the proper motivation.

She opens the box. I can't see the ring, but when I see the way she looks at it and how happy she is, I start to tear up a little myself.

Danny puts the ring on her finger. The girls cheer and then start singing again.

I gently nudge her shoulder. "I think this is yours," I say and pass her the candle.

Danny winks at me, and Lori gives me a huge grin. Now, she understands.

She and Danny blow the candle out together.

Someone turns up the lights.

Danny says, "Hey, I understand there is usually serenading after this. How 'bout we head outside?"

Danny and Lori lead the way with me tagging along right behind them.

I've got to see this! I can't imagine what Danny had to promise to get some lowly freshman football players to come sing to his girlfriend.

This could be a *total* disaster.

This was the part he and Phillip planned on their own.

I just hope, for her sake, she's not embarrassed if it's totally pathetic.

But, as we come out the door, I literally see a *sea* of red.

I gaze around at the mass of people that Danny and Phillip have assembled.

There is what appears to be the *whole* football team dressed in red practice jerseys, pretty much every fraternity boy at the school wearing his house letters across his chest, and—*my God*—what must be the majority—*no kidding!*—of the school's marching band! They are wearing assorted red shirts, shorts, and their big band hats.

Like magic, when Danny appears, the music begins. The team's fight song. After that, they play a song everyone knows, and everyone sings along.

I sing the first few lines and then start humming, "Hum, hum, hum, hum, hum, hum, hum, hum, hum …"

Uh, I really should have learned the words to this song.

Well, one thing's for certain! No one's likely to forget this candlelight ceremony soon!

This isn't an engagement.

It's a wedding pep rally!

After a few songs, the serenading stops, and the event takes on a life of its own. Everyone has come out of the neighboring houses and dorms to see what's going on, and pretty soon, it becomes one big street party. The band keeps playing, and everyone starts dancing. I'm standing on the steps of the sorority house, watching the whole spectacle in amazement, when I see Phillip waving at me from across the street.

I was wondering where that boy was hiding.

I also can't help but notice how exceptionally hot Phillip looks tonight. He's wearing a team logo T-shirt and a pair of baggy khaki cargo shorts. Nothing terribly exciting, but *damn* if he doesn't look good in it.

He and Danny still work out together. Danny has been trying

to bulk up a bit in preparation for the pros, and I realize that Phillip has bulked up a bit, too. I mean, he's always had a great chest and arms, and I don't know, maybe it's because I see him every day, but I really haven't noticed how great he looks. I especially like how big the muscles that go from his neck down to his shoulders have gotten.

Wow!

I run down the stairs, across the street, leap into his arms, and scream, "Phillip!" I throw my arms around his neck and give him a quick kiss on the lips.

"What was that for?" Phillip yells in my ear as he grabs my hips and starts dancing with me.

"I don't know." I shrug. "I can't believe you guys did all of this. I'm so proud of you both!"

Honestly, I really don't know why I just kissed Phillip. All the romance in the air must be adversely affecting me. That, or it's because Phillip looks so hot. I mean, it wasn't much of a kiss, just a quick little peck, but for some strange reason, I don't think I would mind kissing him again.

Phillip intensely looks at me for a second, *evidently* reads my mind, and gives me a kiss on the lips. This one is just a bit longer than my peck, but still, it's just a friend-type kiss.

I ask, "What was that for?"

Phillip just smiles and shrugs his shoulders, like, *If you don't need a reason, neither do I.*

We dance together for the rest of the evening. We're both just so happy for Danny and Lori.

WE'RE WALKING HOME when Phillip asks me, "So, are you bummed you never got to pass your candle?" He's holding my hand and swinging my arm irritatingly high while we walk.

"Well, since I haven't found a guy who can put up with me for longer than about three months, I'd say it's probably for the best."

"Gosh, what a spectacle that was. Would you ever want to be surprised like that in front of so many people?"

"I don't know, Phillip. Part of me says no, way too flashy, but most of me says yes 'cause, God, what a romantic thing it would be to know that a guy planned all of that *just for me*. It would be pretty amazing." I sigh and shake my head. "But I really don't think I'm gonna have to worry about it."

"Why? Never getting married?"

"No, I just can't seem to find a guy who can handle me."

"You are pretty tough to handle," he replies while bumping his shoulder into mine.

"Yeah. Well, you and Danny are the only ones who can seem to do it, and darn it, now, it's official; Danny's off the market."

"I guess it's back to just you and me, Princess."

"Yeah," I say, wondering if that's a good thing or a bad thing.

play spin the bottle again.

APRIL 25TH

THE NEXT MORNING, I get up fairly early and am pouring myself a cup of the coffee that Phillip makes me every morning before he leaves.

He is such a morning boy.

Lori comes out of Danny's room and joins me in the kitchen.

"So, do I finally get to see this ring?"

"See it? I thought you helped design it."

"Yeah, well, see if I ever help him with anything again. He wouldn't let me see it when it was finished. He said you *had* to be the first one to look at it."

"Really?" she says, all flushed and happy.

She holds her left hand out to show me. I notice she has already perfected the pose of the engaged.

And *wow!* The ring sure did turn out beautifully. It's perfect for her.

"How did you know I've always wanted a marquise cut diamond? I don't remember us ever talking about it," she says while putting two pieces of bread in the toaster.

"We didn't. Danny bought the diamond on his own. Did he know that's what you wanted, or did he buy it because it's the diamond shape that looks most like a football?"

"Well, I might have mentioned it once in passing now that I think about it."

"I only got to help with the setting."

"Really?" she says again.

I don't think she can believe that Danny did all of this himself.

Really, neither can I.

He's usually not so romantic. I guess he's never had to be that way. I suppose you don't have to work too hard to romance girls when they are throwing themselves at your feet. Still, it's good to know that a guy can be romantic when he finds the right girl.

Maybe there is hope for me.

Sadly, one of the guys who tried to "romance" me this week thought saying, "Hey, wanna get drunk and hook up?" was romantic.

Even sadder, I actually considered it.

So, maybe not.

Somewhere, my prince is waiting.

Ha!

Actually, I don't think he's waiting. I think he's hiding from me.

But back to Lori.

"You know, Lori, other than helping with the setting, all I did was tell him about the ceremony. Well, that, and make the candle. Phillip got some pledge to deliver it."

"I knew I was right about you." She laughs and then takes a bite of her toast.

"Honestly," I say over my coffee cup, "I was a bit worried about him getting the football players to do the serenading. Afraid it might be terribly pathetic or totally cheesy. I have to say, I was floored to see the whole fricking marching band there. So, what do you think?" I grin. "Was it worth the wait?"

"Yeah." She smiles to herself, dreamily remembering last

night. "It was definitely worth the wait. Could you believe all that?"

"Not really. Oh God, what kind of wedding are you gonna have? How in the world will you top last night?"

"Actually, there is something we wanted to talk to you and Phillip about. Danny and I decided last night that, with him having to report to training camp soon, we're just going to get married on a beach somewhere in Mexico. Probably Cancun."

I interrupt her, "What are your parents going to say? Aren't they going to freak out about that? Will they go, too?"

"Well, sure, they will definitely be there, but the wedding will be very small. Like probably only our immediate families and you and Phillip. We'll have a big party when we get home. I'm going to book the trip today. Danny and I are hoping you and Phillip will come and stand up for us at the wedding. You ready to be my maid of honor? Gosh, I can't believe it! It's only a few weeks away!" She's chattering away and practically bursting with excitement. "We'll leave right after graduation. So, will you do it? Will you come?"

"I wouldn't miss it for the world," I say.

And I mean it.

"On another note," she says as she gets up, pours herself another cup of coffee, and rinses her plate in the sink, "I saw you dancing with Phillip last night. You know, I think you two belong together." She sits back down and stares at me. "So, have you guys ever dated or anything?"

"No, to dating. Yes, to anything," I say with no expression, just to tease her.

She gets a big smile on her face.

"But don't get too excited. The last *anything* was in eighth grade when Phillip attacked me during a game of Spin the Bottle. Oh, and, well, I sorta kissed him last night."

Her eyes get huge. "You *what*? Tell me about it!"

"Uh, well, it was just a peck—well, two pecks—but we were just excited for you and Danny."

"Have you thought about kissing him again? He is so handsome, Jade. You two would be adorable together, and you get along so well. Don't you see the way he looks at you with those puppy-dog eyes? I really think he's, like, in love with you."

Not very subtle, is she? I suppose, since she's all happy and engaged, it'll now become her mission in life to marry off the rest of us.

"Uh, I don't know about the puppy-dog eyes. And, sure, he loves me. We're best friends. And, as far as the kissing goes, no, I haven't."

Really, I haven't.

Fine. So, last night, I *might* have thought about it for a second but only a second.

Well, okay, maybe I have thought about it for more than a second because she's right; he is very handsome. And I have to admit, I really enjoyed having his strong arms wrapped around me while we were dancing, and I even enjoyed our two little kisses.

I try to change the subject by saying with a smile and a wink, "But I can tell you about the time I slept with Danny."

She's heard the prom story before, so she rolls her eyes at me and will not be distracted. "Well, Jadyn," she says with a wicked grin as she walks out the door to head to class, "I think maybe it's time you play Spin the Bottle again."

AROUND NINE THIRTY, Danny strolls out of his room, looking bleary-eyed. It takes him a while to get going in the morning. His dark blond hair is sticking up all over, there are pillow marks on the side of his face, and he's wearing nothing but a pair of baggy sweat shorts.

He looks adorable.

And happy.

"So, what do you think? We pulled it off." He grins while sliding onto the couch next to me.

"We? How 'bout you and half the school? It was really amazing, Danny. I was thoroughly impressed."

"So, I'm actually getting married," he says as his stomach growls. "I don't suppose you'd make me a celebratory omelet, huh?"

I smile and close the textbook I was reading. It really doesn't take much persuasion to get me to stop studying.

"Oh, I suppose," I say like it's a big inconvenience.

He moves to a barstool and watches while I get the ingredients out of the fridge.

I crack three eggs into a bowl, whisk them, and stir in some milk. I put a little butter in a pan and sauté some mushrooms. Then, I pour in the omelet mixture.

It's amazing how good a cook you become while living with two hungry boys.

"Think she's the right girl?" he asks me, still rubbing his eyes.

"Don't you think it's a little *late* to be asking that question?"

"Nah, I could always call it off."

"Yeah," I say as I cook the omelet. "And you would be a fool. Lori is perfect for you. It's weird because you are so different from her. You know, you and I really are a lot alike. I mean, we both love to have fun, are wild, larger than life, always ready for the next challenge, the next adventure, the next dare. But, on the downside, Danny, sometimes, I think you and I could float around aimlessly. We're like kites. We just go wherever the wind blows us even if it's not the best place to be. Lori is like a great kite flyer. She understands that you need enough string to go on your adventures. She even encourages it and helps you soar." I smile at him, add some cheese to the top of the omelet, and flip it onto a plate. Setting it in front of him, I add, "She also knows when you need to be brought back to earth. She grounds you, Danny. In a very good way."

I need someone like that, I think.

He smiles and shoves a big bite of omelet into his mouth.

"Plus," I remind him, "she's booking travel arrangements as we speak."

"This is really good. Thanks," he says and takes another bite. In between chews, he asks, "So, are you and Phillip in?"

"I know I am. I haven't seen Phillip this morning, but I think we both know what his answer will be."

"Jay," he says, pausing to put another forkful in his mouth and chew. Then, he waves his empty fork at me. "Why don't you just sleep with Phillip and get it over with?"

"What?"

"I *saw* you dancing together last night." And he just shakes his head at me.

Lose another boyfriend?

APRIL 25TH

PHILLIP IS AT his last fraternity meeting, and Danny is out with Lori. I'm home alone, lying on the couch in my PJs. I've been absentmindedly spinning an empty beer bottle on the coffee table while channel-flipping between *16 and Pregnant* and *Gossip Girl* and drinking a couple of beers.

Well, maybe more like four or five.

I think I might be slightly depressed and, well, maybe getting slightly drunk, too.

Phillip opens the front door. I take a good look at him. Lori is right; he is *so* handsome.

My heart literally flutters every time I see him.

He walks into the living room and scans my row of empties. I watch the sexy backside of him as he walks to the kitchen, grabs a beer from the fridge, and then plops down on the couch beside me. He opens the bottle with Danny's bottle opener that plays the NU fight song. My mind swirls back to dancing with him last night.

Maybe.

"What's up with all the beer? Lose another boyfriend?"

I ignore his comment.

"Wanna play Spin the Bottle?" I surprise myself by asking.

"You know, it's been a while since I've played, but aren't there usually more than two players?" He squints at me, wondering what joke I'm trying to play.

"Yeah, stupid idea." I sigh a little bigger than I should.

What the hell was I thinking?

"Hey," Phillip says as he leans forward and holds both hands up in the air in front of his chest, "I said nothing about it being a stupid idea." He gestures toward the bottle on the table. "Spin away. Hell, you don't even have to spin. I'll kiss you anyway. Do you want me to kiss you?"

"What about *Moaning Monica*?" I roll my eyes when I say her name.

In case you can't tell, I don't particularly care for her.

That girl is always moaning about something.

Usually me.

"Uh, well"—I get the feeling he would like to ignore the question—"it seems, she broke up with me today."

"Why?"

He laughs. "Well, it might've had something to do with our wild dancing last night."

"I didn't realize it was wild."

"Yeah. Well, what's worse is that I didn't even realize she was there. She never crossed my mind. I was having too much fun with you."

"What did she say?" I'm trying hard not to smile and show my happiness about his unfortunate breakup.

Sorry, but, *yay!* That girl was not nearly good enough for Phillip.

"I don't know." He runs his hand back through his hair, leans back into the couch, and takes a pull off his beer. "It was something like, when she saw you and me dancing, she just knew that what she had always suspected and I always denied was true."

"And what's that?"

"That you and I have—and I quote," he says while making quote marks in the air, "a 'thing' going on."

"A thing?" I laugh.

"Yeah, a thing."

"That's ridiculous," I say. "We're just friends; we have been for a long time. I mean, God, somewhere, there are pictures of us as naked babies together. And we're just, you know, comfortable around each other. We're able to hang out and have fun *without* having things happen."

Then, I stop and realize it's not the first time I've heard this.

"Why does everyone think that?" I ask him seriously as I rest my chin on my fist. "I mean, I've done way more with Danny. How come no one *ever* accuses us of having a thing? I don't get it."

"Um, well, could it be the fact that I always seem to run out on my dates to rescue you, and he never does?"

"You've never done that, have you?"

"Princess ..."

"No, I'm serious." I put my hand on my chest. "I always take care of myself. I've never needed to be rescued."

"Oh, really?" Phillip chuckles. "What about all the times you've had flat tires? Who has come and changed them? What about when you hit the deer or the time you ditched Richie Rich at winter formal or the time you had the huge fever and I had to take you to the hospital?" He pauses, giving me a grin. "Shall I continue?"

Okay, so he might be right.

And there is nothing I hate more than not being exactly right.

In fact, I'm getting a bit irritated right now.

"You didn't have to come and do those things. I could have figured it out on my own. And I didn't know you, like, left dates to do them. You didn't have to do that. You could've been like Danny and said to just call Triple A or whatever."

"I know I didn't have to do it. I wanted to. I guess," he states, sweetly looking at me with his adorable brown eyes, "like you"— he pauses and stares intently at me—"I haven't met anyone who makes me want to stay with them more than I want to go and rescue you. What can I say?" He rolls his eyes at me. "You've made me play your knight in shining armor for so long that I just can't seem to get it out of my system."

God, he is adorable.

He laughs lightly and looks at me. I can tell by the intensity in his eyes what he is about to say is important.

He puts his hand on my knee and leans toward me. "Seriously, you are kinda special to me." Then, he adds sneakily, "Now, speaking of Spin the Bottle, should I start?"

"Would you really kiss me, Phillip?" I ask, scrunching up my nose.

"I think I might be able to be persuaded." He grins, grabs my arm, and throws it up over his shoulder. "Wanna try to persuade me?"

My face is so close to his. I could easily start kissing him. I'd only have to lean forward just a bit.

"No. I mean, *really*? What if we kissed and then we dated and then you got mad at me and ended up hating me like most of my other boyfriends? I couldn't stand to lose my best friend. I'm going to bed," I decide suddenly, getting up off the couch and walking quickly toward my room.

"So, you want to play the game in there, huh?" Phillip asks with laughter in his voice as he nods his head toward my bedroom.

"No!"

Then, I hear him chuckling behind me, and it makes me mad because that boy knows all too well how to get under my skin.

Way Too early.

APRIL 26TH

THIS MORNING, PHILLIP brings me coffee in bed.

It's six thirty a.m.

Way early for me, but for Phillip, it's the perfect time to get the day started.

He and Lori are both the kind of people who sign up for eight a.m. classes. Danny and I try to never start ours until at least ten or eleven.

"Thanks," I say, taking the cup from him. "Coffee in bed. You must want something."

"I do." He looks squarely at me.

He is sitting on the edge of my bed. I fight the temptation to just grab him and pull him in with me.

"So, what do you want?"

"You."

"What?"

"I want *you*," he repeats. "Go out with me for real, Princess."

"I can't."

"Really? So, what was last night all about?"

"Oh, nothing really. Well, Lori and I had been talking. She just asked if you and I ever, you know, dated or kissed or anything. I told her not since eighth grade. Remember Spin the

Bottle?"

"Yeah. So, you thought you might want to play it with me again?" His head is cocked slightly sideways, like a puppy that is trying to understand me.

I hope he can. I'm not sure I do.

I shake my head. "Maybe. Yes."

"Well, at least that's progress." He laughs.

"Progress? What kind of progress?"

"Don't tell me you can't see it. God, Princess, I swear, everyone sees it but you." He shakes his head at me like I'm completely clueless.

I might be. But, in this case, I know exactly what he is talking about.

"I see it, Phillip. I even *feel* it, but I *choose* not to cross the line. I care too much about you to throw our friendship away on a fling." I set my coffee down and cross my arms in front of my chest, indicating that my word on this is final.

"Who said anything about a fling? And you crossed *way* over that line with Danny, and you guys are still friends." He is sort of muttering to himself now. "Of course, you would've never lasted anyway. You're too much alike, think way outside the box, hate to be told what to do. Always right, even when you're wrong."

"True, we probably would've fought like crazy." It surprises me that the thought of Danny and me together still seems to bug him. "But what's that got to do with us?"

"Probably? You *do* fight like crazy."

He can't seem to get off the Danny subject, so I give in on that point and say, "I know. That's why he and Lori are so great together. She's so grounded. She's just like …"

Then, I stop.

I realize what I was about to say and think back to yesterday's conversation with Danny.

The kite thing.

Oh. My. Gosh.

Does Phillip fly me?

Is he just like Lori, hanging on and letting me do my thing, all the while keeping me safe and close by?

Is he perfect for me?

Phillip interrupts my thoughts by saying, "Finish your sentence."

"Um, no." I shake my head.

I can't.

"JJ," he warns.

"*Fine.* I was going to say, um, she's just like you."

"And?" he prods.

"And you're probably perfect for me." I sigh big. "See? See the problem? I have a major conflict of interest here."

"A conflict of interest?" He looks at me like I'm nuts.

"Yes."

"What exactly do you mean?" Phillip needs to know this because he is so exact about everything.

"Well, everyone thinks you and I *belong* together. Part of me agrees. We get along great. I love to be around you, but the conflicting side of me thinks I shouldn't risk it. And, besides, I really don't think we should worry about what other people think."

"Fine. So, what do you think?"

"No fair. You go first. What do *you* think?"

Phillip takes a moment, gathers his thoughts, and says carefully, "Well, I do think we have a fair amount of *chemistry*."

"Chemistry?" I laugh. "Are you serious? You treat me like your sister."

"No, I do not. I'm much nicer to you than I am to my sister. Trust me when I say, I have feelings for you that are probably illegal to have about a sister."

I laugh nervously. I did not know this at all.

"I know, in your mind," he says, poking me on my forehead, "you think of me as a brother." He switches his line of thought and says, "Do you ever feel tingly when I hold your hand?"

"Um ..."

"Do you get excited to hear my voice at the end of the day? Do you like to be with me?"

"Uh ..."

"People are right. You and I *definitely* have a thing. What they don't understand is that we've never *acted* on it. I'm thinking we should," he says confidently.

"You do?" I'm surprised.

"Well, what have we got to lose?"

"Uh, duh. Each other. And I *really* like you, Phillip."

"No, Princess, you don't *like* me; you are totally *in love* with me. You're just too stubborn to admit it."

I look at his eyes because, surely, he must be joking, but he appears very serious.

"Fine," I say, temporarily giving in and avoiding the love topic. "I'll go out with you sometime. Where do you want to go?"

"Mexico."

"Mexico?"

"Yeah, trial run. If it doesn't work out, no one needs to know. We'll just come back to the way things are now," he adds, scowling.

"How's that?" I ask, puzzled.

"You torturing and teasing me and then walking away."

"I don't do that!"

"You did last night."

"Phillip, don't you get it? I don't want to lose you. You're my family, *my only family*. I'd be alone if it wasn't for you." I swear, I'm about ready to cry. My eyes start tearing up, and I choke out, "Why can't you get this?"

"You're not going to lose me." He runs his hand through my

messy hair and down the side of my face.

Oh, that feels so good. I melt slightly and close my eyes for a minute.

"How can you say that? How can you be so sure? You know my history. I *always* lose the guy!"

"Yeah, well, that's because they're *always* the wrong guy."

"And you think *you're* the right one?"

"Yeah, I do. I'm the one," he says, pointing to his chest.

I picture him as Tarzan. *Me. Take you. Jane.*

Then, I focus back to what he is saying.

"I've been here for you all along. I've listened to you cry about other guys. I rescue you, take care of you when you're sick, hug you when you're sad, tell you you're beautiful when you look terrible." He looks me straight in the eyes and is dead serious when he says, "Princess, I've *always* been the one."

I give up.

"I know," I sigh. "So, Mexico, huh? And you promise, if it doesn't work out or we fight, we agree to pretend it never happened?"

"What happens in Mexico stays in Mexico," he says with a twinkle in his eye and a big smile on his face.

"Let me think about it," I say diplomatically.

He takes the coffee cup away from me and sets it on my nightstand. "While you're at it, think about this."

Then, he leans in and kisses me right on the lips.

Very thoroughly.

I can't help but kiss him back. I completely relax, all defense slipping away.

Damn.

Then, he stops, gets up, and walks out my door without another word.

Wow.

And he's right because I can't seem to think about anything else.

Stop thinking so much.

MAY 17TH

FINALS ARE OVER, we've all managed to graduate, and I'm on the beach in Cancun, Mexico. Phillip and I are walking hand in hand in the moonlight.

It's a very romantic setting.

I can hear the sound of the ocean lapping the beach. The moonlight is shimmering off the water and in the sky.

It even feels romantic.

The sand is rough between my toes, and the water keeps coming up onto the beach to caress my bare feet.

Phillip stops and kisses me, and it's really wonderful.

When I kiss Phillip, I feel like I'm home, like I'm exactly where I belong. It's a weird and wonderful and very scary feeling.

Maybe he's right. Maybe I am in love with him.

If only I wasn't so afraid of losing him.

"Stop thinking so much," he says, reading my mind. "Where is Miss Spontaneous when I need her? Any other time, and you'd be dancing on the beach, making out with the guy. Do me a favor, Princess; relax and enjoy this."

I try to relax, and I have to admit, the kisses help.

I can tell Phillip would like there to be more going on than kissing, but every time he presses the issue, I feel myself pulling back.

I am just not ready.

We kissed.

MAY 18TH

THE NEXT MORNING, it's *amazing* because Danny and I are the first ones at our breakfast table. I thought for a second that we were the first ones up because that never happens, but Danny informs me that Lori and Phillip went out for an early morning run, and the parents are already golfing.

Typical.

"So, how did it go with Phillip last night?" He raises his eyebrows up and down, hoping to hear some juicy details.

"Well, we kissed."

"And?"

"And ... that's it."

Danny shakes his head and rolls his eyes at me, like I'm a stupid idiot.

"Danny, what am I supposed to do? I just feel all this pressure, like I have to do this, not like I want to. It's like I'm being told what to do. And you know that, when someone tells me what to do, it usually makes me do the exact opposite. You of all people should understand that."

"I do understand, but it kind of seems like you're looking for excuses." He studies me closely. "You're not letting what happened between us affect you on this, are you?"

"Oh, you mean the *it would ruin us* part? Um, yeah. That's the part that scares me the most." He is still shaking his head at me, so I say, "You don't think, if I go out with Phillip, it will ruin our friendship?"

"No, I don't. I think it will enhance your friendship. Surely, you understand what different people Phillip and I are. Hmm, I guess maybe now might be a good time to confess."

"Confess what?"

He runs his hand through his hair and sighs. "I was so afraid of you on prom night; I literally drank myself sick."

"You were afraid of me?"

"Well, I was afraid of what I—*we*—might do. I mean, I really wanted you, Jay, and I have to admit, there have been many times that I've kicked myself for not going for it." He tilts his head and looks at me. "But I didn't want to take advantage of you. I mean, you'd been through so much in such a short time. Jake. Your parents. Combine that with the fact that it would've been your first time. I don't know. It just didn't seem like the right thing to do. I was afraid you would regret it and hate me. I just couldn't live with that."

"Did you know that I wanted you to take advantage of me?"

"Yeah, I kinda did. Why do you think I was so nervous? You can be very persuasive, Jay. I was afraid I wouldn't be able to say no."

"Why didn't you just tell me?" I shake my head, trying to comprehend this. "Wait, that's not right. That night, you wanted it, too. I saw the condom by the bed!"

"Yeah, well, at that point, I was drunk and not thinking with my head. Thank God I passed out because I think it would have ruined us. At that point in your life, you needed stability, not fun. You and I both know, the times when we hooked up a little in college, it was always just for fun."

"That, and your win record," I tease him. "So, what makes

you think it will work with Phillip? I'm serious, Danny; I really need to know this."

"Well, there's something else I should probably tell you." He leans across the table and says softly, "Prom night, when we all slept together, I woke up before you did. Guess what I saw."

"I don't know. Did I look gross? Was I drooling?"

"No, silly. You're adorable when you sleep. What I saw was you all snuggled up with Phillip. He had his arm wrapped around you. Your head was on his chest. And that's when it hit me. I think, even when we were little, I knew you two had a special bond, something I wasn't part of. I'll even admit that it was kind of a blow to my ego, but it worked out okay. It made it easier for me to tell you what I did. I mean, I knew we'd never last romantically. We're too much alike. But I also knew you'd be fine." He pointedly looks at me. "*Because* of Phillip."

He leans back in his chair and continues, "Christ, you two are perfect for each other. You're already like an old married couple anyway. You just don't get any of the fun benefits ... and I *know* you like the fun benefits."

I shake my head at him. "You'd better be there to pick up the pieces if this all blows up in my face."

"You know I will," he says, and I believe him. "Jay, is there anything you've ever really gone for in your life that you haven't gotten?"

"Um," I say, not knowing quite how to answer.

"Go for it," he demands. "Visualize your target."

"Oh, shut up, Danny."

Danny gives up on the conversation, and we go through the breakfast buffet. We are eating and chatting about what we're going to do today when Lori shows up.

She kisses Danny and then takes a seat. "So, what are you two conspiring about?"

"Oh, I'm just trying to talk Danny into marrying me instead,"

I tease.

"Now, there's a match made in heaven," Danny says, teasing Lori, too.

"A marriage made in hell is more like it," Lori fires back.

"Hey, I lived with him for three years, and we got along just fine." I put my hand to my chest, pretending like I'm insulted.

"Yeah, only because Phillip was there to play referee," Lori counters.

Jeez, she's just full of piss and vinegar this morning. Obviously, the run wasn't long enough.

"Did I hear my name being taken in vain?" Phillip says, sneaking up behind me and kissing my neck. He whispers softly in my ear, "Morning, Princess."

I close my eyes for a second to drink in his words, the sound of his voice, his musky smell. I block out everything in the world but him. I have to admit, I love having him so close to me.

He sits across from me and claps his hands together. "So, what's going on this morning?"

Lori answers his question by saying with a laugh, "Jade is trying to talk Danny into marrying her instead of me."

Phillip rolls his eyes.

"Fine," I say, trying to redeem myself. I don't understand why Lori and Phillip think this is so hilarious. "If I can't marry him, then I will be his bachelor party." I smirk and smile seductively at Danny.

"Whatever," Lori says and shakes her head at us.

Danny winks at me.

"So, what's on tap for today, Miss Cruise Director?" Phillip asks Lori, ignoring me and changing the subject.

"Well, I'm going to have a long day of lying on the beach, doing nothing but watching the ocean, while Manuel brings me a whole bunch of drinks with little umbrellas," she answers dreamily.

"Sounds perfect," Phillip replies in an equally dreamy voice.

Danny and I glance at each other, worried. Because sitting still all day might damn near kill us or, at a bare minimum, drive us insane.

Lori rolls her eyes and says, "Here, you two. Don't look so dejected. There are lots of activities." She slides Danny and me each an itinerary across the table. "I took the liberty of booking a few things to keep you two out of trouble."

"It won't work," Phillip says.

Like Danny and I ever get into trouble.

Okay, maybe, sometimes, our plans don't come to fruition exactly like we planned, but, hey, we always manage to have fun.

Danny gave me a cute magnet for Christmas last year. It said, *The trouble with trouble is it always starts out as fun.* That pretty much sums up our relationship.

I grab the list off the table and read it.

09:00: Sailing
10:00: Volleyball tournament
12:00: Trip to private island and lunch
02:00: Nap time
05:00: Happy hour at the beach bar and then rehearsal
07:00: Dinner with family

"Lori," I say, "you have to do something while you're here."

"Jade, believe it or not, lying on the beach counts as some-thing. Besides, we're going to lunch together. It'll be fun. We're riding WaveRunners out to the resort's private island."

"Yeah, and I hear the island is *clothing optional,*" Phillip tells us and leers at me.

Great. Now, I have something else to worry about for the next three hours.

Danny and I try out sailing. It's okay but not as thrilling as I expected because there isn't much wind. Next, we head to the two-on-two volleyball tournament. This is a very fun activity because Danny and I kick butt and win the whole thing.

Naturally!

After that, we set out to meet our beached friends.

We find Phillip and Lori sitting on beach chairs under a palm tree, doing exactly what they said they would do. Drink. Lori seems to be a bit drunk, and Phillip is not far behind.

"Hey, we were watching the volleyball tournament from here. You guys did great!" Lori says, and then she kisses Danny a little too passionately.

Phillip gets up, grabs me around the waist, and says, "And looked great, too. I really like the new bikini." Then, he kisses me passionately.

What is in those drinks?

Love potion?

But I decide I like Phillip like this. He's very loose and fun. We have a great time riding the WaveRunner out to the island. I stupidly let him drive, but I enjoy it immensely because I'm able to wrap my arms around him and just hold on tight. I love the feel of the wind on my face and my hair flying back behind me. I feel free.

When we get to the island, Phillip jokes with me and chases me down the beach, trying to catch me so that he can *help* me take off my top. When I finally let him catch me, he just throws me into the sand and kisses me. It's great fun, and I'm totally at ease with him. I don't feel the least bit pushed. Maybe this will work after all.

WE GET BACK to the resort, and Danny asks Lori if she's ready for a nap.

I'm sorry, but neither one of them looks the least bit tired.

"Hey," I blurt out, "you're not even married yet. Why don't you save something for the honeymoon?"

They just look at me, laugh, and leave.

Phillip, who has sobered up some, leers at me. "You know, I'm feeling pretty worn out myself. Why don't you come take a *nap* with me?"

I consider it for a minute.

No, I decide. *Too soon.*

"No way. We're going parasailing. Come on." I grab his hand and lead the way.

LATER ON, WE meet Danny, Lori, and their parents for happy hour and tell them all what they missed out on by not parasailing. It was exhilarating and scary and a total rush. The kind of stuff Danny lives for. I loved it and had so much fun with Phillip. I really do like being around him.

I get the feeling they don't think they missed out on much though. They look at each other with dreamy eyes. And they share these glances, like they know a big secret that no one else knows.

It makes me feel kind of jealous.

I would like to feel that way about someone someday.

I gaze at Phillip and wonder if I could ever look at him like that.

AS SOON AS we finish with dinner, Lori and Danny excuse themselves. Evidently, they are still *tired*.

As she is leaving, Lori says, "Don't keep her out too late, Phillip. We have yoga class at eight with full spa treatments after."

"Eight?" I say with a groan. Phillip gives me those stern eyes of his, and I say, "Sounds lovely." I force a smile at her. It is her wedding after all.

Phillip and I decide to go dancing. I think that sounds like great fun because then I can get Phillip a little drunk and loose again.

I'd like to dance with him all night and maybe, *just maybe*, take him back to my room later.

Phillip and I have each had three huge margaritas and are out dancing when two guys, who Danny and I killed in the finals of the volleyball tournament, come dancing up next to us. We are all sort of dancing together, and I have to admit that I'm loving the attention. I thought today that the guys might be gay, but the way they are dancing with me, I'm inclined to think not.

At one point, I turn back around toward Phillip, and I don't see him. I look over at our table, and I still don't see him.

Weird.

He must have gone to the restroom.

The guys and I dance to a whole bunch of fun songs, and the waitress keeps coming around with these cool shots. Her serving tray has a bunch of glow-in-the-dark necklaces on it, and you get one with each shot you order. She must be selling them well because the dance floor is glowing with them. Nearly everyone I see has at least one necklace on.

I've had two of them, I think.

I look down at my chest and see that I do indeed have on two necklaces, so I must have had two.

See? I'm not messed up.

The not-gay-after-all guys order us another round when she comes by again.

I do one more shot, put on another necklace, excuse myself, and head to the restroom.

Why is it, when you're in the restroom at a bar, you suddenly realize *just* how screwed up you are?

The stall is spinning around me, and something in my brain makes me realize that Phillip has been gone for a long time.

Disappeared.

Hmm. I wonder where Phillip has gone.

I think I will go and look for him.

I don't say good-bye to the not-so-gay guys and start off down the beach.

"PHILLIP. OH, PHILLIP. Wherefore art thou, Phillip?" I sing and dance my way across the sand.

Where am I going again?

Oh, yeah.

Find Phillip. Then what?

Take him back to my room.

Ooh, that sounds fun!

I think I see someone sitting on a beach chair up ahead of me and am surprised to find out that it is Phillip.

He's sitting in a beach chair.

Did I say that already?

Why is he doing that?

He is supposed to be dancing with me and having fun.

And I have been having so much fun.

"Phillip! Oh, Phillip, why are thou art out here, Phillip?" I ask him as I slide onto his lap and run my fingers through his hair.

I love Phillip's name. It just *rolls* off my tongue.

I also feel very romantic.

Amazing how that happens after a whole bunch of drinks.

Maybe those glow-in-the-dark shot thingies had love potion in them, too.

"Why did you leave me, Phillip?" I pout while trying to look sexily at one of his eyes, but I keep seeing two. Well, four total actually.

That kind of looks freaky.

He must be drunk to look so bad.

"I didn't really feel like dancing with a crowd."

I think Phillip is mad at me. *Why would he be mad at me when we're having so much fun?*

I know what takes a guy's mind off being mad. Kisses.

So, I kiss him, but he pushes me off his lap and stands up.

That's weird.

"JJ, I'm not going to do this. You don't want *this* or *me*. You made that painfully clear tonight. You didn't even try."

"I did try, Phillip! I was having a great time! You're the one who left me."

I'm getting mad because he is speaking to me in a very accusatory tone.

Like I did something wrong.

He's the idiot who left me with two not-so-gay guys.

"Phillip, I don't get it. You say you want to be with me, but you leave me. You say you want to dance with me, but what? All of a sudden, we can't have fun and dance and party like we always do? It seems to me you haven't made much of an effort. And then, after I come find you and kiss you, you get all pissy with me. I don't like it, Phillip. I thought you wanted to kiss me, Phillip."

"I had a lot of fun with you today, JJ, but you totally blew it tonight. I thought that you wanted to be with me, only me."

I look at both Phillips and say, "So, that's what this is all about? You're on a jealous little rampage? Grow up, Phillip!"

Good-bye, Phillip.

I stumble away from him and run up the beach.

Why am I stumbling?

It must be these stupid sandals. They are giving me problems, and they must come off!

Now.

I sit in the sand even though I'm getting my new dress all sandy. I take the stupid sandals off and throw them down the beach.

Phillip follows me, grabs each one of my sandals out of the sand, and says, "You're picking a fight with me, JJ."

What? Am I no longer Princess?

That's three JJs in a row, and no one is even around.

"I'm not going to fight with you," he continues.

Doesn't he know that I don't want to fight with him either? In fact, I want to do the exact opposite of that tonight.

But I don't tell him that because he's being a jerk.

"Why? Might you have to show some e-mo-tion?" I yell. I get up and try to brush the sand off of my dress. "I'm through with this," I say.

"Yeah, well, I'm through with it, too. This is your fault. I understand you wanted to have fun, but you're supposed to want to have fun with me, not other guys. You didn't even try. In fact, I think you were purposely trying to push me away. I'm the one who gives up." He throws his hands up in the air.

He's very upset with me, I think.

And he's fighting with me.

Didn't he just tell me that he wasn't going to fight with me?

Is he drunk?

"You ever decide you want to try this for real, you know where to find me. It's your move," he says, acting very crabby.

Then, he walks away.

Hey! Wait! He's not supposed to leave me. He's supposed to kiss me!

I watch him walk further and further down the beach and notice that not once does he look back.

Oh, this is *so* not at all how I wanted this night to go.

I sit in the sand and sob.

Phillip comes back either a few minutes or a few hours later. I'm really not sure.

I look up at him through mascara-filled tears.

"Come on, Princess." He sighs as he scoops me up off the sand and carries me to my room. "I'm not going to be able to sleep unless I know you're safe."

I'm never drinking again.

CANCUN

MY GOD! WHAT is that noise?

I think someone is slamming a sledgehammer against my door.

Why are they doing that?

I practically fall out of bed, and when I do, I am genuinely surprised to see that I'm still wearing my dress from last night. And it's all freaking sandy.

Whew. I feel a little fuzzy, but I *must* make that noise stop.

I look through the peephole in my door and see Danny. I fling open the door, let him in, and crawl back into bed.

"Jeez, Jay, you look like crap," he says in a booming voice.

It hurts my head.

"Why are you still wearing that dress? Oh, wow, did you just get back from Phillip's room?"

"Danny, could you *please* talk a little bit quieter?" I beg and bury my head under the sandy pillow.

"O-kay," he says more quietly, quickly appraising the situation and taking charge. "Go wash your face and get dressed." He looks at my dress and says, "As in not the dress you wore last night. I'm taking you to breakfast. You need to eat and take some Advil." He looks at me with real concern. "And I hate to say it, but you might even need a drink. We've got less than an hour to get you ready to meet Lori."

Oh God. I feel awful, but I do as I was told; I drag my butt out of bed and go into the bathroom.

I wash my face, brush my teeth, and pull my hair back into a ponytail.

I have a sudden feeling of déjà vu. It's all very blurry, but I vaguely remember being in here last night with someone.

Was it Phillip?

Was someone throwing up?

Was it me?

I think it was, and I think Phillip helped me get here.

So, why am I wearing my dress?

Why isn't he here, in bed with me?

I have a feeling that things didn't go exactly as I had planned.

But, wait, I remember!

I think he was mad at me.

Then, I remember the not-so-gay guys and arguing with Phillip.

Me crying on the beach.

Oh, not good.

The only good thing I remember is, I'm pretty sure it was me who threw up last night.

That means, I might actually survive this day.

I open the door to the bathroom and am startled.

Danny is standing right in the doorway with my yoga outfit in his hands.

I forgot he was here.

"Put this on," he bosses.

I do, and after sliding my feet into a pair of flip-flops, we head to breakfast.

JUST MY LUCK, when we get there, Phillip is there.

He shoves his remaining food into his mouth and says to Danny, "I've gotta run. See you on the golf course at ten."

He doesn't say a word to me.

Doesn't even acknowledge my presence.

I frown.

Danny, who can't help noticing the frigid climate between Phillip and me, asks, "What's up with you two?"

"Nothing," I say, putting on my sunglasses.

Where is Manuel? Someone really needs to get him to turn down the sun out here.

It is way too bright. It's making my head hurt.

"Stay here," Danny orders, leaves, and comes back with a huge plate filled with all of my favorite things for breakfast.

None of it looks very appealing.

"Eat something, Jay. And drink some water."

Shall I tell him that I'm not really in the mood to be bossed around? Probably not. It's his wedding day; I should try to be nice.

So, I pick up a triangle of toast and take a teeny bite.

Danny hands me a mimosa and commands, "You'd better drink this."

Yuck.

"I can't, Danny. I am so never drinking again."

"Like I've never heard *that* before."

Danny is teasing me. He seems to think this is hysterical.

Yeah, 'cause it's not him for once.

So, I go against my better judgment and do as he said. I drink the mimosa and am surprised that, after a few sips, it's not half bad.

But then Danny makes me feel sick again when he asks slowly, "J-a-y, what did you do to Phillip?"

Me?

"Nothing, Danny. I swear, absolutely nothing."

He shakes his head in apparent understanding. "Ah, well,

that's the problem then."

"Danny," I cry, "the night was a flipping disaster."

"Why?"

"It's not my fault, Danny. Really, it isn't. We were dancing and having a great time, and in my mind, I pictured us dancing, and then I was going to invite him back to my room. I had such great plans."

"I'm proud of you. So, what went wrong?"

"Well, then those cute guys that we killed in volleyball yesterday came over and started dancing with us."

"I thought they were gay," he interrupts.

"Me, too, but they didn't act like it last night," I say, raising an eyebrow and shaking my head even though it hurts to do so.

"Anyway, we were all dancing together, drinking, and having fun. And Phillip didn't say a word. He just left me. I thought he had gone to the restroom or something, and I kept waiting for him to come back, but he never did."

Danny looks at me with a shrewd eye. "So, you were dancing and drinking, and knowing you, you were flirting with these guys. And you're surprised that Phillip left you? What are you, stupid, Jay?"

Hey, that's not very nice!

"No wonder he's mad at you. It was supposed to be a date. You were supposed to be with *him*, not other guys. I'd be pissed at you, too!" He gives me a disgusted look.

Hey, you were just complimenting me on my plan.

Traitor.

"I'm a flirt. You know it. Phillip knows it. It's never bothered him before because he knows I'm harmless. Maybe he needs to loosen up." I pause, thinking. "But, honestly, Danny, even though he says it's what he wants, I'm not convinced Phillip really wants this either. I mean, if he did, he wouldn't have given up so easily." I shake my head at Danny. "Regardless, now, I give up."

"Can you honestly tell me you gave it your best shot with him?" He looks at me with squinty-looking eyes, and I have a sneaking suspicion he doesn't believe that I did.

"Over the years, I've seen the many ways you can wrap a guy around your finger." He rolls his eyes at me. "I should know. Phillip is not immune to you. I think that, if you had really tried with Phillip, he'd probably have married you last night."

I sigh.

"Did you try, Jay?"

"Yes. No. Oh, I don't know! I know he expected things to progress, but I was very clear that I wanted to take things slow. That I didn't want to be pushed. I hate being pushed."

"It doesn't sound like he was pushing you at all. It sounds to me like you were pushing him away."

I take off my sunglasses, so Danny can see just how miserable I am. "Look, I did try. I told you, I had big plans for last night, and now, I'm miserable. And not because I drank too much, but because I think I am in love with him. And I've probably already lost him. I want things to work out so much, but at the same time, I find myself holding back. I'm so afraid I'll screw things up."

"And I think that's exactly what you need to do. Screw things up."

"What?" I ask, completely missing the double entendre.

Give me a break! I'm having a rough morning here.

"Sleep with him, Jay," Danny says very seriously. "Get it over with before you lose him."

SOMEHOW, I MANAGE to get through the day. I do yoga with Lori without throwing up, although my instructor makes some snide comment about me looking a little green.

I make it through the massage, which is normally really relaxing but made me nauseous. After the massage, we break for lunch, and they bring us some healthy and crappy-looking spa food. I beg them for a cheeseburger and fries, and, yay, they bring it to me. Lori and I have champagne with lunch, and I'm starting to feel almost normal.

After lunch, we're both getting pedicures and manicures, and then I'm scheduled for a detoxifying body wrap.

Now, that is something I need.

Suck all the alcohol out.

How much do you want to bet the yoga instructor set that one up?

During our pedicures, Lori finally brings up the subject of Phillip. She doesn't know about the disaster last night, and I have no intention of telling her.

"I saw you at breakfast the other morning," she says, like she knows some big secret. "When Phillip whispered in your ear, you just melted. Your eyes got all dreamy-looking. You know, I have *never* seen you react to any guy like that."

She does an imitation of how my eyes looked. She looks ridiculous, and I'm sure she's exaggerating.

"You're a smart girl. You always amaze me with your ability to see the world as your great big playground. You can see miles into the future, so why can't you see a good thing when it's right in front of your face?"

"Phillip," I state, knowing full well what she means.

"Yeah, Phillip. You know, Danny thinks so, too."

"I know. He told me once after he dumped me."

"He didn't dump you."

"Oh, I know," I say with a wave of my hand, "but it bugs him when I say he did. Sorry, it's an old habit."

"You know, I know *all* about the flag bikini, Jade. I've even seen that sad, tattered little picture."

"He still has it?" I'm surprised. "You know, I love it that it doesn't bother you. A lot of girls would have a problem with it."

"Well, I think Danny has kind of a been-there-done-that attitude toward you."

"*Been there* maybe," I say, "but never done *that*." I grin at her and then frown and say, "Unfortunately."

"No. Fortunately. Because, if you had, he's right; you probably wouldn't have stayed such good friends."

"Why? Is he that bad at it?"

"Well, I think you could expect that he approaches it the same way he does everything else in his life," she says cryptically.

But I understand completely. "One hundred percent focus and full-out energy." I sigh and shake my head.

Figures.

"Jadyn, the end result is, I'm not jealous. Whatever works. He signed a six-year, forty-eight million-dollar contract. I don't care if he visualizes himself playing football with a donkey and a naked clown. Hell, I'd blow the picture up and hang it on the living room wall if I thought it would help his game."

I squint my eyes at her.

"Okay, maybe not, but my point is that I understand your friendship with Danny, and we *both* value it."

"So, brilliant wife-to-be, why do you think I should risk my friendship with Phillip by dating him?"

"Because you're perfect together." She pauses for effect. "Jade, it's like you were made for each other."

"That's all great, Lori, but I think it might be too late. But you don't need to hear about my problems; this is your wedding day." I smile. "We're only going to talk about happy things."

"Did something happen between you two last night?"

"No."

"Oh," she says, understanding. "Is *that* the problem?"

"Evidently," I say with a roll of my eyes.

LORI AND DANNY'S wedding is held on the beach at sunset.

We stand beneath a beautiful white archway that's laden with tropical flowers and smells heavenly. The hotel's wedding planner must have weddings down to an art because they say, "I do," and kiss just as the big orange sun is sneaking below the horizon. It is the simplest yet most beautiful and romantic wedding I've ever seen.

It's intimate and personal.

I think, if I ever find a man crazy enough to marry me, it needs to be on a beach just like this.

I recovered from my massive hangover, and because I had been pampered all day, I have to say I looked pretty darn good at the wedding. Unfortunately, Phillip, who was looking damn fine himself, didn't seem to even notice. He was cordial and overly polite to me at the reception dinner with everyone.

And, as maid of honor and best man, we did have to dance together and toast the happy couple. But, the whole time, he was stiff, and I just wanted to cry and beg him not to be mad at me. I even thought about telling him I was sorry, although I'm still not convinced I did anything wrong. I also thought about telling him that he might be right about me being a little in love with him, but I couldn't. I wasn't sure he'd believe me.

Before we had come here, I had pictured in my mind how much fun Phillip and I would have at our two best friends' wedding. Needless to say, my picture didn't happen.

AS SOON AS Danny and Lori left, Phillip said, "Good night," and walked away.

I thought about going dancing to try to make myself feel better, but I couldn't.

I thought about going to his room, but I didn't know what I'd say.

So, I went straight to my room and kept hoping he would knock at my door.

Of course, he never did.

I know it's over between us. It got completely screwed up.

What am I going to do without my best friend?

Like it never happened.

HOME

PHILLIP BASICALLY IGNORED me for the final day of the trip, so I was pleasantly surprised when we got back home, and he was true to his word.

He acted like it'd never happened.

I guess what happens in Mexico *really* does stay in Mexico.

We still talk every night on the phone. It felt a little forced at first, but we slowly worked our way back to normal.

I moved to Omaha where I have a job with an engineering firm. Phillip is living at his parents' house for now and working at his dad's company.

My romantic life is, well, not exactly going the way I'd like it to, mostly because I haven't figured out what to do about Phillip.

So, I'm sort of dating this cute guy who's in a band.

It's a perfectly mindless fling.

And perfectly mindless is *perfect* right now.

THE SUMMER FLEW by with work and the move and the guitar player. Soon, there is a chill in the air at night, and even though the days are still hot, you can practically feel fall. More importantly, football season in the air.

I haven't gotten to see much of Danny lately. He went to

Wisconsin for training camp and was named backup quarterback. I try to talk to Lori and him every few days and am just thinking about calling them actually when my phone rings.

I look at the caller ID and am happy to see Danny's name.

"So, you're still coming down for the game on the eleventh?" he says without even saying hello.

"Hello, Danny, and it depends on how good my seats are."

"Oh, they're very good, Jay baby. You're sitting next to Phillip."

I'm not sure what has happened to Danny since he started playing professional ball, but he says *baby* a lot. He and I have spent a lot of our time on the phone, discussing the fact that I might very well be in love with Phillip. Actually, we have determined that I *am* in love with Phillip and what my possible options are. I swore to him that I would talk to Phillip about how I feel tonight while we get ready for the game-day party we're having.

The party is an annual event celebrating the first game of the season. We've done it since high school. The venue has changed a lot—sometimes tailgates in Lincoln, sometimes at different houses—but the guest list stays pretty much the same. It's a fun way to keep up with old friends, and I'm really looking forward to it.

"I probably shouldn't tell you this, but did you know that Phillip is going out with Monica again? I think it's getting serious."

"Really?" I'm surprised by this news because I got the distinct impression from Phillip that she was just bugging him again. "It doesn't sound serious to me."

"Well, I think Phillip might be afraid to tell you."

"Why? I'm dating someone, too."

"Jay, a drummer—"

"*Guitar player,*" I interrupt and correct him.

"Does not count. I'm just trying to impress upon you the importance of your doing something this weekend."

"I know, Danny. I know what I have to do. It's still just a bit scary to me."

"I understand that, but I'm afraid, if you don't, you'll lose him *for good* and to someone like Monica."

"My life sucks."

"Well, I expect to hear a progress report on Sunday night. And, Jay?"

"Yeah?"

"There had better be some *progress*," he stresses and hangs up.

I'm so sick of phillip!

SEPTEMBER 1ST

I PULL UP to my condo on Friday after work to find Jimmy, the guitar player, waiting for me. Jimmy has long hair and really does have a rock-and-roll-star thing going on. My friends think he is really hot. He is, but he's nothing compared to Phillip, and Phillip is the only thing I can think about lately. Jimmy is just a decent diversion.

"What are you doing here?"

"I came to take you with me."

"With you where?" I reply, not following him.

"It's so exciting, Jadyn. The band is playing at The Bash tonight. There was a cancellation, and they called us to play at the last minute. There will be a bunch of music industry people there. This could be our big break, and I want you there with me."

"But I told you last week, I have to go to Phillip's house tonight to get all the food ready for the big party tomorrow."

"Of course," he snarls, "Phillip is much more important than I am."

Yeah, I think but don't say it.

Instead, I say sweetly, "You know I care about you and your career, but I have thirty-two people coming to the party tomorrow, and they're expecting something to eat! And the game is early—eleven thirty. There's no way I could get everything made in the morning; I haven't even been to the grocery store yet!"

Jimmy pushes me away. He looks angry. I have never seen him look this way before.

"I am so sick of *Phillip this* and *Phillip that.* I'm sick of being compared to Mr. Perfect. As a matter of fact"—he grabs me by the wrist hard and looks straight into my eyes—"you're done hanging out with Mr. Perfect. You're coming with me tonight."

I wrench my arm away from him.

I don't like to be told what to do, and I'll be damned if he's going to do the telling. I look straight at him and speak very slowly, so Mr. Dense can understand, "I'm going to keep my plans for tonight. I'm sorry I can't go to your concert. If I didn't have people depending on me for this, I would change my plans and go with you, but I can't. You'll just have to deal with it."

"That's it. It's time for you to choose."

He is furious with me.

"Choose what?"

What is he talking about now?

"Between Mr. Perfect and me. You know, everyone thinks the two of you have something going on. I always say it's not true, but now, I'm not so sure. Maybe the real reason you want to go has more to do with *cooking with Mr. Perfect* than *cooking food.*" He adds, "In fact, if you don't go with me tonight, we're through. So, choose."

Okay, that's it. He's pushed me too far.

"Let me get this straight. You want me to choose you, someone I have known for, like, two seconds, over someone I have been friends with for, like, my entire life? Well, let me tell you, Jimmy, the choice is easy." I wave bye-bye with my hand and say, "Goodbye."

"I knew the two of you had something going on the whole time. I'm outta here." He storms out the front door and yells, "You'll miss me when I'm famous!"

I do have feelings for him.

SEPTEMBER 1ST

As I'M DRIVING to Phillip's house, my insides are churning over my fight with Jimmy, the guitar-playing jerk. I mean, I would have stopped dating him soon anyway. I was just sort of planning on keeping him around as a backup. You know, in case things didn't go well with Phillip this weekend.

Now, it appears I'm flying solo.

Of course, I can't be too upset, and, well, he was kind of right about Phillip.

I do have feelings for him.

Very strong ones.

Of course, they are a whole mixed-up mess—confusion, frustration, denial, happiness, sadness, and the strongest one of the bunch, *chickenshit.*

And that is not like me.

I am so not a chicken about anything else in my life.

I have rock-climbed, surfed, parasailed, and bungee-jumped. I even drive too fast on a daily basis.

You'd think this would be easy. But, instead, I feel like I'm jumping out of an airplane without a parachute.

I mean, wouldn't *everyone* be a chicken about that?

JIMMY'S COMMENT ABOUT *cooking with Mr. Perfect* cracked me up, but it also gave me a great visual. Maybe I can get Phillip to cook with nothing on but an apron. Or, better yet, maybe I should do that. Do you think he'd notice?

Well, sure, he would; he's a guy.

The more important questions are, *Would he like it, and would he do anything about it?*

I am so hoping that he will give us a chance. I'm also hoping that Moaning Monica will not be involved in this whole affair.

You know, when Danny told me that he thought Phillip might be getting serious with her, I truly felt like I was going to throw up.

And that is not a very nice feeling.

Last week, I went to the bookstore and bought a hardcover copy of *Our Town*. That's the play we were reading in AP English when my parents died. I have been thinking about the play lately. I knew that its main theme is for people to remember to stop and smell the roses. I remember promising myself that I would always try to live life to the fullest, and I think I've done a pretty good job of it so far. But there was something else from that play that I know I wanted to remember, and I couldn't seem to remember it.

I had hoped, if I thought about it hard enough, I would remember it in a dream because I do that sometimes, but it didn't work, so I had to go buy the book and reread it. I'm glad that I did because I like the story, and I found what I was looking for. It was the part that says something about us wasting opportunities at every moment.

That was the part I was trying to remember.

And, now, I see why it's been bugging me.

It fits.

I know that I can't waste any more opportunities with Phillip.

I can't, and I won't.

God help me.

I PULL UP to Phillip's house, get out of the car, and knock on the front door. It used to be that I would just barge right in, but I'd like to think I have grown up *some*. I take a minute to look around at the houses and the empty lot. In one way, it really doesn't seem that long ago that I was camping in the backyard, playing dragon fighter with Phillip, playing catch with my dad, and punching Danny in the mouth.

But, in another way, it feels so very long ago.

I have so many wonderful memories of growing up here, but I also feel a longing to create a whole bunch of new ones with Phillip. I feel like I'm standing in the doorway of my life, trying to decide if I should go in or not.

When did I become so philosophical?

I sound like an old sap. Next thing you know, I will be crying and getting out the old videos.

What in the world has Phillip done to me?

PHILLIP'S MOM COMES to the door. She's holding a dish towel and wiping her hands on it. "Hi, JJ! Come on in. I was just finishing up."

I follow her into the house and sit on a barstool in the kitchen. The kitchen island is filled with all sorts of tailgating equipment and massive amounts of food.

"I was just trying to get everything packed before Doug gets home. We decided to drive down to Lincoln and spend the night. The game is early tomorrow, and we won't have to worry about traffic that way. The Diamonds should have the RV here any minute."

Our parents always went to a lot of college games together. When Danny started school there, the Diamonds bought a big RV to tailgate in. And do they tailgate! You have never seen so much yummy food and excessive amounts of alcohol. When we were in college, Phillip and I always made sure we stopped by before we went to the game. It was often our best meal of the week.

"JJ," Phillip's mom says, "I hope it's all right with you, but I made double batches of everything I cooked for tailgating. I thought you could use it for the party tomorrow. Save you two a lot of work."

"Really?"

I'm surprised and thrilled about this. She makes great stuff. *Plus*, I think naughtily, *less time working leaves more time for play!*

"That's so awesome because you know I think everything you make is wonderful. Thank you so much for doing that." I hop up, give her a sincere hug, and sit back down. "Oh," I say, practically drooling on the counter, "did you make any of those yummy little sausage puffs?" I love those tasty little things. "And what about that fiesta dip?"

"I made both of them, dear. I know they're your favorites." She smiles at me, like she is about to tell me a big secret, and I realize for the first time that Phillip has her exact smile. "I even went a *little crazy* and bought some of those red tortilla chips. I hope they taste the same as the regular kind." She hands me a spreadsheet of all the food she made, saying, "Here's the list of what's here and how to cook it."

My, she is very organized. I should make lists because it never fails that, when the party is over, I discover something in the back of the fridge that I forgot to serve.

I look over the list and see it's pretty extensive. Barbecued brisket with mini dinner rolls, veggie tray, cheeseball and crackers, cheese dip, Swedish meatballs, sausage puffs, summer sausage and cheese tray, fiesta dip with red chips, Go Big Red cupcakes, and mint brownies.

"I think I'm in heaven. Go Big Red cupcakes and mint brownies! You're spoiling me." And, thinking about them, I say like a little kid who wants cookies before dinner, "Can I have a brownie now?"

"Sure," she says and gets me a brownie.

I really love this woman.

"Phillip's going to have his work cut out for him tonight, just trying to keep me away from those brownies, but, other than that, I don't know what we're going to do with ourselves all night."

Well, I actually do have a *few ideas* in mind.

She smiles a knowing smile. I hope that mind-reading thing doesn't run in the family. But I'm worried because I get the feeling she knows *exactly* what I just thought.

"I thought it might be nice for you and Phillip to spend some time together without having to worry about the party." She pauses and then says, "I have a question for you. Have you and Phillip ever thought about dating each other?"

I wonder if she already knows about Mexico. I kind of hope not.

"Um, well, we did talk about possibly dating in May, right before Danny and Lori's wedding."

"And?"

"And we kind of had a trial run in Cancun, but things didn't go very well. We've managed to stay friends though."

"Did you sleep together?"

Uh, that is probably not information I want to share with you.

You are his mother, for goodness' sake.

At first, I think I'm not going to answer this question on the grounds that it might incriminate me, but I figure that, in this case, the truth is way cleaner than her imagination, so I tell her the sad truth, "No, we didn't."

There. End of story.

But she's not done with me yet.

"Have you *ever*?" she asks in a very matter-of-fact tone, like we're discussing the weather and not my sex life with her son.

Well, lack of sex life really.

This is getting a little too personal, don't ya think?

But, once again, I tell her the truth, "Uh, no. Never." I shake my head.

She looks surprised at this news and has a questioning look on her face, like she doesn't believe me.

"Hmm." She has her finger up to her mouth, like she's thinking very seriously about something.

This ought to be good.

"You know, JJ, you girls today have it rough. Back in my day, if you really wanted to get a man to marry you, you just seduced him and got yourself pregnant."

This woman continues to shock me. I mean, I've never thought of myself as uptight about this stuff, but I gotta tell you, I'm feeling pretty tight right now.

Like I can't get any air.

I must need some milk and quite possibly another brownie.

As I refill my plate, I stammer, "Uh, yeah, but it doesn't quite work like that anymore."

She dismisses my statement with a wave of her hand. "Well, it should. And it would work in Phillip's case. He has good values and would do the right thing."

Is it just me, or does that seem a bit twisted? I mean, if Phillip's morals were so good in the first place, then he wouldn't be getting anyone pregnant, would he?

Then, I put two and two together and realize this is her roundabout way of, not so subtly, telling me that I should seduce her son and get myself pregnant!

I'm shocked. Beyond shocked.

I am, I don't know, double shocked.

Practically speechless.

No, I *am* speechless.

I have my mouth open, and I can't say a thing. I can't even take a bite of this brownie. And it has all that yummy, gooey red mint stuff on the top. I just stare at the piece on my fork.

It's like we were playing freeze tag and someone just yelled, *Freeze.*

And I did!

But I don't have to say anything because she continues with, "You know, I really worry about what would happen should Phillip decide to marry someone besides you."

How did we get to babies and marriage from food?

And, now, she's got him marrying someone else? What's wrong with her?

"What do you mean?" I think I must have gotten lost somewhere because I'm really not following all of this.

"Well, you know, most of Phillip's girlfriends have felt a bit threatened by your relationship with him. And I'm just afraid that, if he marries someone who feels that way, well, you need to know that I would have to do whatever makes *her* feel comfortable."

Then, she pulls out the big guns.

"We might not be able to include you in everything, like we do now."

Oh, that hurts.

That thought makes me want to cry.

I look at her with sad puppy-dog eyes and say, "You mean, if Phillip marries someone else, you're going to kick me out of the family?"

"Now, JJ, we'd never be able to get rid of you."

Like I'm a puppy that she's thinking about taking to the pound.

"I am just trying to impress upon you that the situation could prove to be difficult in the future." Her eyes look warmer.

Apparently, we're not talking about the weather anymore.

"I'm not sure if Phillip has any desire to date me, let alone marry me. Have you talked to him about any of this?"

"No, but I know how he feels about you. It's quite obvious."

It is?

Still?

She thinks Phillip might actually want to marry me?

I get a brilliant idea. "You could just adopt me. Then, no one could complain, and you wouldn't have to get rid of me."

She's too quick for me though because she says, "Wouldn't it just be easier to give it a try with Phillip?"

"Probably," I say, telling her the answer she wants to hear.

I know she'd never shut me out of their lives, but she does bring up a good point.

Some of Phillip's girlfriends *have* had a problem with me.

Okay. Most of them.

But I swear, I'm always nice to them. So, it can't be because of anything I've done. I mean, most of them seemed pretty nice.

No, that's not exactly true.

I think back and realize that I can't think of even one girl Phillip's dated that I really liked.

Could all those girls see it in me?

Have I been experiencing latent jealousy all these years?

No, that can't be it. I just think the girls realized that, if Phillip had to choose between them and me, he would always pick me.

And he would.

That's one of the things I like best about him.

I suppose it's time I return the favor.

Hey, wait, I already did.

Today.

I chose Phillip over Jimmy. Yay for me!

I hear Julie talking to me.

"JJ, what are you thinking about so hard?"

"Um, just about what you were saying. You're right. None of Phillip's girlfriends have ever liked me much."

She smiles big at me. She likes being right.

"They were jealous of you. Phillip has feelings for you that are very strong, and feelings like that are hard to hide. Ashley told me just the other day that she thinks Phillip has always been in love with you."

"I know. I think I've always felt the same way."

Oh crap!

I can't believe that just slipped out of my mouth!

She really smiles at that.

Boy, she is good, that sneaky woman.

Somehow—maybe she put truth serum in the brownies—she's already gotten me to admit that I love Phillip.

She should be an interrogator.

She'd feed people sweets and have them confessing to everything before they even realized what she was up to.

I've already said enough to incriminate myself, and she is the closest thing to a mom that I have, so I might as well tell her the rest of the truth.

'Cause this is the part that worries me.

This is the chickenshit part.

"I've been kind of afraid to do anything about how I feel because I don't want to mess things up and lose him. Lose our friendship. Because *that* I couldn't take."

She gets out a bottle of wine, uncorks it, and pours me half a glass. "You shouldn't think of it as *losing* your friend, dear. You should look at it as *gaining* something *a whole lot better*."

I look at the half-glass of wine in front of me. *God, she's got visuals.*

"That's kind of like the whole *is the glass half-empty or is it half-full* thing, huh?"

She raises an eyebrow at me. I'm afraid, if I don't succumb, she might stoop to torture.

"I get it," I say, laughing and holding up my hands in defeat. "Really, I get it."

Then, she walks over to a bookcase in the family room, pulls a picture frame off the shelf, and sets it in front of me.

The picture is of Phillip and me together as babies.

We're naked, of course.

I wonder if our parents ever stopped to think there might be something slightly *wrong* about having us naked together *all* the time. Maybe I need to go to a shrink and have them hypnotize me to pull out my early memories. Maybe it's their fault that I can't commit.

I consider saying this for a second but think better of it and just look at the picture.

Another visual.

I have to wonder, *Did she plan all this, or is she just winging it?*

Because, if she's winging it, then I need to sign up for lessons on manipulation from this woman. I have always considered it one of my stronger skills, but I realize I'm a total novice compared to her.

I look at the picture again. You know, this is the first time in my life I haven't flinched or cringed upon seeing a picture like this.

God, I *must* have grown up somewhere along the way.

I surprise myself by thinking that I now agree with what Mom always used to say.

"You and Phillip are just so adorable."

We would probably have beautiful children.

Whoa.

Wait.

Did I really just think that?

I am shocked at the things *my own mind* has been thinking lately. It's like it has a mind of its own!

I must be smiling at the picture a little too dreamily.

"You would have adorable children," Julie says, reading my mind.

Evidently, that talent *does* run in the family.

"That's part of the reason I made all the snacks for your party."

"So, Phillip and I can have an adorable baby?"

You've got to be kidding.

She laughs. "Well, not exactly. I just thought it would be nice if you could spend some time *alone* together. I think it would be good for both of you. And, while you're at it, would you *please* tell Phillip how you feel about him? That Monica girl drives me nuts."

I smile at that 'cause *me, too.*

And then she gets a big smile on her face and adds, "And I guess, if I get a grandbaby out of the deal, all the better."

I knew she had an ulterior motive.

This whole conversation is very unexpected and sort of weird, but a lot of her comments hit home. But I really didn't need any convincing; I had already decided.

I want Phillip, and I'm not going to let anyone, even Moaning Monica, get in my way.

Scratch that.

I am more grown up than that.

Monica is not the problem.

I am.

And, this time, I'm not going to let *myself* get in the way.

Something special just happened.

SEPTEMBER 1ST

MRS. MAC LOOKS at the clock and gasps, "Oh, look at the time! Is there anything else I need to take?" She refers to her spreadsheet. "Summer sausage. I almost forgot. JJ, will you run out to the garage freezer and get two packages of summer sausage?"

"Sure." I mean, it's the least I can do.

So, I go out to the garage. They have one of those huge chest-style freezers. The kind that you can fall into and never be found until someone else needs something frozen.

I hate these things.

And, of course, I see that the summer sausage is at the very bottom in the back.

Figures.

I'm leaning over, bent practically in half, trying to reach it.

And the stupid garage door is open. I hear blaring music coming from up the street. I recognize one of my favorite songs.

Great. It's getting louder. I suppose the new cute neighbor boy is gonna drive by and see my butt stuck clear up in the air like this. Not a pretty picture.

I almost have my hands on the sausage when—*honk!*—a car horn scares me, and I very nearly fall in.

I manage to work my way back upright and turn around to

see Phillip driving into the garage in his recently purchased little red BMW. He's got the top down, the music blaring, and his hair is all messed up.

He looks sexy!

It is at that moment, I decide I'm done thinking.

Click.

Brain officially turned off, body officially turned on.

Yikes!

I walk over to Phillip's car door, turn my back to it, jump up over the door, and land with my butt on his lap and my legs dangling over the side.

That was kinda slick. I didn't know that doing the high jump in track would come in so handy someday!

Phillip catches me and says, "You know, I think I could get used to seeing your butt hanging out of the freezer every day when I come home." He gives me a big, wonderful smile and says, "I was hoping you were already here."

His arm is holding up my back, and he's looking into my eyes.

"Yeah, well, you might change your mind when I tell you about the real interesting conversation I've been having with your mother."

"Really? About what?" The way he asks makes me wonder if he already knows exactly what we were talking about. His voice has this, *You're going to tell me a dirty joke, aren't you,* tone to it.

"You."

"Uh-oh," he says, although he doesn't sound the least bit worried.

I pull my legs into the car, tuck them under me, and flip around, so I am facing him. It's more comfortable; plus, I like looking straight into his eyes.

"Yeah," I say, poking my finger into his chest. "Uh-oh for you."

"Why's that?"

"Well, I think she wants me to try to seduce you."

"Keep sitting on me like this, and you won't have to try very hard." His eyes are playful.

Oh.

I look down and realize that not only is this a more comfortable way to sit, but it's also significantly more intimate.

I'm straddling the poor guy.

Shame on me!

He laughs. "In fact, you'll be lucky if I let you out of this car."

I smile at him, trying to make him think I was smart enough to plan it that way.

"Oh, come on, Phillip. I thought you'd play at least a *little* hard to get. Be a challenge."

He looks at me seriously. "What are you trying to say?"

I let my voice drop its playful tone because he needs to know I am not joking around about this. "Look, you said I'd have to come to you. So, here I am, and you'd better write this down because it doesn't happen very often. I admit it. I was wrong, and you were right. I didn't really try in Mexico. I was scared and stupid, and I preferred to have you mad at me than not with me at all."

"I know this." He is softening but still has a stern look in his eyes. "So, no holding back this time?"

"That's right," I state firmly with a nod of my head.

"And no games?"

"What, am I gonna have to get a lawyer? I think maybe you need to make some concessions, too. You did leave me with two strange guys."

"Fine. What do you want?"

"No bossiness," I say with a sweet smile.

"Deal." He is grinning from ear to ear, and I can tell this makes him happy, but evidently, he is still not completely convinced because he lowers his voice and says, "So, you're *really* going to give this a try? A *real* try?"

"No, Phillip, I'm so through *trying*. I am *doing*."

I curl my fingers into his shirt, pull him closer, and plant a big kiss on his lips. I keep kissing and kissing and kissing him.

I'm kissing him with every ounce of pent-up passion I've been holding inside me for however long I've loved him. His hands are in my hair, so it's hard to determine right now when that exactly was. Oh, who cares? This just feels so incredibly right.

Finally, I think.

I might never stop kissing Phillip.

Ever.

Of course, it is at this moment that I'm startled by another loud, echoing *honk, honk!*

I open my eyes and slowly tear my lips away from Phillip's. His dad is honking and turning into the driveway.

Phillip grins at me, but his eyes are smoldering. "Dad followed me home from the office. I was under strict orders from Mom to make sure he got here on time. They're heading to Lincoln tonight with the Diamonds."

"Yeah, your mom told me," I say back, still staring into his eyes. We're just sitting here, staring at each other, and I know I should probably move or get out of the car or *something*, but I sort of don't want to. I'm afraid I might break the spell.

Something special just happened here, I think.

JUST THEN, PHILLIP'S mom walks out into the garage and says, "JJ, did you fall in the freezer?" She sees me sitting on Phillip's lap in the rather intimate position, laughs, and shakes her head. "You work fast. Heck, if I'd known my powers of persuasion worked so well, I would have suggested this to you years ago."

I'm embarrassed, to say the least, but, hey, she kind of asked for it.

I extricate myself from Phillip's lap, and we both get out of the car.

I notice that he can't seem to take his eyes off of me. In fact, he is gazing at me with such intensity that it's making me blush.

Thank God the Diamonds pull up in the RV. Mrs. Mac becomes a drill sergeant. She knows something has happened and wants everyone out of there quick. They get everything loaded up and leave.

Phillip and I are all alone.

Finally!

I'm sitting on the kitchen counter, and he is standing between my legs, his arms wrapped around me.

"Well," Phillip says, "what do we have to do to get ready for this party?"

You've got to be kidding me!

I know Phillip is very practical and always needs to get everything finished and in order.

But, *come on!* Isn't this what he wanted?

Okay, fine. I guess I'll just have to persuade him not to be so practical.

So, I start kissing him, but it's not working quite as planned because, although he is kissing me back, in between kisses, he is asking me questions.

"Did you go to the grocery store?"

Kiss.

"No."

"Did you pick up the beer?"

Long kiss.

"No."

"Did you make a list?"

Longer kiss.

"No."

"Did you do *anything*?"

"Not yet."

Then, I jump off the counter, lead that boy up to his room, and lock the door.

It's time to finally do what everyone seems to think we have already done.

Because I really need to know.

STILL SEPTEMBER 1ST

A FEW HOURS later, he remembers the party. "You know, we really need to get out of bed. There must be a ton of stuff to do."

"Actually, we have nothing to do. Your mom made everything. I think she was hoping this is exactly where we would spend our time. She really did suggest that I seduce you. It might even be on my list."

"I can't believe she said that." He tilts his head. "You know, come to think of it, I had a suspiciously similar conversation with Ashley today. She was a little less blunt though. She said I needed to get off my ass and do something. I think they were working in tandem."

"So, were you going to?" I ask. Because I *really* need to know.

"Going to what?"

"Do something."

"I'm pretty sure I already did." He laughs as he traces my jawline with his finger.

I smile, remembering *exactly* all that he did, but that's not what I meant. "I mean, if I hadn't completely thrown myself at you, what would you have done?"

"Well, as stubborn as you are, I probably would've had to throw you over my shoulder and carry you up here, kicking and screaming."

I give him my mad face.

"But then," he says as he kisses my shoulder, "I would have done something like this. And something like this." He kisses my neck. "And something like this." He kisses my ear. "And something like this ..."

Okay, I get the picture.

And I am so loving the way it looks.

A FEW *MORE* hours later, and we're both starving.

For food, I mean.

It's nearly ten o'clock, and, well, we never did get any dinner. I run downstairs to raid the refrigerator and bring up a tray of cheese, some crusty bread, and a bottle of red wine.

"Isn't that supposed to be for the party?"

"There is so much food; I don't think anyone will miss it."

"Probably not, but I missed you while you were gone, Princess. You were down there much too long."

"It only took me about two minutes." I shake my head and roll my eyes at him while I set the tray on his nightstand.

"Two minutes too long," he replies as he grabs me, throws me on the bed, and kisses me.

"Phillip," I say, finally wrenching my lips away from him, "it's taken you twenty-two years to get me into bed; two minutes should feel like a blip."

"Twenty-two years? Don't flatter yourself. Maybe, like, eight years." He gives me a naughty grin. "But I'll tell you this; now that you're finally here, I'm not wasting another second."

YES!

We feed each other cheese and bread and drink some wine.

Unfortunately, the crusty bread was not the best choice because, now, there are crusty crumbs all over, and I really thought I was being careful to avoid that. Since his mom is such the expert on all things seduction, I'm surprised she didn't tell me about this. I use my hand to try to sweep the crumbs onto a plate.

"Remind me to properly thank my mother for making the food and for whatever it was the two of you talked about."

"Phillip, I had already decided about this before I got here"—I smile naughtily—"but I am following her advice to relax and enjoy you."

He laughs. "So, did you, uh, *enjoy* me?"

"Uh, yeah, very much so." I kiss his neck and whisper in his ear, "And I think I would very much like to enjoy you some more. *Right now.*"

I'M LYING, ALL snuggled up with Phillip. He's sleeping, and his breath is tickling my neck. I know I should be getting some sleep, too, but I can't.

My brain decided to kick back on now that my body is so worn out.

I just keep thinking about how incredibly happy I am. I want to pinch myself to make sure it's not a dream. I feel like the luckiest girl in the world. Part of me kind of wants to kick myself for not doing this sooner, but I don't. I'm too happy. I feel … well, it's hard to describe, but I'll give it a try.

You know how sometimes you go shopping and find a great dress? You try it on, and it fits you and looks great on you in the store. So, you buy it and take it home.

But then, when you put it on because you are getting ready to go somewhere, you feel like it's just not quite right.

Like maybe something is missing.

So, you keep looking at yourself in the mirror, trying to figure out what it could be, what it needs. You try on different shoes, another hairstyle, some dangly earrings, a rhinestone necklace, maybe even a wrap. But, no matter how you seem to mix it up, there is still something missing.

Oh, you look *good*, maybe even *great*, in the dress.

Just not *fabulous*.

You don't have that glowing look because, deep down, you're not confident in the dress.

That's kind of how it felt with all the boys I've dated in the past.

Something was always missing.

I'd try to rearrange them or me or what I was doing, but no matter what, I couldn't quite get it right. And the fix is a *really* mysterious thing.

I think it's because the fix is an emotion. A feeling. It's not really a tangible item.

I mean, I've made a few drunken mistakes.

Who hasn't?

Well, okay, Phillip. But he is so not normal when it comes to that sort of thing.

He's always in complete control.

And I have to say, it's always been a trait of his that sort of bugged me. I'm always trying to get him to loosen up. But, tonight, I've learned there are *many* benefits to being with a man who's in control.

Ahhh.

Oh, sorry, I got lost there for a minute.

What was I talking about?

Oh, yeah. I was saying that I've made a few drunken mistakes, *but* for the most part, if I was with a guy, it was because I thought he might be *the one*. Or at least someone who I thought I might want to try to *make* into *the one*.

After being with Phillip, I can tell you that I could put absolutely anything on in my closet, and it would look perfect.

Well, except for the bridesmaid dress I had to wear for Katie's wedding. Nothing could help that!

And not because of the outfit, but because of how I feel inside.

I am positively one hundred percent completely complete.

It's like the line from that *Jerry Maguire* movie. *"You complete me."* I always thought it was some cheesy movie line. I know that every girl, me included, melted when Tom Cruise spoke those wonderful words.

But, come on. You complete me? Get real!

And that's how you feel when you don't understand. I've been going through life, not even *knowing* that I was incomplete.

I'm telling you, this is something they should teach you in school.

I'm a college graduate, and I didn't even know that I had been walking around all this time, slightly defective.

But I don't care anymore because I know it to be true.

With Phillip, I am complete.

I yawn, snuggle up closer to him, and fall into a blissful sleep.

Who cares what day it is.

SEPTEMBER 2ND

I'M AWAKENED AT dawn.

No kidding.

By Phillip kissing the back of my neck.

Okay, so maybe things with Phillip won't be totally perfect after all. I mean, this morning-boy thing is probably going to drive me crazy. He'd better not expect me to start getting up early with …

Oh.

Phillip starts doing something to me that I am too polite to talk about, but I can tell you this; it's worth being woken up for.

Oh!

Maybe I will become a morning girl after all.

IT'S ALMOST NINE, and we're still in bed, trying to get motivated to do something besides stay here all day. The game starts at eleven thirty, and everyone is due to arrive around eleven.

Speaking of arriving, I realize I *still* don't know if Monica is coming to the party.

So, I ask bravely, "Um, Phillip, what about Monica?"

He looks at me kind of funny.

"Look, I know you've gotten kinda serious with her lately,

and, well, I just need to know if she'll be here today. You know, so I can prepare myself."

Phillip pulls me close and runs his hand through my hair. God, I love it when he does that. Then, my mind wanders to all the other things he does that I love, and I swear, I blush from just *thinking* about them.

"Why in the world would you think Monica and I have gotten serious? I was just telling Danny the other day that she's been driving me nuts."

I blink my eyes.

Hard.

I am going to kill Danny.

He told me that to make me jealous!

He manipulated me.

And it worked!

Now, he will try to take the credit for us being together, and he will *never* let me forget it. We'll be sitting in wheelchairs at the old folks' home, and he will *still* be telling me that I owe him. And I don't think I can take that!

"Danny told me."

"Danny lies," Phillip says, smirking.

Yeah, I know.

"That little ..." I start to say a bad phrase about Danny, but Phillip just laughs and kisses me.

I'm back in dreamland.

"We *really* need to get up and get things ready," I tell him.

"Nah, I think we should just lock the door, turn off the lights, and not come out all weekend."

I am tempted. Very tempted.

But our consciences get the best of us, so we get up and do everything on Mrs. Mac's list. While Phillip runs into town to get beer, I take a quick shower and get ready.

I'M LOOKING AT myself in the mirror, now thinking that I really wish I hadn't waited so long to get together with Phillip. Aside from all the fun we might have missed out on, I think about *how many days* I could have looked like *this*!

I mean, I look beautiful.

Incredible.

And I *never* look this way. Kind of cute maybe but not this!

Whatever *this* is, if I could bottle it and sell it, I would be very, very rich.

Quite frankly, I don't know how I'm going to get through the party today. I feel like people are going to take one look at me and know. There's a permanent grin on my face, my knees are weak, and my eyes are smoldering, like there's a fire in them that can't quite get put out.

I might as well be wearing a flashing neon sign. *I slept with Phillip!* Flash. *I slept with Phillip!* Flash.

I don't think anyone will be able to miss it.

And I'm worried about this because I really don't want people to know yet. I don't need any coaching or advice or pressure.

I want to savor this.

Oh. And I have a *big* confession to make.

I think I might have found my prince.

I always knew I would, and I know, *technically*, he's not a prince, but I don't think you necessarily have to be royal to be a prince.

I mean, he acts like a prince, and he treats me like a princess.

He always has. What more could a girl ask for?

I'm half-tempted to look at the sky and yell up to my parents, *I told you so!*

But then I remember they always hoped I would marry Phillip, so I guess we're even.

I can't believe that I'm actually *thinking* about marrying him.

It is *way* too soon to have thoughts like this.

PHILLIP GETS BACK with the beer, and I don't get to attack him again because people have started showing up early.

Damn them!

What? I missed him.

And, surprisingly, no one notices my neon sign.

This is amazing to me because, every time I look at Phillip, I swear, it flashes all the dirty little thoughts I'm having about him.

I have fun catching up with Katie and her husband, Eric. They just bought a new house and are all excited about it. Lisa brought her new boyfriend, Parker. I like him a lot, and they seem really good together. Other than her big crush on Danny, she hasn't always had the best taste in men.

I'm happy for her.

Heck, I'm happy for everyone today.

I can't seem to wipe the happy off of my face.

Brandon, Joey, and Neil are here, too, and a bunch of other old friends.

I get the big spread of food out onto the kitchen island. While I'm doing that, I can't help but watch Phillip. He's talking and laughing. He's got such an easy way about him. He makes everyone feel comfortable and welcome, and he's so sweet and so handsome and so … everything I need.

PRETTY SOON, THE game gets started.

After getting everyone else situated, I realize that there is nowhere left to sit, except on the floor. So, I get brave and plop down across Phillip's lap. He's sitting in a big, cushy chair, and I sit across the arms in the opposite direction. I figure this move will surely blow our cover, but no one seems to think it is all that unusual.

I am really *worried* about my friends.

They are not very perceptive people.

A LITTLE BEFORE halftime, I run to the garage to get more ice out of the dreaded freezer. As I come around the corner, I nearly collide with Phillip, whose hands are filled with bottles of beer. He sets the beer down, grabs me around the waist, and kisses me wildly.

"Do you know how *badly* I've been wanting to do that?" he asks when he finally stops kissing me.

"Yeah, I think I do."

He caresses my cheek and declares, "I love you."

Those three little words wake up my previously dormant brain.

"Phillip, don't say that. Okay?"

"Why not? I mean it."

"Phillip, I know you love me. I love you, too, but do me a favor." He starts to roll his eyes at me, but I give him a stern look and say, "This is important to me. Please don't tell me that you love me until you've spent some time with me, and we have a better idea of whether this will all work out."

A flash of irritation crosses his face. He thinks I'm looking for a way out, but I am *so* not.

"Look, I just want you to wait until you can honestly tell me that you're *in* love with me. And I'm not talking friend love either." Then, the chicken inside of me goes out onto a big and scary limb. I bite my lip and say, "I'm talking *real* love, like the *forever* kind."

He smiles at me and kisses me again very sweetly. "I can live with that. Mostly because it means you're serious about this, about us." He kisses the tip of my nose. "It also tells me you're actually thinking about forever with me. I really like the way that sounds."

"We should probably get back in there," I tell him, but he ignores that.

"So, you were *desperate* to be with me last night, huh?" he teases and then flips my hair behind my shoulder and kisses my exposed neck.

He's never gonna let me live this down.

"Yeah, I was prepared to beg," I say flatly, trying to keep my cool. But what I really want to do is kick everyone out of the house, drag him upstairs, and see if I can make *him* desperate.

"You know, I think I *definitely* heard some begging last night." He gives me a huge grin.

I laugh at that because I know *exactly* what he is referring to.

And, uh, I *was* begging.

He's got his hands up the back of my shirt, and I swear, my skin is practically sizzling. I'm tempted to look over my shoulder to see if there is smoke, but instead, I come back with, "Oh, really? Well, what I want to know is, when did you get so religious? I haven't heard God's name spoken that many times in church."

We laugh at each other, and Phillip says, "You know, I keep wishing this game would just end so all these people would go home. I couldn't care less if they win or lose."

Phillip doesn't care if our team wins or loses?

Wow!

Now, that's saying something.

In fact, that might be the *best* compliment I've gotten in my entire life.

Are you still in bed?

SEPTEMBER 3RD

SUNDAY MORNING, PHILLIP and I are awoken around ten by my loudly ringing phone. Yeah, it's unusual for Phillip to sleep in, but I did keep him up late last night.

I grope around for the handset and can't find it, so I hit the speaker button on the base.

"Hello?" I say groggily.

"JADE!" Lori's screaming voice echoes into my room.

My God, she can't possibly know about Phillip and me already.

Can she?

"You don't sound awake. Are you still in bed?"

"Uh, yeah, but that's okay. What's up?"

"I AM *SOOOO* EXCITED! OH, I JUST CAN'T BELIEVE IT! YOU'RE. NEVER. GOING. TO. BELIEVE. IT!"

"Believe what?"

"I'M PREGNANT!"

"Oh, Lori, that is *so* awesome!" I look at Phillip, who just rolled over toward me when he heard the news. He has a great expression on his face, and I'm so excited that I start to say, "Phil—" Then, I stop quickly.

Because I am not in bed with Phillip right now as far as my

329

friends know.

"What did you say, Jade? Did you say—"

I interrupt her, "I said, that's awesome. *Phil*-ipping awesome."

"No, you didn't. You said Phil—oh my God! Is *Phillip* there? Am I on speakerphone? Phillip, if you're there, you'd better answer me."

I shake my head at Phillip, but he doesn't do as I said.

Sure, *now*, he's a rebel.

"Yeah, I'm here, Lori," Phillip confesses. "Congratulations. This is so great. I bet Danny is just ecstatic."

"Um, well, he doesn't exactly know yet."

"He doesn't?" I ask, surprised.

"No!" she says and starts talking very fast. "I know I should have told him first, but after he left for the game this morning, I was getting ready and realized it'd been a long time since I had my period, and I looked at the date and saw I was, like, *two weeks late*! I'd been so busy trying to get this house all painted and decorated that I hadn't even noticed. So, I ran to the drugstore and bought a home pregnancy test. I was standing here alone when it said *Pregnant*, and I just *had* to tell someone! And I didn't want to call Danny right before his game and just tell him on the phone, like I was asking him about the traffic or something. I mean, I want to do something *special*." She pauses for a moment. "*Hey, wait a minute! Did you say you were still in bed?*"

I am so busted.

"Uh, yeah," I admit sheepishly.

"*Finally!* It's about time! Phillip, how did you talk her into it? I told you it would work out. She is just so stubborn."

"Hey! You're on speakerphone. I can hear you."

Phillip kisses me and says teasingly, "I didn't have to do anything, Lori. She just couldn't resist me any longer and begged for me."

Uh, that's not exactly right.

So, I stand up for myself and say, "I probably shouldn't bring this up now that you're pregnant and stuck with him, but you should know that your *wonderful* husband is a manipulative liar."

An evil laugh fills my room. "You mean, the little Monica *exaggeration*? Oh, Jadyn, honey, that was all me."

Phillip laughs. He thinks this is just hysterical.

I shake my head. "So, you're both liars. It's no wonder you're perfect for each other."

I see I'm not going to win this one. It's a rare thing, but I know when I'm beat.

I give up.

Where's the white flag?

Lori sighs peacefully. "This is almost the perfect day. I'm pregnant. You guys are together. Now, if Mark Conway could just get bonked on the head again, Danny could—oh. My. Gosh. I can't even believe I just said that or even thought it! I'm so awful. That is just *awful!*"

She sounds like she's going to cry.

And then she does.

She's an emotional wreck. She's never like this.

"I would never want that to happen to anyone. Oh my God, what is wrong with me? Can hormones mess with your brain like this? Please forget I said that." She takes a big, loud breath. She is in control and businesslike again.

Man, pregnancy must be an emotional roller coaster ride because she has gone through, like, four moods in less than two minutes.

"Anyway, so does this mean, you two can share a room next Monday night after the game? That would be great because then I'd only have to get one guest room done. These construction workers are just moving so slow."

"Sure," I say, "and if we're not still together by then, Phillip will gladly sleep on the floor."

"You guys are going to watch the game today, aren't you?" she asks.

"Yeah, you know we wouldn't miss it. And you know Phillip; he always spoils me, so we're going to Hooters." I laugh.

Phillip grabs me because he thinks I am a naughty girl for saying that.

And, when he starts kissing my stomach, I have a hard time thinking, but I do hear Lori say, "Cool. Maybe you'll see me on TV. I'll wave to you. And when Danny calls to tell you the good news …"

"We'll act surprised," Phillip and I say at the same time.

PHILLIP AND I go to Hooters and get a table right in front of the big screen. We order a bucket of beers and drummies, hot and extra crispy.

I know most women hate Hooters, but they really do have good wings.

The team isn't playing very well even though they have most of their starting players in for this last preseason game.

About three minutes into the second quarter, the defense intercepts a pass, and the offense rushes back out onto the field. On the first down, the play gets totally blown up, and the quarterback, Mark Conway, gets sacked.

He goes down hard.

And he doesn't get up.

Lori must be going crazy. She'll be convinced that she somehow caused this.

While the trainers are out on the field, the camera shows Danny warming up on the sideline. They go back to the picture of the quarterback on the field. He tries to sit up, looks like he doesn't know where he is, and is laid back down.

The game announcers say it looks like he got his bell rung. Again.

Evidently, he has a history of concussions.

Danny runs out onto the field and stands with the rest of the team.

It takes a few minutes for the trainers to look at the quarterback and get him carted off the field.

During this time, the commentators talk about Danny's college career, and then they flash on Lori.

"His wife," they announce.

Lori waves.

At us, I know!

I stand up and wave back.

On TV, we see her grab a sign from a lady next to her, flip it over, and furiously write on it.

The commentator starts to say, "I wonder ..."

But, before he can finish, she holds up the sign. It says, **I'M PREGNANT!**

The announcers love this, and you can see that she is now up on the jumbo screen in the stadium.

The crowd is clapping and screaming.

The TV cameras flash back to Danny in the huddle, and we watch as one of the big linemen pats Danny on the back and points up to the screen. Danny looks up at it.

Unfortunately, we can't see the look on his face, but I just know he is smiling at that!

The ref blows the whistle, and play resumes. Danny claps his hands once, and everyone takes their formation. Danny immediately throws a beautiful, deep fifty-two-yard pass straight into the end zone.

Touchdown!

The crowd goes wild. So do Phillip and I and pretty much everyone in Hooters. All of a sudden, many Nebraska fans are now Kansas City fans.

Everyone loves a winner.

The defense is pumped and feeding off the noisy crowd, who feels hopeful again. They cause a fumble, and Danny is back on the field. He leads the team sixty yards straight down the field where the running back takes it in from the six-yard line.

The game is very exciting and ends with Danny brilliantly winning.

AFTER THE GAME, the media is all over him. They tell him what a great game he had and want him to speculate on whether *he* should be the starting quarterback.

Danny takes it all in stride and says very appropriately, "Mark Conway is our team's starting quarterback. He's our leader, and I just went out there today and tried my best to fill his shoes. I really have to give all the credit to the offensive line. They took care of me and made my job very easy. I had all day to throw the ball."

"So, how do you like KC so far?" a reporter asks.

"Well, I came here from Nebraska, home of the greatest fans in college football. So, I feel right at home here, in KC, home of the greatest fans in professional football."

What a suck-up, I think. Of course, I know he's serious.

Another reporter says, "And this is quite a day for you personally as well. Congratulations. So, what did you think when you saw your wife on the big screen?"

"Well, it certainly took my mind off how nervous I was," Danny replies simply.

Now, there's an understatement if I ever heard one.

So far, so good.

PHILLIP HAS BEEN staying at my house all week. We've been getting along very well and managed to fly under everyone's radar, except for Danny, Lori, and Phillip's parents. I mean, I've always been comfortable around him, but Danny's right. This way has many benefits, and I am really liking them. Phillip has been good and hasn't told me he loves me, and I haven't been letting my mind screw things up.

So far, so good.

We're sitting on the floor in front of the TV on Wednesday night when Phillip says, "Princess, let's go on a *real* date this Saturday. You free?"

"I don't know," I say, but then he grabs me and tickles, so I scream, "Yes! Yes! I'm free!" When he finally lets me up from tickling and kissing me, I say, "So, where are you taking me?"

"Somewhere nice," he says, not really answering. "Well, a little nicer than Hooters anyway."

"Phillip," I whine.

But he just sits there with his arms crossed in front of him.

"Fine. No more kisses for you until you tell me."

"Oh, okay. I thought The View Room. So, do I get a kiss now?"

The View Room is our city's nicest and most romantic restaurant. It sits at the top of a local hotel and overlooks Omaha and the Missouri River, which, from that far up, actually looks pretty instead of yucky and muddy.

"Yes, that sounds perfect," I say and kiss him, "and romantic."

"That's kind of the idea."

WHEN I WAKE up on Saturday morning, Phillip's not in bed, but there's a little note lying on my nightstand that says, *Be here at 5:00. Can't wait!*

There's a little heart drawn above where he signed his name.

I should mention that I'm very proud of the fact that I don't freak out and try to analyze or interpret all the possible meanings of the heart.

Because it just doesn't matter.

My first date with phillip.

SEPTEMBER 9TH

I LIE IN bed, staring at Phillip's note. It makes my heart feel warm. I close my eyes and relive our week together. I've had such a wonderful time with him. I really could picture myself marrying him. And, evidently, the chicken in me has flown the coop because it's not even that scary of a thought anymore. I probably should get up. I think I'll pamper myself and spend most of the day getting ready. I really want to look great tonight. So, I get up, have a bowl of Frosted Flakes, and decide to start by giving myself a pedicure.

I'm digging through my bathroom closet for pedicure supplies when my doorbell rings.

I run to the door and look out the window. I see a huge bouquet of roses with two legs. I open the door, and the deliveryman, who does have more to his body than just two legs, hands me a massive bouquet.

Wow!

There are three—yes, three—dozen beautiful, long-stemmed red roses in a huge vase.

I just stand there for a minute and breathe them in. They smell wonderful!

Gosh, I wonder who they're from.

Actually, I'm just teasing. I have a pretty good idea who they're from.

Phillip.

Wow! He's really getting into this whole first-date thing.

I mean, no one ever sends flowers like this before a first date. But I guess this isn't your typical first date. I mean, we have had an amazing week together.

And rarely do you get them after the first date because the guy would be all afraid to look like he was crazy about you even if he was.

Guys would think that wasn't cool.

But Phillip knows I love flowers, and knowing him, he probably knows exactly how many times and from whom I have gotten flowers in the past. My record is two-dozen pink roses from Jason O'Connor. Jason was from a very wealthy family, so Phillip irritatingly called him Richie Rich. Jason was adorable, but he could be a bit arrogant and tended to drink a lot. Bad combination. He got wasted at my winter formal, got mouthy, and started a fight. I'd had enough, so I left him at the dance. The next day, he sent me the flowers as an apology. I accepted the roses but not his apology. One of the few times I have actually followed Phillip's advice on boys.

So, Phillip knows that three-dozen roses is by far the biggest arrangement I have ever received—or practically seen, for that matter.

I'm just ready to close my door and go into the house when Phillip's sister, Ashley, comes walking up the sidewalk. I can just see her through some of the stems.

"Hey, JJ. Wow, those flowers are gorgeous! Are they from *anyone* I might know?"

"Well, I don't know. I have so many men in my life these days."

Actually, that's how it used to be. I always had lots of boys around, and I liked it because it meant I didn't have to get serious with any of them. And, in retrospect, I probably didn't get serious with anyone because I'd always had Phillip.

I'm happy to say that, for one whole week, there has been only one man in my life.

And has he been *in* my life. I can't seem to get rid of him.

He wants to be with me every second.

And guess what.

That's not even bugging me yet! So, things are going really well!

"What are you doing here?"

"I came to pick you up."

"Oh, I'm sorry, Ash, but I'm already sort of spoken for."

"Very funny." She rolls her eyes at me.

I walk back inside and put the gorgeous bouquet on my kitchen table. It dwarfs it. This flower arrangement is so big; it looks like it should be in the lobby of a Vegas casino. Oh, I don't mean that they are tacky or gaudy in any way. It's just so very large!

"So," Ashley says, "big first date tonight, huh?" She frowns at me. "Hmm. You don't look like you're ready."

"Uh, no, I'm not since the date doesn't start for, like, seven hours. I kinda thought I'd pace myself, Ash, but I was just getting ready to paint my toenails."

"Not anymore. We are going to get you beautiful."

Like I'm not already?

"We are?"

"Yes. I'm taking you to Bloom Beautiful Spa, that new place."

"Wow! I've heard that place is incredible."

"It is, and I don't want to be late, so we have to leave. Now!"

Ashley is still very bossy. I'm glad she's married because, now, she has someone else to boss around.

BLOOM IS A great place. I love it!

Ashley and I are immediately treated to a glass of wine. When I question her about drinking wine at ten o'clock in the morning, she just raises her glass to me, takes a drink, and says, "Hey, it's five o'clock somewhere."

We sit and relax for a bit. Ashley is babbling on about something, but I'm kinda tuning her out because my mind is on Phillip.

I thought it was pretty cool that he left me a sweet note this morning, but then, wow, the flowers were amazing.

And, now, the spa?

I've known Phillip for a long time, and he has only sent flowers to a girl twice—once being Valentine's Day and the other ... I forget really why, but they were both *way* back in high school.

Really, that seems a bit odd to me now that I think about it because Phillip has had quite a few girlfriends.

They just never seemed to last.

I wonder if that was my fault.

And, if it was, I'm glad.

Sorry, but I am.

Phillip has always given me flowers on Valentine's Day. They were not, like, delivered or anything, but he would usually stop at the grocery store and buy me a sweet little bouquet.

I used to tease him, telling him that he must have a secret crush on me, and he would jokingly tell me that he only did it because he was afraid I wouldn't get anything from a real guy, and then I'd be horrible to live with. He has always been so sweet to me. I seriously do not know why I never hooked up with him before this.

Maybe I knew deep down that he was worth more than that.

The other night, I asked him why he never tried anything with me, and he said he was waiting for me to make a move.

I was like, "So, you really didn't want to?"

And he was like, "No, I just—I don't know. It just never felt like the right time, and I didn't want to be like all the other random guys."

And I was like, "Chicken."

And then he attacked me.

Mmm.

I hear my name being called, and it breaks my daydream.

I stand up and ask Ashley, "Hey, did Phillip plan all the spa stuff, too?"

She just smiles that sneaky smile of hers. She loves knowing stuff that you don't know.

My first treatment is a gingerbread body scrub. After nearly an hour of having my body scrubbed and massaged, I'm feeling amazing. I go back to the relaxation area, curl up on a chaise, and read the latest *Cosmo*.

Well, I am specifically reading an article about how to please my man, which I am hoping could be, um, useful tonight.

Ashley comes out of her treatment room and says, "Isn't this place just heavenly?"

She looks all limp, like they poured her out of the room, and she is practically drooling. I think she is really enjoying herself.

My name is called again, this time for a pumpkin enzyme facial. Afterward, my skin feels so smooth, and I must say, I smell incredible.

Seriously, Phillip will not be able to resist me tonight. I smell like pumpkin bread and gingerbread cookies, which are two of his very favorites!

We are served a wonderful, yummy lunch and more wine. I'm really quite relaxed, which is probably a good thing because, if I wasn't, I might be thinking about tonight, about Phillip, about our future, if we have a future—all that scary stuff.

And, all of a sudden, I am really, surprisingly nervous for our date.

I know that sounds silly, having known Phillip forever, but I want it to go well.

It needs to go well.

I think that, in my mind, I have always thought Phillip kind of crushed on me, and I've always felt sort of in control of our friendship, but now … I'm thinking that I did my fair share of crushing as well, and, well, I really think I love that boy.

I mean, I think.

I'm pretty positive—well, practically, completely, mostly positive—and I really want to make a good impression.

Like a knock-his-socks-off impression.

Next up is a side-by-side pedicure with Ash. Ashley and I have fun during the pedicure. We talk and laugh about all the stupid stuff we did as kids and how Phillip and Danny used to be scrawny little things. And how that has *really* changed. I mean, they are both very hot and very not scrawny.

After a blissful pedicure, I have sparkly, bright red toenails. What is it about painted toenails that make you feel so sexy?

Next, we get our nails done. French manicure for me and bright fuchsia for Ashley.

"OKAY, TIME FOR hair and makeup," she says, floating down the hall in front of me.

She leads me to Rico's styling chair. Ashley and Rico start discussing my hair, like I'm invisible and I have no say in the matter.

Ashley is telling him, "This is a very special occasion. I really think it needs to go in a pretty updo."

And I'm thinking, *Very special occasion?*

Kind of special?

Sure.

Special?

Yeah.

Very special?

I don't know.

It's not like it's prom. I mean, yes, I want to make a good impression and look amazing, but it's still *just* a first date!

Rico says, "No, I do some-zhing differ-int."

Different? Now, that worries me.

I could end up with purple hair or something. Plus, from personal experience, I have learned updos don't stay up so good if the guy you're with likes to play with your hair. And Phillip is *always* messing with my hair. I have to admit that I love it. Honestly, I love pretty much everything that boy does to me.

So, I take control and say, "You know, Phillip always sees me in a ponytail, so I definitely want my hair down. Maybe you could do some of those sexy waves all the stars are wearing these days?"

Rico considers my request by running his fingers through my hair. "Ch-es, I zink wee could do zhat. Perfecto."

TWO HOURS LATER, my body has had about all the relaxation and primping it can take. Aside from my sexy toes, pretty nails, and tasty body, I'm sporting long, sexy waves and a face full of artfully applied makeup.

I look and feel great.

"Almost perfect," Ashley says, appraising me in the mirror.

"Almost?"

What else could there be?

"Well, you can't wear sweats there, can you?" Ashley snips in her sassy way.

ASHLEY DRIVES ME back home and lugs a beautifully wrapped box and a gift bag into my house.

"I have a couple of presents for you," she teases. She knows I love presents. "But, first, champagne."

She pulls a bottle out of the bag and opens it without getting it all over. That's a talent I didn't know she had, and I'm impressed because I always seem to make a big mess with champagne. I get a couple of flutes from the kitchen and hand them to her.

"Sit down." She pours champagne into our glasses and dramatically raises her glass into the air, like she's in front of an audience and not just me. "I propose a toast. To one of my best friends, someone who is like a sister to me. I hope that, someday, my brother will get off his ass and make us sisters for real."

I hesitate on that toast.

"Drink," she bosses.

When the queen says drink, we drink.

"Ash, that's very nice, but don't you think you're jumping the gun a little?"

"No, I don't. And we're going to toast again. This time to the fact that, with this date, you are headed down the road to becoming my sister."

"Ashley, I can't drink to that."

I mean, I seriously hope that's the road I'm heading down, but she doesn't need to know that.

She gets testy with me and says, "Well, what *will* you drink to then?"

"Gosh, I can drink to the fact that I am indeed on a road."

She grins at me.

I shake my head and say, "This road is long and windy and could have many forks in it as well, and it is a possibility, albeit a small one, that one of those paths could *possibly*, eventually lead to marriage someday."

She drinks to this.

I swear, I'm going to be drunk before my date.

A horn honks outside.

"Crap. So soon? It's only four thirty. He is not supposed to be here until five. We're not even ready yet," she mutters as she heads toward the door. "I hate being rushed."

"Uh, Ashley, it's ten till five. Is Phillip out there? I mean, it's okay with me if—"

"No, he's not out there," she says, quickly interrupting me, "but the limo is."

I watch Ashley run out my front door and think, *A limo?*

Ashley comes flying back in the house. "I told him we needed a few more minutes."

"Oh! I've got to get dressed, Ash. Come help me decide which dress to wear. I have four different ones, but I just don't know who I want to be tonight."

"*Who* you want to be?" She laughs at me like I'm nuts. "What do you mean?"

"Well, come in my room, and you'll see."

Ashley sits on my bed, watching me.

I'm cheap entertainment, I think.

I pull the first dress out of my closet. "Okay, so this dress is kind of *sexy, wild me*," I say, holding up a slinky red wrap dress. I put it down on the bed and grab another one. "This one is more *conservative me.*" I hold a little black dress in front of me and then place it on the bed. "This third one"—a flowing fuchsia-and-gold paisley dress with a scalloped hem—"is *creative, kind of artsy me.* And the last one"—a simple cream silk dress—"is *demure, innocent me.*"

I still have no idea who I should be. Really none of them seem quite right, and that's not the way it's supposed to be because I look great, and, you know, I feel complete.

And then I start to panic a little.

"Ashley, what does Phillip like? Who should I be?"

"JJ, don't freak. He likes you. *All of you*," she says, rolling her eyes at me and apparently insinuating I have multiple personalities.

She runs in the kitchen, grabs the big box, and sets it on my bed. "Why don't you open this and see if it'll solve your problem?"

So, I open it.

And I think she is very right.

Problem solved.

Nestled in the box is the most beautiful dress I have ever seen. It's made of stretchy ivory lace, lined with a golden-colored silk.

It's the kind of dress in which, from a distance, you look naked underneath the lace.

I know this because a girl from my sorority had a top made this way, and when we walked in the bar, the boys practically went crazy and couldn't get over there fast enough to see her up close.

They really thought her shirt was see-through.

Needless to say, they were disappointed.

Scattered on the ivory lace are millions of little iridescent ivory sequins, which I see now that I get it out of the box are not ivory but more golden, almost the exact color of my hair. The sequins shimmer when I move the dress.

The cut of the dress is, well, pretty damn sexy, and it isn't even on my body yet! The top part of it is a halter. It's cut low in the front, and the skirt is straight and short.

I can't wait to try this thing on. *I sure hope it fits!*

I put the dress on, and it fits like a glove. The neckline plunges down and shows off my, um, assets, and the skirt makes me look skinny. I love it! I grab the satin and rhinestone sandals I wore to Danny and Lori's wedding and put them on.

Ashley and I look at my reflection in the mirror.

"Now, you look perfect!" Ashley beams.

And that is a really good thing because Ashley is not a very complimentary person. I mean, she doesn't give out many compliments. So, I must look good.

Very good.

I look at myself in the mirror. One more time!

It's amazing! This dress is perfect. It's sexy, demure, wild, and creative, all at the same time.

Just like me.

Phillip will love it.

"Where did you get this dress?" I gush.

"I didn't get it. Phillip did."

"Seriously?"

"Yeah, believe it or not, he did. My brother, the guy who bought me Scooby-Doo slippers last Christmas, bought *this amazing dress*. I didn't think he had it in him. Evidently, he saw it a few weeks ago when he was in Kansas City, visiting Danny and Lori. He had Lori go back to the store and buy it."

He did?

Wow!

I should take him shopping with me more often. I didn't know he could find such great stuff.

ASHLEY HANDS ME my glass.

Another toast, God forbid.

Then, she gives me another gift. "Hurry, open this."

She is getting awfully bossy now, but I know she can't really help herself because that trait definitely runs in the family.

I open the package, and inside is a silver link bracelet.

"It's beautiful," I say as I start to put it on.

"Wait," she says and hands me a smaller box.

I open the little box, and inside is a charm. It's a rose.

"Here, let me put it on for you," she says, snatching them out of my hands.

I just stand and watch. She gets the bracelet and the charm the way she wants it and puts it on my wrist.

"All right, the limo is waiting for you. You'd better get out there." She looks at me like she's never going to see me again. She is really acting weird.

"Thanks, Ash, for everything," I say as I give her a hug.

Then, she gets all teary-eyed.

What's going on with her?

I'd blame it on PMS, but I hate when I have important feelings that are glossed over as PMS. So, I won't.

"Um, isn't Phillip going to come get me at the door? I mean, the flowers, the dress, the champagne, the bracelet, and he isn't even going to walk up to the door and get me? What, is he just going to honk and wait in the car? Jake used to do that. It drove my dad and Phillip nuts. They said it meant he didn't respect me."

Obviously, they were right.

As if on cue, the limo honks.

"I told you. Phillip isn't in the limo, JJ. He's meeting you ... um, somewhere ... else. You need to *go!*"

Okay! So, I'm going.

I take a deep breath, but then I stop quickly to smell my roses and realize that, in all the excitement, I haven't opened the card.

I open it quick.

The card has no signature. There is just a big heart drawn in the middle. I still have no idea what the heart means exactly, but it really makes me smile.

"JJ, stop stalling. You really have to go, or you will be late for ..."

"Late for what?" I ask, holding my heart card up to my chest.

"Um, for your dinner reservations," she tells me, but I get the feeling she's not being one hundred percent truthful.

not exactly

SEPTEMBER 9TH

"YEAH. WHATEVER," I say to myself as I walk to the limo.

The driver opens the door for me, and I ask where we're going, where we'll meet Phillip. The limo driver just shrugs and tells me to have a glass of champagne and enjoy the ride.

More champagne. Yikes.

The whole limo thing is really a surprise, and I must say, I like it! I know Phillip wants this date to be special and to make an impression.

Although, I have to say, he was pretty *impressive* last night, but I really probably shouldn't talk about that.

Where was I? Oh, yeah. Spa and flowers and jewelry.

Like lions and tigers and bears, oh my!

Sorry. You know, I often wonder what incredible things my mind could hold if it wasn't filled up with lines from every movie I have ever seen.

Anyway, wow!

He really has gone to an awful lot of trouble and expense for this. So, I fully intend to enjoy it and maybe try to *repay* him later.

I pour myself a flute of champagne, take a sip, lean back, and enjoy the ride. We head out of the city, eventually to the town, and then the neighborhood where we grew up. Before I know it, we are at our old grade school.

The limo driver stops the car, walks around to the other side, and opens my door.

He obviously expects me to get out.

So, I get out, look at him in confusion, and say, "Now what?"

"Walk back to the swings," he says after consulting a list from his pocket.

Remind me to get my hands on that list later.

I look down at my light dress and satin shoes, and then I look at him like, *Are you nuts, boy?*

He ignores my look, so I say, "Are you sure? I don't think I should go back there. My shoes will get dirty."

Actually, I kind of whine.

"You have to."

Oh, really? I think.

This is ridiculous. It makes no sense. *Why would Phillip get me all gorgeous, buy me a beautiful dress, and then send me out into the dirt?*

Then, it dawns on me *why* I'm here.

Our first kiss. Oh, that's so sweet.

He must be meeting me here.

I RUN DOWN the dirt path that curls around the building, not even worrying about my shoes. I expect to find Phillip waiting for me on the swings, but I am disappointed to see only a boy swinging. I walk over, sit down on the swing next to him, and sigh.

Hopefully, the swing doesn't get my dress dirty.

"Now what?" I mutter to myself.

To my surprise, the little boy stops swinging and says, "Here." He hands me a little wrapped package and runs away.

I look around in all directions, figuring Phillip is bound to turn up. But he doesn't, so I open the package. Inside is another charm—a swing. *How cute.*

I add it to the bracelet and figure, *What the heck?* I'm already sitting on it; swinging on it isn't going to get me any dirtier.

So, I start swinging, and pretty soon, I'm swinging as high as I can. I close my eyes and let my stomach go all fluttery. I'm really enjoying myself until I hear that damn limo driver honking his horn at me.

I've already had about enough of his rude honking.

Maybe I'll have a word with him when I get out there. But, as I walk back, I decide I look much too beautiful to get all pissed off, so I just get into the limo.

We don't go very far because our next stop is Phillip's house. Finally, I get to see my date. Unfortunately, when we pull in the driveway, I notice that Phillip's car isn't there.

Shoot.

THE NAZI LIMO driver comes around again, opens my door, and says, "Go inside."

Doesn't this man know that I hate being told what to do?

I swear, if I wasn't relying on him for my transportation, I would tell him to *knock it off!* I look straight at him and scream, *KNOCK IT OFF,* in my mind, and it makes me feel a little better.

I barely get to the front door when it swings open to reveal Phillip's parents.

"Oh, JJ!" Julie cries. "You look beautiful!"

I notice that she and Mr. Mac are very dressed up.

"Wow! You guys look great yourselves. Where are you going, all dressed up?"

"Oh, there's a fundraiser at the Piedmont tonight. We're just getting ready to head there," Doug tells me.

The Piedmont?

"Did you know Phillip and I are having dinner at that hotel?"

"Um, uh, no, we didn't. The View is a wonderful restaurant

though. I'm sure you'll have a great time, dear. This is for you," she says, thrusting a box into my hand and deftly changing the subject.

I open it and there—surprise, surprise—is another charm. This one is a heart with little red stones scattered around the edges.

"Thanks," I say.

Before I can hug her, Mr. Mac hands me another box. I open it. It's a red capital N—for Nebraska football.

"I love it," I say and give them both big hugs.

"Oh, JJ, I wish your mother were here to see you tonight," she gushes and looks like she's going to cry. "You look just perfect."

That's nice, but come on, people, it's a *first* date. We probably don't need to go getting all emotional just yet. I know Phillip is going to a lot of trouble, but, um, how 'bout we get past, like, the *second* date before we go getting all teary-eyed.

She gives me another hug just as the Nazi limo driver honks his horn again.

"That's my ride. And he's so polite. Um, do you guys know if I'm ever going to see my date? Did Phillip tell you where he's meeting me?"

"Oh, Doug, look at the time," Mrs. Mac says, glancing at her watch. "We've got to get going."

They hustle me out the front door and into the limo without answering my question.

I LEAN BACK in my seat, let out a big sigh, and decide to have some more champagne.

Is it just me, or are all the Mackenzies acting a little strange about this whole first-date thing?

Is something going on here?

I feel like I'm missing something. It's nowhere near my birthday. And it's not like they are coming on our date. *Surely,* he wouldn't have invited them. No, he said romantic. I must just be paranoid. They are simply excited that Phillip and I are finally together. And that's a nice thing. I wouldn't want to have in-laws who didn't like me.

God, there I go again. Actually thinking about marrying Phillip. Although I guess it's not that big of a deal. I remember, in high school, always trying on a boy's last name to see if it sounded okay. If it fit. Trying on a last name is very important because you wouldn't want to fall in love with some guy, only to find out that your name would end up being something weird or all rhymey like Mary Barry—or worse, something gross like Jenny Tayla or Amanda Lick.

Okay, so let's see. Just for fun.

Jadyn Reynolds-Mackenzie.

No. Too long.

JJ Mackenzie.

Jadyn James Mackenzie.

Not bad. Doable, I'd say.

All of a sudden, the driver stops the car. I look out to see that we are ... uh, where are we? I peer out the windows in all directions and determine that we are ... definitely in the middle of nowhere.

Like, all I can see is a gravel road and lots of corn.

Great. The limo driver is probably some psychotic serial killer, and now, he's brought me out here to finish me off. Just as I'm thinking about my options, he startles me by lowering the window separating us. It's been up the entire trip.

Crap.

My purse wasn't big enough for pepper spray. Now what?

I smile at him sort of nervously. He smiles back and hands me a little box.

I open it and see that it's a cross charm.

I look outside again and realize that this is probably the exact spot where Phillip pulled off the road and yelled at me before his dad called us on the night my parents died. Well, actually, I might have yelled at him.

Hmm.

Not a particularly happy memory, but a strong one nonetheless. And definitely a time in my life when Phillip was there for me. He was my rock. I don't think I could have gotten through it without him.

I feel the car go forward as the driver rolls the partition up.

Yippee. Maybe he's not going to kill me.

We drive for about half an hour. I can see that we are going back toward Omaha, and it even appears we are headed downtown.

Hopefully to the Piedmont and my date.

I look at my bracelet full of charms and think, *This is nice and all, but doesn't it seem like a bit much for a* first *date?*

Actually, it seems like a bit much for *any* date. Although I don't think I could even categorize this as a date yet. Because, technically, it takes two people to have a date, and I refuse to count the limo driver.

This has been more like a scavenger hunt.

Not exactly the romantic evening I had in mind.

Maybe this thing with Phillip isn't going to work out.

Where the *&%# is that boy?!

SEPTEMBER 9TH

THE LIMO DRIVER pulls up to the Piedmont. The Piedmont is the coolest hotel in town. It's in an old historic building that has been completely renovated. The doorman opens my door. I slide out and look around for Phillip.

I don't see him, so I walk inside. I've never gotten to stay at this hotel, but if the lobby is any indication, the rooms must be beautiful. The lobby has a huge, high, old-fashioned tin ceiling. There are marble columns and crown molding that must be at least two feet thick.

A bellman walks over to me and hands me a notecard.

What is this? And how the heck does he know who I am?

Just go with the flow, Jay, I tell myself, trying to stay calm.

I read the note. It says, *Take the elevator to the 16th floor.*

No signature. No heart.

I get on the elevator and see from the sign that the restaurant is on the sixteenth floor.

I am telling you, if Phillip isn't there, I'm done with this date because I'm sick and tired of being on it alone!

The elevator doors open to a dimly lit hall that leads into the restaurant.

Still, no Phillip.

Damn that boy!

Where is he?

I mean, I'm not complaining, but I have been on this whole scavenger-hunt/date-extravaganza thing for over two hours now, and I still haven't seen my date.

Okay, so maybe I'm complaining a bit, but I can't help it.

I want to *be* with him.

THE MAÎTRE D' is obviously expecting me because he says, "Miss Reynolds, please follow me," and leads me to a big, cozy leather-wrapped booth.

And guess what.

Phillip is actually here!

He sees me, gives me a big grin, and stands up. He sweetly kisses my cheek and then lets me slide into the booth before him.

Finally! Some manners! Much better than the horn-honking, bossy Nazi limo driver I have been spending my time with.

"You're late," he says.

I give him an angry look before he kisses me again.

He is teasing me, I think.

Phillip looks very handsome. He's got on a dark brown suit that matches his eyes. Under the suit, he's wearing a light-blue shirt and a really cool brown-blue-and-orange tie. And, I will admit, when I got here, I had my panties in a bit of a wad and was kinda irritated with Phillip. But, the minute I look at him, it all melts away. I'm pretty sure that means I do love him.

"You look incredible," he tells me.

And I'm pretty sure he means it because his eyes are just riveted on me.

It makes me feel both nervous and powerful at the same time.

I think I could get away with just about anything in this dress.

Hmm. Maybe I'll give it a try.

"Well," I tell him, shaking my head, "I have been having *quite* the date without you. How did you ever find a limo driver who was a former male dancer? *He was so cute.* It was like having my own mini bachelorette party before our date. It was really nice of you to let me get that out of my system before we got too serious. Thank you so much!" I say very sincerely and very much lying.

"The limo driver *danced* for you?" Phillip asks in disbelief.

For a second, I see a little jealousy cross that cute face of his.

"Isn't that why you hired him?" I ask innocently, trying to control my smile.

"*No,*" he says angrily, but then he sees my smirk, grabs me, kisses me again, and says, "You are so full of it. I can't believe I just fell for that."

I laugh.

It's good to know I can still get to him.

"Seriously though, I suppose I should thank you for the limo ride even though I didn't like that you weren't there. And let's see ... the incredible roses and the spa and the bracelet and the dress ..."

"I think the dress was for me," he interrupts. "You look ... beautiful, incredible, sexy ... *everything.*"

Phillip keeps beaming at me. This dress feels practically magical. It might very well be, based on the way he's looking at me.

It's like he's mesmerized, he's hypnotized ...

Hey, that reminds me of a movie line.

Oh! I know!

"Why, this car is automatic, it's systematic, it's hydroomatic."

My mom and I loved to watch *Grease.* My friends always thought Danny Zuko was so cute, but I preferred Kenickie, which isn't a big surprise now that I think about it. I mean, if Phillip had to play one of the T-Birds from *Grease,* he'd definitely play Kenickie. But *only* because of how he looks—as in hot—'cause, let's face it; Kenickie was kind of a jerk, and Phillip is so not.

The waiter comes over and pours us champagne, so I shove

the movie and Kenickie to the back of my mind.

"You know, Phillip, I really should eat something before I drink any more." I barely get the words out of my mouth when another waiter starts setting an array of appetizers on our table. Phillip has obviously planned out this portion of the date in detail as well.

I immediately dig in.

I mean, I do it gracefully.

"You know," I say between bites of crab cake, "your sister has us, like, practically married already. I thought we were going to try to keep this a secret."

"Did you really think Mom could keep this to herself? After the plotting the two of them have been doing? They're already congratulating themselves."

"I know. I just don't want them to get the wrong idea about us. I mean, it's been a week. We don't even know for sure what's going on yet."

"We don't?"

"Well, I mean, we're having great fun and all, but …"

"Here," he says, interrupting me *again* and handing me another little box.

Another charm. Fabulous. Can't wait to open it.

I'm sorry, but I've had about enough of these little things.

But, still, I try to look surprised and pleased as I open the box.

Oh crap. Now, I feel bad for thinking that.

I really do love this charm. In fact, it's my favorite. It's a little princess crown with pink jewels on the tips of the crown's points.

Phillip raises his champagne glass in a toast. "This charm is my way of promising to always treat you like a princess."

Okay, so the princess crown and what he said make me melt a little, but come on!

I have about had it with all the romance.

This is *so not Phillip!* He's a take-me-to-Hooters, watch-football, play-darts, go-jogging-with kind of guy. Not this mushy sap.

What has happened to him?

So, being the blunt girl that I am, I say, "Okay, Phillip, what gives? What's with all this romance stuff? I've had almost as much as I can take. This is so not you."

He smiles sweetly. "Well, I just wanted tonight to be a night that you would never forget. I wanted it to be very special."

Very special? There are those pesky words again.

"Have your previous boyfriends ever done anything like this?"

"I think you already know the answer to that, Phillip"—I roll my eyes at him—"and, *no*, they have not."

So, I add the charm to my bracelet and eat another crab cake.

The waiter comes over.

Yay! He's here to take my order, and I'm starved. Okay, I'm thinking a big steak, some garlic mashed potatoes … but then I notice he doesn't have his little pad out.

Instead, he sets another box on the table in front of me.

I think I'm on present overload. Can't I just play with what I already have?

But I want to please Phillip, so I smile at him and start to untie the bow on the box. At first, I think this is another charm, but I realize this box is bigger than the others.

Charm earrings perhaps?

"Wait," Phillip says.

He grabs both of my hands in his and looks into my eyes. "First, I want to tell you that I love you, that I'm in love with you. I know you wanted me to be serious when I said it, and I am. Princess, I have loved you for as long as I can remember."

I smile at him, and I know he's serious. I feel the same way.

Then, he slides out of the booth, walks over to my side, kneels down on one knee in front of me, takes my hand in his, and says, "Will you marry me?"

"Wait! What? What was that last part? I thought you said—"

Phillip doesn't respond to my question or my shocked look. Instead, he slides back into the booth next to me, unties the ribbon on the box, and opens the lid.

And what's inside is *definitely* not charm earrings.

What's inside is a ring.

An engagement ring!

Absolutely. The. Most. Beautiful. Engagement. Ring. I. Have. Ever. Seen.

Yet it looks strangely familiar to me.

But why?

I've never seen a ring like this. It's so beautiful!

I look at Phillip, and then it hits me. "Oh my God, this is the ring I sketched."

I am stunned.

I look at him, flabbergasted. That's a very weird word, but no other word can accurately describe the way I must look.

Phillip smiles and pulls a little folded-up piece of paper from the top of the box and hands it to me.

"No way," I mutter and shake my head.

I unfold it, and there is my drawing.

He kept it.

Has he always known?

I mean, did he keep it because he knew months ago that he wanted to marry me?

I look at the ring again. A gorgeous two-carat emerald cut diamond in a platinum setting with baguette diamonds on the crisscrossed sides.

I am staring at perfection.

This ring belongs on my finger.

I am dazed.

"So, will you marry me?" Phillip says, jolting me back to reality.

"Phillip ... no. I can't marry you. We're on our first date. What am I going to tell everyone? *I know you didn't even know we were dating, but on our first date, we got engaged.* It's like the time in my sorority when one of the girls passed her candle and when she blew it out, we were all like, *Which one is she marrying?* Because she was dating, like, two different guys. I don't want to be that girl, Phillip. Everyone will think we're nuts."

I pause for a minute. "You can't get engaged on your first date." I put my hand on his cheek, kiss him, look into his eyes, and say sincerely, "I'm not saying I don't want to marry you. I mean, that possibility seems very intriguing to me, but don't you think we should see if we can make it past, I don't know, maybe the third date or something?"

Phillip sits there very calmly. He's known me long enough to know that this is not necessarily my final answer, that I'm working things out in my mind by saying them. I tend to speak what my mind is thinking.

It does get me in trouble sometimes. But I'm done talking. This is ridiculous. I said no. What more is there?

Phillip leans over and whispers in my ear. He reminds me of something that happened so long ago that I completely forgot it.

And then, well, all of a sudden, everything makes perfect sense.

Hmm.

"So, let me ask again," Phillip says patiently. "Will you marry me, Princess?"

I smile and say, "Yes!" as he slips the ring on my finger.

Apparently, you *can* get engaged on your first date.

And, you know, it's not like we have to tell anyone right away. Right?

"So, can we kind of keep this our little secret?" I ask Phillip. "Like, we'll start letting people know we're dating, and then, maybe in a few months, we can announce the whole engagement thing?"

"Uh … sure," Phillip responds.

That should work out just fine, I think.

"So, can we order now?"

"Um, well, we need to run downstairs real quick first."

I give him my dejected look.

He sighs big at me and gives me an *is your stomach all you ever think about* look. "Just quick and then we'll eat, I promise."

He drags me out of the booth and down to the mezzanine level.

Now, normally, I would ask a million questions about where we are going that's so freaking important and why we can't at least eat first—stuff like that.

But what can I say?

I'm still a bit dazed by the ring, but I'm also seriously dazed by, well, everything!

All of it! The roses, the dress, the spa, the limo, the charms, the ring. He really put a lot of thought into this. And I'm starting to grasp the fact that he's loved me for a long time.

Why didn't I ever see that?

Maybe *I'm the one* who's not so perceptive.

Phillip leads me into a ballroom.

There are people mingling and talking and a band that looks like it's getting ready to start playing.

"This is the fundraiser my parents are at," Phillip tells me while scanning the room.

So much for not telling anyone. I'll have to stress that this is just between us and that we will tell people in our own sweet time.

As I look for his parents in the crowd, I'm surprised to see a few people I know. Like, a couple of the girls from Phillip's office.

Hmm, maybe this is a fundraiser that Mr. Mac's company is hosting or something.

But then, over in the corner, I spot our friends Brandon and

Neil.

Wait a minute.

"Hey, Phillip, Brandon and Neil are over there. Why are they at this party?"

He ignores my question and points. "Hey, there's Mom and Dad."

But, when I see Katie and Eric, I know something is going on.

Why are all these people I know at this fundraiser?

Katie is not the fundraiser type.

And what is it raising funds for anyway?

Why isn't there a sign?

Finally, I say, "Phillip, what is going on here?"

He looks at me with a huge grin, holds up his hands, and happily says, "*Surprise!* This is our engagement party."

I blink hard.

What? You've got to be kidding me.

This is keeping things quiet?

I stand there and stare at him, dumbfounded. I'm sure my mouth is hanging wide open. *The boy is nuts.*

"Excuse me? You were so confident that I would agree to marry you on our first date that you planned a surprise engagement party?"

"Well, not just me." He grins proudly as he takes my hand. "My family helped a ton, and Danny and Lori, too." He is so excited about this.

Who is this man?

He has taken on some alter ego, and I don't like it one bit!

Phillip quickly kisses me and says, "Let's go up on stage, thank everyone for coming, and tell them it's official! Now, we can party!"

I look at the stranger standing in front of me and pull my hand out of his with as much force as I can muster.

"You arrogant son of a bitch," I say. Well, maybe I growl it.

It's hard to say for certain.

But I can tell you this. I am fuming, smoke-flying-out-of-my-ears mad as I take the engagement ring off my finger, shove it into Phillip's hand, and march toward the stage. The march to the stage feels like it takes forever because there are a million thoughts running through my mind.

Did all these people come here because they really thought I'd say yes?

Or did they come for the fireworks of me saying no?

Do they wish us well?

Or hope to see us fail?

I reach the stage and tentatively walk out on it. One of the band members hands me a microphone, and I know I really need to say something to all these people.

"Phillip and JJ sitting in a tree, K-I-S-S-I-N-G ... "

Great! Now, I'm having flashbacks to when I was ten.

As I survey the crowd, I see many of the friends who tortured me with those songs, except they're all grown up now. Well, *sort of grown up*. I half-expect them to break out in song.

Unfortunately, they are just standing there, staring at me.

I might die of embarrassment.

Actually, I wish it *were* possible to die of embarrassment. Then, I could drop dead, and I wouldn't have to do what I am about to do.

Part of me wonders how in the world I got here to begin with. Phillip and I have been friends for a really long time and only decided to have a real relationship, as opposed to the totally platonic one we'd always had, all of *a week ago*.

And, well, it has been really incredible.

I mean, Phillip is *incredible* in ways I didn't even imagine!

Okay, so I might have imagined a little.

Anyway, as of about six minutes ago, we were out on a romantic first date.

Then, he had to go and blow the whole thing all to hell by asking me to marry him.

Can you believe that?

Me neither.

And, as if it wasn't unbelievable enough that he asked me to marry him on our first date, he was so *damn* sure I'd say yes that he planned this huge *surprise* engagement party.

Tonight. On our first date. Like, right now!

On stage, I shudder and mentally prepare myself. I have to tell everyone who came here tonight that there is *no way* I'm going to marry that boy!

I put the microphone up to my mouth and say, "Well, it took me a little while, but I *finally* figured out this *isn't* a fundraiser."

Laughter, all around me.

"Now, I know you all came here tonight, expecting to surprise me with an engagement party." I pause for a minute. "Well, at least you got the *surprise* part right." I chuckle.

Oh, I'm failing miserably up here. Just do it, JJ. Get it over with.

"Actually, Phillip did ask me to marry him tonight. And I have to tell you all that, well, I said NO."

The crowd sighs. I glance over at Phillip's mom. She looks like she's going to faint, but I continue. I'm in too deep to stop now.

"I told him that it's crazy. That this is our first real date, and, God, *what would people think?*"

I try not to look at Phillip, but I do. He's standing very still, staring at my perfect ring, probably wondering how his magical plan went so astray.

But I go on, "So, he told me that he loves me, that he has always loved me, and *who cares* what people think anyway? But I'm thinking, *I do.* So, I say NO again."

The crowd goes, "Aah," and then is silent.

What am I doing? If I say no tonight, will Phillip still date me, or will he give up on me forever? And what in the world would I do without him?

Just as my life about blows up in my face, I spot Danny and Lori in the crowd, and something very important clicks in the back of my mind. I flashback to the conversation Phillip and I had after their engagement.

He asked me if I'd ever want to be surprised in front of a whole bunch of people.

Didn't he?

And I told him yes.

Didn't I?

Because I thought it would be so cool to know a guy had planned all of it for me.

My God, I asked for this!

He did it all for me.

All of it.

The spa, the dress, the limo, the charms, the ring, the party. He did it because it's what he thought I wanted.

I look at Phillip again and melt. He's still my Phillip, my handsome prince. He still loves football and cars and darts and, well, *me.*

So, I decide.

For good this time.

What's my mantra?

Say it with me now!

What the hell?

I continue speaking to the crowd, "But then Phillip reminded me of something that happened so long ago that I had completely forgotten it."

I start to get tears in my eyes.

"He reminded me of when we were ten, and he gave me my first kiss. We were on the swings out behind school, and right after he kissed me, he got up and ran away. Then, all of a sudden, he stopped, turned around, and yelled back, 'Will you marry me someday?'" I smile big at everyone as I remember this, and tears start streaming down my face.

"And I yelled back to him, 'YES!' And so he said that, if people asked, I could tell them that we'd been secretly engaged for the past twelve years. *And so*"—I close my eyes for a second and think, *Here goes nothing.* I open them and look straight at Phillip—"you will probably all think I am *very* crazy, but I *had* to say YES again tonight!"

Everyone screams and laughs and claps.

Phillip looks up at me, smiles a huge smile, runs, and leaps up onto the stage with me. I wrap my arms around his neck and give him a really big kiss because I know in my heart that I've just made the very best decision of my entire life.

Phillip grabs my left hand and holds it out, so everyone can watch him put the ring back on my finger where it definitely belongs!

He smiles at me and says, "Princess, don't ever take that off again."

I kiss that boy and then say very seriously, "You know, if you want to be my husband, you've really gotta stop being so bossy."

The End
Well, not really because I truly feel like my life is just beginning.

ABOUT THE AUTHOR

Jillian Dodd is a *USA TODAY* bestselling author. She writes fun romances with characters her readers fall in love with—from the boy next door in the *That Boy* trilogy to the daughter of a famous actress in *The Keatyn Chronicles* series.

She is married to her college sweetheart, has two adult children, and has two Labs named Cali and Camber, and she lives in a small Florida beach town. When she's not working, she likes to decorate, paint, doodle, shop for shoes, watch football, and go to the beach.

www.jilliandodd.net

CPSIA information can be obtained
at www.ICGtesting.com
Printed in the USA
BVHW070710200820
586808BV00001B/1